FOUR FREEDOMS

ALSO BY JOHN CROWLEY

Lord Byron's Novel: The Evening Land

The Translator

Little, Big

THE ÆGYPT CYCLE
The Solitudes
Love & Sleep
Dæmonomania
Endless Things

OTHERWISE: THREE NOVELS
The Deep
Beasts
Engine Summer

Novelties & Souvenirs: Collected Short Fiction

In Other Words: Essays and Reviews

FOUR

John Crowley

FREEDOMS

WILLIAM MORROW

An Imprint of HarperCollins*Publishers*

This book is a work of fiction. References to real people, events, establishments, organizations, or locales are intended only to provide a sense of authenticity, and are used fictitiously. All other characters, and all incidents and dialogue, are drawn from the author's imagination and are not to be construed as real.

HarperCollins books may be purchased for educational, business, or sales promotional use. For information please write: Special Markets Department, HarperCollins Publishers, 10 East 53rd Street, New York, NY 10022.

FIRST EDITION

Designed by Kate Nichols

Library of Congress Cataloging-in-Publication Data

Crowley, John, 1942–
  Four freedoms / John Crowley. — 1st ed.
      p. cm.
  ISBN 978-0-06-123150-6
  I. Title.
  PS3553.R597F68 2009
  813'.54—dc22   2008046338

---

09 10 11 12 13 OV/RRD 10 9 8 7 6 5 4 3 2 1

For LSB, after all

PRELUDE

In the fields that lie to the west of the Ponca City municipal airport, there once could be seen a derelict Van Damme B-30 *Pax* bomber, one of the only five hundred turned out at the plant that Van Damme Aero built beyond the screen of oaks along Bois d'Arc Creek (Bodark the locals call it). The *Pax* was only a carcass—just the fuselage, wingless and tail-less, like a great insect returning to its chrysalis stage from adulthood. I mean to say it was a carcass then, in the time when (though signs warned us away) we used to play on it and in it: examining the mysteries of its lockboxes and fixtures, taking the pilot's seat and tapping the fogged dials, looking up to see sky through the Plexiglas windows. Now all of it's gone—plane, plant, fields, trees, and children.

There is a philosophical, or metaphysical, position that can be taken—maybe it's a scientific hypothesis—that the past cannot in fact exist. Everything that can possibly exist exists only now. Things now may be expressive of some conceivable or describable past state of affairs, yes: but that's different from saying that this former state actually somehow exists, in the form of "the past." Even in our memory (so neuroscientists now say, who sit at screens and watch the neurons flare as thoughts excite them, brain regions alight first here and then there like vast nighttime conurbations seen from the air) there is no past: no scenes preserved with all their sights and sounds. Merely fleeting states of mind, myriad points assembled for a moment to make a new picture (but "picture" is wrong, too full, too fixed) of what we think are former states of things: things that once were, or may have been, the case.

That B-30 was huge, even what was left of it. The lost twin fin-and-rudder section—those two oval tails—had stood nearly forty feet high. The hangars where it had been assembled had been huge too, some of the biggest interior spaces constructed up to that time, millions of square feet, and flung up in what seemed like all in a day; Van Damme Aero had designed and built them and the government agreed to buy them back when the war was over, though in the case of the B-30 buildings and shops there wasn't a lot to buy back. The wide low town, Henryville, spreading out to the southwest beyond the plant in straight rows of identical units to house the workers, went up just as fast, twenty or thirty units a day, about as solid as the forts and rocket ships we'd later make of cardboard cartons with sawed-out windows and doors. The prairie winds shook them and rattled their contents like dice boxes. While it stood it was a wonder written about and photographed and marveled at almost as much as the Titans of the Air that it was set up to serve; how clean, how new, how quickly raised, all those identical short streets paved in a week, all those identical bungalows, the story was told of a woman who found her own each day by locating the ladder that workmen had left propped against the side of it, until one day it was removed while she was gone, and when she returned she wandered a long time amid the numbered and lettered streets trying to orient herself, looking in windows at other people's stuff not much different from hers but not hers, unable to think of a question she might ask that would set her on the way toward her own, and the sun getting hot as it rose toward noon.

When the sun at last set on any given day (there weren't really weekends in Henryville or at Van Damme Aero in those years) those on day shift would return in the Van Damme yellow buses and be dropped off at various central nodes, like the Community Center and the post office; the buses would cycle around downtown Ponca too at certain times and the workers would get off loaded down with grocery bags from the Kroger. By eight or nine the air outside the bungalows was cooler than the air inside, and people'd bring out kitchen chairs and armchairs to sit in on what some people called the lawn, the strip of pebbly dirt tufted with dry grass that ran between the street and the front door, and open a beer or a soda pop. A Thursday night in May, when the day shift was coming back and people were calling out the open windows or turning their radios outward that way for the dancing starting up in the still-hot street, Rollo Stallworthy brought out his long-necked banjo and began the lengthy process of tuning it up, each sour note stinging like a little pinprick. Rollo, foreman in Shop 128, did this with great care and solemnity, same as he would finger your finished control panel wiring or panel seals. Then almost when nobody was interested at all in looking or listening to the process any longer he'd start hammering on, a skeletal rattling of notes, and sing out stuff that nobody'd ever heard of and that only seemed to resemble the cornball music you expected. It was funnier because his expression never changed behind the round glasses and that brush mustache like Jeff's in the funny papers.

"*Teenie time-O*
In the land of Pharaoh-Pharaoh
Come a rat trap pennywinkle hummadoodle rattlebugger
Sing song kitty wontcha time-ee-o!"

Horace Offen, called "Horse" for as long as anyone knew and for almost as long as he himself could remember, sat at the rackety kitchen table in the unit he shared with Rollo, his portable typewriter open and a piece of yellow copy paper rolled in it. Horse almost never tried to write in the heat of the frypan bungalow but on the way back from the plant that day an idea had begun forming in his mind for a new piece, a new *kind* of piece in fact, not just another press release about how many million rivets, how many kids drank how many gallons of milk in the nursery and how that milk came from the cows that ate the hay that grew in the fields that went for miles beyond the plant's perimeters—the "house-that-Jack-built" gimmick, a good idea you could use only once, or once a year anyway—no this was something different, something beyond all that, something maybe anybody could think up (and Horse Offen knew that he tended to think up, all on his own, a lot of good ideas that a lot of other writers had already thought up) but which wouldn't be easy to do really right, and was maybe beyond

Horse's powers—a thought he found at once chest-tightening and elat-
ing, like placing a bet bigger than you can afford to lose. The first lines
he had written on the yellow sheet looked brave and bold and just a
little anxious, the same as he felt:

> I am *Pax*. *Pax* is my name, and in Latin my name means
> Peace. I am not named for the peace that I bring, but for
> the peace that I promise.

The hysterical fan on the counter waved back and forth over Horse
as he tapped the sweat-slippery keys of the typewriter. There was
nowhere, nowhere on earth he had been, as hot as this plain. Horse felt
lifeblood, precious ichor, extracted from his innermost being in the
salty drops that tickled his brows and the back of his neck.

> In my belly I carry terrible weapons of war, and I will not
> stint to use them against the warmakers. But with every
> bomb dropped there comes a hope: that when the winds
> of war on which I fly are stilled at last, there will never
> again be death dropped from the air upon the cities, the
> homes, and the hopes of men and women.

An awful pity took hold of Horse Offen, and a chill inhabited him.
What words could do; how rarely they did anything at all when he
employed them!

Belly was wrong. It made the bombs seem like turds. In my *body*.
Outside, the nightly ruckus was kicking up, Horse could hear a radio
or a gramophone and Rollo's ridiculous banjo, the most inexpressive
musical instrument Man ever made. People calling from lawn to lawn,
bungalow to bungalow; laughter, noise. The ten thousand men and
women.

> These things I know, although truthfully I have not yet
> been born. When at last I come forth from the huge han-
> gars where ten thousand men and women work to bring
> me and the many others like me to birth, I will be the larg-
> est and most powerful weapon of the air ever built, the

latest child of all the thinkers and planners, the daredevil pilots and the slide-rule engineers who made this nation's air industry. Yet I am a new generation. The Wright brothers' first flight was not longer than my wingspan of TK feet. When the men and women with their hands and their machines have given me wings, they will be so broad that a Flying Fortress will be able to nestle beneath each one, left and right.

Was that true? He thought it was. It would need some checking. When he'd first started writing press releases at Van Damme and submitting copy to the *Aero,* the editor (little more than a layout man in fact) had asked him what the hell this TK meant. Horse had worked briefly for Luce (well he'd been tried out for a couple of months) and he sighed and smiled patiently. TK means To Come. Information or fact to come. Why TK then? Because that's the way it's done. The way the big papers do it. *Time. Life. Fortune.*

The workers who build my growing body come from every state in this nation, from great cities and little towns. They come from the Appalachians and the Rockies, the Smokies and the Catskills, the Blue Ridge Mountains, the Green Mountains, the White. They are men and women, Negro and white, American Indian, Czech, Pole, Italian, Anglo-Saxon. They are old and young, big and small, smart and stupid

Inspiration was leaking away, and Horse was where he had been before, writing what he had written before. But there was a place this was meant to reach, Horse felt sure, whether he could reach it or not. That voice speaking. Why did it seem to him female? Just because of all those ships, those old frigates and galleons? He had almost written *to bring me and my sisters to birth.*

They believe that they came here just because the work to be done is here, because they've got sons or husbands at the front, because they saw the ads in the papers and listened to the President's appeal, because they want this war to be won, and most of all they want it over. And that is my promise. But this they do not know: that it is I, *Pax,* who have drawn them to me. Here to this place I drew them before I existed, I drew them to me so that I could come to be: and as I grew, I reached out to more and more, to every corner of this nation, calling the ones who would rivet, and weld, and draft, and wire, and seal, and

With a sudden cry Horse Offen yanked out from the typewriter the yellow sheet, which parted as he pulled, leaving a tail behind. Oh God what crap. What was he thinking? Outside the fun was rolling, summoning Horse, offering a Lucky Lager, an It's-It ice-cream bar. He closed the lid of the typewriter and locked it shut.

A few units down, Pancho Notzing entertained the Teenie Weenies, the ones anyway who hadn't been moved to other shifts in the last reshuffle of forces, which somewhat broke up that old gang o' mine. From an oddity of the settlement's geometries, certain of the corner units, like Pancho's, had a wider spread of ground around them, so Pancho's was the place to wander to at day's end. Pancho'd piled up stones he'd found around the place left over from construction and built a barbecue grill, topped with a rack of steel that had served some function at the plant, airplane part, something, but that nobody seemed to need or to miss when Pancho appropriated it. He burned branches of blackjack oak, winter-broken and gnarly, that he picked up from the roadsides, and lumber scavenged from the building sites. People brought their meat rations, steaks and chickens and the odd out-of-ration local rabbit, and Pancho slathered them with stuff he claimed he'd learned to make on a hacienda in Old California long ago. Wearing his hat and an apron over his gabardine pants, he flipped and slathered and plopped the meats on platters and talked.

"Happiness," he was saying to those waiting for meat. Cooking and serving didn't interfere with Pancho's talk; nothing did. "I am a person who knows people. I think I can say that. I've worked all my life. I take man as he is: a creature of his needs and his desires. Nothing wrong with it—I take no exception to it, even if I could. It seems to me that we have no business telling people what they should or shouldn't want.

Happiness means meeting the desires a person has, not suppressing them."

"Happiness is a plate of ribs, Mr. Notzing," said a young fellow, raising his plate, sucking a greasy thumb.

"Have more," said Pancho, flipping a rack and watching the happy flames leap up. "Nobody in this present world has enough pleasure. They feel it, too. The poor man never gets enough, and he hates the rich man because the rich man supposedly gets his fill—but he doesn't. The rich are eternally afraid that the poor will take away what pleasures they have, they indulge themselves constantly but never feel filled—they feel guilty. Meanwhile they hoard the wealth, more than they can ever spend or use or eat or drink."

"Are you saying," Sal Mass chirped up, "Mr. Notzing, sir, are you saying money don't buy happiness?"

Pancho Notzing was immune to sarcasm. Those close enough to hear her odd chirpy voice laughed. Old Sal.

Sal was the only one of the Teenie Weenies (except for her husband, Al Mass) who really was one, and not only in the sense that she was an actual midget. Ten years before she had played one of the little characters in a promotion for a canned food company; she'd flown, she said, ten thousand miles and into three hundred airports, dressed as the Lady of Fashion, her husband, Al, as the Cook, inviting people aboard the Ford Trimotor they traveled in to look over the cans and packages of food, the Pepper Pickles, the Chipped Beef, the Hearts of Wheat, the Succotash, the Harvard Beets, the Soda Crackers. Handing out free samples and little cookbooks. She knew she disappointed the children who came, because the Teenie Weenies in the funny papers were really teeny, no larger than your thumb, and she and Al were small but not that small, and now and again she'd get a kick in the shins from some kid who wanted her to be at least smaller than he was, which is what all kids wanted she decided, though it didn't explain why grown-ups came and clambered into their plane and made much of them. What Sal wanted was to fly the Ford herself, but no amount of solicitude, or pleading, or showing off, or anything could get the pilot to do more than laugh at her. Hell with him. Al just read the paper and smoked his cigar and snorted. Hey, Hon, here we are in the funnies—see, this week I try to figure out how to cut up a grape with a saw—Jesus. A little later that food company fired them and from then on used a couple of little kids instead for half the price. That was 1941, and Sal and Al got hired by Van Damme Aero's West Coast plant to work on their A-21 Sword bombers, getting into the small spaces no one else could get into and riveting. And their selling job went on too, as Sal showed up again and again in company promotions, in the newsreels, in Horse Offen's stories, wearing her bandanna and miniature overalls. Al stayed just as mad as ever, midget mad—well, he was one of those angry midgets she knew so well, he had a right, she paid no attention. When Van Damme built this plant in the middle of nowhere (Al's characterization) and started on the B-30 there seemed at first no need for midgets, the whole plane was open from end to end and no space too small for a normal-size worker. But they accepted Sal and Al anyway when they applied to go out to the new plant, which Sal thought was white of them; Al just snorted.

"Well," she said to Pancho, though not for him alone to hear, "I guess happiness is overrated. Not all it's cracked up to be."

"I'm no Utopian," Pancho said. "I would never say so. I am a modest fellow. I know better than to demand too much of this world. Nothing's perfect. You try to build the best world, the best society you can. I am not a *u*topian but a *best*opian."

All this time the moon had been rising into the cloudless air over Henryville, nearly full and melon-shaped, huge and gold and then whiter and smaller as it climbed. The sounds of the banjo, the radio music, and the people's voices moved with the sluggish air block to block and reached into the bedroom where Prosper Olander sat on the edge of Connie Wrobleski's bed with a Lucky Lager of her husband's growing warm in his hand. He was listening to Connie, who was telling her story, which was in a way the story of how she happened to be here in bed with Prosper. She'd stop often to say things like *Oh jeez I don't know* or *I never expected this,* that meant she was giving up trying to explain herself, and at the same time keeping the door open to going on, which in time after a sigh she did, only to stop again to question herself or the world or Fate. Prosper listened—he did listen, because what she had to say was new to him, the part that was proving hard for her to say, and he liked her and wanted to know what she thought—but always as he sat his eyes went to the pair of new crutches now propped in the corner. Boy were they something beautiful, he couldn't get enough of an eyeful, they leaned together there gleaming new, preening, proud. They had been built at the plant just for him by machinists on their breaks, and they were, as far as Prosper knew, the only pair like them in the world: slim strong light aluminum tubes with hinged aluminum cuffs covered in leather to go around his forearms and posts for his hands to grip, clad in hard rubber. They weighed nothing. His poor underarms, eternally chafed from the tops of the old wooden ones he had used for years—the parts of himself he felt most sorry for, while everybody else felt sorry about his ski-jump spine and marionette's legs—the skin there was healing already.

"Oh if I don't shut up I'm going to start crying," Connie said. Connie's husband was in basic training a long way away, and he'd be off to war most likely soon thereafter, and here was Prosper beside his wife in his house, in nothing but his skivvies too; but there was no doubt in Prosper's mind that they two weren't the only ones in Henryville, or Oklahoma, or in these States, who were in similar circumstances. It was the war, and the war work, and those circumstances wouldn't last forever, but just on this night Prosper seemed unable to remember or imagine any others.

"Don't cry," he said. "Don't cry, Connie."

These crutches. Look at the slight dog-leg each one took in heading for the ground, each different for his different legs. These crutches were, what, they were angelic, they were spiritual in their weightless strength and their quick helpful patience. God bless them. His own invention. He tried not to show it, in the circumstances, but he couldn't help thinking that in a lot of ways he was a lucky man.

PART ONE

1

For a time after the war began, the West Coast would go dark every night in expectation of air attacks. Who knew, now, how far the Japs could reach, what damage they might be able to inflict? We mounted citizen patrols that went up and down and made people draw their shades, put out their lamps. The stores and bars along the boardwalks and arcades that faced the ocean had to be equipped with light traps, extra doors to keep the light inside. In cities all along the Pacific we looked up from the darkened streets and saw for the first time in years the stars, all unchanged. But every once in a while, startled by some report or rumor, the great searchlights of the coastal batteries—eight hundred million candlepower they said, whatever that could mean—would come on and stare for a time out at the empty sea. Then go off again.

Van Damme Aero was already in the business of building warplanes before hostilities commenced, and after Pearl Harbor their West Coast plant was fulfilling government contracts worth millions, with more signed every month. A mile-square array of tethered balloons was suspended just over Van Damme Aero's ramifying works and its workers like darkening thunderclouds, a summer storm perpetually hovering, so that from above, from the viewpoint of a reconnaissance plane or a bomber, the plant was effectually invisible. More than that: the sheds and yards and hangars not only seemed not to be there, they also seemed to be something, or somewhere, else: for the topsides of all those balloons had been painted as a landscape, soft rolling hills of green and yellow, with here and there a silver lakelet and the brown furrows of farmland, even (so they said down under it, who would never see it and went on rumors) the roofs of a village, spire of a church, red barns and a silo. A pastorale, under which round the clock the A-21 Sword bombers were riveted and welded and fitted with engines and wings, and the huge Robur cargo seaplanes were given birth to like monster whales. Even when the danger of an invasion of the mainland seemed to have passed (leaving us still jumpy and unsettled but at least not cowering, not always looking to the sky at the whine of every Cub or Jenny), every day the Van Damme Aero workers coming to work dove under that landscape and it was hard not to laugh about it.

From the Van Damme shop floor where Al and Sal Mass then worked with a thousand others you could see, if you knew where to look, a bank of broad high dark windows behind which were the conference and meeting rooms of the Van Damme directors. Guests (Army Air Corps generals, government officials, union bosses) brought into that wide low-ceilinged space, to look down upon the ceaseless activity below—the windows faced the length of the shop, which seemed almost to recede into infinite working distance—could feel superb, in command, and they would be awed as well, as they were intended to be.

On a day in the spring of 1942 the only persons assembled up in there were the engineering and employment vice presidents and their assistants, and Henry and Julius Van Damme. On a streamlined plinth in the middle of the room was a model of a proposed long-range heavy bomber that Van Damme Aero and the rest of the air industry and the appropriate government agencies were trying to bring forth. Julius Van Damme kept his back to the model, not wanting to be influenced unduly by its illusory facticity, the very quality of it that kept his brother Henry's eyes on it. It was canted into the air, as though in the process of taking a tight rising turn at full power. It wasn't the largest heavier-than-air flying thing ever conceived, but it would be the largest built to date, if it were built, maybe excepting a few tremendous Van Damme cargo seaplanes on the drawing boards; anyway it wasn't a tubby lumbering cargo plane but a long slim bomber, designed to inflict harm anywhere in the world from bases in the continental United States. It had been conceived even before December 1941, back when Britain was expected to fall and there would be no forward bases any closer to Germany than Goose Bay from which to run bombers. The plane was designated (at the moment) XB-30, the X for experimental or in plan. B-30 would be its model number in the complex rubric of the American air forces. As yet it had no name. The Model Committee was making a preliminary presentation of the latest mock-up and specs. It was somewhat dim in the huge dark-brown room, the brilliantly lit shop floor below giving more light than the torchères of the office.

"In this configuration, six pusher twenty-six-cylinder R-400 Bee air-cooled radials, each to drive a seventeen-and-a-half-foot three-bladed propeller." The chief of engineering made dashes at the model, ticking off the features, his long black pencil like a sorcerer's wand summoning the B-30 into existence. "Wingspan's increased now to 225 feet with an area of, well, just a hair over 4,000 square feet, depending."

"Depending on what?" Julius said, picking up a slide rule.

"I'll be making that clear. The wing, as you see, a certain degree of sweepback. Fuel tanks within the wings, here, here, each with a capacity of 21,000 gallons. Wing roots are over seven feet thick and give access to the engines for maintenance in flight."

Julius unrolled the next broad blue sheet.

"Twin fin-and-rudder format, like our A-21 and the Boeing Dominator now in plan, though lots bigger naturally, thirty-five-foot overall height." Here the engineer swallowed, as though he had told a lie, and his eyes swept the faces of the others, Julius's still bent over the sheets. "Sixty-foot fuselage, circular cross section as you can see. Four bomb bays with a maximum capacity of 40,000 pounds in this bottom bumpout that runs nearly the length of the fuselage. Forward crew compartment pressurized, and also the gunners' weapons sighting station compartment behind the bomb bay. A pressurized tube runs over the bomb bays to connect the forward crew compartment to the rear gunners' compartment."

"How big a tube?" Henry Van Damme asked.

"Just over two feet in diameter."

Henry, who was claustrophobic, shuddered.

"Crew has a sort of wheeled truck they can slide on to go from one end to the other," said the engineer.

For a while they gazed at it, the paper version and the model still climbing. The dome of the forward crew compartment, pierced with a multitude of Plexiglas panels, swelled from the slim body of the fuselage like a mushroom cap from its stem but smoothed away underneath. A snake's head, a.

"I hate the pusher engines," Henry said. "They make the ship look dumb."

"They're necessary to get the damn thing off the ground," Julius said, turning back to the specs unrolled before him. "Just that little bit more lift."

"I know why they're necessary," Henry said. "I just think *necessary* should be *elegant* as well, and if it's not it means trouble later."

Julius, without nameable expression, raised his eyes from the rolls of specs to his brother.

"*Might* mean trouble later," Henry said to him. "Possible trouble. Often does."

"Oh I don't know," Julius said. He sat back in his chair and felt for the pipe in his vest pocket. "I remember Ader's Avion back a long time ago. That day at Satory. How elegant that was."

"Yes," Henry said. "The Avion."

"Piss elegant," said Julius. His lack of expression had not altered. To the chief of engineering he said, "The Avion looked like a bat. Exquisite. Even folded its wings back like one, to rest." Julius made the gesture. "Only trouble, it couldn't fly."

"Well I hate to tell you what this one looks like," Henry said.

Julius turned then from the specs and gazed, deadpan, at the absurdly elongated fuselage, with its swollen head and the two big ovals at its root.

2

The day that Henry Van Damme and his brother had spoken of was a day when Henry was twelve and Julius ten, a day in October of 1897, when following their tutor and their mother, young and beautifully dressed and soon to die, they came out of the Gare du Nord in Paris and got into a taxicab to be driven to a brand-new hotel in the Rue St.-Philippe-du-Ruel (their father liked new hotels, as he did motor cars and telephones). Waiting for them at the desk, as they had hoped and expected, was a large stiff envelope, and the boys insisted that their tutor immediately set up the gramophone that went everywhere with them in its own leather box. Their mother had difficulty even getting them out of their wool coats and hats before they sat down in front of the machine. Jules was the one who cranked it up with the slender Z-shaped crank of lacquered steel and ebony; Henry (whose name was Hendryk in the Old World) was the one who slit the seals of the envelope and drew out carefully the Berliner disc of cloudy zinc. He knew he was not to touch the grooves of its surface but it seemed a deprivation hard to bear: the pads of his fingers could sense the raised ridges of metal as though longing for them.

Their tutor affixed the disc to the plate of the gramophone and slipped the catch that allowed it to rotate. It was one of only a handful in existence, though the boys' father was confident of changing that:

he, like Berliner, could see a day not far off when communication by discs small enough to fit in a breast pocket or slip into an envelope, playable on machines that would become as common as telephones, would bring the voices of loved ones (and the instructions of bosses and officials too) anywhere in the world right to our ears, living letters.

The tutor placed the stylus on the disc's edge, and it was swept into the grooves. "My dear boys," they heard their father's voice say, speaking in English with his distinctive but unplaceable accent. Hendryk felt his brother, Jules, who sat close beside him bent to the gramophone's horn, shiver involuntarily at the sound. "I have some good news that I think will interest you. I'll bet you remember a day five years ago—Jules, my dear, you were only five—when you saw Monsieur Ader fly his Avion, the 'Eolus,' at Armainvilliers. What a day that was. Well, next week he is to make a test flight of his latest machine, the Avion III, called 'Zephyr.' The flight—if the thing does fly—will be at the army's grounds at Satory, on the fourteenth of this month, which if my calendar is correct will be three days after you hear this. It is a beautiful machine. Monsieur Ader's inspiration is the bat, as you know, and not the bird. Take the earliest morning train to Versailles and a carriage will meet you. All my love as usual. This is your father, now ceasing to speak." The stylus screeched against the disc's ungrooved center, and the tutor lifted it off.

"And what," he asked the boys, "do we see in the name of this new machine?"

"Avion is a thing that flies, like a bird," said Hendryk. "*Avis,* a bird."

"Zephyr is wind," said Jules. "Breeze." His hands described gentle airs. "Can we listen again?"

Henry Van Damme and his brother were Americans, born in Ohio of an American mother, but their father—though he spent, on and off, a decade or more in the States—was European, a Dutch businessman. He disliked that term, which seemed to name a person different from himself, but Dutch alternatives were worse—*handelaar, zakenman*—redolent of strong cigars and evil banter and low tastes. If he could he would have described himself as a dreamer; he wished that *entrepreneur* meant in French what it had come to mean in English, the glamorous suggestion of risk and romance.

His sons grew up on trains and steamships, speaking French or Dutch or English or all three at once, a compound language they would use for years to keep their secrets. Their education was conducted in motion, so to speak, and staged as though by an invisible mentor-magician as a series of adventures and encounters the point of which seemed to be to discover why they had occurred, and what each had to do with the preceding ones. At least that's how the boys made sense of it—they worshiped their father, and their young British tutor amiably turned their attempts at exegesis into standard lessons in mathematics or language.

Eudoxe Van Damme (he had been christened Hendryk, like his son and his father, but found the name unappealing) was a large investor in mechanical and scientific devices and schemes, about three-quarters of which failed or evaporated, but one or two of which had been so spectacularly successful that Van Damme now seemed impervious to financial disaster. He had a quick mind and had trained it in science and engineering; he could not only discern the value (or futility) of most schemes presented to him but also could often make suggestions for improvements that didn't annoy the inventors. His son Hendryk, large and optimistic, was like him; Jules was slighter and more melancholy, like his mother, whom he would miss lifelong.

The Berliner discs weren't the only sound recording device Van Damme had taken an interest in. As a young man he had assembled a consortium of other young men with young heads and hearts to develop the phonautograph of Scott, the machine that produced those ghostly scratchings on smoked films representing (or better say resulting from) sound amplified and projected by a horn. It could even produce pictures of the human voice speaking, which Scott had called *logographs*. The great problem with the Scott apparatus was that although it produced what was provably a picture of sound, the sound itself could not be recovered from the picture. Van Damme was interested in this problem—he was hardly alone in that, for problems of representation, modeling, scalability, were absorbing the attention of engineers and mathematicians worldwide just then—but he was even more interested in the claim that the machine might be able to receive and amplify sounds—and voices—from the other world, a claim that Van Damme spent a good deal of time thinking how to establish, or at least investigate. His money and his support did seem to have results: a revamped phonautograph, though shut up alone in a carefully soundproofed room, had nevertheless produced films showing the distinctive traces of human voices. When at length the problem of retrieving from the Scott films the sounds that had left their shadows there (a process requiring great delicacy and never truly satisfactory) Van Damme saw to it that these logographs from the soundproof room were also processed: and what certainly seemed to be human voices could indeed be heard, though far less distinctly than the ones caught in the usual way. Van Damme told his sons that it sounded like the striving but unintelligible voices of spastics.

Unfortunately the more reliable gramophones of Berliner caught nothing in soundproof rooms but the noise of their own operation.

These enterprises took time and travel, but it was above all flight— heavier-than-air, man-carrying flight—that most engaged Eudoxe Van Damme's imagination and his money in those years. Hendryk and Jules arrived in Paris in that autumn of 1897 from England, where with their tutor they had visited Baldwyns Park in Kent and seen Hiram Maxim's aircraft attempt to get off the ground. What a thing that was, the largest contraption yet built to attempt heavier-than-air flight, powered by steam, with a propeller that seemed the size of a steamship screw. Old white-bearded Hiram Maxim, inventor of the weapon still called by his name around the world, and builder of the hugest wind tunnel in existence. That July day when the boys watched, it actually got going so fast it broke the system of belts and wires tying it down like Gulliver, tore up the guardrails, and with propellers beating like mad and the mean little steam engines boiling went rocketing at a good thirty or forty miles an hour, and almost—almost!—gained the air, old Hiram's white beard tossed behind him and the crew knocked about. It was impossible not to laugh in delight and terror. If M. Ader's delicate beings of silk and aluminum rods were rightly named for gods of breath and wind, that one of Maxim's should have been called Sphinx—it was about the size of the one in Egypt and in the end as flightless, though Maxim wouldn't admit that and later claimed he'd felt the euphoria of earth-leaving and flown a short distance that day.

M. Ader too would remember the day at Satory differently than others would. Eudoxe Van Damme met his boys and their tutor at the field at Satory, drizzly breezy October and chilly, not like the blue into which Hiram Maxim had thrust himself. Van Damme looked as elegant as always, even in a large brown ulster; his soft fedora at an angle, waxed mustaches upright. More than once he had been mistaken in train stations or hotel lobbies for the composer Puccini. Around the field gathered in knots were French Army officers, M. Ader's backers. As Maxim did, these Frenchmen expected the chief use of "manflight," as Maxim called it, would be war.

"I can't say I think much of his preparations here," Eudoxe told his sons as they followed after his quick determined footsteps over the damp field. "You see the track on which the machine will run. Observe that the track is *circular*—M. Ader will start with the wind at his back, presumably, but as he rounds *there* and *there* the wind will be first athwart, then at his head. Ah but look, do look!"

The Avion III "Zephyr" was unfolding now on its stand. Dull daylight glowed through its silk skin as though through a moth's wing. Its inspiration was indeed the bat—the long spectral fingerbones on which a bat's wing is stretched modeled by flexing struts and complex knuckles. Tiny wheels like bat's claws gripped the track. Incongruous on its front or forehead, the stacks of two compact black steam engines. "He claims to be getting forty-two horsepower from those engines, and they weigh less than three hundred pounds," Eudoxe cried, hurrying toward the craft, holding his hat, his boys trailing after him.

The attempt was a quick failure. Fast as it rolled down its track it could not lift off. Like a running seabird its tail lifted, its wings stretched, but it wouldn't rise. Then those contrary winds caught it and simply tipped it gently off its weak little wheels to settle in the damp grass.

In the few photographs taken of the events at Satory that day, Eudoxe Van Damme is the small figure apart from the caped military officers, facing the disaster, back to the camera, arms akimbo to express his disgust, and the two boys beside him, their arms extended as though to help the Avion to rise.

"Now, boys," said their father in the train compartment, "what can we see to be the primary error of M. Ader?"

"Copying the look of flying things," said Hendryk.

"But not . . ."

"Not their, their—not their reasons."

Eudoxe laughed, delighted with this answer. "Their reasons!"

"He means," Jules said, "the principles. It can't fly just because it looks like something that can. Leonardo thought that was so, and he was wrong too, that if a thing has wings that look like a bird's . . ."

"Or a bat's . . ."

"Then they will function in the same way," said the tutor, who tended to get impatient and pony up the answers the boys were fishing for.

"Very well," said Eudoxe. "Of course just because it resembled a bat, or a pterosaur, did not necessarily mean it would *not* fly. And what other error, related to that first one, did we see?"

"It was badly made," said Jules.

"It was very *well* made," said their father. "The fabrication was excellent. My God! The vanes of the propellers, if that was what those fans were supposed to be—bamboo, were they, interleaved with aluminum and paper and . . ."

"Scale," said Hendryk.

Eudoxe halted, mouth open, and then smiled upon his son, a foxy smile that made them laugh.

"It's *too big*," cried Jules.

"Ah my boys," said Eudoxe Van Damme. "The problem of scale."

"The giants of Galileo," the tutor put in, with a reminding forefinger raised. "Who could not walk without breaking their legs, unless their legs were the size of American sequoias. We have done the equations."

"Weight increases as the cube of the linear dimensions," Jules said.

But that principle was a simple one, known to every bridge builder and ironworker now; the harder concept of making models that modeled not simply the physical relations of a larger object but also that object's behavior was still to be solved. Ostwald had not yet published his paper "On Physically Similar Systems," wherein he asked a question that would haunt Julius Van Damme lifelong—if the entire universe were to be shrunk to a half, or a quarter, of its present size, atoms and all, would it be possible to tell? What would behave differently? Helmholtz's dimensionless numbers could relate the motions of small dirigibles to great unwieldy ones such as had never been (and might never be) made. But the small flying "bats" like those the Van Damme boys played with worked by twisted rubber strings that turned a screw, craft that might carry miniature people on tiny errands in toyland, always failed when scaled up to carry actual gross fleshly people. Something was wrong.

"Poor Monsieur Pénaud," said Eudoxe Van Damme, and the boys knew they were to hear again the tale of the day when Eudoxe Van Damme saw the planophore and its inventor. "I was a child, your age, Hendryk. What a day it was, a beautiful day in summer, the Jardin des Tuileries—I could hear the music of the fair. An announcement had been made—I don't know where—that Monsieur Pénaud would conduct an experimental flight of his new device. A crowd had collected, and we waited to see what would happen."

Van Damme paused there, to extract a cigar from the case in his pocket, which he examined without lighting.

"And what happened, Papa?" the boys asked, as they knew they were supposed to.

"I saw flight," said Eudoxe. "The first winged craft that was heavier than air, pulled by a screw propeller, stabilized by its design, that flew in a straight line. It flew, I don't remember, a hundred and fifty feet. Flight! There was only one drawback."

The boys knew.

"It was only two feet long."

The boys laughed anyway.

M. Pénaud had come out from a carriage that had brought him onto the field. The crowd murmured a little as he came forth—those who didn't know him—because it could be seen that he was somehow disabled, he walked with great difficulty using a pair of heavy canes; an assistant came after him, carrying the planophore. M. Pénaud himself—slight, dark, sad—turned the rubber strings as the assistant steadied the device and counted. The strings were tightened 240 turns—that number remained in Van Damme's memory. When it was fully wound, M. Pénaud—held erect by the assistant from behind, who gently put his arms around his waist, as though in love or comradeship—lifted and cast off the planophore, at the same time releasing the rubber strings.

The craft dipped at first, and the crowd made a low sound of awed trepidation, but then it rose again, and so did the crowd's general voice, and it flew straight and true. The crowd began to cheer, though M. Pénaud himself stood motionless and unsurprised. Eudoxe Van Damme by his nurse's side found himself as moved by the inventor as the invention, the flight over the earth less affecting than the crippled man just barely able to hold himself up and keep from lying supine upon it.

Well, the world thought that M. Pénaud had invented a wonderful toy, and so he had. But he believed he had discovered a principle and had no interest in toys. He thought he could scale up the planophore to carry a man, or two men. "If I'd been twenty years older, I'd have helped. I'd have known he was right. I'd have come to his aid." The Société Française de Navigation Aérienne, which had praised the planophore, gave Pénaud no real help. He asked the great dirigibilist Henri Giffard, who first encouraged and then ignored him. And one day in 1880 M. Pénaud packed all of his drawings and designs and models into a wooden box shaped, unmistakably, like a coffin, and had it delivered to M. Giffard's house. Then he took his life. "He was not more than thirty years old."

The story was done. The principle was enunciated: what is small may work, what is large may not, and not for the reasons of physics alone, though those may underlie all others. The boys were silent.

"Oddly enough," Eudoxe Van Damme said then, "Giffard himself committed suicide not two years later. And still we do not fly." He lit his cigar with care; he seemed, to his elder son, to be standing on the far side of a divide that Hendryk would himself one day have to cross, because he could just now for the first time perceive it: on that far side there was enterprise, and failure; possibility and impossibility; cigars, power, and death. "It may be, you know," he said to the boys, "that we may one day solve the problem of how it is that birds fly, and bats; and at the same time, in the same solution, prove also that we can never do it ourselves. How tragic that would be."

Of course the problem was solved, it did not exclude mankind, and Eudoxe Van Damme lived to see it solved, though by then he was largely indifferent to a success like that.

In the days after the Great War, when the Wright brothers planned joint ventures with the Van Damme brothers, ventures that somehow never came to fruition, the Wrights used to talk about how they had played ("experimented" they always said, those two didn't play) with those rubber-string-driven bats that Hendryk and Jules were sending aloft, at the same time, not far from the Wrights' Ohio home. The Wrights, though, weren't simply marveling but trying to figure out what caused the bats to behave so differently at different sizes. The machines, as willful and pertinacious as living things, as liable to failure, beating aloft in the summer twilights.

It was odd how many pairs of brothers had advanced the great quest. So often one luminous brave gay chance-taker, one careful worried pencil-and-paper one, issuing warnings, trying to keep up. The Lilienthals, fussy Gustav and his wild brother Otto, who not long before the Van Damme brothers watched the Avion III not fly, killed himself in a man-bearing kite: Gustav was absent and thus had not done the safety drill he always did. Hiram Maxim had a brother, Hudson, who resented and plotted against him. The Voisin brothers. The Montgolfiers, for the matter of that, back in the beginning. The Wrights: Wilbur the daredevil, so badly hurt in a crash when careful Orville had not been there to watch out for him. Never the same after.

And the Van Dammes.

Henry sometimes wondered if there was something about brotherhood itself that opened the secret in the end. For what the Wrights learned, and learned from gliders, and from M. Pénaud's planophores too, was that a flying machine, so far from needing to be perfectly and completely stable, was only possible if it was continually, controllably, *un*stable, like a bicycle ridden in three dimensions: an ongoing argument among yaw, pitch, roll, and lift, managed moment to moment by a hand ready to make cooperation between the unpredictable air and the never-finished technologies of wood, power, and wire. It was a partnership, a brotherhood. There never was a conquest of the air. The air would not let itself be conquered, and didn't need to be.

Madame Van Damme, née Gertie Pilcher of Toledo, died of peritonitis aboard the Bulgarian Express on her way to meet her husband in Constantinople. The train was passing through remote country when she was taken, and a decision had to be made whether to stop the train and take the woman by carriage to a local hospital that would be unlikely to treat her properly even if it could be reached, or race forward as fast as the tracks could be cleared to Philippopolis, where an ambulance would be waiting. Her own last words, before she lapsed into fevered nonsense, were a plea that they not put her off into the forest and the night, and though that could be discounted, no one—the conductors, the porters, the medical student found on board who had diagnosed her burst appendix—felt capable of contradicting her. She died just as the brakes were applied at the station approach, the cry of steel on steel and the gasp of escaping steam accompanying her passing spirit. The two boys, who had been put in another compartment after kissing their mother's hot wet cheeks, awoke at the sound.

It seemed somehow appropriate to them, in the years that followed, that their education in motion stopped with their mother's death. They began then to be enrolled in stationary schools, where they studied the same things every day along with other boys. There were no more Berliner discs delivered to their train compartment or waiting for them at the desks of hotels; their father's letters became less frequent though not less loving, as he spent more and more time resting at resorts and spas where nothing ever happened. The boys began their studies together, both committed to science and engineering, but soon drifted apart; Jules the better scholar of the two, chewing through difficult curricula at great speed and asking for more, Hendryk preferring friendships, sports, reading parties in the mountains.

Then in 1904 Jules went to Germany to study energetics with the great Boltzmann at the University of Vienna. Hendryk left school and took up his father's enterprises, trying (he understood later) to reawaken his father's passions by asking to be educated in his business, insofar as it could be learned—Eudoxe Van Damme had apparently continually flouted in his actual dealings the principles he tried to teach his son, indeed this seemed to be the greatest lesson, but one that could only be grasped after all the others had been learned. Still merry, still beautifully appointed, Eudoxe Van Damme resisted his son's attempts to interest him in new adventures: his heart had died on that station platform in Bulgaria and would not be awakened.

Jules worshiped Herr Professor Doktor Boltzmann, fighting to be admitted to his classes, never missing one of his public lectures. He wrote to Hendryk: "B. says the problem of flight will not be solved by endless experiments, nor will it be solved by work in theoretical mechanics—the problem's just too hard. He says it will be solved by a clear statement of principles, and a new formulation of what is at stake. But that's as far as I follow him."

Perhaps to fend off Hendryk's attempts to bring him back into the world, Eudoxe Van Damme decided that his older son too needed more mechanical and technical training, and found a place for him at the University of Manchester. Hendryk agreed to go, if he could work in one way or another on the problems of heavier-than-air flight. The solution to the problem—which in Hendryk's mind would, when found, lift his father's heart as well as the world's—was about to be reached in America, in fact in the boys' dimly remembered home state, though for a long time Europe didn't hear about it, and when told of it it wasn't convinced. At Manchester the engineering course was both practical and theoretical, there were both workshops and seminars, everyone talked physics and machine tools equally, and in the summers you could go up to the kite-flying station at Glossop on the coast and build huge kites to sail the cold sea winds. The great topic was how to power a man-bearing kite with an engine, and there was much discussion of the pretty little French Gnome engine—those were the days when engines, like flying machines, were so different from one another they went by names. There were Americans and Germans at Glossop, flying the kites developed by the American westerner and naturalized Britisher Samuel Cody, a kinsman (so he asserted) of Buffalo Bill. A German-speaking young man whom Hendryk befriended flew Cody-type kites by day and worked on the equations for a new propeller design by night. "He is called Ludwig," Hendryk wrote to Jules. "Though it seems his family call him Lucky, so I do too, though it annoys him. In fact he is Austrian not German, a family of rich Jews. He too wanted to study with Boltzmann. He's told me he envies you. How strange that you have gone to Vienna to study while I befriend a Viennese here! We talk about flight, language, mathematics—he talks and I listen. He has two brothers—no—he *had* two brothers, who both committed suicide. Imagine. He told me this after many glasses of beer and has not since spoken of it. Write to me, Jules, and tell me how you are."

That summer the Wrights brought their flier to France, and after that there could be no longer any doubt. The great race of the nations had been won by the least likely of them, the one whose government and armed forces had invested next to nothing; won by two bicycle builders without university degrees. At Glossop the students and professors pored over the report and the photographs in *L'Aérophile,* but Hendryk's new friend Lucky seemed to lose interest in the pursuit of further advances; Hendryk worried for him. It was as though he felt an equation had been solved once and for all. He put aside his kite models and his propeller design. He told Hendryk that on an impulse he had written to Bertrand Russell at Cambridge to ask if perhaps he could study philosophy there. If he was accepted, he said, he would be a philosopher; if he proved to be an idiot, he would become an aeronaut. Hendryk got him to apply for a patent on his propeller design, thinking he might put some Van Damme money into its development; he shook Lucky's hand farewell at the train station.

What the young Austrian had seen as a conclusion, Hendryk Van Damme knew to be a beginning: he felt that sensation of elation and danger and glee that comes when an incoming sea wave, vast heavy and potent, lifts you off your feet and tosses you shoreward. He had had no letter in months from his brother, not even in response to the Wright news; then came word at the university that the great Boltzmann had committed suicide, no one knew why. Still no letter for Hendryk from Jules. Hendryk left Manchester the next week, caught the boat-train from London, thinking of the pilots of the purple twilight crossing the narrow seas one day soon, surely soon now, and in Paris boarded the express for Vienna. At the last address he had for his brother he ran up the stairs and knocked on the door, but the concierge below called up after him to say that the young Dutchman was gone.

Just as Lucky had never after spoken of his brothers, Henry and Julius never after spoke of the succeeding days. How Hendryk searched the city for his brother, growing more alarmed; sat in the Schönbrun park fanning himself with his hat (he was already running to fat and worried about his heart) and thinking where to look next; tracing, from the bank his brother used and the engineering students at the university, a way to a certain low street in the Meidling district, and a desolate room. Jules had descended there because he had no money, because his father had sent none, had sent none because Jules had asked for none, because he had ceased to answer his father's letters. Hendryk found him shoeless and shirtless on his bed, in his cabinet only a vial of prussic acid he was unable (he told Hendryk later that night) to muster the energy to open and swallow.

Henry was right, that there was an industry to build; right that he would not win his share in it without his brother by his side, to keep his craft in trim. It wasn't surprising that all his life from that time on Henry Van Damme thought of suicide as the enemy, a universal force that Freud had discovered (such was Henry's understanding of what he'd learned of Freud's ideas, beginning that year in Vienna); nor that, close as it was bound to brotherhood and to death, flight nevertheless seemed to him to be the reply, or the counterforce: suicide was the ultimate negation, but flight the negation of negation itself.

The doctors at the brand-new Landes-Heil und Pflegeanstalt für Nerven- und Geisteskranke where Jules was treated would not explain to Hendryk and Eudoxe what Jules suffered from, though they took grave credit when it passed. Jules wouldn't say what had occurred between him and the doctors: he would only say that whatever had been so wrong with him was now all gone forever. The brothers were from then on inseparable in business, their contrary qualities making them famous, nearly folkloric, figures in the capitalism of the new century, its Mutt and Jeff, its Laurel and Hardy, its Paul Bunyan and Johnny Inkslinger. Henry, so big, so ready for anything—he loved speedboats and race cars, ate what the press always described as Lucullan feasts, married three times, walked away from the crash of his first Robur clipper singed and eyeglass-less and still grinning—was a match made in the funny papers with unsmiling lean Julius, his eternal hard collar and overstuffed document case, a head shorter than his brother.

When Van Damme Aero received the 1938 Collier Trophy for achievement in aeronautics, Henry was seated at the luncheon next to the President; he watched as the President lifted himself, or was lifted, to a standing position to deliver a brief, witty speech in Henry's honor. Then an aide seated right behind the lectern, sensing that the President was done almost before his peroration was finished, half-rose and unobtrusively put a cane into the President's hand, and helped him again to his seat, slipping the locks of his braces while everyone looked elsewhere or at the President's radiant grin. He lifted his old-fashioned to Henry, who raised his glass of water in response.

"Mr. President," Henry said, "I believe you would enjoy flying."

"I couldn't do it," the President said, with dismissive modesty, still grinning.

"You sail, don't you, Mr. President?"

"I do, and I enjoy it. Always have."

"Well, air is a fluid. Managing a craft in the air is in many ways the same."

"You don't say."

"I assure you."

It wasn't really so—after all a boat skims the surface of one fluid while passing through another that is fluid only in a different sense—but at that moment it seemed true to Henry Van Damme. It seemed important to say.

"The controls require a lot of foot power, as I understand," the President said mildly, affixing a Camel in a long cigarette holder.

"A technical detail, easily altered."

"Well." He tossed his head back, that way he had, delighted in himself, the world, his perceptions. "I shall put it to my cabinet. I'm sure they'll be happy to see me barnstorming come election time. You build me a plane, Mr. Van Damme, and I will fly it."

"Done, Mr. President."

Henry spent some time with his engineers, designing a small light plane, neat as an R-class racing yacht, that could be controlled entirely by hands, and delivered it to the White House two months before Pearl Harbor. When Henry and Julius flew to Washington in 1942 to propose what would become the Aviation Board—the great consortium of all the major aircraft builders to share their plants and workers and skills and even their patents among themselves so as to build a fleet of planes such as the world had never seen, and in record time too, as if there were any relevant records—it seemed not the time to mention that pretty little craft. Henry was more tempted to prescribe some remedies he knew about for the weary and hard-breathing man who brought them into his office and spoke with undiminished cheer to them, before turning them over to the appropriate cabinet secretary. Henry said later to Julius in the washroom: The man'll be dead within the year.

3

G laive," said Julius.

"'Glaive'?" Henry asked. "What the hell is that?"

Julius consulted the papers before him. The vice presidents for Sales and Employment waited for the brothers' attention to return to the actual subject of the meeting. "It's a kind of poleax," he said. "Like a sword on a stick." He waved an imaginary one before him, striking down an enemy.

"I don't know," Henry said, lacing his fingers together over his midriff. "Let's not give it a name people have to look up."

Julius shrugged, to say he had sought out the possible names Henry had asked for and wouldn't dispute Henry if Henry had an idea he liked better. All the Van Damme Aero military craft had the names of ancient weapons: the A-21 Sword, the F-10 Spear.

"Mace," Julius said. "Halberd."

Henry stood; his special chair, designed by himself to accommodate and conform to his movements, seemed to shrug him forth and then resume its former posture. He approached the wide windows, canted like an airship's, that looked down on the floor where the A-21s moved in stately procession, growing more complete at every station, though so slowly it seemed they stood still. Even through two layers of glass he could hear the gonglike sounds, the thuds and roars, the sizzle of arc welders.

"You won't be able to build it like you build these," he said. "It's too damn big. You'll have to go back to the old way. Bring the people to the plane, a team for each. It'll cost more, take more time."

The vice presidents were solemn.

"Nor can we build it here," Henry said. He'd said that before. "Is there land we can extend into?"

"Not contiguous to this plant."

"How about the farms and fields?" The present plant had been built where once a walnut orchard had stood; they'd said about it then that the orchard had taken thirty years to grow and had come down in thirty minutes.

"Almost all of them are producing for the armed forces now," Julius said. "Making a mint. If you want them you'd have to get the government to invoke eminent domain. Could take a year."

"Very well, you're right, it's a bad idea, take too long, cost too much. We just have to find someplace new, someplace we can throw up a lot of big buildings very quick."

"Very quick," Julius said. "I'm already working on it."

"Lots of land out there," Henry said, motioning eastward. "Across the mountains. Land that's flat. Empty. Cheap."

Julius sighed, and made a note, or pretended to.

The vice president for Employment crossed his legs and slipped a folder from his case, signaling his readiness to report. Henry turned to him.

"If you're planning a very large expansion," he said, "we'll have a labor problem. It's hard enough to collect 'em in the cities. If you head out into the desert someplace, I don't know."

"Not the *desert*," said Henry mildly.

"We're doing all right now," the VP said, looking at his numbers. "But it's tight. Men with skills are the tough job. Otherwise we're making do, with women, the coloreds, the oldsters, the defectives, the handicaps. We'll soon be running out of them."

"Go out into the highways and the byways," Henry said. "Bring in the lame, the halt, and the blind."

"No place to house them if we can find them," the VP responded.

Henry Van Damme could just at that moment see, down on the floor many feet below, two men gesturing to each other strangely, but not speaking. Deaf men, he realized, talking with their hands. He remembered reading about them in the last issue of the *Aero*. *No problem for THESE fellows communicating on a noisy shop floor!*

"We'll build them houses," Henry said. "Houses are easy. Sell them on the installment plan, no money down. Or rent them. Surely we can design a little house. Or get a plan someplace. Build it cheap."

He turned to face them all, though mostly they saw his broad silhouette against the windows.

"Clinics," he said. "Free clinics. Dentists. A staffed nursery, so the ones with kids can come work. This isn't hard. They'll come if you give them what they need."

"You'd think," said the Employment VP, who had a son in the Army Air Corps, "they'd come to help win the damn war. Not ask for so much at a time like this."

"They're just men," Henry said. "Men and women. No reason to blame them. They want what they need. We'll get it for them. We can and we ought to."

On the floor now a piercing horn began to blow, not urgently but imperiously, in a steady rhythm. Henry turned back to the windows to watch; the line was about to move. The far doors slid apart, opening onto the falling day. The last ship on the left end of the U-shaped track was moved out, finished; a new unfinished one was poised to move in on the right end. All the other ships moved down one place.

"*Pax,*" Henry said.

"What?" Julius looked at his brother.

"The name," Henry said. "For this new plane. Not a sword or a spear or a hammer or any weapon."

"And why not?" Julius asked incuriously.

"It's not going to be for war," Henry said. "If the war even lasts long enough for this plane to get in it, it'll be the last one built. You know it."

Julius said nothing.

"It'll be a peacemaker, peacekeeper. Or nothing."

"All right," Julius said, uncapping his pen.

"*Pax,*" Henry said. "Remember."

4

Ponca City was an oil town, made rich by successive strikes, none greater than the fabulous Burbank pool discovered in the Osage country. Around there in the 1940s we could still get those comic postcards of hook-nosed Indians piling their blanket-wrapped squaws and papooses into Pierce-Arrows bought with their royalties. In Ponca City, oil money built the pretty Shingle Style mansions, the great stony castle on the hill, the Spanish Oriental movie palace, the new high school (1927), and the straight streets of houses that by the time the war started were beginning to look settled and placid, tree shaded and shrubbery enclosed. Beside the proud little city another one arose—the towered and bright-lit one of the refinery. Its tank farm spread to the southwest, uniform gray drums picked out with lights. All day and night the flare stacks burned off gases, sometimes blowing off a bad batch with a noise like thunder and lighting the night, millions of cubic feet, "darkness visible," as though the city beyond was a nice neighborhood of Hell. By the time the Van Damme brothers settled on the empty land outside the city for their plant and town, the oil boomers were dead or bought out, the oil was just a steady flow, the natural gas was firing the town's ovens and refrigerators, but the smell of crude and the wastes of the refinery lay always over the place; locals had ceased to notice, or liked to say they had.

Van Damme Aero worked out an arrangement with the Continental Oil Company, taking up land a couple of miles to the north of the refinery dotted at wide intervals with the black nodding pumps called grasshoppers. A hundred blue Elcar trailers came first, bringing workers and engineers and surveyors to build the settlement that Julius jokingly called Henryville and then wasn't able to change, not to West Ponca or Bomber City or Victoryburg. It was Henryville. A spur line of the Atchison, Topeka and Santa Fe was laid to reach the Van Damme acreage, and while huge Bucyrus steam cranes, brought in on railcars, lifted and fitted into place the steel beams of the plant buildings, surveyors laid out the streets, all lettered north to south and numbered east to west, with hardly a natural feature to be got around, though Henry Van Damme insisted that as many trees as possible be left, to breathe out healthful ozone. Even before the sidewalks were laid or the tar of the roadways was hard the houses started to arrive in boxcars, and the workers offloaded them and they went up like things built in a film where magically everything takes but a second, people flit like demons, and buildings seem to assemble themselves. The Homasote company's Precision Junior was the model chosen, fifty-six of them a day sent out ready to go, all the lumber—sills, plates, joints, rafters—cut to size and numbered like toys to be assembled on Christmas Eve for Junior and Sis. Homasote: a miracle building material made from compressed newspaper, heavy and fireproof and gray, strangely cold to the touch. It took two and a half days to set a house up on its concrete slab, then they'd tarpaper the flat roof, hook up the water and electricity, and spray the outside walls with paint mixed with sand to give the stucco effect. Metal-framed windows that never quite fit, the wind whispered at them, woke you sometimes thinking you'd heard your name spoken.

Van Damme signed on with the Federal Public Housing Administration to borrow the money to build the houses and public buildings, and the FHA guaranteed the mortgages, which you could get for a dollar down; you could own the house for $3,000, or lease it, or rent it, or rent and sublet (there'd be guest entrances in the houses for subletters to enter by, or for others to use who might not want to bang on the front door toward which the neighbors' windows were turned). You got a stove and a tub and, most wonderful, that gas refrigerator, Van Damme'd insisted, and got them all as necessary war materials. Faint crackle of the ice cubes in their metal trays when you opened the door.

A couple of large dormitories (Henry Van Damme had toyed with *lodge* and *residence* and *habitation* before giving in to the standard word) were put up too, one for women and one for men, this because of the bad Ford experience at Willow Run, where a mixed-sex dormitory had quickly become a mass of troubles, lots of keyed-up well-paid workers looking to unlax, nonrationed rum flowing, parties moving from floor to floor, high-stakes strip poker only one rumored aberration, the whole system falling into depths of vice, lost work time, and bad press before being segregated.

The whole settlement filled fast, and even the trailers were left there when the job was done, to put more people in—eventually most of the colored workers were housed there, *happier with their own kind* said the VP for Employment, you had to conform to local customs if you could and Oklahoma had the distinction of being the first state in these States to establish segregated phone booths. Van Damme Aero had addressed the workforce problem by shifting their West Coast employees (*associates* as management named them, *workers* as the union went on stubbornly calling them) to the Ponca City plant, and hiring new people for the older plant from among the migrants always coming in. Van Damme paid a bonus to the associates who'd go east, then pretty soon raised the bonus, what the hell, and that's how Al and Sal Mass and Violet Harbison and Horse Offen and so many others had been *summoned* (Horse Offen put it that way in the *Aero*) to Oklahoma *and that wind that came sweeping down the plain,* which were being celebrated at that very moment on Broadway far away. Some of the associates were originally from there, having left the dust bowl farms and sold-up towns to get in on the good times on the Gold Coast, and now strangely come back again. As more were needed and Van Damme's recruiters went nationwide and the word spread about the new city as foursquare and purposeful and wealthy as the communes dreamed of by Brigham Young or Mother Ann Lee, people began arriving from everywhere else, shading their eyes against the gleam of it coming into view in the salty sunlight.

Prosper Olander began his journey from a northern city with its own aircraft plant, though not one that would hire someone like himself. He was headed for the West Coast, like so many others (when the war was over it would be found that four million of us came out from where we lived to the West Coast, and most never went back). On a winter morning he stood on a street corner of that city, by the stairs that led up to the tracks of the elevated train that could take him to the city center where he could buy a ticket for the West; he had money enough in the wallet tucked into the inner pocket of his houndstooth sport coat, and another fifty that his aunt May had sewn into the coat's lining, which he'd promised to return if he never needed it. A woolen scarf around his neck. Everything else he had decided to bring was packed into an old army knapsack that was slung over his shoulders, somewhat spoiling the lines of his jacket (he thought) and smelling a bit musty, but necessary for someone like himself, propelled by his arms and his wooden crutches.

He hadn't moved from where he stood for some minutes. He was contemplating the stairs leading up to the El, and thinking of the stairs that would certainly lead down into the station when he reached it. He'd never been there, had never before had a reason to go there. And so what if he got a cab, flagged one down, spent the money, got himself to that station—could he get himself inside it? And then the high narrow stairs of the train coaches he'd have to mount—he'd seen them in the movies—and all the stairs up and down from here on, as though the way west were one long flight of them.

Alone too, it was certain now, though he hadn't set out alone.

He turned himself away from the El as a laughing couple went by him to go up—he didn't care to appear as though he himself wanted to go up and couldn't. Across the street a small open car was parked by a sign that said NO PARKING! and showed a fat-faced cartoon cop blowing an angry whistle and holding up a white-gloved hand. Leaning against the fender was a small elderly man, arms folded before him, one foot crossed over the other, looking down the street as though in some disgust. Waiting for a tow? Prosper Olander, unwilling to think of his own dilemma, contemplated this man's. Expecting a woman? Stood up? Prosper had reason to consider that explanation. The man now turned to where Prosper stood in the tiger-striped shadows of the El, and seemed to ponder Prosper's condition—but people often did that. At length—for no real reason, maybe just to be in motion—Prosper walked toward the man and the car. The man seemed to come to attention at Prosper's approach, unsurprised and already rooting in his pocket for the coin he assumed Prosper was about to ask him for—Prosper was familiar with the look. Prosper pointed to the car.

"Out of gas?"

"Not quite," said the gent. "But near enough that I have decided I won't go farther without a plan to get more."

"Can't get any, or can't find any?"

"Both." He looked down at the machine, an old Chrysler Zephyr, gray and dispirited and now seeming to shrink in shame. The plates were from a neighboring state. "You may know there's a shortage on, though you yourself may not have experienced it. I don't know."

"I've heard," Prosper said.

"I was doing pretty well, what with one thing and another," said the man, "until on driving into this town I began to run low, and all the gas stations I passed were all out, or so they claimed."

"Uh-huh."

"Then a gasoline truck went by me, going the other way," he said. "Good luck! You could tell by the way he drove—slouching around corners—he was full. Gravid you might say. A line of cars had figured that out and were following him. I turned around and got in line too, but I was cut off by others on the way, and fell behind, and was further supplanted till when the station was reached I was far in the rear. I do not like to battle for precedence or advantage. I don't do it."

"You're a lover not a fighter," Prosper ventured.

"Well. By the time I got my heap up to the front of the line—after every car passing by wedged itself in too, and a fight or two had broken out—the well was dry. I had just enough left to get me this far."

"They say the shortages are local. Farther south they have a lot."

"The Big Inch," said the gent.

"The what?"

"The great pipeline that'll bring oil from down there up this way. When it's done."

"Oh."

"We make do now with the Little Inch."

"Oh."

"In any case finding the gas wouldn't have done me much good. I have one stamp left, and no more till next month."

"What kind of ration card do you have?" Prosper asked.

The fellow looked up at him as though surprised, maybe, that someone like him would know to ask this question, which could hardly be of much interest to him. "The miserable A," he said. "My employer was unable even to get me a B. He was told salesmen could take the train. I think not."

Prosper said nothing. A salesman.

"And yourself?" the man said. "Alone and palely loitering?"

Not knowing why he should do so, Prosper decided not to pass this by. "I was going to take the El downtown," he said. "But those stairs are a little beyond me."

The man looked at the stairs, the iron framework of the El, as though seeing them for the first time. "Inconvenient," he said. He indicated the knapsack. "You are prepared for a journey."

"I was going west to look for work."

The salesman didn't look surprised or amused by this ambition, though Prosper'd expected the one or the other. "So a ride downtown wouldn't take you far. I see that now."

"And there'd go your gas, though I appreciate the offer."

For a moment they stood together, Prosper and the salesman, both feeling (they'd confess it later to each other) that there was another remark to make, that Destiny had put them in speaking relation and they hadn't yet said the thing Destiny wanted them to say.

"The name's Notzing," said the salesman then, and put out his hand—a little tentatively, thinking perhaps that such a one as Prosper might not take hands, or not be able to—Prosper saw those thoughts also, also not unfamiliar to him. "Call me Pancho." The way he said it, the first syllable sounded like *ranch* and not like *launch*.

"Prosper Olander," Prosper returned, and took the salesman's hand before it retreated. Then he took from inside his coat a small paper booklet. "This might help you out," he said.

Pancho Notzing reached for the thing, a look of baffled wonderment beginning to break on his face that he struggled to conceal. The booklet was a C gasoline ration booklet, the most generous ranking, reserved for doctors, ministers, railroad workers, people on whom we all depended (that anyway was the idea). It was chock-full of coupons. It was unsigned.

"A man could go far on this," he said.

Prosper said nothing.

"I wonder how you came by it," he said. "Issued to you perhaps in error?"

"Not exactly." The book remained in Pancho's hand, as though still in passage between them. "Where were you driving to, anyway?"

"I don't really have a destination. I have my route, of course, and my territory. But to tell you the truth I have been thinking of quitting."

"Really."

"I don't suppose you're offering those to me for sale."

"That would be a crime," Prosper said.

For a moment neither of them said anything more, the conclusion evident to each of them already, only the question of who was to broach it remaining. Barter was a thing we all in those times resorted to; Mr. Black was a man we knew.

"I have been to the West," Pancho said then. "The Mission country. The land of Ramona. The hacienda at sunset. The primrose blooming in the desert."

"There's a windshield sticker that goes with it," Prosper said, reaching again into his pocket. "I have that too."

"I understand all the big plants are hiring. Everyone can do his part."

"They say."

Pancho straightened, and with a final glance at the C booklet, he put it in the breast pocket of his jacket. "You shouldn't be made to suffer indignities, if you're headed out to help build ships or airplanes. Ride with me, and we'll make our way. I'm in the way of changing jobs myself."

"You don't say."

So sporting the new C sticker on the windshield, the Zephyr set off in the direction of the sunset; when it ran out of gas just yards from the next pump, Prosper took the wheel as the old man pushed, and together they rolled it to the pump, Prosper pulling up gently on the hand brake lever as instructed to bring it to a stop. The attendant, a plump young woman in a billed cap and leather bow tie—there were lots of women manning the pumps now, with the male pump jockeys off at war—watched as Prosper pulled his crutches from the back seat and got out to stand next to Pancho, who was panting with effort and pressing a hand to his breast. They presented their C booklet, which Pancho had signed, and the girl tore out a stamp, then expertly unlimbered the hose and wound the handle of the counter to put in their allotted gas. No one spoke. The pump bell rang off the gallons. Above them the red Flying Horse beat skyward. When she was done she cheerfully washed the windshield with a sponge, her rump in the trousers of her brown coverall moving with her motions. She took Prosper's money and went to make change while the two men stood not speaking by the car.

"All set," she said, returning with the change.

"Thanks," said Prosper.

"Thanks," said Pancho.

"Oil change?" she asked. "Check those belts?"

"No, no thanks."

The car started with a cough, dry throat needing a moment to recover.

"Bye," said the girl, and gave them a smart two-finger salute. "Drive under thirty-five."

"Bye," said Prosper.

"Bye," said Pancho.

The two of them didn't speak again for some time after that, conscious of having done a wrong, not quite knowing whether to congratulate themselves or shake their heads over the ways of the world that had forced them to it, or just shut up; Pancho never would ask Prosper, in all their journey together, where he had come up with those stamps, and Prosper didn't volunteer the information.

Pancho had a couple of last calls to make, he'd told Prosper, and then a stop at the home office in the next city, where he'd leave his sample cases, his last orders, and his resignation. He roomed with his widowed sister, he said, when not on the road, which he was most of the time; he'd wire her about his plans. Then they'd head for the south and then the Coast.

"What was it you sell, or sold I guess?" said Prosper when the Mobil station was far behind them and his city growing thin and passing too.

"Fabrics," Pancho said. "Commercial mostly. To the trade. Damasks, *matelassés,* shantungs, broadcloths, velours. Specialty silks. Done it for thirty years, a traveler in fabrics."

"Why don't you want to do it anymore?"

For a time Pancho seemed to be choosing among various answers he might give, opening his mouth and making introductory sounds, then shutting it again. "Ah, for one thing," he said, "the business is changing. I'm getting too old to keep up. All these new man-made wonder fabrics. Nylon, rayon, spray-on, pee-on, who the hell can keep them straight or pitch them in any way that'd be useful, well whoever can, *I* can't. Then this war, the big companies supplying the war department are taking all the business, sucking up all the supplies, the cotton, the silk, all of it, if you're not selling to the government forget it. Rationing: how are you going to sell fine fabrics to manufacturers who are cutting back every day? When the women are wearing unlined suits and the men are leaving the pocket flaps off their jackets and the cuffs off their trousers? You tell me."

Prosper could not tell him.

"More than that and above it all," Pancho said, "I violate my own best sense of how a man should live. I have done the same work for decades, never changing, never learning, without friends beside me, without associates, without the refreshment of change, without delight." He turned to Prosper. "Not that this makes me in any way different from millions."

"I shouldn't say so," Prosper said.

"Well and you?" the salesman asked him.

"Ah. Well I was privately employed."

"Ah."

They said no more for a long time. Prosper studied the places they passed, that seemed to come into being merely by his entering them, and then to persist behind him as he and Pancho and the Zephyr made more. Fields and farms appearing, then after a time the outskirts of a town, sometimes announced with a proud sign (GREENFIELD—A FRIENDLY TOWN) and the totem pole of the local lodges and clubs, Masons, Lions, Odd Fellows. The last and least farms passed, then the more decrepit and dirtier businesses, the ice-and-coal supplier and the lumberyard, then the first paved streets of houses and neighborhood shops, maybe a mill with its strings of joined workers' houses like city streets displaced. The better neighborhoods, a white church or a stone one, big houses with wide yards and tended shrubbery, but the biggest one an undertakers'. Then downtown, brick buildings of three and four stories, hero on a plinth, the larger churches, a domed granite courthouse on Courthouse Square.

"Well take a good look," said Pancho a little bitterly when Prosper noted these trim towns, each different but all alike. "These places won't last. They'll be drained of population. They're the past, these old mills. People'll go where the work is, and that's the big plants in the big cities or the new cities now a-building. That's the future."

"I'd like to see the future," Prosper said. "All the wonders."

"You are a Candide," Pancho said. "You think this is the best of all possible worlds. Or will be."

"I can't be a Candide," said Prosper.

"And why not?"

"Because I've read the book."

Esso station, five-and-dime, A & P. Pancho contemned the big chain stores, displacing local businesses, substituting standardized needs and ways of meeting them for individual taste and satisfaction.

"They say that this new finance capitalism's efficient. Actually it's inefficient, and the more the owners are divorced from the operations of it the more inefficient it can get. They claim 'efficiency of scale'— they don't know that when you scale something up it doesn't always work the same. It's just as when a great corporation claims the same right as an individual to the freedoms guaranteed by our forefathers in 1776. A nice piece of sophistry. As if Nabisco was not different from a man running his own bakeshop here in this town."

The bakeshop Pancho pointed to looked welcoming. It was called

Mom's and had red-and-white calico curtains in the window, and Prosper thought of calling a halt to buy some supplies, but Pancho hunched over the wheel seemed unlikely to hear, and then Mom's was gone, and the Ball Building, and the fire station. The railroad tracks, after which the houses grew poorer and fewer, some streets of Negroes, then scarcer, with vacant lots and abandonment (the hard times hardly gone) until once more fields and farms began, much like the earlier ones but not them. Tractors plowing in contour lines like marcelled brown hair, because spring was rushing upward toward them as they went down.

Sometime after dark they came upon a long low establishment roofed in Spanish tile (so Pancho said it was) with a floodlit sign in front that commanded that they DINE-DANCE and offered them STEAKS CHOPS CHICKEN, though it was unlikely that it'd have much of that these days, or much of anything to drink either, but by then the Zephyr'd been traveling a long time; the road had been bare of other choices, and didn't look to be getting better.

"It's a law of life," Pancho said. "Turn down the pretty-good place and you'll wander for hours and find nothing as good, end up in a greasy spoon just closing its doors. Trust me. Years on the road."

Attached to this place was a cinder block motel, red-tiled too: a string of red-painted doors, each with a wicker chair beside it and a window with a calico curtain like Mom's bakery. Prosper thought that calico curtains were perhaps to be a feature of travel, and made a note to watch for more. He had never left the city of his birth before.

"Mo-tel," Pancho said. "Motor-hotel. A hotel, but one without bellhops, a cigar stand, newspapers, a front desk, room service, a Western Union office, or any other of the common amenities."

"Two dollars a night," Prosper said, pointing to a sign.

"You have an endless capacity to be pleased," Pancho said gravely. "That is an enviable quality in youth, and a good thing for a traveler to have."

The room that the key given to Pancho let them into was small and spare, and clad in honey-colored knotty pine, a thing that Prosper had never seen or smelled before—like living in a hollow tree, he thought. A single lamp between the two beds was shaped to resemble a large cactus and a sleeping Mexican. The beds were narrow and the pillows ungenerous; there was a shower but no tub. A rag rug on the linoleum floor nearly caught a crutch and spilled him: Prosper was opposed to linoleum floors, and to rag rugs. But still he loved the place immediately, and would come to love all motels, with but one shallow stair up to the little cloister that protected the doors, sometimes not even that, out of the car and in, and there you were.

He deposited his knapsack and Pancho lugged in a suitcase and his sample cases, washed his hands, and they went to eat in the wide building fronting the motel. Prosper had never been in one of these either, though he knew right away what name to call it: the air of weary gaiety, glow of the cigarette machine, couple drinking over there with another male whose role was unguessable, blond waitress with challenging eyes and bitter mouth—"A *roadhouse*," he said to Pancho. "Just like in *True Story*."

"Just like in *what* true story?" Pancho asked.

Prosper told him to never mind.

There were, amid the items crossed off on the menu, enough to make a meal, and whiskey, a surprise. They each ordered one. Pancho, having rapidly downed his, described to Prosper the principles of Bestopianism, which he claimed were in fact not different from the principles of natural life and common sense. "This isn't hard," he said. "You ask: What makes a person happy? Not one thing that will make all men everywhere happy, but this person here and now. And next question, How's he going to get it? That's all. Answer those questions. Let every person answer the first. Society should answer the second."

"Uh-huh," Prosper said. "So what's the answer?"

Pancho regarded him with a penetrating look, and for the first time Prosper discerned the penetration might be due to a slight cast in one of his close-set wide-open eyes. It made for a furious or accusatory look Prosper didn't think he meant.

"The answer," he said, "is the wholesale reorganization of human society so that the natural impulses of humankind are allowed free development."

"Aha." It was clear to Prosper that he was not saying this for the first time. "And what are these impulses, would you say?"

Pancho placed his hands on the table in oracular fashion. "You know. Think a minute, you'll be able to make a list. We are made by

Nature with these desires, yet every political system and moral system is bent on repressing or extinguishing them—either by force or by convincing us our natures are evil and must be repressed. As if that were possible. As if the industrial society could crush our desires for variety, for pleasure, for worth, for interest, for satisfaction. As if two incompatible people locked in the legal institution of marriage could force themselves to love, when their deep, true, innocent passions remain unfulfilled."

"You mean," Prosper asked, "free love?"

"Free love, truly free, isn't possible now. In a society rotten with money values and venereal disease the idea's laughable. But yes. In a society correctly made, where human feelings and passions and needs are understood and met, not repressed or denied or despised, yes. Free love; mutuality; everyone a suitor to many; many loves for each one. A Passionate Series in harmony. Old, young, everyone. The old in our society suffer a loneliness that can hardly be imagined, because they are cast out of the possibility of the love relation."

"Everybody just going at it, then? Grandpa, Grandma, the kids?" Prosper tried not to grin disrespectfully.

"Not at all," said Pancho. "Not in a harmonious society, such as you, my boy, have never experienced and perhaps cannot conceive, which causes you to laugh at these possibilities. Of course even in the Harmonious City to come, some will be satisfied with a brute connection, and will find many who are like spirited, if they are allowed. Some are naturally satisfied only with a lifetime devotion. Others not; they enjoy intrigue, titillation, variety—they are like gourmets to the plain dinner-eaters." He sopped bread in his gravy. "Then there are those whose *spirits* are the part that is most invested, who care less for the physical, though no love relation is without the physical. And so on."

"Sounds complicated," Prosper said.

"The complicated is always the true," Pancho said. "The simple is false and a lie."

"I'll remember that," Prosper said.

When their Salisbury steaks were done and the greasy paper napkins balled and tossed on the plates, Pancho said he'd retire, but Prosper decided to sit a while, have another drink, see if something happened, he couldn't say what. The bandstand remained empty, and the few folks who arrived to take the tables or occupy the bar—a couple of men in uniform among them—seemed to be fruitlessly awaiting the same thing, whatever it was—intrigue, maybe, titillation—and after a time Prosper went back across the courts to his room.

Pancho lay in his bed, pajamas buttoned up to the neck, his gray hair upshot, reading from a small leather-bound book, a Testament Prosper supposed.

"No," Pancho said. "A poem, in the form of a play, by Percy Shelley. *Prometheus Unbound*. Though it has served me in some ways as a scripture."

"Oh," Prosper said. He got out of his jacket, rummaged in his knapsack to find his toothbrush and tooth powder, and went into the bathroom; brushed his teeth, washed his face with a dingy cloth, and made water, propping himself on one crutch. He flushed, and looked into the damp-smelling shower stall, hung with a rubberized curtain. To use it he'd have to turn it on standing, then sit to take his braces off while it ran, then hump on his bottom over the lip and under the stream. If the water changed temperature meantime, he was out of luck. Don't forget the soap: if he left it in its wire basket above, he wouldn't be able to reach it once he was in.

Maybe tomorrow.

He returned to his bed and sat. From now on, wherever he went, he would have to lay plans for himself, and think of everything. He hadn't seen that clearly till now.

Pancho kept his eyes on his book while Prosper removed his pants, unstrapped each of his braces in turn and with his hands pulled his legs free. He laid the braces on the floor and managed to pull down the coverlet and sheet and put himself within.

"Good night, my friend," Pancho said then, and closed his book.

"Good night."

Pancho pulled the chain of the lamp. He lay back against the pillow, arms alongside him, gray hair upright, palms down; Prosper would find him just that way in the morning.

Prosper lay awake in the light passing from outside through the drawn shade and the calico. He tried to imagine all the things that he would have to be prepared to do, to put up with, to get around or over.

He tried to feel sure that they would each be accomplished or avoided somehow, even though he would have to face them alone, without Elaine. That would make up for Elaine's skipping out on him at the El, and going on without him. She had urged him that far, she had made him be that brave, but she'd been unable to believe in him any further, and left him there at the bottom of the stairway. But when he found her again he'd show her that he had done it. When he found her, out there by the sea in the sun where she'd gone and he was headed, he would be able to tell her *See? I'm here, I made it, alone. You didn't think I could but I did.* She'd be sorry and amazed. And he'd say *It's all right: it's all right now.*

In the late afternoon of the next day they reached the city where Pancho's fabrics company had offices. Looking somehow determined and stricken at the same time, Pancho left Prosper in the double-parked car, pulled out his sample cases from the trunk, and disappeared into a closed-faced building; reappeared an hour later without them. Prosper had fended off a traffic cop by showing his crutches, claiming his driver'd be out any minute. Pancho started the car and drove for a time without speaking. Then he said:

"Prosper, not one thing written in all the books of philosophy or morals over the last three thousand years has made one damn bit of difference to human beings, or added one jot to human happiness. They say what should be: not what is. I've learned more about the corruptions of the human spirit in that office, in that business, where for thirty years and more I was robbed and hoodwinked and taken, than I could have in any book. More about human nature in a smoking car. More about the frustrations of desire in a boardinghouse. Don't talk to me about philosophy."

Prosper didn't. They checked in that night at a downtown hotel, one supplied with all those things Pancho had said motels didn't have, plus a barbershop and a shoeshine stand. As Pancho had his shock of straw-stiff hair cut, sighing at the barber's worn wisecracks, Prosper read magazines. Here was one on whose cover a young woman modeled a uniform that an airplane company was issuing to all its women employees. Inside, the article was titled "Working Chic to Chic" and showed the same young woman in various situations, wearing the new outfit, which satisfied all the requirements of the job but could be worn anywhere. It was a deep blue (the article said blue), a pair of high-waisted slacks and a tunic the same color, with company badges on the shoulder and the breast pocket. All you had to do was swap the tunic for a nice blouse or sweater and you were dressed for a date or a dance. There were pictures of the young woman in full uniform on the wing of a plane, gazing into the clouds; then holding an electric tool of some kind; then, tunic-less, laughing at a bar, holding a drink, the same slacks, and two—maybe three—servicemen around her for her to ignore. The girl's name was Norma Jeane.

Prosper closed the magazine. Norma Jeane on the cover stood with her back to the camera, hand on her hip and her head turned back to smile at Prosper, like Betty Grable in that picture. No girdle for her.

"So get this," the barber said.

Prosper sought out the article again, flipping the big pages, unable to locate it, pages filled with tanks and planes and advancing and retreating armies, generals and statesmen, the united nations. Here.

Norma Jeane. He envied her; envied her soldiers, her smile. Many suitors for each one. The plant where she worked building airplanes with her tools was in Oklahoma. Van Damme Aero's brand-new plant for the making of their huge new bombers, using the most modern and up-to-date methods and materials. A workers' paradise, it's said, and workers are pouring in from all parts of the country to sign up for the thousands of jobs. Skilled and unskilled. Old and young.

Oklahoma. If he remembered his geography right they would pass through there on their way to the Coast. They had to.

"Say," he said, looking up, spoiling the barber's punch line. "I've an idea."

5

We weren't where we were in those times because we had been thrown or removed to there. We didn't think so. We felt we had impelled ourselves, like the faring pioneers and immigrants driving their wagons or pushing their barrows who somewhere somehow along the way stopped and *settled* as a bird does on a branch or a catarrh does on the lungs: those pioneers whose grandchildren we were, now again pulling up stakes, uprooted in the *mobilization,* the putting-into-motion, that began before the real war did and continued all through it. True, in some places we stayed on where our fathers and mothers and grandfathers had first settled, but even so we were caught up in that motion if our parents and grandparents had happened to settle in places that those on the move were now headed for or drawn to—seemingly *blown* to, you might think seeing them, as by one of those comic tornadoes that lift a boy on a bicycle or a chicken coop full of chickens or a Ford car with Gramps and Gram inside and set it down unharmed somewhere else. Those stories always made the papers, and the new migrant herds did too, arriving purposefully, getting off trains carrying their bags and kids, pulling into town in panting jalopies with bald tires, looking around for a place to stay. Alarming, sometimes, to those already there and living in the homes and going to the churches and the shops they thought were theirs.

Those trains go both ways the locals would now and then say to new-comers whose ways they didn't like. People from elsewhere were more different from you than they are now. They came from farther away.

Pancho Notzing with Prosper beside him reached Ponca City the next afternoon and they were immediately caught up in the stream of traffic headed out of the city—every Ponca spare room, hotel bed, guesthouse, and shed held a worker or two that hadn't got accommodation in the dormitories or houses of Henryville, and the second shift was about to begin. Yellow Van Damme buses, yellow bicycles that Van Damme loaned out free to workers, cars of every description all going out along roads not meant for much traffic beyond a leisurely touring car going one way and a hay wagon going the other: tempers could get frayed, including those of the folks on their porches by the roadside watching.

Getting a job at Van Damme Aero Ponca City was like being drafted by a tornado. A hundred people were involved in nothing but looking you over, asking you questions, filling your hands with forms, examining you, putting you through tests, chivying crowds from one station to another in a wide circle (though you couldn't see a circle) until you reached where you'd started from, but now with all you needed to be an employee. Now and then as you were blown around you heard vast noises outside the processing center, the big Bee engines starting up, horns sounding, wide steel doors rolling open—that's all it was, but you didn't know that and jumped a little each time. They sorted you into shifts, sent some home to come back the next morning or midnight to begin, and some they simply put to work—especially the skilled men, who'd arrived dressed for it, and not in a suit and a pair of wingtips or a frock and stacked heels, and who had their own tools in sturdy cases. If you wanted that Van Damme Aero uniform for work, and they suggested it would be a very good thing, you got a ticket for one and could pay it off out of your first pay envelope, or take a little out for three weeks or four. There wasn't a stair in the place: Van Damme wanted every space accessible to the fleet of electric trucks that scooted everywhere, pulling trailer-loads of materials, running unguessable errands, tooting their little horns and flicking their lights. Pancho and Prosper were immediately drawn apart, stepping into two different intake lanes and swept inward in different directions. Prosper kept up with the crowd, though he spent longer in Physical Examinations than most, and at the end he got a time card, and instructions, and a form to fill out to get a badge.

Prosper Olander had a war job. He started on the first shift, next morning.

Pancho Notzing, also taken on, was looking pale and somewhat asweat when Prosper found him by the car in the parking lot.

"I don't know if I can do this," the older man said. "I would like to be able to refuse."

"It seems good to me," Prosper said. His shirt was damp at the arms from all the walking. "Are you antiwar?"

"Well not in the usual sense maybe," Pancho said. "I regret the stupid waste. No one would go to war if their lives were gratifying, if their associations gave them satisfaction, if they had pleasure and delight. They go because they can't think why they shouldn't. Their leaders are filled with rage and envy and fear, and no one laughs them down."

"You have to defend yourself."

"Ah yes. Well. Perhaps. In defending ourselves we may also change ourselves, without seeing that we do, and for good too. These vast engines of destruction. The vast System that's needed to build them and send them on their way. We don't know the outcome."

He said it as though he did know the outcome, and Prosper—not only to forestall him from saying so—said, "Let's get some dinner. Speaking of pleasure."

They went back to Ponca, looking at a night spent in the car, as there were very likely going to be no rooms for miles around. A square meal at least they ought to be able to get, they thought, and they had to wait long enough for that, standing listening to the chat on the line outside the Chicken in the Rough on Grand Avenue (animated neon sign over the door whereon an enraged rooster took a swing at a golf ball, and was next shown with a busted club, and then again).

"Dance lessons?" they heard one man ask another in some surprise.

"Thursdays. Tuesdays I got bowling, Mondays the checkers tournament."

"Mondays the Moths play the Hep Cats. First game of the season. They say Henry Van Damme's throwing out the first ball."

Once inside they had a further wait at the counter, Ponca City's longtime dry laws modified to allow mild beer for the duration, and glasses and steins crowding the length of it. Prosper worked in beside a tall person in the Van Damme uniform, minus the tunic with badge and name, the blue slacks and a shirt just fine for off-hours, as promised. Not Norma Jeane. Two blue barrettes held back her black hair, done in a Sculpture Wave he guessed, though maybe it was natural. A very tall person. She took no notice of him, looking down the bar away, but (Prosper thought) at no one in particular.

"Mind if I smoke?" he asked her.

"I don't care if you burn." She turned slightly toward him to let him see her uncaring face, and she noticed the crutches under his arms. "Oh. Sorry."

He offered her a smoke, which she declined. "You work at Van Damme?" he asked. The woman looked at him with kindly contempt, who doesn't, what a dumb line.

"I just got hired," Prosper said.

"Is that so."

"Doing something I've never done."

"Yeah well. They have their own ideas. I was a welder when I came, but no more."

Prosper saw Pancho waving to him, he'd secured a couple of seats.

"Care to join us?" he asked the woman, and as all his remarks so far had done, this one seemed to rebound gently from her without making contact. He straightened carefully and stepped away with what he hoped was a certain grace. As he went to where Pancho waited he heard laughter behind him, but not, he thought, at him.

Baskets of fried chicken, laid on calico paper as though for a picnic, and French-fried potatoes; paper napkins and the bottled "3.2" beer. Pancho looked down at this insufficiency. One of his beliefs was that if all people received a real competence for their labors, or simply as a birthright, they could just refuse poor food until it was replaced with better.

"And what did they say they'd be putting you to doing?" he asked Prosper.

"Well they didn't," Prosper said. "As I was explaining, there." He gestured to the counter. Pancho looked over his shoulder; the woman Prosper had spoken to passed a glance in their direction, maybe a hint of a smile, and away again.

Day Shift workers went into the Van Damme works through a bank of

glass doors, even as the Victory Shift workers exited through another bank, looking worn and depleted. The heels of incoming workers made a din on the tiled floor; Prosper was like a stick in a stream as they swept around him, and he had to be careful not to get kicked and lose his footing—they gave him space, when they saw him, but they didn't always see him. Prosper had washed his face in a Conoco gas station toilet, but his cheeks were stubbly and his collar gray; he felt a cold apprehension he hadn't felt yesterday.

Where the entrance narrowed to stream the workers past the time clocks, he handed the cards he'd been given to the clerk behind a window there, who saw something on them that caused him to pick up a phone. He flipped a switch on his PBX and waited a time, regarding Prosper with steady indifference; he spoke a name into the phone, hung it up, and pointed to where Prosper was to stand and wait. Pancho had long since gone into the interior beyond. Prosper had time to fill up with a familiar but always surprising anxiety as the workers went past him, some glancing his way. Far more women than men, like a city avenue where the department stores are.

"Olander?"

Prosper stepped forward. The man who'd called his name, without actually looking for him, was a long thin S-shaped man, knobby wrists protruding from his sleeves. He wore a tie and round horn-rims. He motioned to Prosper to follow him along into the plant.

"Through here."

Prosper Olander had never been in a cathedral, but now he felt something like that, the experience of entering suddenly a space so large, so devoted to a single purpose, that the insides of the heart are drawn for a moment outward and into it, trying to fill it, and failing. It wasn't perpendicular like a cathedral, or still and echoey, it was loud under long high banks of lights; but it was so huge, and the numbers of people and tasks that filled it so many, that it took a moment before Prosper's stretched senses even perceived that what was being scrambled over and attended to were units, were all alike, were the bodies of airplanes. Even then he could doubt the perception: was it really possible that things this big (and still they were only parts of things that would have to be a lot bigger, reason told you that) were meant to fly? For a second you could feel that they were something more like brooding hens, and the workers were helping them lay and hatch the actual airplane-sized airplanes out of their vast insides.

The supervisor or foreman he followed, as he would come to know, was Rollo Stallworthy, and a kinder man than he appeared. Prosper followed after him as fast as he could down what would have been the cathedral's nave, between the plane bodies on either side, Rollo giving no quarter. Prosper could travel fast but not for long, and eventually he had to stop; Rollo Stallworthy after a moment's solo progress divined something was wrong and looked back to where Prosper panted.

"Oh. Sorry."

"It's fine," Prosper said. "Just give me a minute."

Just then a very large man consulting with others at one of the long tables that at every station held blueprints and paper in piles caught sight of Prosper, and signaled he'd like a word.

Prosper waited. Rollo nodded respectfully to the big man and put his hands behind his back.

"New hire?" said the man. His face was the size of a pie and crossed with gold-framed eyeglasses. Prosper nodded. The man pointed to his legs and his back.

"Tabes dorsalis?" he asked.

"No," Prosper said.

"Been to the health clinic?" the man said. Prosper thought he'd never seen such yardage of seersucker expended on a single suit. "Got your health card?"

"Yes."

"Go on over. May well be something they can do for you."

"All right," said Prosper.

"Carry on," the man said cheerily, and turned back to his table.

"That was him," Rollo said as he set the pace again. He grinned back at Prosper.

"That was who?"

"Himself. Henry the Great. Here on an inspection tour. He doesn't miss a thing."

"Well say," Prosper said.

"You're fortunate he didn't give you a pill to take," Rollo said. "His pockets are full of 'em."

What Rollo had been given was the job of finding something for Prosper to do. Rollo'd already shown himself ingenious at tasks like this, and lay awake at night sometimes (none of his own supervisors knew this, they just assumed Rollo could do it and so they told him to do it) putting together his crews and subcrews so that everybody could work just as hard and fast as they were able. The short, the strong, the old, the weary and querulous, the whites who'd work next to blacks and the ones that wouldn't, the helpful and patient ones you could put next to the stupid truculent ones and get the best out of both. He'd been thinking about this lame young man he'd been assigned, who was actually in worse shape (Rollo was now convinced, having studied him without staring rudely) than he'd been described as being by Intake.

"All right," he said, and they slowed beside a station that seemed like other stations, beneath the long unfinished hollow body of a plane, which was far larger to look at from beneath even than to see from the door. Workers were riveting panels of the aluminum skin in place, one outside with the gun and the other on the other side with the bucking bar that turned the rivet's end (he didn't yet know this). Rollo began talking in a voice so slow and deliberate it was actually hard to follow, though intended to be easy, describing Prosper's job, which would involve assisting in keeping records of tools and materials used and needed at this station, new orders filled or pending. He understood Prosper'd not be able to take it all in right off, but a little practice would put that right, it wasn't a hard job but it was exacting. And Prosper tried to listen, but his eyes were drawn up and around, to the women in their coveralls, their caps, their heavy gloves and saddle shoes and sloppy socks, till they began to look down at him too, and smile and wave and welcome him. Colored women and old women and young women of many shapes, perched on narrow footholds, handling power tools with grace and equanimity. The repeated *tzing* of those guns, like bullets fired every which way in movie cartoons.

"You'll shadow me," Rollo said. "Till you get familiar with them all."

He seemed to mean the forms and stamps he was gesturing at, which Prosper at length looked down at. "Yes," he said.

"You'll do fine."

"Yes," Prosper said. "I think I will."

Prosper and Pancho spent that night on couches in the men's dormitory, and then got beds in the plain bare rooms there, but it wasn't long before a house on Z Street became available. Despite all of Van Damme Aero's efforts to attract and keep workers, the turnover rate was almost as high as in the rest of the war industries, people getting homesick, men's deferments running out and not renewed, women quitting when their men were demobilized or when they'd earned enough for a down payment on a real house in a real place; or they just couldn't adjust, despite Van Damme's psychologists, and they went back to where people acted and thought the way they once supposed everyone everywhere did.

The Z Street family that departed sold Pancho their two beds and the other sticks of furniture they'd acquired, they could afford better now, and Prosper and Pancho picked up other things—Henryville was a ceaseless rummage sale of lamps and tin flatware and radios and deal dressers; one fringed pillow with a painted satin cover showing sunset over Lake George migrated from bed to couch in houses from A Street to 30th, holding up heads and tired feet, until it wouldn't plump and was so soiled that night had fallen on its pines. The house had two bedrooms and a living room, and that sublessor's door on the side, and a yard a little bigger than the others, but otherwise (Pancho thought) belonged on Devil's Island for its cheerlessness and separation from all the identical others. Wave of the future he said sadly, unless things changed. Prosper was delighted with it. Like a motel, it had no basement, no attic, no high porch with a cliff of steps, nowhere in it he couldn't go or couldn't use, it was all *his* as much as it could be anybody's. He stood looking out his window at the rectangles of the house opposite his. It was identical to his but had a carport over the miniature driveway roofed in a strange ribbed translucent green material Prosper'd never seen before. "Fiberglass," said Pancho, somewhat bitterly. "It's a fabric and a wool and a plastic. No end to its uses."

"Nice," said Prosper. "Keep the Zephyr dry if we had one." Pancho (as Prosper had hoped) turned to eye him in disgust.

It was on that day, as Prosper was making his way across the vast parking lot from where Pancho had to park among the thousands, that Horse Offen in his little Van Damme electric car stopped beside him to offer a lift. Pancho had already gone on ahead, at Prosper's urging, don't be late.

"Say, thanks," Prosper said, figuring a way to climb aboard as Horse watched with interest.

"Don't mind if we go a roundabout way?" Horse asked.

"No not a bit. I'm early." He tended to be, until he was sure how long a trip like this one would take him, on average.

Horse was out with pad and camera to write up a feature for the *Aero*. He'd already done the sports scores and the winning suggestion of the week (some kind of improvement to a wing jig that Horse didn't quite get) and needed more. He questioned Prosper as they rode, how long he'd needed the crutches, where he'd come from, what he'd done before, which seemed mostly to be not much. Nothing there for Horse.

"Any hobbies?"

"Well, I don't have many of my tools here, but I like drafting and lettering and so on. Working with pens, commercial art."

"But that's not your job here."

"No."

"Well hey. Who knows. We can use people in my shop who can do that kind of work. If you want to apply."

Prosper maintained a silence, one that Horse couldn't know resulted from a kind of awed embarrassment, that what he most wanted would be offered him right here and now, or the hope or suggestion of it.

"So after all this. What's your goal?"

After a moment's thought, or silence anyway, Prosper said: "I would hope one day to achieve greatness."

"Aha. In what line?"

"I don't know that yet."

Horse allowed himself a laugh, but thought it sort of served him right, getting an answer like that in response to a tease—a "goal," after all, for someone like this gangly Plastic Man with the snappy fedora.

"Here we go," he said. He stopped the little car and dismounted. They were within the central building; Prosper could see the shop numbers receding into the distance, toward his own. "Well, my two gals aren't here yet," he said looking around. "Let me take your picture. Never know when I might use it." Prosper lifted himself off the car, set himself on the shop floor, and drew himself up, insofar as he could. Horse thought of a title—"Aiming for Greatness"—and laughed again as he looked down at Prosper on the screen of the Rolleiflex. Just then Prosper saw behind Horse two women, a very tall one and a very short one, both dressed for work, but headed their way.

Horse turned. "Ah say, how are you, ladies?"

It seemed to Prosper that the two women knew Horse pretty well and treated him with a kind of impatient tolerance. "Meet our new employee," Horse said, indicating Prosper. The smaller woman was definitely small, a midget Prosper supposed, not with the brawny shoulders and big head of one or two such people he'd known. The other, the tall one, he recognized.

She recognized him too. "We've met," she said, as though she thought something was amusing.

"That's right, we have," Prosper said. "I don't think I caught your name, though."

"I don't think I tossed it."

Horse said the names—small Sal Mass and tall Violet Harbison, been around a good while, Vi plays for the Moths, the best softball team in the industry. As he made the introductions he conceived the idea of lining up all three of them and taking a picture and running it with some kind of joke about a sideshow or something, "So Where's the Fat Lady?" but of course that was stupid. The two women, though, went together naturally: they worked in the same shop. No forced humor there. They just happened to be the shortest and the tallest. And Vi was a stunner in a kind of unsettling way. They both wore the flying "E" badges awarded for effort, and that, of course, would be the lead, but he still planned to call the story "The Long and the Short of It," all in good fun.

Prosper watched Horse set up his shot, clicking off a surprising number, this way, that way. He got Sal to climb a stepladder and sit, to bring their two heads together. Finally he asked Vi to maybe hoist Sal on her shoulder, or hold her in her arms like (he didn't add) a ventriloquist's dummy, or something cute. They looked at each other and then at him, and shook their heads.

During all that time, all that posing, Vi Harbison, untouched it seemed however Horse tried to catch her soul with his camera and his wisecracks, kept glancing toward Prosper Olander as though she'd like to ask a question, or make a remark, that couldn't or oughtn't be asked or made here and now, when shift was starting, both for him and for her; and Prosper noticed that, and *his eyes answered hers* as they sometimes put it in the issues of *True Story* magazine he'd read, and he thought he knew where he stood. Both she and Sal waved as Prosper was carried off with Horse.

"Tough broad," Horse said to Prosper as he negotiated the crowded pathways through the building. "A ballbuster, frankly. In my humble opinion."

"The tall one? Violet?"

"Her," Horse said. "But the midget's no honeydrop either."

The Teenie Weenies all live in Teenie Weenie Town, which is hidden under a rosebush in a backyard not so very far away from you or me. The path through the town leads past the sauce dish which is the Teenie Weenies' swimming pool, and the syrup can that is their schoolhouse, and the teapot where the Chinaman lives. A glass fruit jar is a greenhouse, a coffee can a workshop. Several Teenie Weenies live together in a house made from a shoe. The trail leads on to the garden and to the Big People's house, where the Teenie Weenies some-times go, to find things the Big People no longer want or won't miss.

Today the Teenie Weenies have come upon a toy that a Big People child has lost. It is an aeroplane! It is made of "balsa" wood and is very light, though not to the Teenie Weenies. The aeroplane works by a rubber band, which is wound up tightly and then released to turn the propeller. Some of the bravest of the Teenie Weenies have decided to see if the plane can fly! Perhaps they will use it to fly to other places, where there are other Teenie Weenies they don't know. The Lady of Fashion has been offered the first trip, but has declined, and left the experiment to the Policeman, the Admiral, and the Cowboy. The Scots-man and the Carpenter are at work thinking of a way to turn the rubber band that gives the power.

"The worst idea they've had yet," Al Mass had said when the Sunday paper showed this panel. "If they can get that thing wound up and let it go, good-bye Cowboy, good-bye Admiral, good-bye Policeman. I won't miss them three. They always were a pain in the keister."

It was this panel of *The Teenie Weenies* that had long ago given the workers at Shop 128 their name: the picture of the long fuselage, the graceful wings, the delicate wheels in the tall grasses (tall to the Teenie Weenies), and the crowd of people around it and on it, laboring to make it go: the Cook and the Dunce and the Lady of Fashion, Tommy Atkins and Buddy Guff, the Clown, the Indian, Mr. Lover and Mrs. Lover holding hands, Paddy Pinn the Irish giant all of four inches high. There had been a Jap once, but he was gone now, though the clever Chinaman remained. So they themselves, Shop 128, varied and unique, with different souls and different skills and Passions, none interchangeable with any of the others (as Pancho Notzing insisted), not *fungible* no matter what the bosses or the government or the union thought. They even had an Indian, though his black-satin hair was cut short as a scrub brush and he wore the same work clothes as everybody.

Shop 128 was one of twenty stations where the fuselages were put together with their wings. Fuselages entered the Assembly Building from the Fuselage Building, and finished wings—all but their wingtip sections—were lifted out of the Empennage Building by overhead crane cars and carried into Assembly. When the wing section was hovering suspended over the fuselage, a select team, all men but one (Vi Harbison), guided it as it was lowered into place. Then the remaining Teenie Weenies climbed the rolling ladders and scrambled upon the assembly to rivet it and connect all those wires and snaking tubes. Al and Sal Mass, and others not so small as those two, were the riveting team on that narrow pressurized tunnel that ran from the forward compartment to the rear. Sal on the inside loaded her gun with a rivet, drove it into the predrilled hole, and on the other side it met the bucking bar—a piece of steel the size of a blackboard eraser, curved to lie flat against the aluminum surface—held in place by Sal's bucker, Marcie. The rivet struck the bucking bar and was flattened, making a seal; if the seal looked good to Marcie, she tapped once on the aluminum; if she wanted Sal to give it another hit she tapped twice. It was so loud all around that Sal had to listen hard for those taps. It was (she said) like dancing with a guy you couldn't see or touch. Sal was the only riveter on the team willing to work with a colored woman when they were both new on the job ("What do you think I care?" Sal'd said), and now they were the best team in the shop, maybe the floor, and everybody wanted Marcie, but she and Sal wouldn't part.

The growing ship then moved up the floor, gaining new things, ailerons and wingtips and tables and chairs and lights. When the whole ship was furnished and complete, the vast central doors opened on mechanical tracks—it took some time—and a fleet of three little tractors came to draw it out onto the tarmac, everybody not busy doing something else standing to watch and clap as the impossible thing, wings drooping slightly like an albatross, ghostly in the purity of its yet unlettered unmarked duralumin, Plexiglas ports still blinded with black paper, crept into the sun. It took so long to move into place beside its sisters on the field that everyone soon went back to work.

The three buildings were actually one building, the walls between them formed by two lines of offices, machine shops, tool distribution, production control, big glass windows through which the workers on the floor could see the supervisors and designers and computers inside, all of them just as busy as they were in their white shirts and ties. Henry Van Damme had wanted those glass windows. He was also the one who chose the new fluorescent lighting for those offices, which also hung high over the shop floor in vast rectangular banks, the first building this size lit solely by the cool magic-wand bulbs that many workers had never seen before they arrived here, that made it bright as day but somehow unearthly. Along that row of offices was the Press and Publicity Office where Horse Offen turned out the *Aero*. Henry particularly wanted that office open to the shop. He read the *Aero* with great interest, cover to cover each week: Horse Offen knew it, and knew that suggestions reaching him from higher up might well be coming from the Mountain Man himself.

Horse's office contained the mimeo machines and a little Harris Automatic photo-offset printer, with a man and an assistant to run it, real IPPAU printers, who stamped the International Printing Pressmen and Assistants Union bug on the last page of every issue of the *Aero*. They also printed reports, spec handbooks, notices, calendars, and every other thing that the incoming workers were handed or saw or read or were advised and counseled and warned by through the day and night. Just today Prosper Olander was working on lettering the new series of *Upp 'n' Adam* cartoons that would appear large-size around the shop floor and in the toilets and lunchroom, and small-size in the *Aero*. At least one idea for an *Upp 'n' Adam* had definitely come from Van Damme himself, who thought the two clowns were funny and instructive, a big fat one and a little skinny one, always grinning even when stepping on abandoned tools, shocking themselves with worn wiring, wasting rivets, sleeping on the job as the drill press went haywire *(Hey Upp! Get Your Sleep in Bed—Not on the Job!!)* or making other messes that wags could alter with a crayon into the vulgar or obscene—Horse marveled at the human male's capacity for inventive crudity. The art was done off-site and mailed in, but Prosper did the words with his lettering pens, making clusters of exclamation marks like cock feathers. He did Anna Bandanna too, whose posters conveyed more sober remarks, and longer ones, directed at female workers. He'd just finished one of those and it lay on his table ready for photography.

" 'Don't let that time of the month keep you from doing your best, girls!' " Horse read, looking over Prosper's shoulder. " 'Get the straight story, not the old myths—Ask for Pamphlet 1.1 at the Nurse's Station!' "

"What's the straight story?" Prosper wondered.

"Straight story is, Buckle this pad on it and get back to work."

Anna Bandanna posters were easier because the picture never changed, it was only she, bust of a great broadly grinning woman in a polka-dot bandanna, the straps of her overalls visible on her shoulders; red wet mouth, maybe fat, eyes alight. Prosper'd heard her referred to as that damn Aunt Jemima, and there was a resemblance, if only the strength and joy and white teeth. He got very used to looking into that receptive but frozen face.

"You're not going to believe this," Horse said, "but I had a dream last night about that woman."

"Really?"

"Really. I dreamed she and I. Well."

"I dreamed about President Roosevelt," Prosper said.

"Swell," said Horse. "He running for a fourth term?"

"Well we talked about that. I gave him my advice."

"Oh good. You had a high-level meeting."

"No no," Prosper said, remembering it. "It didn't seem that way. We were at a picnic. A few others around. Then he and I went for a walk, up into the woods. Talking about this and that. Just ordinary matters."

"Yeah?"

"Yeah." It had seemed morning, the sun and the path; they talked about nothing in that easy way that friends do, friends who gain sustenance from the mere exchange of true words. His to the President, the President's to him. It felt good to be able to help him.

"So he was *walking*?" Horse asked pointedly, as though he had a surprise for Prosper.

"Yes."

"He can't."

"Well, no. I guess he has trouble with it anyway. But he was. So was I."

"You didn't think anything of it?"

"I usually walk all right in dreams. Run up stairs, you know. Like everybody. I bet so does he."

"In your dreams you can walk," Horse said, and for a moment a kind of wondering pity seemed to invade a face not really suited for a feeling like that. "Man oh man that's . . ." But he couldn't or didn't say what it was. He returned to his typewriter, shaking his head.

Prosper, yes, could walk in his dreams, run too; that same morning he'd awakened in the warmth of one, where he'd been running, running across an open field under the sky, readying himself to launch from his hands a great weightless paper-and-wood model airplane, like the one the Teenie Weenies found; almost aloft himself, he'd lifted it to the sky like a heartful of hope.

At four o'clock the Day Shift changes to the Swing Shift. The Day Shift workers down tools, pack their toolboxes, head for the lockers; the women fill their dressing rooms, yakking and laughing or weary and silent, showering and changing into their actual clothes and hanging their boiler suits and overalls and standard-issue uniforms in their lockers, tossing in their scuffed shoes and limp socks, but some don't care and after a swift hand wash and a reapplication of lipstick are out the door, only a hop to their houses anyway and, for many, no husband there to keep up standards for. Marlene, a new inside riveter, said good night to her team, and "Good night, see you tomorrow," to Marcie, who waved back. Then on the way out of the plant it occurred to Marlene that that was the first time she'd ever said *Good night, see you tomorrow* to a colored person.

Other Day Shift workers go right from the floor to the cafeteria, and get their big meal there now, when the evening has cooled the place. They often skip lunch, it's too damn hot to eat at the set hour in that plant all made of metal—it's like one of those fold-up aluminum picnic ovens they sell that are guaranteed to cook just by heating up in the sun. Today a lot of people just took a Popsicle or an ice-cream bar from the snack trucks that circulated around the floor as break time moved, the frosty insides revealed when a lid was opened, the momentary cold breath heavenly. Now they were ready for dinner (or supper, depending on where you came from in these States and how you learned to name your daily meals) in the Main Dining Commons as you were supposed to call the cafeteria, though no one did.

The cafeteria's the source of some of Horse Offen's best statistics—five hundred pies an hour coming out of the ovens, three automatic potato peelers peeling fifty pounds a minute and slicers slicing and dumpers dumping them into batteries of French fryers over which a mist of hot oil continuously stands. The thousands of Associates served every hour. The specially designed dishes of unbreakable Melamine, washed by the largest washing machines allowed under wartime regulations. There's a stage at the far end for shows and War Bond promotions, and at the entrance, before the food service area, Henry Van Damme decreed a fountain—white porcelain, round, a wide-lipped gutter surrounding a column from whose many chromed faucets or pipe-mouths thin streams of warm water pour when the foot treadle is stepped on. Not everybody but almost everybody pauses there to wash, as the large sign urges them to do, before they enter the serving lines beyond.

"He's not a normal person," Prosper Olander was telling the Teenie Weenies around him, which included Francine, who might be the Lady of Fashion, though dressed now like everybody in bandanna and overalls. "You should see him. Not even the photographs show you how big he is. I mean he looks big in them but in the flesh he just takes up more room. He's a behemoth."

"Well be he moth or be he man," Francine said, with a Mae West shrug to one shoulder, "he can put his shoes under *my* bed any time." The other women at the table—they were all women—laughed at that; they said things like that around Prosper they wouldn't have around other men.

At the next long table some of the women were reading from an article in *Liberty* magazine about the new world to come after the war, and how men and women and even children will have been tested in that fire, and how they'll deserve the bounties of peace that the end of the war will bring, when our enormous war power will be turned to other uses.

"Well I don't know," a dark and somewhat saturnine woman said. "I sorta can't see it that way. I can't see that this'll come out right for us."

"Who's this *us*?" the reader wanted to know.

"Us who are getting these jobs, putting in these hours, earning this overtime. Us here in this country, where we never were bombed, just Pearl Harbor, nowhere in the States, and we're not going to be. And over there people starving and getting killed—I don't mean soldiers, everybody's soldiers die and get wounded, I mean people who don't fight. People like us."

"Hey we've made a sacrifice. Every one of us."

"Yeah? Seems to me we're actually doing pretty well. Seems to me."

The women around her were variously dismissive, or scandalized, or affronted. Some wanted to respond, wanted to tell her to shut up, they were all doing what they could, but they didn't say any of that.

"We're doing too well out of this war," she said at last, but more to herself than to the rest. "It's not right."

She looked around herself then. No one who'd heard her was looking her way.

"Well what do I know," she said, returning to her meat loaf. "I'm just a clog in the machine."

Elsewhere, Larry the union shop steward was *holding court*, as Pancho Notzing described it, at a table near to the one where Pancho sat today. Pancho turned now and then to glare at him. Larry is something of a bully, which many workers think is an all right thing, since he's their bully, and he's won something or wangled something or mitigated something for a lot of them. Most of those at his table were men.

Loud enough so that Larry was sure to hear it, Pancho himself expatiated. "You know what they want to do," he said. "They want to put the whole population under the control of the government. They want a labor draft—manpower to be shifted to whatever task the military deems necessary. Conscription of free labor! Male and female!"

"A crank case," Larry said to his chums. He thumbed secretly over his shoulder, indicating Pancho.

"A what?" one of them asked

"Yeah. One of those crank cases who comes along with some big homemade idea about how people should live, how the society ought to change, all out of his own brain."

His chum was still regarding him puzzled. "Crank case?"

"Crank. Nut case," Larry said testily. "Jeez."

"Dear Mrs. Roosevelt thinks this regimentation should simply continue after the war," Pancho said. "And very likely it will. The monopolies, the government, the army, and the unions will share out the world, and we'll be forced into a single mold, no more different from one another than gingerbread men."

"Why don't you shut up, old man," Larry said, turning his chair suddenly with a scrape. "Nobody wants to hear your guff. This union's fought the company *and* the government for workers' rights, and—"

"You just wait till this war's over," Pancho exclaimed, still facing the crowd at his own table, who were now curious to see what would happen next. "You'll see. The unions, the government, the military, the corporations, they'll all knit together"—here he interlaced his own fingers—"into one big grinding machine to grind our faces. We'll all be rich as Dives and miserable as worms." He dabbed his lips with a paper napkin. "The *union*," he said, as though that were all that needed to be said about *that*, and tossed the napkin down.

Larry was out of his seat now, and still Pancho, nose lifted, declined to notice him.

"You damn fool, you can keep your opinions to yourself, or I might just jam 'em down your throat!"

Pancho arose and said something to his table about those without reasons, who used blows instead. Larry threw a chair out of the way to get at Pancho and now around him people were getting to their feet and yelling *Hey hey* and other cries to quell argument. Pancho in a graceful rapid move pushed up both his sleeves even as he took an old-fashioned boxer's stance, the backs of his fists to Larry. Larry appeared startled at Pancho's ready-Eddy defense and jutting chin, and backed away, kicking the chair instead. "Ah go sit down, y'old dope. Who needs your advice."

Pancho maintained his posture for a moment more, then sat again, dusting his hands.

That seemed to those at the tables a forbearance on Larry's part, as he was known to be a brawler not only practiced but ruthless—he'd told how as a younger man he'd carried a set of brass knuckles, and he'd won fights by slipping them on in his pocket while he and the other man Stepped Outside, then he'd clip the other guy with a disabling punch before the mutt knew what was happening, and slip off the knuckles before he was caught with them: a history he seemed proud of. He was smart enough, though—he said now, glaring at Pancho's back—not to start a fight in the damn cafeteria.

"Oh, he's one smart fella," Pancho said. "Oh yes."

"One smart fella, he felt smart," said Al Mass across from him. "Two smart fellas, they felt smart—"

"Shut up, Al," said Sal.

At midnight the Swing Shift ended and what longtime factory workers always called the Graveyard Shift but now throughout the war industry was called the Victory Shift began, special commendation and maybe a couple of cents more an hour for those who took it on and worked through the dark toward dawn: a contingent of Teenie Weenies including the Indian and the Doctor (of veterinary medicine, he hadn't practiced in the years since he took up the bottle). Somehow the stillness of the deep midnight, or the ceasing of certain jobs done only in the daytime, made the shift quieter: maybe it just seemed so. Conversation seemed possible. At three in the morning they had begun talking about people in the news who could or couldn't sing.

"Norman Thomas had a fine voice," Vilma said. "I stood once in a crowd that all sang the 'Internationale' with him. I could hear him loud and clear. A fine tenor voice."

" 'Arise you prisoners of starvation,' " a union man who'd overheard sang out, hymnlike. " 'Arise you wretched of the earth.' "

"How long till lunch break, anyway?" said Lucille the spot welder.

"You know who couldn't sing," somebody else said. "Huey Long. I saw him in the newsreel singing 'Every Man a King.' He waved his finger like this but couldn't keep the time. He looked like a spastic."

"I'll bet the President has a fine voice."

"I know his favorite hymn is 'Our God Our Help in Ages Past.' He sang it on that ship, the time he met Churchill. They had a Sunday service right on the ship. They both sang."

The Doctor hearing this began to sing:

"Our God, our help in ages past,
Our hope for years to come,
Our shelter from the stormy blast,
And our eternal home."

Somebody else took it up, as though unable not to, the way some people can't help blessing someone who sneezes, no matter how far off the sneezer, how unheard the blessing.

"Under the shadow of Thy throne
Thy saints have dwelt secure;
Sufficient is Thine arm alone,
And our defense is sure."

It was harder to hear it now, amid the noise of the place, but it was clear the song was being passed on, sometimes a couple of people stopping what they were doing to sing a verse; and some of those who sang or listened to the old words heard them anew, here on the Victory Shift gathered around the wingless *Pax* like ants around their queen:

"A thousand ages in Thy sight
Are like an evening gone;
Short as the watch that ends the night
Before the rising sun."

And farther aft, where the pop of rivet guns punctured it:

"Time, like an ever rolling stream,
Bears all its sons away;
They fly, forgotten, as a dream
Dies at the opening day."

Coming back around like a little circling breeze to where Vi, Lucille, and the fuselage team worked. A colored man strapping wire within the fuselage could be heard taking it up, a light sweet tenor like Norman Thomas's, you wouldn't have thought it from such a large man, it was so surprising that some around him stopped work to notice, while others shook their heads and didn't:

"Like flowery fields the nations stand
Pleased with the morning light;
The flowers, beneath the mower's hand,
Lie withering ere 'tis night."

Those who knew the hymn well recognized this as the last awful verse, and they could begin again on the chorus, comforted or not, in agreement or not, or simply able to remember a hundred Sundays in a different world:

"Our God, our help in ages past,
Our hope for years to come,
Be Thou our guard while troubles last,
And our eternal home."

But now it's morning, and Vi Harbison sits on the bed with Prosper in his bedroom in the house on Z Street, trimming his nails with a pair of little scissors. Pancho Notzing's on the Day Shift but Prosper on this day has been moved to Swing Shift, so the house is theirs. The sensation of having his nails cut is one that Prosper can't decide if he enjoys or not: it recalls his mother, who used to do it, grasping each finger tightly in turn; seeing the dead matter cut away, something that should be painful but was only forceful. And the feeling of pressing the exposed fingertips into his palms. Vi's doing it because Prosper scratched her as he put a finger, then two, far up inside her. She wasn't going to have that. There was a lot this young man needed to learn.

"There."

And since she's naked there on the bed, because she'd stopped him from going farther before she performed that operation, Prosper reaches out and circles the globes of her breasts with his hands, the newly sensitized fingertips, like a safecracker's sanded ones, assaying the yielding curve of flesh.

"Okay?" he asked.

What he loved to see, had loved ever since he was ten and it had been Mary Wilma's step-ins and jumper: the pile of a woman's discarded clothes on the floor, his own too, the astonishment of nakedness. They went down together. Time passed.

"Okay so," she said.

They lay face-to-face. She held his eyes with hers, but not as though she saw him; she was looking, with a gaze of some other sort, down into where he went; her face was like that of a blind woman he'd known back when he worked for The Light in the Woods doing piecework: how she'd sorted rivets into bins by touch, looking with her fingers, eyes on nothing.

"That," she said.

"This?"

"No. Ah. That."

Now he too was looking within, looking with a clipped finger's end. It lay under a soft fold falling just below where the brushy mountain ran out and the bare cleft began. It too was soft but soft differently, satin not velvet. Now he'd lost it again. Found it. It seemed to grow or peep out at his touch.

"Everybody has this?" Except for his own finger's movements they were both still.

"Every woman does. Ah."

He examined it, tiny movements so that he, his little searching self, didn't get lost. It did seem to remind him of an arrangement or complexity he'd encountered before but hadn't actually perceived, not as a separate thing or part that needed a name. The Little Man in the Boat, she'd said. Here was the boat, the covering fold. Here the man. The slick moisture made it seem to roll beneath his finger like an oiled ball bearing in its socket. She moved then, earthquakelike, to lie on her back, and he had to begin the search again, in a new land. "Little man," he said. "Why a little man, why not a little woman?"

"Hush."

"Why not though."

"Because ah. Because it's ah, a little man. That's the name. Ah. My little man."

Another seismic heave and she turned another quarter turn over so that her back was to him. He pressed close against her and she took his arm and drew it around her and directed his hand again downward, her own now atop it, lightly, reminding him (when he thought about it later) of his aunt May's hand resting on the planchette of the Ouija board and waiting for its subtle movements. She lifted her outside or upper leg a little. "There," she said. But soon she grew restless, or dissatisfied, or encouraged—Prosper tried to gauge her feelings—and rolled again, now onto her stomach, and her legs opened as though grateful to be able to, and they lifted Vi up a bit. This was a challenge for Prosper, he'd learned, since his own legs weren't up to the power requirements, but Vi had a way of hooking her lower legs over his to keep him steady and in place, and she could help too in getting him or it in past the gatekeepers and on into the interior, which she now did, with a seemingly pitiful small cry.

"Now you be careful," she gasped into the pillow. "Prosper. You be careful. You know?"

"I know."

This being the second time that morning he thought he could do all right, in fact it felt a bit wooden and abused after having gone on in, but she again drew his hand around and onto her to go find that Little Man he'd met, which now he could easily do, not nearly so little this way, why hadn't he identified it before; and with everything then set and going, the round and round along with the in and out, like rubbing your stomach while patting your head, the train left the station, picking up speed wonderfully, amazingly: even as he began making sounds of his own he was able to marvel at it.

"So how do you know these things," Prosper said later. **The bed was** mussed and suffering, not really meant for two if one of them was Vi. "Who taught you?"

If you lay still in that dry air, as the heat rose you could feel the sweat pass off you even as it was produced. They lay still. They had stopped touching.

"You just know," Vi said. "It's part of me. I know about it."

"But those names," Prosper said. She knew names for what she had and what he had, what they did, what came of it, some of them useful, some funny.

"Oh. I learned. From somebody."

"Man or woman?"

"Man."

"Tell me," Prosper said.

"Why should I?"

"Why shouldn't you? All these things are educational." He put his hand on the rise of her thigh. He thought how soon you can get used to being naked alongside someone naked, so that the two of you can converse just as though you were dressed, and how that ought to be odd but somehow isn't, which is odd in itself. "Isn't that so?"

"You might be asking out of jealousy. People can be jealous of people's old lovers. Former lovers. They pretend to ask just out of curiosity but it's a nagging thing, they're jealous even if they don't know it. They think they just want to learn something about someone, but it poisons them to hear it."

"Really?"

"Really. It's like bad earth." She rolled away from him and looked upward at the ceiling, which seemed to be hammocking ever so slightly downward. "Poisoned through the ear. And they asked for it too."

"No. I just wanted to know. About you. What you did, what you thought, before. I'd like to know."

She turned her head toward him, and he could see that she was considering him. Her eyebrows rose, asking something, more of herself than of him: but she smiled.

"Tell me," he said, smiling too.

"Tell you. Tell you what."

"Start at the beginning."

"No," she said. "I won't."

"So start in the middle. Like *True Story.*"

"Like what?"

"The stories in *True Story* always start in the middle. 'Little did I know when I saw the dawn come that day that by nightfall I'd be locked up in jail.' You know."

"You read *True Story*? It's for women."

"I used to."

"Little did I know I'd find myself in bed with a ninny." She reached down to pluck the crumpled and somewhat soggy pack of Luckies from the pocket of her shirt, where like a man she kept them. "Okay," she said. "Here goes."

7

ittle did she know: that when the great worldwide storm rolled over at last, after hovering so long undecided, it would leave the land remade by its passing, the way spring storms and the sun following them can change the brown prairie to green almost overnight or overday: that it would move her farther than she had ever thought to move, though not as far as she had once dreamed of moving. She'd gone out to the Pacific Northwest first, looking for work, coming down after a long trip into a port city along swarming roads filled with others also ready to go to work if they could find someplace to stay. There were ten shipyards slung out into the bay and a ship was being launched every month, soon it would be every twenty days, and it was easy to find out how to get to the employment offices, as easy as following the crowd funneling into a ballpark, and after you signed up at one—whichever you came to first, you couldn't know which was the better place to work but the work was all the same and you had lots of company no matter which one you picked—they told you about places to look for a room or at least a bed, and where *not* to look if you were a young single girl in a summer dress and a thin sweater carrying an old suitcase tied up with a length of twine. Not even if you were a girl just a little short of six feet, wide-shouldered and big-handed with a touch-me-not coolness in your long narrow eyes.

It was less than a week since she'd left the ranch and her father's house. Six weeks since her youngest brother had left for the army induction center, following his older brothers. Ten since the bulldozer had covered with dirt the corpses of the last sick cattle shot by the government agents and her father had shut the door on those agents as though he'd never open it again for anyone.

Bad earth they'd called it, stretches of prairie that were somehow naturally poisonous, whose poisons could be drawn up into plants that stock would eat. Maybe for a long time eating the plants hadn't hurt them, maybe not for years, but then there'd be a change in the groundwater, or some new plant would start growing there and take hold—a kind of vetch, they said, was one—and it could suck up so much of the poison it could kill. Kill a sheep in an hour, a heifer in a day; leave cattle with the blind staggers or their hooves softening and sloughing off, too weak to feed, had to be shot, so poisoned they couldn't be sold for slaughter even if they lived. Government gave you a penny on the pound. She herself had to sell the horses; they were smarter than the cattle and stayed away from the garlicky smell of the bad-earth weed, but there was no way now for them to earn their keep. Without them the ranch seemed to her to be, and always to have really been, a hostile stretch of nowhere, no friend to her. Her father was planning (if you could call it a plan) to hole up with the government payment till his two sons came home and they could start again, fence off the bad earth. Vi wouldn't stay just to keep his house for him and wait. She thought—she knew—she could have done what was necessary to get going again, the bank loans, the inspections, meat prices were soaring, but she wasn't going to talk him into letting her. Wouldn't and couldn't. Even a woman could make $2,600 a year as a welder, and she planned to send most of her pay home.

He'd driven her out to the county road where the bus stopped once a day and never said a word. She wondered if he'd go home and put a shotgun to his head the way his uncle had done in the dust-storm days. Just when the bus appeared far off raising its own cloud he took a crushed roll of bills from his pocket and peeled off a ten and some ones, and she thanked him meekly, but she'd already taken more than that out of the bank, where she'd had an account ever since she turned twenty, three years before. She hadn't told him or anyone, not knowing then what the money was for. It was for this.

"Bye, Daddy. Take care of yourself."

"So long, Vi."

"I'll see you when the war's over," she said, but he didn't smile.

The bus was filled with soldiers, only a few country people in among them, and they stirred as one when Vi climbed the stair; one leapt up to help her lift her bag into the netting overhead, a little ferrety fellow, she let him think he'd helped. She took the seat they competed to offer her, and for a time tried to make conversation, which she'd never been much good at, especially the kind that had no purpose, or rather had one hidden in the commonplaces. She gave them a word picture of the cattle dying and stinking in the sun, how she'd pulled the ropes to help the tractor drag them into the pits, sometimes pulling apart the longer-lying bodies, all the time followed by the crows: and they mostly fell silent, some because they knew what she meant and what it had been like, some because they didn't. A day and a night passed.

In the dark and the dawn she expected to be anxious and afraid. But her heart felt cool. She passed through towns she'd never seen, the trucks at the feed store, the tavern and the post office and the bank like the ones in her town, the school and the churches, but not the same ones, and beginning to grow different as she went west: why different she couldn't say. She couldn't sleep even when the darkness outside the window was so total she could see only the dim ghost of her own face, a person who'd left home to find war work. Now and then what she was doing came back to her in the middle of some bland string of thought and her heart seemed to collapse into her stomach and her breasts to shrink, the feeling of diving into water from a high rock. But it only lasted a second, and she wasn't even sure it wasn't a good feeling, in its way.

By the next night Vi was done with bus travel. She was filthy, she felt limp and wound up at the same time, and the trip went on forever, since the bus was forbidden by company policy to go faster than thirty-five miles an hour to save gas and rubber, and even when the driver picked it up a little, it did no good, because the stops were calculated at the set speed, and you simply waited longer at stops. In any big town she could have got off and found the train station, but she had paid for the trip, and anyway in the fusty odor and noise of the bus, amid the changeful crowd, she felt cocooned, waiting to come forth but not yet ready.

That night they came to a broad crossroads, two great stripes of highway at right angles, that had collected gas stations and bars and a long diner around itself. Vi could see, as the bus downshifted and slowed, a line of military vehicles, two-ton trucks, bigger trucks, smaller ones, strung out just off the road, thirty or forty or more. When the bus turned in to let out its passengers to eat and drink and use the toilets, it passed a crowd, apparently the drivers of the vehicles, going to or coming from the diner, gathering to talk or smoke a cigarette before starting out again west where the vehicles were pointed—that's the thought that occurred to Vi. Over at the big garage behind the diner, which came into view as the bus drew up to park, two of the hulking brown trucks had their hoods open and were being worked on under lights on tall poles. It was also clear now in the lights of the parking lot that all the drivers in their jackets and caps were women. Not soldiers but women, some in skirts, most in trousers. Vi getting off heard their laughter.

There were several in the diner, waiting maybe for the disabled vehicles to be fixed, crowded into the booths or seated on the stools. They were all ages, some as young as Vi, some as old as her mother had been, some as old as her mother would now be. The soldiers from the bus who banged into the diner looked around in awe, no place they'd expected to find themselves, an army of the opposing sex. They couldn't help but engage one another, though some of the boys were over-whelmed and some of the women shy, maybe about the bandannas turbanning their heads or their lipstick worn away or not even applied that day, the ends of their dungarees rolled high.

They were drivers for a plant building military vehicles, in convoy to deliver the trucks to the port where they'd be put aboard ships (the women assumed) and sent out. Why not put them on flatcars, send them by train? The women laughed, asked each other why not, but no one knew for sure, maybe the trains were so busy now and the trucks were needed quick.

They moved aside, pushed over, let the newcomers share their booths, take their places at the counters, sit with them at their burdened tables that two harried waiters and a colored busboy tried to manage. Vi sat down next to a woman with her hair in a swept-up Betty Hutton do, a cap perched on it so small and far back as to announce its uselessness, point out that its wearer wasn't really a cap-wearer at all. But her nails were short and darkened at the moons.

"Where you headed?"

Vi named the city on the sea, the same to which the convoy was going.

"Whatcha doing there? That's a long ways from home. Trying for a job?"

"Right. Welding. I read about it."

The woman, whose name was Shirley, looked Vi over in some admiration. Vi thought to drop her gaze, thought she ought to, but Shirley held it. Vi wondered how old she was: ten years older than she? "You'll do all right," she said. "You going alone?"

"Yep."

"You ever do anything like that? Welding?"

"Well on the ranch. A little acetylene torch, fixing hay rakes and things. My brother was better."

"This'll be different," Shirley said. She laughed. "When I got a job at this plant, I was working in the yard, they came and asked, You ever drive a truck? And I said Sure. I mean I'd driven a pickup, you know, how hard could it be? So I was signed up. They took me out and showed me this thing. I couldn't even see how to get *into* it. Then there's four forward gears and an overdrive. Two reverse. I said Huh? They said Oh there's a chart right there on the floor. All the slots are numbered. Easy."

"Was it?"

"Well let's see. It took me a half an hour to get the motor running without stalling. Another half an hour to figure out how to back up without stalling."

"How much training did you get?"

"Training? That was the training. We left next morning."

Shirley enjoyed Vi's face for a moment, then put out her wet-lipped cigarette in the dregs of her coffee. "Listen," she said. "Long as we're headed for the same place, why don't you ride along with me?"

Vi, who'd told herself to be ready for anything, wasn't ready for this, didn't have a name for the feeling the offer wakened in her.

"I paid for a bus ticket all the way," she said.

"So what?" Shirley said laughing. "I'm not going to charge you. And I'll get you there faster." She bent toward Vi. "I'd like the company," she said. "Gets lonely in the dark. You can keep me from falling asleep too."

So Vi went and woke the bus driver asleep in his seat and told him she wasn't going any farther; he looked at her like he'd not heard, then nodded slowly without speaking. She got her bag from the overhead rack and dragged it away down the bus steps and only then heard the driver call after her, but not what he said. Shirley was waiting for her and they went together out to where the trucks were starting their engines, turning on their great lights.

"So this isn't against the rules?" Vi asked. "What if they kick me off?"

"There's no they," Shirley said. "There's just us."

It *was* hard to get into, no running board, only a sort of rung, you stood on that and pulled the door open, then took a jump to another step and in.

And it was hard to get the big thing going. Shirley pulled the choke, feathered the clutch, worked the long gearshifter into the wrong then the right slots, all the while letting out what in an old book Vi'd read was called "a string of oaths" and then doing better after she calmed herself, and crossed herself.

The trucks moved out into the empty night highway. Vi could see the vehicles far ahead pulling one by one into line like a great glittering snake whipping sidewise very slowly. Then Shirley's, with a judder and a roar. Vi was on the move now for sure: later she would remember it as the moment when she was put into motion not *away* but for the first time *toward*, toward whatever the world was bringing into being, everything ahead.

They picked up speed. High up off the road Vi bounced in her hard seat as though she might lose it and end up on the floor—she thought of the miles ahead and wondered if she would regret her impulse to climb in with Shirley, who was gripping the steering wheel hard but at least no longer bent forward as though impelling the 10-ton all by herself. Vi's job was to help keep an eye on the truck ahead, watch for its dim brake lights. If something happened far up the line, if the lead truck had to stop, then the following trucks would have to stop in turn, but the gap between a braking truck and the still-moving truck behind it would shorten as the stop went down the line, till the trucks far back would have to stop fast, so you needed all the time you could get.

"It's why we're driving through the night," Shirley said. "We got a truck this afternoon had to go off the road to keep from hitting the one ahead. Just like a train derailing. The one truck turned out so's not to hit the one ahead, and the one behind *that* one had to turn out not to hit *her* and got bent and went into the slough there, and altogether it took some hours to get us all out and going again."

Night went on. Vi tried to watch the truck in front, hypnotized by its swaying. She only realized she'd fallen asleep when she felt a sharp smack on her arm.

"Hey," Shirley said. "You're supposed to be keeping *me* awake."

"Oh," Vi said. "Oh sorry."

"So talk to me," Shirley said, turning back to the road. "Tell me your story. What do you love, what do you want, what makes you laugh, who'd you leave behind. All like that. Make it exciting."

Vi laughed and suddenly wished she could do that, but the story she could tell—all that she was willing to tell—was more likely to put a hearer to sleep than keep one awake. She told Shirley about how her mother had died when Vi was eighteen, a cancer, and her father had moved his kids out to the ranch where his own mother still lived alone. Vi'd just graduated from high school in the town they lived in then—not a big town, not a real city, but it had had a picture show and a couple of restaurants and a normal school that Vi had enrolled in, hoping she could figure a way to get to the state college—she was smart and knew it, and had done well in school, her favorite teacher was working to help her. She spent a year attending the normal school, but in the end she'd gone out to the ranch with her father and brothers. "The boys were young," she said. "I couldn't let Daddy go it alone. Grandma wasn't well either."

"Sure," said Shirley.

"Anyway," Vi said, and then no more.

"So this was what, four, five years ago?"

"Yes."

"Great time to go ranching. Or farming. Around there where you were."

"Yeah well. We didn't do so hot."

There came a pause then in the cab, a brief mournful or memorial moment: everybody remembered, times on the farm that had been so bad you didn't need to say anything, only a fool would feel the need to say something, and the worst was all over now—but you didn't say that either, it wasn't good luck or good sense to say so. But Vi had to at least finish the story, which in her own case or her family's didn't get better. Bad earth, failure, war and her brothers enlisting, things staying so bad it was almost laughable, like some pileup of disasters in a comedy picture.

"So no regrets about leaving," Shirley said, reaching for the pack of smokes on the truck's dash. "That's good."

Vi wouldn't say yes or no.

"A fella you left behind? Not even that?"

"No," Vi said, looking ahead. "No fella."

"No cowboy serenading you with a git-tar?"

Vi laughed. Another reason to leave town and school and go out to the empty places: that's what her father thought, and Vi for her own reasons, but concerning the same matters, had guessed it was advisable: what she went away *from,* which didn't count now, not right now anyway, beside Shirley in the truck. "I got a nice smile from Gene Autry once when he came to the opera house in the next town," she said. "But he didn't follow up."

They laughed together, and went on into the night, which was at last beginning to pass, the ragged edge of the mountains that they were to cross now distinguishable from the greening sky; they sang some of Gene's hit songs, everybody knew them.

"Sometimes I live in the country
And sometimes I live in the town
Sometimes I take a great notion
To jump in the river and drown."

Somehow, all the next day after she climbed at last down from the 10-ton in the port district where the trucks lined up to be loaded onto ships, and she and Shirley'd said good-bye amid the stink of the exhausts and the shouts of the dispatchers, after they'd hugged and laughed at their momentary friendship, Vi kept thinking of Shirley. She imagined Shirley observing her, observing her behavior in the street and in the employment offices and out onto the street again, Shirley noting how Vi did things that *she*'d do in a different and maybe a better way, and Vi explaining to Shirley why she did what she did. Shirley would remain in Vi's brain or spirit for a long time, listening to her, approving her, surprised by her, commenting on her, as though those hours beside her in the truck had been enough to pass something of Shirley and her cool bravery into Vi, to see her through: like Virgil and Dante.

The women's hotel, when she reached it, had no room for her, and by the look of the white-haired pince-nez ladies who ran it never would— one glance at Vi and her shabby suitcase was all it took. They were delighted to direct her to the YWCA, a wonderful place they were sure would suit her. Vi set out for this place, and reached it feeling wearier than she ever had after any day's work on the ranch: the pavement harder on her feet and legs than any hardpan; the constant draw of thousands of faces passing you on the street, the constant need to look away from them if they caught your eye, just as they looked away too; the air filled with sounds to be listened to, radios blaring from stores, car horns urgent but mostly meaningless, gunshot backfires, police whistles, sirens announcing disasters that maybe she should run from but couldn't see (for the first time she became keenly aware that you can shut your eyes but you can't shut your ears). And there were no rooms at the Y.

"Nothing? I've walked a long way. I've got a job, starting tomorrow."

"I'm so sorry," the woman at the desk said, and she seemed to mean it; she was no older than Vi, and badly frazzled. "I can put you on our list. I mean people come and go so fast here, you know, they get more permanent places, I'm sure there'll be something soon."

"Well," Vi said, not turning away, hoping she'd somehow be taken on as a desperate case and her problem solved, even when the frazzled woman moved off to busy herself with other things and avoid Vi's eyes. Vi looked around. Something calming and bounteous about the place, a couple of oil portraits, old lady benefactors Vi guessed, the wicker furniture and the bookshelves. They had a gymnasium, just for the women! Vi thought she could live here forever. But she couldn't just hangdog it here in front of the desk, it wasn't going to work.

Turning to look for a solution she saw a woman seated in the lobby regarding her intently, who then raised two fingers to summon her. Vi, with a glance at the receptionist's back, went to where the woman sat, a pretty plump brunette Vi's age.

"I know you need a place," she said to Vi in a hurried undertone. "Look, you can stay in my spot. I work the late shift, and you can have the bed till I get back."

"Really?"

"Yeah. They don't like us doing that, though, so you know, mum's the word."

Closer to her now, Vi saw that the girl's eyebrows were carefully plucked and redrawn, like a movie star's, and her makeup done with care.

"Okay?" she said.

"Oh. Yes," Vi said. "Yes, sure, thanks so much. My name's Violet."

"Terry," said the girl, and held out a hand, limply ladylike, but the nails short and what seemed to be small burns on thumb and knuckle. "It's 302 upstairs. Just go around and down to the gym, then up the back stairs from there."

"Okay."

"See you in a bit. They won't mind if you rest here. Read a magazine, something."

"Okay."

She was gone. Vi watched the seams on her stockings flash: where'd she get those? Then carelessly she drifted through the lobby, picked up a paper, sat down out of sight of the desk. Women came and went, yakking and laughing and calling to one another, some in work clothes and boots or saddle shoes, some in dresses and hats, some toting lunch pails or toolboxes. After a while she got up and followed the sign down to the overheated gym, which was empty except for a couple of large women on stationary bicycles; Vi could hear the echoey splash of the pool and smell chlorine. Then up the narrow back stairs to knock at the door of 302.

The room was tiny, a narrow bed, a little dresser with a mirror, a white curtain in a window that looked out at nothing. Terry was redoing her makeup, getting ready to go, she said. She did her lips with a dark lipstick, not the stick itself but a brush she wiped across the obscene little red tip poking from the cartridge. Vi asked her what work she did.

"Welding," she said. She named the shipyard, famous for its speed, a great tycoon had *streamlined* the works, they called him Sir Launch-alot in the papers. Terry plucked a sheet out of a box of Lucky tissues and pressed her lips on it. "Where you going?"

Vi took from her bag the form she'd been given and read the name.

"Hey, that one's out on the island," Terry said into the tiny mirror. "You'll have to take the ferry out."

"That's what they said," Vi said.

"Why'd you pick that one?"

"Well," Vi said, feeling Shirley in the room too, wondering too, "I guess because they said they have a softball league. I thought I could play."

Terry looked at her without judgment but conveying clearly that Vi was a greenhorn and didn't know the basics. "They all have softball leagues," she said. "And bowling leagues and glee clubs and theatricals. Anything you want. Anything to make you happy."

Vi said nothing, afraid that if she asked further she'd find out she'd made a dumb mistake.

"You play softball?" Terry said kindly. "You like it?"

"Yes." Vi decided to make the claim for herself, not be shy. "I played on a good team in high school. WPA built the town a diamond and stands. We were all-state, 1935. I played at normal school too for one year."

"Well." Terry looked at her and nodded, smiling, as though a child had told her of some little accomplishment. "Real teams."

"My brothers were stars. Baseball. It was all they cared about. They taught me. I'm good." She tried to say it plainly, as though she'd said *I'm tall.* "Anyway it would be fun to play. I thought."

"Sure," Terry said, popping her lipstick into an alligator bag. "Let me tell you how you get out there tomorrow, okay?"

How many stories she had read of people on journeys—there was
Kidnapped and there was *Alice in Wonderland* and *Pinocchio* and so

many more—and in them the one who's on the journey meets persons, one after the other, who either help or hurt him—sometimes seeming to offer help but then turning on him, sometimes gruff or rejecting but then kind underneath. Some of them seem to know a secret about the traveler, or to want something from him. That's how the story proceeds: sometimes going from bad to good, sometimes bad to worse before becoming good again. Her journey wasn't turning out like that, not that she'd expected it to. Everybody was pretty kind but mostly preoccupied; you asked them for what you needed and sometimes they could give it but mostly not and they passed out of your attention and you went on. It didn't *pile up* the way it did in books: it was come and go, over and gone.

But Shirley stayed in her consciousness, speaking and questioning and a little doubtful, or surprised and admiring; and Terry too, her makeup and her burns. And then the three women in black leather at the ferry's rail.

She'd been early at the dock, making for the streetcar with the others, standing on the open platform and clinging on, thinking in a kind of euphoric fear that at any minute she'd be knocked off and tumble down the impossibly steep hill that the little car trundled over, bell clanging. The air was rich and cold and watery, nothing she'd seen or smelled before, clouds of pale birds—gulls!—descending and arising from the sea-edge where she got off. After the crisp brassy trolley bell the deep imperious horns, hurry up, she was carried along under the noses of high black ships being loaded by sky-flown cranes, and through the gate and onto the little ferryboat, cars creeping in three lines into its belly and people crowding the decks. Then out onto the sea, or the bay at least, black heaving water and the insubstantial city seeming to float away behind. Vi held tight, as though she might float away too. She saw three women, chums apparently, laughing together, one leaning on the rail on her elbows and looking down, one beside her hands in her pockets. The three were all dressed alike, in jackets and trousers of what could only be black leather, heavy as hides, collars up against the smart breeze, and high boots laced with a yard of thong. Their hair was covered, except for one's blond forelock escaping, in bright bandannas knotted at the front. And on the back of each jacket was sewn or stuck a big red *V* in shiny cloth, their own idea obviously.

People turned to look at them, intrigued or cheered or a little shocked, but they didn't notice, used to it maybe. Vi had always thought of herself as brave—her pa said so, her teacher, but she knew it anyway—but she'd always thought of brave as something you did alone: being alone in what you did and doing it anyway was what was meant by being brave. Only when she saw those three (and she couldn't have said it then, couldn't until she'd thought about it, had seen them often in her mind, their open faces, joshing one another or looking out over water) did she know that there could be a way of being brave together, a few together.

The first thing she'd have to do, they told her and her class of new hires, would be to get some good strong boots. Shipyards are just dangerous places. Dungarees are good but in some jobs you'd be better off with a pair of welder's leathers. You'll pay for those yourself; you might go down to the Army-Navy store, they've got the stuff. You'll have a locker and you can keep your work clothes here if you don't want to wear them in the street, lot of girls don't (Vi thought of Terry, brave too). Now come along and we'll start you with some basic training.

So she became an arc welder, stitching precut forms together to make bulkhead walls and then other parts of ships ("it's a lot like doing embroidery," their trainer said, as he obviously had said many times to women before, but Vi'd never done embroidery so it was no help to her), and on the Swing Shift she and others would pick up their rod pot, stinger, wire brush for washing off the slag and getting that perfect bead, and the long lead for hooking up to power, looped over your shoulder: watch out for somebody cutting into your lead, detaching you at the middle and hooking themselves in, hey what the hell! Sixty feet overhead the crane car ran on its tracks, the huge steel plates suspended from it that were chunked in place with that vast noise, the welders lowering their masks and moving in. Vi wore her ranch overalls and a sweatshirt of her brother's, didn't buy leathers for a while, feeling somehow she had to earn them, like a varsity sweater or a jockey's silks; but the sparks from a carbon arc off a steel plate could burn badly, right through your brassiere—Terry, shaking her head, gave Vi cream for the burns.

Off-hours she looked for a room, but it was tight. You couldn't just get a room in some cheap portside hotel, it looked bad, a girl in a flophouse, but sometimes when she found a house with a sign in the window, ROOM FOR RENT, she'd be told it was taken already, only to find out later that some man had come after her and got it, tough luck sweetheart. After a week of sneaking into Terry's room at the Y she got lucky, the union found her a room to share in an old mansion downtown that had been swept into a bad neighborhood in the Depression and never recovered, cut up into small rooms sharing the vast marbled baths, a dusty ballroom on the third floor where the women danced and got in trouble. Her new roommate had been sharing with her sister, but her sister's husband had been invalided out and she'd gone home to care for him. She'd left behind her gloves, Vi's now if she wanted them, her good lunch box, and an Indian motorcycle, an ancient one-lunger on which the two of them had got to the docks each day, now to be Sis and Vi's transportation, each of them in their welding gear and black turbans, Vi up behind so tall she could see over the driver's head: rolling onto that ferry where she'd first seen that trio with the V-sign on their backs, herself one of them now.

Pretty soon she started playing ball.

8

After the first tryouts Dad said to her: "You've played some."
"Some."
"Okay. You want to pitch."
"If I can."

He smiled. "You can," he said, "if you can. You certainly may."

Hearing that the man who'd be coaching her team (and a couple of others too) was called Dad, she'd expected a grizzled codger, tobacco chewer, old-timer. Dad wasn't old; he was an engineer, with a wife and kids, doing necessary war work. The ball teams were his relaxation. He spoke little and smiled less, and Vi had to keep herself from staring at him, trying to figure him out. She'd find out later that he'd noticed that.

Everyone who signed up to play was sorted randomly into the four women's teams the shipyard fielded—the Rinky-dinks, the Steel Ladies, the Stingers, the Bobtails. Just about anybody was allowed to play, but a rough order was apparent, and if you were better than the team you were put in, Dad pushed you into a different position on another one, where maybe you wouldn't look good for a while, so nobody'd feel jealous, and then he'd give you the position you could really play, and the team would rise in the standings.

They played not out on the island where the shipyard was, but at a little ballpark on the mainland, three diamonds laid out regulation softball style, where there was a constant rotation as shifts began and ended, some teams practicing, others playing. They played each other, they played teams from the other shipyards and war plants, they played the WAVEs from the base, they played a team from the government offices and one from the port authority. Vi was amazed at how seriously most people took it, as seriously as they took their jobs. The Stingers (her team) had uniforms, baggy and gray but uniforms, and Dad wouldn't allow you to play in a game if you weren't suited up—sometimes Vi heading for a game straight from her rooming house had to wear hers on the trolley out to the field, and back again sweaty and bedraggled and feeling foolish. The whole of downtown was no larger than a ranch, but getting around in it took forever, trolleys and buses and on feet weary from a day's work. It was hard, and the game the women played was played more fiercely than Vi had ever played it, no kindness in it, no forgiveness for errors, no encouragement yelled out by the other team just to be nice. She loved it that way. It was great to learn you could weld, learn you could drive a crane a hundred feet over the shop floor, or run a drill press as big as a double bed, but playing real ball was even better. Vi thought so.

She'd never really had a coach before, but she could tell Dad was hardest on the players he thought were the best; they were all playing just for fun, supposedly, but Dad played to win as if it weren't. He caught Vi out for being lackadaisical, for letting runners steal bases because she didn't check, for smiling, for giving away her pitch in the way she stood, the way she composed her face—he said she looked one way when she threw a fastball and a different way for a curve. She didn't believe him, or didn't believe it could matter, and laughed, but his face was stony.

"Softball's a game of thinking," he said. "You gotta think, Vi. Because the ball goes so slow, and can't go far. They say baseball's a game of thinking too, but then along comes Ruth or Williams and it turns out it's a game of muscle after all. But softball's a thinking game all the time. And the pitcher's the player that's thinking the game."

"I think."

"You think too much. *When* you think. I can read you like a book."

He made her pitch to him, hitting pitch after pitch, lightly laying them out behind her, to right field, left field. The harder she tried the easier it seemed for him to do it.

"Come on, girl. Fool me. Trip me up, take me out. What are you waiting for?"

Dad could make her want to cry, but he could also make her refuse to cry: she looked back at him, her eyes slits like his, gum clenched in her jaw. Her arm ached. She threw as hard as she could until at last she decided she hated him so much she didn't care what he thought of her, stared fiercely at him and wound up and threw a lazy slider that he whiffed. The catcher missed it too.

"Practice over," Dad said calmly.

Night had fallen suddenly. She, the stolid little catcher, and Dad were the last players left. Vi was faced with a walk to the trolley and a long ride back to the mansion. Dad put them both in his Dodge coupe.

"It's out of your way," Vi said.

"You don't know what's out of my way."

He drove the old car top down, shifting with a sort of beautiful caution to save both transmission and rubber: they went on without speaking, though Dad once looked over to Vi, conscious that she was watching him, and smiled. He dropped off the catcher at her house on the hill and took Vi down toward the harbor, though even Vi could tell the other order would have been quicker.

"I've got to send you home," she said at the door of her place. "House rules." At which he slowly nodded, knowing from the way she put it (she knew he knew) that she wouldn't if she didn't have to; and halfway down the block he turned the Dodge around and came back, and she was still standing there on the doorstep just as though she'd known he'd do that, though really she hadn't, had simply stopped in midspace awaiting something—the same thoughtless mindless not-expectant awaiting (she'd think later) as before a kiss. They went up the stairs and she left him in the alcove and knocked at her own door. Sis answered, she was just dressing to go out because tonight the picture changed at the Fox, and Vi said Okay and waved her good-bye, at which Sis closed the door slowly and in some puzzlement. Vi took Dad's hand and together they went up to that ballroom on the third floor, the parquet and the spooky peeling gold wallpaper illuminated by the streetlights coming on. Vi wound the gramophone and put on whatever record was on the top of the pile, just the right one of course, because by now it was evident that this was one of those times when nothing could go wrong, even things going wrong would be funny and sweet and right. It didn't surprise her that Dad was one of those men who can dance as well as they play ball, or swim, or drive a car. After a while they knew that Sis had gone to the movies and they went downstairs.

They left the lights off but this room too was lit by the streetlights, the city never dark, not the way home had been. She wept a little, and wouldn't say why; Dad thought he knew why but he was wrong. It was the dark V of his throat and his burned forearms in the dimness, the long white body and its stain or smudge of black hair from breastbone down to where his penis rose: reminding her of someone else, back where she came from, and all that had happened between them there, which seemed now not only far away but long ago.

"So he taught you more than ball," Prosper said to Vi in Ponca City.

"He didn't teach me how to play ball. I knew."

"Well I mean."

"Yes."

"And he was the first man you'd been with?"

"No," Vi said. "No, actually, Prosper, he wasn't."

"Ah well then who—"

"Never mind," Vi explained.

It was practice the day of a game with the Bomberettes from the air-craft plant, and—Vi afterward couldn't actually remember the sequence of events, and had to believe Dad when he told her how it happened—the second baseman, trying to catch a runner headed for the plate, beaned Vi square in the back of the head.

The second baseman was being comforted—she felt terrible—when Vi came around. Dad had brought her a Coke bottle full of water from the bubbler at the edge of the field. While she sipped, he felt within her heavy hair for the bump beginning to grow. "She's okay," he said. "Just give her room."

They all stood around.

"All right," Dad said, that way he had, it made you jump: they went back to the field.

"You're okay," he said to Vi. "You can pitch today."

It took Vi a while to respond. "Oh?"

"Sure."

"And what if I'd rather stay in bed with a bottle of aspirin."

"No no," said Dad. "We need you. We need to win this one."

"And why so." She had a hard time hearing herself speak.

"Well," he said after some thought, "one reason, there's a lot of money riding on tonight."

She thought he'd said "a lot of muddy riding" and tried to make sense of that, an image from the ranch forming in her mind. "What?" she said.

"A lot of money," he said. "We're doped to win. The smart bettors have been watching you. I mean you particularly. The book is still giving odds against us, though, and they want to get in on this before the odds change."

"What the hell are you talking about?" said Vi. She usually never used a bad word, except around her brothers. Times change. Dad sat down beside her, the bottle of water in his hands, and gave her a sip now and then as he explained.

There had never been a time like that for gambling: so much money flowing into our pockets, so little to spend it on. The horses and dogs got record purses, and an average Sunday bettor was dropping a hundred dollars at the races, but the trouble was getting to the track—we weren't supposed to be wasting gas traveling for amusement, and it was said that War Resources Board agents were coming to the parking lots and conning the license plates for cars from far away, issuing warnings, maybe even canceling your precious B sticker so you'd stay home.

There were the endless poker games too, their pots growing, the amount won every wild night exactly matching the amount lost, a continuous float moving from back room to dormitory to rooming house to basement around the war plants. We'd bet on checkers tournaments, on ladies' pedestrian races (a dozen dames wig-wagging along heel-and-toe toward the tape like a flock of geese), on donkey basketball. Of course there were bookies, it was the golden age of vigorish, their multiple phone lines ringing one after the other (one bookie's operation had twenty phones crowded on a desk, a sort of homemade PBX with all the receivers dangling from a wall of hooks). They made book on the remains of major league baseball, where you couldn't see DiMaggio or Williams, who were fighting the war, but there was Stan "the Man" Musial, for some reason exempt, and there was Pete Gray of the Browns, who had one arm, master of the drag bunt, no surprise; the Yankees brought back smiling old-timers like Snuffy Stirnweiss and Spurgeon "Spud" Chandler, who doffed their caps to the ironically cheering crowds. There was the women's pro ball league, founded by a chewing gum magnate, playing what was actually softball at the beginning. And there were the leagues of the war plants, an East Coast, a Middle, a West Coast, playing for free, their standings known only to the unions and companies that sponsored them and to the ferrets of the betting book that laid the odds, which went unmentioned in the Green Sheet; you had to read the plant news releases and the back pages of small-town papers, better you had to have seen a team play, aircraft plant against Liberty Ship builder, welders against riveters, Bay City Bees versus Boilermakers Lodge 72 Sledges, the roster changing every week as workers were hired or quit or were drafted. It was the women's teams that were the ones that were followed, oddsmakers discovering a new science in judging the tenacity, speed, spirit of coeds and housewives and waitresses.

It had to be hush-hush or the bosses and the government would start wondering what this had to do with winning the war, but that only made it more attractive, a secret Rube Goldberg machine you put money into at one end and it came out double at the other or disappeared entirely. Like any honorable sportsmen, the coaches and managers wouldn't bet, and neither would the players—mostly—but the unions and the industries wanted their teams to win: all the gifts and the time off they gave the best players and the little kickbacks for the coaches hotted up the atmosphere, and staying high in the standings meant getting and keeping the talent, which meant figuring how to convince a pitcher or a first baseman to quit one plant and take a job at another.

"You're not telling me you've got money on this," Vi said to Dad.

"If I did I wouldn't say so," Dad said. "I'd say no."

"Are you saying no?"

"I'm saying no."

"So big help that is."

"Listen," Dad said, and he helped Vi to her feet. "I want to win. I want to see you play with the best team I can give you. I want the shop to be proud of the team and you, so next day they can think about how well you did when they go in to work to make ships and send them out to fight the war. There's the reason. Okay?"

Vi stood, feeling the world turn about her a bit, then slow, settle, and stop. She bent to pick up her glove and the world stayed still. She was okay. "Okay," she said.

The Stingers won that day, beating that "point spread" that was evolving among the West Coast bookies just at that time, a new way of managing the rolling tide of betting money and the unknowability of outlandish semipro and amateur teams. That was a good day, with a special commendation from the front office read out over the loudspeakers from which issued on most days the news of battles, of quotas met, ships launched, and announcements of War Bond drives. Then with amazing suddenness (amazing if you hadn't lived there long enough to witness it) the dry season ended and the rains came; every game was washed out until they just gave up and called it a day, tossed the bats in the musty canvas bags and pulled up the sodden bases and locked them in the dugouts. The end. Vi and Dad and the others went back on the line, working double shifts now and then to make up for lost time and wages, but for the two of them also because it was easy on the Graveyard Shift to find a place deep in the belly of a growing ship that foremen weren't going to wander into, one with piles of cotton wadding or insulation to lie on. Reflected glow of a flashlight turned away into the darkness. Echo of their noises off steel walls, walls she had maybe made herself, how odd, but they two not the only ones to have found their way down there, repellent litter of cigarette butts, pint bottles, used condoms, a bulletin had had to be posted about it, Let's Keep Our Work Spaces Neat. Too cold anyway soon enough, always cold and damp, clouds parting for a moment only to gather again like helpless weeping. Vi thought she was getting athlete's foot, not fair, since she wasn't an athlete anymore. Sis said *she* was getting athlete's foot up to the knee. Vi learned that the mere clammy difficulty of getting warm together could kill a romance that was already chancy at best, illicit, homeless, always needing to be arranged, willed into being. As the rains fell steadily Dad's six-month exemption from military service ran out. He could have got a new exemption without difficulty, but he chose not to. It was not Vi but his wife and kids who saw him off for basic training at the station.

A couple of months later—spring coming, blue sky visible now and then, that smell in the air—Vi was told by the new manager of the Stingers that she had an opportunity to go down to the Van Damme

Aero works, get a job building planes, easier work for better money. Van Damme Aero had one of the best softball clubs in the league, except for the pitching, which had long been weak. They were eager to get Vi and had offered to persuade a good shortstop and one of their top catchers—they were deep in catching—to take jobs up here in the shipyards, if the benefits were right.

"Play all year round down there," the manager said to Vi, though finding it hard to look her in the eye. "Season never ends."

So she'd gone south, and then west to Ponca when the offer came; she played for the Van Damme teams, meeting new people. Men too. Never anything serious. She told Prosper about one or two, dismissive, not letting out of her locked heart the details he'd have liked to know.

"Oh well," she'd say. "The trouble with *that* one was, the beginning of the end came before the beginning."

Prosper lifted his legs with one arm and swung them out of the bed to put his feet on the floor, and sat up. "I know what you mean," he said.

"Yes. 'Love grows old, and love grows cold, and fades away like morning dew.' Like the song says."

"Yeah. That's sort of been my experience," Prosper said.

"Oh?" Vi smiled, taking notice, her eyes soft for once, and she spread out in the bed as though the coarse sheets were silk and she liked the touch of them. "You got a lot of experience?"

"Some," he said.

"Going way back?"

She was amused, apparently thought his claim was sort of funny, extravagant or unbelievable, though he was trying to speak modestly. "Pretty far," he said.

"Really." She rolled over and propped her broad cleft chin in a hand. "You're not that old."

Prosper shrugged one shoulder.

"I wouldn't have thought," she said. "I mean, no offense, but it wouldn't seem you'd get around a lot. See and be seen. You know. Some things you might not get around to doing."

"Well not so many."

"Uh-huh."

There were, actually, plenty of things Prosper hadn't ever done, and some that he hadn't done in years. He'd never gone to the public library in the city where he'd grown up, never managed the long flight of stairs up to the far-off double doors of the local one, or the even longer flight (why "flight," Prosper'd often wondered) to the even farther-off doors of the central one downtown. Before his operation he'd gone on city buses and on streetcars, when he could scoot up the stairs like a monkey—everybody compared him to a monkey, his sloping back like a knuckle walker's and his long arms and big hands reaching for handholds; something narrow about his pelvis too like the narrow nates of a chimp. But by the time he reached what neither he nor anyone around him then knew to call puberty (those gloomy films that Vi had seen in high school—the ones shown in two versions, male and female—weren't shown to the special classes, as though there were no need for Prosper and the others to have the information) he could no longer mount the steps of a streetcar, couldn't bend his knees when locomoting, only when seated, with the locks on his braces slipped. That was after his operation. He'd been to the movies, before that operation; after it, getting to the pictures from his house had been the hard part, and before his uncles Mert and Fred had taken him in hand and begun squiring him around in the auto he'd missed a lot of good pictures.

Yes, lots of things undone, but lots of things done too, and many (he might say "many," though without any *basis for comparison* as Pancho would put it) were of the kind Vi doubted.

"So tell me," Vi said, still amused, seeming ready to hear something funny, funny because it wouldn't be what he claimed it was. She'd know the difference. "Your turn."

"Tell you what? You know my story."

"These *experiences,* Prosper," she said, "is what I mean."

"You want to hear?"

"I do. It's your turn. You tell me, and I'll just listen."

"Okay."

"Don't leave things out."

"Okay."

She lifted a forefinger gently to his lips, but as though to open them rather than seal them. "Tell me," she said.

PART TWO

L ike the disabled and transected body of the *Pax* B-30 that once lay in the long grass of the field over Hubbard Road from the Ponca City Airport, the orthopedic hospital where Prosper Olander spent two childhood years was still around long years after he left it. It was one of those great brown-brick institutions that were built to mark a city like Prosper's as forward-looking, scientific, up-to-date. Two others weren't far away: the reform school, and the state school for mental defectives. They had opened one after the other, starting with the state school twenty years before Prosper was born, public ceremonies and speeches from grandstands fronted with bunting, the buildings in brown photographs looking raw and alone on their wide plots of treeless land. They're all gone now: the state school abandoned and derelict, the reform school torn down for an office building, Prosper's hospital subsumed into a medical center and unrecognizable. But such places remained, though having changed their meaning: from works of benevolence they became dark holes in our child society, places to which the failed and the unlucky were remanded. You too if you put a foot wrong. *You're gonna end up in reform school.* They remain in our dreams.

Prosper was nine years old before the curvature of his spine became something out of the ordinary and started gaining him nicknames, and looks, pitying or repelled or amused. The few doctors his mother took him to (for diphtheria, when he nearly died; for tonsilitis, his tonsils snipped with a miniature garotte; for a broken thumb) all told her that he'd grow out of it, most kids did. He didn't. In the fourth grade he was sent to a special class for the first time, as much for dreamy inattention and a kind of cheerful solipsism as for his back and his pigeon-toed knee-rubbing walk; he'd go in and out of special classes like a relapsing criminal as he went from school to school, when he was allowed into school at all. His teacher that year, Mrs. Vinograd, took an interest in him; she had ideas on posture that she thought he illustrated.

"Prosper, come here and stand before the class. Take your shirt off, please, dear. Yes. Now stand in profile, so the class can see clearly." Cold pointer drawn down his naked back. "You see how Prosper's spine differs from the normal spine. Here it curves *in* where ours are straight. This pushes the abdomen forward and causes the chest to recede." Taps of the pointer, front and back. Prosper loved and feared Mrs. Vinograd, her long torso arising high and straight from her solid hips like a hero's statue from its pedestal, her eyes large, darkest brown and all-seeing; and he didn't know whether to exaggerate for her the sticking out of his tummy, to illustrate her remarks, or to straighten up, as she otherwise wanted him to do. "Doctors call it the Kit Bag Stoop. As though Prosper were carrying a kit bag, that pulls his shoulders back and down. And what is the cause of this deformity, whose real name is *lordosis*?" They all knew, all called out. "Yes, that's right, boys and girls, the cause is Poor Posture. Prosper you may dress again, and take your seat. Ah, ah, ah! Posteriors against our seat backs, dears, chin high, head straight above our shoulders!" There were those who laughed when Mrs. Vinograd said "posterior," but she would take notice of that, and no one wanted to follow Prosper and be ordered to exhibit other forms of Poor Posture, the Obesity Stoop, the Dentist's Stoop ("from eternally bending over patients to extract teeth, don't you see, dears"), or the scoliosis that brings on Da Costa's Syndrome and Irritable Heart.

Mrs. Vinograd was sure Prosper could fully straighten himself out, and if he could he would do better in school, and be able to pay closer attention to what was said to him, and sleep better and awake refreshed; distortion of the food-pipe was giving him digestive problems, she thought (she had come to his house, right to the house where he lived, to talk this over with his mother), and indigestion was making him logy. It had once been believed, she said, that nervousness, irritability, bashfulness, torpidity, and so on were causes of Poor Posture. Now it was understood that Poor Posture itself induces those conditions! Isn't that remarkable? Mrs. Olander, nearly as awed as Prosper was to have opened the door and found towering Mrs. Vinograd on the step in velvet cloche and cape, could only murmur assent and shake her head at the strangeness of it all, as Prosper in his seat pulled himself up, up, up.

He tried hard not to give in to the spine within him, which seemed to want to settle, relax, soften, and give up on holding him upright. Secretly though, unsaid even to himself, he wanted to take its side, sorry for the continual effort he demanded of it. And since the lordosis never got better, he guessed he had done that, somehow thus winning and losing at once. That's how it seemed, later on, when he examined how he had felt then, as a kid; which was like someone looking back at how once he'd struggled to find his way lost in the woods, just a while before he fell off a cliff.

Prosper was a war baby; his father was a soldier, or became one the day after Prosper was conceived. On the night before he'd left for Over There (though actually he'd never got nearer to the front than a desk at Fort Devens) he'd got his wife pregnant. She had a long-standing horror of pregnancy that she could never account for and was ashamed to feel; the next many months as Prosper grew steadily within were filled with a dread she never spoke of and yet efficiently communicated. Not to Prosper; but certainly to her husband, home on leave, hovering at the bedroom door and wondering what to do, wondering if she would die, or sicken irremediably.

Like all the women in her family Prosper's mother-to-be was a believer in Maternal Impression: if you witness a bloody accident while pregnant, your child can be born with a port-wine stain; hear a piece of dreadful news (the kind that all in a day can turn your hair to gray) and the fetus can squirm in revulsion within you (hadn't the women felt this, or heard that it had happened to someone?) and at birth it might appear wrong way around, unable to be got at. So she stayed indoors, and wouldn't answer the telephone for fear of what she'd hear, and sat and felt her substance looted and applied to the new being, as you rob clay from the big snake you've rolled to make the little one. Nothing bad happened, except that she grew hugely fat with little to do but consider her cravings and try to replace her lost insides. When he appeared at last, held aloft by his ankles, Prosper seemed just fine, long and blood speckled, and with a huge dark scrotum and penis (an illusion or temporary engorgement that nearly put a Maternal Impression for good on his mother's spooked heart to see).

Kids growing up, especially the singletons, don't consider their parents to have particular natures, or characters that can be named; they love them or fear them or struggle with them or rest in them, as though they were the weather, or a range of mountains. When Prosper was eight or nine, a girl who lived in the upstairs apartment described his father as a Gloomy Gus, and Prosper, baffled at first, was astonished to feel, as he repeated the words to himself, the great enveloping cloud of his father shrink and coalesce into just a person, a person of a certain kind, a small broody man in a derby and a pin-collar shirt, carrying a sample case, eternally stooped, the Salesman's Stoop.

Maybe he was just made that way. There was no reason for Gloomy Gus in the funnies to be gloomy except that he was, as there was no reason for his brother Happy Hooligan to be happy. That his father's gloom might have a cause was a further step in perception; but it may not ever have occurred to Prosper at all that the cause was Prosper himself, or—even tougher—that his father regarded him as a plenty good reason, a source of troubles. There was the damage done to his wife's soul by Prosper's tenancy of her body. Then the weakness of Prosper's own body, which was somehow responsible for all that had gone wrong in those nine months, and was still wrong. Eventually the doctor bills, and the prospect of more of the same, endlessly. The misaligned boy scuffling beside him as he walked the street, every eye on them (he believed) in curious pity. All Prosper knew was that a lightness would possess him when his father set out on the road, gone for days sometimes; and a contrary melancholy sunset at the man's return. For that he now had a name. He even had, in the name, a justification for wishing he'd *not* return: for the doing of magic in various homemade forms to insure that he stay away, delay, be stuck in snow or in badlands, never darken the door again. And one day he left, as usual, and then didn't return. Just didn't, and wasn't heard from ever after.

This time, strangely, having left his two sample cases behind. Prosper, awed and gratified about as much as he was guilty and stilled, would open the closet door now and then to look at those dark leather lumps, his father's other body, still remaining.

For a time he watched and waited to see if his mother would hate him for her husband's disappearance, which she might suspect her son had brought about by his little deals with the powers—avoiding the cracks on the sidewalk, wishing on dandelion moons and train whistles—and for a time she did regard him in something like reproachful grief. But he was convinced she was as much better off without Gloomy Gus as he felt himself to be; and she almost never mentioned him. She was, as she said herself, not much of a talker. There was so much family surrounding them, and so many of those were disconnected from spouses or otherwise out of the ordinary (two aunts, one each of his mother's and his father's sisters, who lived together; an uncle and his wife and nearly grown kids living in a nearby house with another single uncle in a spare room; a grampa a few blocks away cared for by a grandniece; others whose connection to himself and one another he had not yet worked out) that the jigsaw puzzle piece that was Prosper's part, though changed now in shape, still fit all right.

And the vanishing of his father (and their income with him) brought to his house—at the instigation of those various uncles and aunts and others, his mother wouldn't have known to do it, though Prosper knew nothing of all that—a caseworker from the city welfare bureau. Her name was Mary Mack, and she wasn't dressed in black black black but favored tartans and a tam and was the most beautiful person Prosper had looked upon up to that time, her bright kindly eyes and the plain sturdy way she plunked down her mysterious buckled bag, from which she drew out printed forms and other things. Even his mother smiled to see her coming down the street (she and Prosper keeping watch at the window on the appointed days), though his mother always made it clear to him that Miss Mack's visits were nobody's business but theirs and shouldn't be mentioned anywhere in any company.

Anyway it was another society that engaged most of Prosper's allegiance and concern then, the one made up of personages that grownups don't see or hardly see, as unknown to them as the society of bugs in the weeds, only brought to notice if they sting or fly at you repulsively: the neighborhood's kids. The map of their world overlay the one they shared with their elders (the one marked with the church and the other church and the market and the streetcar stop and the school and the public baths and the free clinic), the same geography but with different landmarks: Death Valley, which was what they called a treeless waste between the back of the bowling alley and the Odd Fellows lodge, where treks and battles happened; the nailed-up—but by them reopened—three-hole privy in the scruffy woods in the slough behind the big hotel, why there, who knew, but ritual required it to be used each time it was passed, by all, girls, boys, young, old, leaders, followers; the railroad bridge abutment where the hoboes slept, where over scrapwood fires they cooked their beans and luckless kids' body parts.

Prosper wasn't the only funny-looking or oddly shaped one among them; any neighborhood gang could show a kid, Wally Brannigan was theirs, who illustrated with a sightless peeled-grape eyeball the incessant adult warning about what happens when you play with sharp sticks and improvised bows. Little Frankie No-last-name had had rickets and walked with an invisible melon between his legs. Sharon was hugely tall, like Olive Oyl. Only Frankie and Prosper among them found it hard to keep up, and Frankie was younger than the others and weepy and didn't count, which left Prosper at the bottom of the heap, helped along sometimes, or mocked, or nicknamed; by one or two of the strong, actively despised. He could hit a baseball pretty well, though sometimes a big swing caused him to lose his balance and fall in a heap, and he rarely beat the throw to first. Then a designated runner was assigned to him, the biggest kid on their side, who had to piggyback Prosper to the bag. Hit the ball, leap onto Christopher's back, be carried at a jouncing run, laughing and sometimes falling together in stomach-aching hilarity halfway down the base path while the rest of the field looked on in disgust—but sometimes bearing down with bared teeth at full gallop, scaring off the first baseman and stamping across the base.

It was Mary Wilma who decided it was not against the rules for Prosper to be carried by the pinch runner, in fact she determined that it was required. Mary Wilma was the smartest kid among them, or at least the most decisive; if something needed to be settled, Mary Wilma came out with a plan before anybody else had even had time to decide what was what, and if she met disagreement she was loud and definite in pointing out why she was right and the other was wrong, which was usually the case.

"Mary Wilma, I don't want to do your idea."

"Well it's smarter than your idea. Prove it isn't!"

"I don't care. I just don't want to."

"Tell me why you don't, stupid bubuncle! Idioso! Come on! I'll believe you if you can tell me!"

She said or shouted them, her directives and her made-up insults, with such fierce delight, her big dark eyes aflame and big mouth smiling, that it was hard to hate her, though everybody at some time said they did; and it was after all she who organized the great watermelon theft, and the Halloween bonfire extravaganza, and the nighttime kick-the-can eliminations. She liked to stage field days, and kept careful score: she ran faster than anybody else, not that she was so fast a runner, or longer legged, she just put so much concentrated heat into it, more than anyone else could summon or cared to summon, her legs scissoring and her eyes fixed on the goal.

Mary Wilma took an intense interest in Prosper, thinking up things he had to do to keep up, ways to put him to use, ways to insult him too.

"Here comes Prosper on his little horsie!" Meaning his odd tippety gait, it took Prosper a while to figure that out; Mary Wilma never said anything meaningless, though it might at first seem so. "What's your little horsie's name, Prosper? Is it a hoobie horsie?"

Of course he yelled back the meanest things he could think of, which amused her further, expert boxer or knife fighter challenged by a child; but he stayed near her, if only because it lessened the likelihood of his getting beaten up, chances of which went up after he started having to wear a back brace of leather and buckles and metal. Mrs. Vinograd made the horrible error—mortal, irreversible, to Prosper—of calling this device a Boston girdle. Which was its name, in fact, but which when said out loud before the class was curtains for the wearer. Mary Wilma on the playground or in the alleys liked to name it too, at top volume, and it was she who began then to call Prosper Coozie Modo, which even those who hadn't gone to see Lon Chaney tormented in the movie (Prosper hadn't) knew to be a killing taunt. Never mind: if he stayed near her he wouldn't be kicked or pelted with dingbats—those who liked the idea of doing that were also the ones most afraid of Mary Wilma, her needle-sharp sense of each of their weaknesses and inadequacies; and she didn't allow group activities she hadn't conceived of.

Her family had a house a few blocks from Prosper's, a whole house that they rented part of to others but whose basement and attic and weedy garden and shed were all theirs, a huge domain, and she brought Prosper there and took him all through it. She revealed its arcana to him only slowly, watching his reaction to certain mysterious or alarming items as though he might not rise to the occasion, as though others before him perhaps had not: in the basement ancient pickled things in jars of murky fluid, which she claimed were babies but surely were only pig's feet or tongues; in the shed a black metal hook that she said had once served her grandfather as a hand, its brutal rusted tip still sharp— what had the old man done with it, to whom? She menaced Prosper with it, and he didn't flinch, though he wouldn't touch it himself. Anyway maybe it wasn't what she said it was, because she was a big liar, as Prosper told her, as everybody told her; she didn't seem to mind.

"Go on," she said, pushing him from behind. They went up the halls to the top of the house, where a rope hung that pulled down a flight of stairs leading to the attic. "You probably never saw this before," she said as the staircase descended gently, treads rotating into place. He shrugged nonchalantly, but he hadn't. Mary Wilma had just had her black hair bobbed, and Prosper couldn't stop looking at the tendons of her neck and the hollow between, like a boy's now but not like a boy's. "Up we go, little Prosper," she said. "Up up up." When they had gone up through the hole in the ceiling Mary Wilma pulled up the stair behind them. It seemed to take no effort at all; Prosper wondered why not.

There were other mysteries to be revealed in the dry dim warmth. A harmonium whose cracked and mouse-chewed bellows could only wheeze spooky groans like a consumptive or the ghost of one. A dress dummy she hugged, calling out Ma, Ma. The dust on these things and in the air, the slatted windows always open, the squeak of the gray boards underfoot, which were so obviously the ceiling of the rooms below.

She had them play cards there on the floor with a wrinkled and dog-eared deck. Go Fish. Slapjack. Then she taught him another one, a good one she said, a better one. It was called Lightning. She laid out a row of cards for herself and one for him, in complicated fashion making piles and moving cards from one to the other.

"Now you take the bottom card of the first pile and put it on top of the pile in the middle. No in the middle. No across-ways. That's the Boodle. You leave that there strictly alone. Now hold out your cards." She bent forward to transfer cards from his hand to hers and hers to his. Some were laid down.

"Prosper! Not there! I told you!"

"You said before—"

"Now we have to start *all* over. Put down eight piles of three cards . . ."

"It was seven before."

She reached to grab his shirt, disordering the cards that were spread in arcane ways over the floor between them. "You listen! Eight piles of three!"

"You said before—"

"Do it!" she said.

He threw down his cards. "You're just making it up. There isn't any game at all, just rules."

She was laughing. "It's fun! It's a good game. You must do it."

Her face was very close to his. "Stop being mean, Mary Wilma," he said. "Why are you so mean? Did somebody beat you with the mean stick?"

She almost fell into him laughing, her laughter seeming to say that he'd found out her secret or maybe that he was the funniest person in the world, fixing him at the same time with her wide unbreakable gaze. "Prosper!" she cried, as though he were a block away. "The *mean stick*?"

"Yes!" he said, unable not to laugh too, and then she had grabbed him again by the shirt.

"Prosper!" She'd stopped laughing, her fierce hilarity remaining though. "Let's take your pants off!"

He didn't look away. "Let's take *yours* off."

She instantly did, reaching up under her dress and pulling down.

She lifted both bare legs in the air and slipped over her shoes the little white bundle. Just as he did it himself every night. "Now you," she said.

Everybody grows up by leaps, and not by a steady climb like a mountaineer's. As though he had just been pulled up by the hair to look over an enclosing ridge, Prosper hung in a space of Mary Wilma's creating, unable then to confute or even really to perceive what she had done: she had taken off her pants but given nothing away, yet she had certainly gone first, leaving him to go next, fair's fair. All that Mary Wilma was, and did, and would be; all that he was and knew, all now altered. He started unbuttoning.

Afterward he always said, when he would ask her (or she would say, inviting him), *Let's go play Lightning:* and a few times up in the attic they did lay out cards in Mary Wilma's meaningless arrangements. But these nongames became briefer and then were forgotten even though the name remained as the name for what they did do. Mary Wilma, after she had played that first trick on Prosper, was as willing as he was to reveal, whipping off her jumper with practiced celerity as Prosper stood before her, new flesh extruding strangely but interestingly from him. "Now what's *this*," she would cry, her hand shooting like a bird's claw to snatch it, gripping as though it might fly away. "What's *this* supposed to be! Huh, Prosper? What?"

As often though she liked to play a pretend game, as though naked-ness relieved her of the heavy responsibilities of leadership and returned her to an earlier time in her life when the world could all be invented. She became or played a vague helpless party, moving as though under water or in a dream, her act for Prosper. "Oh gee"—absent, distrait—"oh look I have forgot my pants, oh dear. Here I am outside and no *cloath-es,* what will I do. Oh my oh dear they all see me, oh they see my posterior, oh boy, my *buttawks,* ooh what will I do. I will sit here and wait for the trolley." Her head lolled, she parted her legs where she sat on an old trunk. "Oh dear now I must pee pee, now what, oh well oh well I guess I just *will,* dum de dum de dum, can't help it, ooh oops." The first time the game reached this point she just pretended, making a sissing noise as her hands feebly grasped air, and the second time too; but the third time, she lifted her dusty knees and regarded Prosper with a face that mixed a hot triumphant Mary Wilma challenge into the fey person she was pretending to be; then she let go, water spraying from the cleft in the girl way, not like his own straight stream, wetting the box and the gray floor. His face and breast hot with amazement and elation.

What they did in the attic (that word *attic* ever after retaining a shadow of secret warm shared exposure for him) didn't change Mary Wilma's ways out in the world with the others, and only later on did it occur to him what a chance she'd taken with him, how brave she'd been, those things they did together were riskier for her than any crazy brave thing she'd ever done, than climbing up to the railroad bridge from the river, than letting Hoopie Morris shoot her in her winter-coated back with his air rifle to prove it wasn't fatal like Hoopie stupidly claimed: because Prosper could have told on her. He could, as she certainly knew; as she would certainly have told on someone if she needed to, to maintain her place. *You know what Mary Wilma does?* Yelled someday when she bossed him or mocked him, as she never stopped doing. *You know what Mary Wilma does?* And she would instantly have been *toppled* as leaders in the news were; her power would have vanished. Tears of rage, he could almost see it. Why would she take that chance?

Because (Vi Harbison told Prosper in Henryville, having heard a brief version of this, the first anecdote or instance Prosper offered, though not one that in Vi's opinion counted) because she trusted Prosper not to.

But why did she think she could trust him, Prosper wanted to know; and if Vi knew, or had an idea, she didn't say.

It didn't go on long, but it didn't end because one or both of them decided to quit, or chickened out, not at all, but only because (as nearly as Prosper could figure it later) it was just at that time that he was discovered by the Odd Fellows, and went away to the hospital, and all that happened thereafter began to happen, one thing falling into the next and the next, until at last he wasn't even living in the same neighborhood, and—though this he never knew—neither was she. What became of them all, she and Hoopie and Wally and the others whose names he couldn't recall, those he had once spent all day with, in school or after, on Saturdays and Sundays? He rarely thought about them afterward, but they certainly were a Passionate Series as Pancho Notzing would later describe it to him—lovers of power and lovers of pleasure, the greedy and the indifferent, the retiring and the unhesitating, an entire spectrum of human temperaments, needs, and wants, enough anyway to make a complete society, the only one he'd ever know himself to be a member of until he came to live and work among the Teenie Weenies still far away then in time and space.

2

That orthopedic hospital, though a source of civic pride pictured on postcards that visitors to town could buy, was not used as much as the founders and supporters had expected: not enough people willing to go have the clubfoot or the gimp leg they'd lived with for years corrected, or with enough money to pay for it. So the local chapter of the International Order of Odd Fellows (whose building, with its name at once comical and sinister, had hung over the wasteland where Prosper's gang had played ball) volunteered to survey the county and learn who was in need, who could be helped, especially among the children; and to raise the money to pay for the surgeries of some. It was Mrs. Vinograd who brought Prosper to their attention, Prosper and one or two others she had observed as well. Despite her belief that Poor Posture could be overcome by will and self-control, Mrs. Vinograd also believed in doctors and the advance of Medicine; she believed in efficiency, in principle and in practice. She didn't tell Prosper or his mother what she had done, though, and when the two moon-faced men in great double-breasted suits appeared at the Olanders' door and announced who they were and their interest in Prosper, he assumed that they had come to claim him as one of their own: an Odd Fellow, as they were; the lodge he was a member of.

When it became clearer what the two wide smilers actually meant by coming there, Prosper's mother lifted four fingers to her chin in doubt or fear. "Oh dear," she said.

"Get you some help, you see," said one, gently, knowing to whom he spoke.

"Well he's been fine this far," she said.

"But he could be fixed right up," said the other Odd Fellow, and tousled Prosper's hair as though he were six, or a dog.

"Oh but an operation," Prosper's mother said. "An *operation?*"

"At no cost to you now or ever," said the first, a salesman.

"But what about his schooling? That's important too."

"We're just here to make sure the boy gets examined, ma'am." He drew out from within his capacious jacket a memorandum book and a gold pen; and they all turned to Prosper.

Examined. To see, first, if it really was possible to fix him right up. On a sloppy winter day Prosper and his mother took the streetcar to the hospital, which stood on a rise above a raw new neighborhood on the other side of the city. They had to cross a construction site on duckboards, then climb up a path and two flights of stairs to reach the doors. There they made themselves known at the window, waited on a bench in the echoey strange-smelling waiting room where hortatory posters had been put up. His mother lifted her eyes to one after another, patted her bosom, moaned almost inaudibly. One showed a funny man about to sneeze, finger beneath his nose, and warned that COUGHING, SNEEZING, SPITTING SPREAD INFLUENZA! Another showed a family man, his wife and child cowering behind him, desperately trying to keep shut a door on the outer darkness where a vague white hideous specter was trying to come in. Tuberculosis. Shutting the door on the thing looked hopeless, though it wasn't probably supposed to.

After a long time a nurse all in white, even to her shoes, called their name and led them down wide high corridors across floors more highly polished than any Prosper had ever seen, gleaming tile seeming to vanish beneath his muddy feet as though he walked on water. Doors opened on either side and he glimpsed people being ministered to, lifting legs or arms with nurses' help or playing slow games with big balls. They were shown into a room to wait with other young people, other culls of the Odd Fellows he supposed, some of them glad to see people in their own case and lifting hands in salute or recognition, some who wouldn't meet his eyes. One a delicate pale girl with white-blond hair carefully marcelled, her spine so out of true it seemed she had been cut in two across the middle and the two parts put back together incorrectly. She shrank farther away as Prosper helplessly stared, as though she could feel the gaze she couldn't meet, and his mother at last pulled his hand to make him stop.

The young doctor he was finally taken to see—hawk-faced, his hair laid tight against his head with Wildroot oil, its odor unmistakable, the same that Prosper's father had used—made one judgment right away. Prosper was to stop using the Boston girdle: it could do him no good, the doctor said. He took it from Prosper and with thumb and finger held it up, fouled with sweat and other things, edge-worn and splitting, as though it were some vermin he had shot. Prosper's heart lifted.

Then he was taken, more wonderful still, to have an X-ray, the nurse telling him it wouldn't hurt and would show what the inside of his body and his bones looked like, but Prosper knew all that, and stepped up bared to the waist smartly and efficiently, put his breast and then each side and his back against the glass as the doctor showed him; it didn't hurt, though he was sure he felt pass through him coldly the rays without a name. Then that was all. Back through the waiting room, still unable to make the pale girl see him, along the corridors and through the doors and down the steps and home. Three weeks later a letter came from the hospital saying that he was being considered as a candidate for surgical correction of spinal lordosis, and setting another date for more examinations.

Prosper couldn't know it, but even that first uneventful journey into the hospital had nearly undone his mother. He did know that she was someone to whom you couldn't bring your bleeding body parts to be bandaged, as she would faint, or say she was about to, and turn away white-faced and trembling; also best not to tell her you'd thrown up, or had sat on the pot with the gripes until a load of hot gravy was passed that flecked the bowl and lid. These things were for you to know. Long afterward, in one of those reassessments that come upon us unwilled, like a sudden shift of perspective in a movie scene that shows the lurking villain or dropped gun that couldn't be seen before, Prosper realized that it was actually his father who had bound up his wounds, carried him to bed in fever, washed out the white enamel basin (*Hasten Jason bring the basin*) with the horrid black chipped spots in it; and that therefore it had certainly cost him something when his father blew.

He would think then: There are thoughts you never think until, for the first time, you do think them. And he would remember his father telling his jokes, salesman's patter, even as he cleaned the boy that Prosper had been.

It wasn't that his mother neglected cleanliness, health, and the body. They were ever present to her mind, a threat and a promise she could never get working together. She had been raised on medicine as though on food: Wendigo Microbe Killer, Kickapoo Indian Sagwa, Hamlin's Wizard Oil liniment, Doctor Flint's Quaker Bitters, cod-liver oil in the winter and sulphured molasses in the spring. After her only child was born she felt she deserved Lydia Pinkham's Vegetable Compound to reverse the bad effects; she sucked Smith Brothers cough drops (which she fed to Prosper too) and was a user of Hadacol, which she found lots better for her headaches than Coca-Cola. And as within, so without: Prosper's earliest memory was of hearing the enormous Hoover starting up somewhere in the house, brand-new then possibly, anyway unknown to him, an inexplicable noise at once roar and shriek and coming closer; moving away; closer again, and evidently seeking him out where he lay in bed. Then to find the great gray floor-sucker thing entering his room, manipulated by his grim-faced mother, therefore not dangerous at all, maybe.

His mother feared germs; her own earliest memory was watching her bedroom stripped of its bedclothes, curtains, and toys, to be burned in the alley after her scarlet fever. The Hoover was her defense, or her offensive, against germs, that and lye soap, naphtha flakes, carbolic, Old Dutch cleanser with the furious punitive bonneted figure on the can that Prosper took as the image of his mother's spirit, and scrub brushes boiled weekly. Prosper, already afflicted by troubles that seemed to get worse as he grew, caused her endless worry, she almost feared to touch him, not only because of what he had inside him but because of what he might have touched in the filthy world outside. Once he brought home a stray dog, sick too, half-carrying it into the house and supposing he might be able to keep it. His mother blocked him and it with a broom from entering, prodding them away desperately and calling on the deities. After that when she was sunk in her cleaning he could sometimes hear her mutter *the dog, that dog.*

So if it had been up to her, Prosper likely wouldn't have gone into that hospital or under that knife, and what would have happened instead was unknowable, and still is. It was Miss Mary Mack, her eyes and eyelashes glittering as though frosted and her cheeks red from the cold, who came to fetch him and bring him back there, which for all he then knew she did out of kindness only: kind too to his helpless inert mother fretting on the kitchen chair with two aprons on. Held his hand when they mounted to the streetcar. Prosper found a certain satisfaction, on his return, in telling his mother how blood had been taken from him, right from the crook of his arm where this gauze was now wrapped, and how he watched it rush out to fill the glass needle, thick and dark as beet soup.

Just before he went into the hospital for the surgery, the Odd Fellows held a little ceremony where the check for the costs was presented to the hospital. The Odd Fellows ranged on the steps of the hospital with the director and a doctor (who had to be persuaded to don his white coat for the picture). Of the children who were to benefit from the lodge's efforts, Prosper and the pale blond girl were chosen to participate in the event, Prosper with a tie of his father's on and the girl in white with a white hair bow so huge that it seemed she might be able to flap it and fly away—and she looked as though she wanted to, stricken, eyes alert as though to danger or downcast in shame. Prosper talked to her. Her name was Prudence, and he laughed a little at that, mostly from fellow-feeling with someone else not named Joe or Nancy, but she only lowered her eyes again as though he'd mocked her. Still he stood protectively by her while the pictures were taken and the man from the newspapers asked their names. "Her name is Prudence. My name is Prosper. *P-r-o-s-p-e-r.* Will the picture be in the paper?"

It was. It appeared the morning he was to go with his mother to be admitted, a little suitcase packed with clean skivvies and socks and a toothbrush and a dictionary (his mother's choice) and some tonics and vegetable pills (likewise). He studied the picture with her. There he was with a big smile that made his mother shake her head, and Pru, her great eyes looking up as though out of a burrow.

"Don't let it turn your head," his mother said, and it was the last thing he clearly remembered her saying to him, though no doubt she said more than that, taking him to the hospital and getting him onto his white bed in the big ward and kissing him good-bye. Maybe because he'd never heard the phrase before, and had to puzzle out its meaning. Once, when months had passed, awake in the night in his plaster jacket immobile in that ward, he thought what she had done was to warn him: *don't let them turn your head*. And unwittingly he had done that, he had let them turn his head, and all that resulted was his own fault.

He'd imagined, for no good reason, that Pru would be given the bed next to his, but in fact she wasn't even in the long room of parallel beds, she was in the ward below, for girls—he learned that when both their wards and others joined in the great sunroom for marching each morning to a Victrola. Three mornings: he saw her each time, and spoke to her, and at last she smiled to see him, her only friend (so her smile seemed to say). Around and around they went as the oompah music played, stopped, and began again, some of them on crutches, others pushing themselves along on rolling frames or staggering rhythmless on legs of different lengths. Pru walked as though always in the process of falling over to her left, as her spine went, but she never did; she held her hands curled up to the breast, as though she held an invisible plumb line there, to see how far from true she bent, and to try and straighten.

"Did you see your picture?" he asked her.

She looked away.

"You looked pretty," Prosper said.

She looked into the distance, as though searching the halting shuffling crowd for someone she knew.

"Do you talk?" Prosper said smiling. "Cat got your tongue?"

He thought the shadow of a smile crossed her face but still she wouldn't speak. The music stopped, skritched, resumed.

On the fourth morning they began to build Prosper's cast, and there was no more morning marching for him.

He had two nurses attendant on him for this, one kindly and calm, the other brisk and dismissive of fears; the one lean and snaggletoothed, the other plump and soft-armed. They had him follow them out of the ward (observed by everyone) and down the hall to a bright room where there was a table covered in rubber sheeting and piles of other things. Talking, talking, first one then the other, they pulled off his nightshirt, which they called a johnny for some reason, and hoisted him onto the table to lie facedown, a little pad for his cheek, the horrid cold rubber under his nakedness. He knew you were not supposed to mind if nurses or doctors saw your posterior.

"He'll be a brave little fella," said Nurse Kind.

"He better be," said Nurse Brisk. "This's the easy part."

They had sheets of black felt and a big scissors, and cut pieces out and laid them on his back from neck to knees, patting and stretching them into place. Then they ran water at a sink and did other things he couldn't see while they talked to each other about this and that, Hoover, the talkies, Rudolph Valentino and Rudy Vallee—for a long time Prosper thought these were the same person, one the nickname of the other.

"Okay dearie, this is going to get a little damp," said Nurse Kind.

"Move a muscle and I'll brain you," said Nurse Brisk, which made Nurse Kind laugh dismissively. Something wet and heavy was laid on him, at his neck, and the nurses ceased their chatter, only murmuring to each other as they worked the wet plaster bandages to fit him before they hardened. It was like nothing he'd ever felt before and the desire to wriggle out of it, clamber up and get out, was nearly irresistible, the nurses must have known it and kept their hands on his legs and head to keep him still while the clock on the wall ticked away.

When they were done, they removed the hardening cast, turned him over and made the front the same way, right down to his groin, leaving a space for him to make water. The back side had a hole too, neatly edged in rubber. They showed it to him when it had all dried and been trimmed and lined with felted cloth and fitted with straps and toothed buckles; it was the last time he'd see the backside till it came off, long after.

Laid in this cast like a turtle—the plastron part could be unbuckled and removed, now and then, but he was told never to get out of the back part—he should not even allow himself to *think* about getting out. He didn't have to lie flat on his back, the bed itself had a crank that could move it up and bring the world into view and his head in right relation to it, gratifying.

In the next bed a boy was looking at him, or seemed to be looking at him, though his head and face were hard to assess, because he seemed to be in the grip of some invisible opponent he wrestled with, straining every muscle. He made sounds that might have been language.

"Did he say something?" Prosper asked the nurse.

"May have," the nurse said, not looking at the fellow. "Sometimes he does. He's a spastic and we don't know what else."

Prosper looked over at the boy in the bed. He was definitely studying Prosper, though with what intentions or thoughts Prosper couldn't tell—not dull or idiotic he was pretty sure. "Hello," he said.

The other seemed gratified to be greeted, and said something back.

"Try harder, Charlie," said the nurse, not looking at him. "Or be quiet. Nobody can guess what you mean."

Charlie rose up in his bed, as though lifting himself by puppet strings, and seemed ready to fling himself out, his mouth working. The nurse turned to him and, hand on his chest and her face close to his, pushed him back. "I've told you about this, Charlie. You lie still and be a good boy. It's for your own safety. Don't make me get the straps."

At this Charlie sank back and stopped talking, though he went on moving; if you watched you could tell that the muscles he gave orders to were constantly revolting or refusing, and he had to continually change the orders, so that he was never quite still. When the nurse had passed to the next bed, Charlie spoke again to Prosper.

"Sheeez a caution. Ain she."

"I'll say," Prosper answered.

"Oooh shth. Shthink she. Is. Muscle Eenie?"

It wasn't hard to understand once you listened. Prosper got it and laughed, and Charlie laughed too. Nurse Muscle Eenie turned to look back at them—like all powerful persons, she had a keen sense of when she was being mocked—but that only made them laugh the more.

Prosper, spending long hours beside Charlie, got good at understanding what he said, and sometimes translated what he said for the nurses, who seemed to have very little patience with him and to assume most of the time that he was muttering nonsense, and would talk back to him as though he were a baby. "He's not stupid," he explained to one of the nurses as Charlie listened. "He's just spastic. If you listen he's not stupid."

"He's not a spastic," said this nurse. "He's an athetoid. There's a difference."

Prosper actually thought Charlie was the wittiest kid on the ward, his jokes all the funnier for being unexpected or hard to decode—it really was hard to tell when Charlie was trying to be funny, though Prosper got that too at last.

The other person who understood Charlie fine was his father, who came often to see him, once bringing Charlie's mother and three small sisters, though all these visitors were too uproarious and Nurse Muscle Eenie made it clear that from now on they were to come one at a time and not *upset the routine* as she said. So it was mostly his father who came, and sat by his bed; his presence seemed to still Charlie's muscles, at least to lower the spasms from a boil to a simmer. It was Charlie's father who explained to Prosper that Charlie's muscles weren't weak, they just wouldn't listen to his brain. They were plenty strong: in fact Charlie was here to get a couple of them released—they'd been holding parts of Charlie tight since he was a baby, and didn't know how to let go.

"So he's gotta go under the knife," said Charlie's father smiling a little sadly. "Right, son?"

"That'll show 'em," Charlie said. He held up his left hand, which curled backward toward his wrist, and made a face at it that was supposed to be tough and uncompromising.

Prosper's mother came too, once, though she had a great reluctance to come too close to where Prosper lay in his cast; she stood a ways off, her hands clasped, as though the left were keeping the right from touching anything around her. Prosper could tell she suffered, though not what she suffered from, and tried to ask her about life out beyond the hospital; he told her about Prudence and about Charlie and his muscles, but she seemed not even to want to open her mouth much and swallow the air in there.

"I'm going under the knife," Prosper said. "Any day."

"Oh Prosper," she said. "Oh Prosper."

Soon the nurse came close: visiting hours were over, ambassadors from the world beyond were to depart. Prosper's mother kissed her son. The ward returned to the state it ought to have, just the children and their noises and cries, the circulation of the nurses, like horses in their sweaty hardworking domineering presence, great rumps and thighs beneath their white cottons or lean hard shins and the crack of their heels against the ward floor. They caught boys out of bed and heaved them back in like grain sacks, threatened and chastened and stilled them with a look as Miss Vinograd had done, though they were gentle with the ones who moved less or not at all, teaming up to move them from their beds to the rolling carts that took them to hydrotherapy or elsewhere, who knew where, and back again. On three, lift.

Prosper's turn at last, after the nurse had rung the curtains around his bed and washed him with some awful carbolic. A long black razor on the tray, opened, and a bowl of soapy water—they shaved his back and buttocks right down into the crack, why, when there wasn't any hair there. Charlie'd said they would: *Doan ledm slice your GNUTS opff*, he'd cried.

They put a mask over his face, and told him to count backward from ten, and that's all he knew of that afternoon, until he knew himself to be back in the ward again, his head at least afloat above a body that seemed not to be his. Nurse Muscle Eenie told him that while he lay there neither in nor out of the world his mother had come to visit him. Charlie confirmed it—a lady came and sat and stood by him; Charlie tried to imitate how she had hovered, how she had wrung her hands. Prosper felt, when they said these things, that yes, she had been there, had looked down on him, but in his remembrance she'd worn a white dress and a white veil, like nurses in pictures during the War, maybe even a cross on her breast, and that couldn't be; the picture persisted, though, and when he was older he'd still be able to summon it up, and question why he'd got it in his mind—maybe he'd mixed it up with a nurse who'd also leaned over him, but the nurses there weren't wearing those angel outfits any longer; maybe he'd got it from a movie, but which one? Anyway he'd somehow missed her, this nonsensical scrap all he had, and she didn't come again. She'd got sick, the nurses told him. She'd sent a message. She was thinking of him, but too sick right then to visit. For days Prosper himself was too sick to think of anything; and when he was no longer sick he was so changed he didn't know how to think of her or where he had come from. He'd been put to sleep in the hospital, and when he awoke fully—when the spell was lifted—he was still there, only now it was where he lived, and always had been.

The next thing he would remember with any clarity was the doctor, his white coat collared like a priest's, who came to hover over him, read his chart and tell him what had happened to him in that limbo. The operation on his back had gone well, the doctor said. He would stand straighter than he had before. He wouldn't be able to bend over quite as well, but he hadn't been able to bend very well before, except at the waist, wasn't that true? It was true. Prosper hadn't yet tried bending over with his new back so he didn't know what the difference would be.

"Better than that," the doctor said. "It won't get worse now. If we'd done nothing it would have got worse."

Prosper couldn't respond to that. They'd told him often, the doctor and the nurses, that he'd get worse and worse if he didn't have the operation, but he hadn't felt himself to be in bad shape, and didn't know what "worse" would mean.

"All right," he said.

"So." The doctor smiled, ready to move on.

"But can you tell me," Prosper said, "how come I can't move anything." He made to move a leg, to show him it couldn't.

"Temporary," the doctor said. "You'll get over that."

Maybe it was temporary, though everything that happened in those days was so new and unknown, any transformation or decline or wasting or empowerment possible, that even transitory states seemed to be forever, no matter what the nurses said; Prosper poked at his unresisting thighs, as cold-skinned as a chicken leg and seemingly no more his.

Each day a nurse removed the front of his brace and washed him. Then the brace was buckled back together, and two nurses lifted him in his brace and with great care and much instructing of each other they turned him over, and let him lie facedown for a time. It was like turning over in sleep, except that it took a very long time, and two other people. After a week, it was different when the nurse came to wash him. He was different. He could feel it: the warm water, the smooth soap, the rough cloth. Not the way he had before, but as though he were awaking with the sun and hearing confused noises not yet resolved into birdsong and kitchen clamor. He could feel it and held his breath. His penis when the nurse lifted and swiped it, swiped under his testicles, suddenly rose and swelled, as though also startled awake. She cleaned his inner thighs and reached deep down between his legs. Prosper thought of looking at the ceiling, or closing his eyes, but couldn't. Without looking away from her job the nurse said, "Feeling a little better, huh?" and at the same time flicked at his crotch with the middle finger of her free hand, the way you do when you want to send something—a spitball, a bug—a good distance; her nail struck sharply against the tender underside of the pink head that was peeking boldly out, Prosper yelped, and the whole collapsed and shrank.

Feeling better. Still his legs remained cold, as though asleep, below the middle of his thighs. In a few days the doctor came again, and lifted Prosper's legs, and laid them down again. He talked to the nurse about Prosper's back, his legs, the healing of his wound (they called it a wound, as though they had done it by accident), and he went away again, with a wink at Prosper that made him wonder.

After a month he came back, and this time drew up a chair by Prosper's bed to have a talk.

"So the operation was a success, and your back is doing well," he said. "But it didn't go as well in another way."

Prosper grew momentarily conscious of the cast he lay buckled in. The doctor was regarding him, maybe with truth and frankness in his steady gaze, but it seemed sinister to Prosper, the intense stare of people in the movies who are about to reveal crimes, or accuse others of them, or change people into monsters.

"The side effects of an operation like this can't be predicted," he said. "It hasn't been done in this way for very long. In the future we will . . . well. In your own case. There's a lot of complex innervation running up that spine of yours. Well up everybody's. And placing the instrumentation can have unintended consequences."

He put a hand strongly but gently on Prosper's leg. Prosper could feel the warmth.

"You've had a certain amount of paralysis."

Prosper nodded, not knowing what the word meant exactly though it was one spoken around the ward. Infantile Paralysis. "The nurse said it would get better," he said. "It already has." He almost told about how he had felt the nurse washing him, the effect it had had and what she'd done, but stopped before he did. "She does the massage every day. I couldn't feel it, now I do."

"Well that's fine," the doctor said without a smile. "But in the long term. You're going to need some help walking."

Prosper pictured two nurses, the nice one, the other, by his side always, helping him along.

"We're going to teach you all about that. How to use some crutches to get along. You'll do fine when you get used to them. Everybody does." He rose. "You'll need a little bracing to keep these legs straight and strong for that. Braces and the crutches. You'll get along fine."

"Okay," Prosper said. The two of them, Prosper on the bed and the doctor above, with everything and nothing to say. "So maybe I'll still get over it someday."

"Sure thing," the doctor said. "Maybe you will."

3

He'd been in the cast for four weeks, with as much at least left to go, when he got a visitor again. His own visitor, not like the actress or the ballplayer who visited everybody, going from bed to bed followed by reporters and helpers and the doctor, smiling and kissing one or two while the flashbulbs went urgently off.

Two visitors in fact: his aunts, Bea and May. Bea was the older sister of his mother, and May the younger sister of his father. Bea was taller and blonder, with heavy curls that seemed to burden her head, and May was small and dark, her hair cut short when it became all right to do that, and unchanged since. He had never seen them apart, so it was also like having one visitor.

"Hello, Prosper," Aunt Bea said. "You remember me. And here's May too."

"Hello, Aunt Bea. Hello, Aunt May. Sorry I can't stand up."

"Oh, now, Prosper," said May. The nurse pushed over an extra chair by the bed so they could sit, both on their chair's edge, both clutching their purses. "So what now's all this they're doing to you? Is all this proper?"

"They have to tug him straight," said Bea confidentially to her.

"Well, I must say," May said, "you're quite the brave fellow, putting up with all this. I never could."

"It's fine," Prosper said. "I'll be doing fine. I might need a little help in walking."

"Oh. Oh."

Charlie in the next bed now stirred, and Prosper—somehow the two kind outspoken ladies made him want to be punctilious and correct—indicated him. "Aunt May, Aunt Bea," he said, "I'd like you to meet my friend Charlie," and here he realized he'd never heard or didn't remember Charlie's last name. Charlie'd come out of his own plaster cast in that week, and his muscles, released from long confinement, were going crazy, having forgotten all that Charlie had tried to teach them or just wild with freedom; he put on quite a show lifting himself in the bed to greet the two ladies, sheets astir and pajamas twisted, head tugged sidewise and mouth working as though he were catching flies around him. But he said "Pleased to meetcha" pretty well, and then said it again, happy with the success of it. The two ladies smiled and nodded, interested, and Bea took from her large bag a small stack of cookies, which she handed around.

"How's my ma?" Prosper asked, eating. "Is she coming?"

Bea and May shared a look—it was a thing they did, that Prosper would become accustomed to, their heads turning together like connected gears to lock in place, and the knowledge, or the unease, or the wonderment or puzzlement passing between their wide eyes and big long ears, you could almost see it in transit. Then both together back.

"She's not been well," said May.

"She's been poor," said Aunt Bea. "She's getting better."

They added nothing to that, and Prosper didn't know what further to ask. Bea cried *Well* and from her bag began to take out more things, books and puzzle magazines, Lucky bars, the bag was like a magician's fathomless top hat; finally half a cake cut in slices. The ward around them, at least those that were mobile, began to be drawn to Prosper's bed like a school of fish to fish food until they were all around and the aunts were handing around cake.

"Prosper, what do you think," May said. "When you're all better and out of this contraption. Would you like to come and stay with us for a while?"

Prosper's mouth was full, so he couldn't say anything, and had a moment to think. He liked the women. Once he'd spent a night at their house while his mother went away to another city to visit a practitioner of some sort, he couldn't remember for what illness, and Bea and May had entertained him royally, ice cream in three flavors, games of Snap and Crazy Eights, dancing to late-night bands on the radio, the two of them laughing and pulling his leg and smoking Turkish cigarettes in holders. He thought they liked him too, something he was never sure about with his parents.

But he said: "I'd have to go home first. To be with my ma."

"Well sure," May said, and looked away smiling to the crowd of hungry jostling boys around her. Bea was helping Charlie with his slice, gazing with admiration at how he wielded his fork and made it to his face with almost every bite, and didn't turn to Prosper, as though she'd heard none of that. May remarked that when Prosper was out the two might get together, he and Charlie, and she wrote down for Charlie her own telephone number, which Prosper thought was remarkable.

Before they left, the aunts brought out one last present they had for him, a long box of dark wood with a brass catch, beautiful and rich, and inside, richer still, laid into the grooves of the paper liner, a spectrum of colored pencils: all in rainbow order, but shading subtly from blue to blue-green to green-blue to green, orange to red-orange, crimson, scarlet. They had all been pointed, not by penknife but by machine, flawlessly. He could hardly imagine disturbing them in their perfection, almost wanted to assure the two women that he never would, never spoil this thing that opened like a promise before him. Later they wondered if maybe he hadn't liked the gift: so quiet. But oh my: the poor kid had so much to think about, didn't he.

The nurses rigged up a table or desk surface hanging upside down from a frame over Prosper's bed and clipped his papers to it, so that even mostly prone he could use his pencils to draw. He started by simply edging his papers with great care in bands of color, thicker and thinner, as though making a larger and larger frame for a picture that he never drew. Then he began making letter shapes, copying from newspaper headlines the strange forms full of barbs and hooks and thick and thin lines, making up the letters that he couldn't find. He made name signs for the beds of the other boys, each of them putting in his own requests as to shape and color and nickname. "We know their names," Nurse Muscle Eenie said, and removed these distractions. He started making only one name, planting the dry sticks of it as though in a garden, where it grew strange buds and blossoms in red, violet, aquamarine, and sienna: the name was PRUDENCE. He'd send them with one of the nurses to deliver to her on her ward, and get back her thanks or none, and draw another.

His aunts came now and then to see him, though never his mother. On one occasion it wasn't they but two uncles, whom he knew by sight but had rarely spoken to before—Uncle Mert and Uncle Fred, bearing a box of chocolates, keeping their hats and coats on. They didn't have much to say. Mert extracted a cigar from his pocket and bit off the tip, was about to light it too as the children stared in glee, too bad the nurse just then told him no. Mert called her Sister. Say, Sister, when's the boy gonna be up and at 'em. Say, Prosper, you look like a turtle in that shell, naw, you look swell, kid. They didn't stay long, though Prosper shone briefly afterward in the ward in their reflected raffish glare; he made up some stories about who they were and what they'd done.

It took four months for Prosper to be broken out of his plaster shell, his skin flaking and gray and the cast itself loathsome as the grave, but himself alive. Two further months to regain the strength in his hips and the long muscles of his thighs that still functioned, and to find out which those were, and make them move. More months to cast his legs and have the steel braces made that from then on he would need to stand and to walk; to learn to put them on and take them off by himself, and lift himself up like a stiff flagpole erected, himself the flagpole sitter, wobbling high atop them, swept by vertigo—awful to know that if he fell, his locked knees would stay locked and he'd go down straight and headlong. To learn to walk with them, first in the parallel bars of the exercise rooms (the very rooms that he had peeked into on his first visit to this place, rooms that he now seemed to have been born and raised in) and after that with wooden crutches under his arms. The Swing Gait: put both crutches out in front of you and then fling your body forward on them, advance the crutches quick enough so you don't fall forward. The more approved Four Point Gait: left crutch tip, right foot, right crutch tip, left foot, like a parody of a man free-walking. When he got good at it he was allowed to compete in the unofficial crutch-racing meets on the ward. On the lower floor he joined the marching again, singing and walking at the same time, a good trick.

He was walking with Prudence (who still rarely spoke but seemed glad, even proud, to have him by her, all he'd wanted) when far off Miss Mary Mack came onto the floor—several of the children were her responsibility, and they sang out in greeting:

"Miss Mary Mack Mack Mack
All dressed in Black Black Black
With the silver Buttons Buttons Buttons
All down her Back Back Back."

Which more than one of the children really did have, under their skin, including Prosper and Prudence, they'd have known it if anyone had explained to them what the doctors had done. When the elephant jumped the fence in the song and didn't come down till the Fourth of July Prudence suddenly sang out all by herself in a high piercing challenging voice Prosper would not have thought she had, that stilled the tall-shoe clumpers and spastics and cripples:

"July can't Walk Walk Walk
July can't Talk Talk Talk
July can't Eat Eat Eat
With a knife and Fawk Fawk Fawk."

In all that time Prosper turned ten and then eleven. He passed from fifth grade into sixth, or would have if he'd gone to school; the teachers who volunteered on the ward never tried too hard to find out who needed to learn what and who already knew it well enough—Amerigo Vespucci, *i* before *e* except after *c,* 160 square rods to the acre. He grew two inches taller, though from now on he would grow taller more slowly. The stock market crash took all of the family money Nurse Muscle Eenie'd put into the Blue Ridge Corporation. Some of the sickest boys vanished from the ward, usually at night, and no notice was taken of their absence, not by the nurses, not by the patients; they weren't spoken of again. Charlie went home, a little less knotted up than before. Let's go, son, his father said, grappling him and lifting him down from the bed. Prudence went home, in the same white dress and bow she'd worn to have her picture taken long ago; straighter now but not all straighter, seeming to handle herself delicately, a tall stack of wobbly saucers that might slump and fall. She smiled for him, though, and showed him that she was taking all the versions of her name he had made home with her. She seemed happier, he thought. He never saw her again.

At the end of the year, his uncles appeared again, without the chocolates this time, but with something to impart that they seemed to have been ordered to tell him but couldn't. Each in turn glanced now and then behind himself, as though the unspoken thing were right behind them, nudging. In the end they only asked several times how he was doing, made a joke or two, and hurried away, saying they'd be back. It was Aunt Bea and Aunt May who, a day after and in the wake of his uncles' failure, had to come to tell him that while he had been in the hospital all this time, his mother had lost ground; had worsened; weakened—they took turns supplying words—and failed. She had died just about the time (Prosper later figured out) he'd first put on his braces.

Whatever else Prosper would remember of that day, the thing that would cause his own heart to fill with some kind of fearsome rain when it occurred to him, the thing that for him would always stand for human grief unbearable and rich, were the tears that stood in his aunts' eyes as they talked to him then, the tremble in their voices. He had never seen grown-ups in the grip of sorrow, and though they came close and put each a hand on him he couldn't conceive of it as being on his behalf; it was their own, and he would have given anything to have been able to say to them *It's all right, don't cry.*

"My God," Vi Harbison said to Prosper in Henryville, or to the world and the air around.

"What," said Prosper.

"You went in with the bent back and came out and you couldn't walk?"

"I can walk," Prosper said.

"You know what I mean. And then just while you were getting better they told you your mother died?"

"They didn't want to tell me till I was getting out. So I'd have some relatives, you know, around. They thought it would be tough if I had to learn it and then be in the hospital alone."

"What did she die of?"

"I don't know. No one said."

"My God." Vi's own mother had passed with her sons and daughter around her, her last labored breath; they'd seen her put into her box and into the earth and the dirt covering her. She knew. "And by this time your father was gone who knew where?"

"Yes."

"My God. You were alone. I can't imagine."

"No I wasn't actually. There was Bea and May. My aunts. Two uncles too."

"Aunts and uncles aren't parents. I mean they can try to do their best, but."

"Well. I don't know. It was different."

"Well it can't have been better."

"You didn't know my mother and father," Prosper said. "You didn't know Bea and May."

4

It will be different when you come out, they all said—Mert and Fred, Bea and May, with different faces at the different times when they said it—and he had pondered that as best he could, but it wasn't easy to think through what that meant, *different*; when he looked forward he saw a world that was all changed but actually all the same, because he couldn't imagine it changed. Once he dreamed of it, all different, but what was different about it was what was gone: his city, the streets, his house and the vacant lots around it and the buildings that had looked down on it. What was in their place he couldn't see.

It was that way, all changed and the same. Mert and Fred came to get him. He could walk out and down the hall and out the door on his own, and all the nurses, even Nurse Muscle Eenie, came out of the wards and offices to say good-bye and watch him go: first using the respectable Four Point, then the faster Swing Gait, an uncle on each side of him, one carrying the bag with his things, their hands at the ready and making for him nervously now and then as though he were an unsteady and valuable piece of furniture they were moving. "Doing fine, son," said a doctor who passed them. He was doing fine.

The long stairway to the street where Fred had double-parked the car was a different matter. Prosper halted at the top, looking down like a mountaineer about to rappel. Then Mert picked him up without a

word, and as though stealing him he took the steps at a good pace,
Fred after him. Prosper, pressed against his uncle, could smell Mert's
seersucker and even his cigar case; Mert's breath whinnied faintly up
his throat.

They tried to hustle him into the car by main strength, but his rigid
legs posed a packing problem that they argued silently over until Prosper made them stop. They stood back and watched as he unclipped the
locks at the knees of his braces and let them down and tucked his legs
into the car.

"Easy as pie," said Fred.

"Shut up, start the car," said Mert. A couple of passers-by had stopped
on the street to gawk at the operation, which Mert wanted to get over
with. "Rubes," he said. Fred got the car going. Prosper in the back seat
laid his head against the leather humps of the upholstery and watched the
city go past, not the familiar streetcar route but another way, chosen—
though Prosper couldn't know it—to bypass his old house.

"Take Main," said Mert.

"Main?"

"Main. Take Main and turn on Pearl."

"Why Pearl?"

"Just do it," Mert said.

The world was rich and huge. That's what was different. It poured
in on him as though it had just come into being, or was coming into
being as the car drove through it: huge sky, air full of odors, streets full
of newborn people in new-made coats and hats, ding of a bicycle bell
like struck crystal. Even the parts of the journey he recognized, streets
and corners and buildings, come upon sideways or at the wrong end,
seemed newer, sharper, bigger.

Then they pulled up before a house he knew, though not, at first,
what house it was. Fred set the brake but let the motor run, and Mert
leapt out and came to get Prosper; manhandled him out of the car as he
had into it, and set him up like a department-store dummy on the sidewalk before the house, which had by now become the house where Bea
and May lived, a house Prosper couldn't help thinking used to be somewhere else.

Fred had got out of the car now and come to stand by Prosper. Mert
brushed his hair with a hand, and Fred set down his bag of things

beside him and stuffed a five-dollar bill in his shirt pocket. Then the two of them looked at each other, came to a silent agreement, and with a quick *good-bye, good-bye* they climbed hastily back into the impatiently muttering auto and went off. As in an old comedy, the door before Prosper opened at the same moment as the car behind him pulled away. His two aunts appeared.

"Prosper!" Bea said, as though amazed, delighted too.

"They're gone," said May.

He had been turned over by the two uncles to the two aunts, who came out to claim him, one gentle hand each on his shoulders, faces with calming smiles bent to look into his.

"Hello, Aunt May. Hello, Aunt Bea."

"Why hello, Prosper. We're glad you're here."

"May," said Bea, "how's he going to get into the house?"

There were two low steps up to the narrow porch and another into the house. If he'd been asked before this day if his aunts' front door had steps up to it, and how many, he wouldn't have been able to say. There was a little bannister for the porch steps, made of coupled plumber's pipes, like those of the practice stairs where Prosper spent many hours. He stepped out from the shelter of their hands, swapped his right crutch into his left hand, grasped the bannister, and with it and the left crutch hoisted himself so that his feet landed on the first step. He steadied himself, feeling his aunts' and the street's and the world's eyes on him, marveling or doubtful. He did it again. Then again, but this time the toes of his shoes caught under the lip of the step. He fell back to start over with a bigger stronger push, swinging his feet *back* and then *over* the lip to land on the porch. A large cat that had just put its head out the open door turned and fled from the sight of him. Prosper turned to face his aunts, who looked at each other and then at him in wonderment. How do you like that. Easy as pie.

Flushed with success, he lifted himself over the threshold and stood in the hall. There was a smell of fusty rug, baked bread, the cat, a potent odor he didn't know was incense, Bea's Fatima cigarettes, window box geraniums. Sun came in through the open lace-curtained windows of the parlor beyond, falling on a dark velvet hassock and its armchair. Far door into a yellow kitchen. Later on, when a sudden memory of his standing that morning in the hall of Bea and May's house would arise in him, Prosper would sometimes feel his breast fill with a sob, though it hadn't done so then; and he never could say just what was gathered so densely into that moment as to cause it. Escape; refuge; exile too. Relief he couldn't have accounted for, and grief he was not yet even able to measure. His aunts' true kindness, and everything that kindness couldn't assuage. Pride that he had come into their house under his own power. New world. Lost life and strength. Maybe more than anything it was his memory of that boy's ignorance, ignorance of the years he would live in the rooms he could see from where he stood, and of all that would befall him there: that boon ignorance.

Bea and May had lived together all of Prosper's life. Prosper had never had much sense of how old they were; he guessed that May was younger than Bea, but he was wrong about that. They were the age of his parents, but in their knockabout freedom they seemed younger, in their fearlessness in the world they seemed older. Bea was dizzier, but May had done crazier things in her life—Prosper would hear her say this was so, but he was left to imagine what the crazy things might have been. She seemed to have come to rest in Bea, and was not tempted now, though Prosper would have liked to see an outburst or breakout of some kind, to know what May might be capable of.

Bea sold cosmetics at a department store downtown, spraying women with little spurts of My Sin or L'Heure Bleue and talking to them about their coloration. She had a wide-eyed soft-spoken cheer that seemed like total honesty, and she was honest, believed that she could suit a woman to a product that would benefit her, and took a dollar for a jar of lettuce oil or patent vanishing cream with a feeling of having done a good deed all around. May worked as office manager in a firm that sold business supplies and furniture wholesale, leather-topped desks and swivel chairs and gooseneck lamps and filing cabinets, as well as typewriters, time clocks, and adding machines. She never regarded her job as her calling, as Bea did hers. She complained about the time it took from her real life, which was lived in the realm of the spirit: her delicate, years-long negotiation with a disembodied child who communicated with May by various means. The child—whose name was Fenix Vigaron—taught May a lot, but also lied to her atrociously, apparently just for the fun of it, and had another friend among the living somewhere in Servia or Montenegro, a friend who got different help, maybe better help (the child hinted with casual cruelty) than she was willing to give to May. No one in her office knew about May's other life; but there, with her journal and ledger and her in-box and out-box, no matter how fast she moved May seemed to herself to be standing still, whereas sitting in stillness awaiting the dead child's touch she seemed always to be moving, however slowly, toward something.

Bea was always glad to get whatever advice Fenix Vigaron had for her, but May was shy about revealing her experiences to others; too many of them believed in things that May didn't believe in for her to talk to them about Fenix. They would go on about how their mothers and lovers and babies had called out to them as they sat holding hands in darkened rooms with paid mediums, but—May wanted to know—how could the only dead souls who mattered to you be just the ones your medium's spirit guide could introduce you to? Wouldn't it be more likely that they wouldn't be acquainted with them, among so many, the Great Majority? It was like running into someone who hails from a distant city where you yourself know one person, and asking, Say do you know Joe Blow, he's from there—and of course he doesn't. May's little angel or devil couldn't give May news of her brother, Prosper's father; she couldn't say if he was actually among them over there now (as May believed), and didn't seem to care either; nor did she ever come to know Prosper's mother, so as to bring any comforting words from her. May told Prosper anyway: your mother's happy now; nothing can hurt her now; I know it's so. Prosper nodded, solemn, as it seemed he should do. Prosper knew nothing then about Fenix Vigaron, though Fenix knew all about him.

The two women had taken on the orphaned Prosper (they'd agreed to regard him as an orphan, though Bea had her doubts) because they could, and because there was no one else not already consumed with their own children, or with the care of some other displaced or incompetent relative, or who wasn't just unsuitable, like Mert and Fred, into whose families (if they could be called that) you wouldn't want to insert any growing innocent.

But how to meet his needs, practical and spiritual, a male child, they themselves not so young and flexible as once they were? He'd have to have a room of his own, and (it took a while for them to grasp this) not at the top of the stairs, where theirs and a little spare room were. The only choice was the downstairs room the women called the parlor, though it was small and dim and they rarely used it, preferring the big bright room that ought to have been for dining. Thank goodness the bathroom was downstairs.

So they sent Mert and Fred a note telling them that their next task was to empty this room of its horsehair sofa and mirrored sideboard and grandfather clock and glass-shaded lamps and store them safely somewhere, then bring in instead a boy-size bed, a dresser and a wardrobe where he could put away his clothes and his, well, his things, snips and snails and puppy-dogs' tails. A desk May provided from work, and a steel lamp to put on it. (This oaken thing, with a hidden typewriter table that pulled out and sprang into rigidity with a snap, a secret cash drawer within a drawer—it was the first item of furniture Prosper recognized as his own, as in fact *him* in another mode; it appeared in his dreams for years, altered as he was himself.)

Mert and Fred didn't appear for this job themselves (they disdained and shrank from the women as much as the women did from them), but eventually a couple of fellows in derbies and collarless shirts arrived in a horse-drawn van and unloaded a cheap and vulgar but serviceable and brand-new set of furniture of the right type, don't ask how acquired, and swapped it for Bea's and May's parents' old moveables, which they carted away without a word.

"Why don't you like Uncle Mert and Uncle Fred?" Prosper asked them as he ate the egg they cooked him every morning, themselves taking nothing but coffee.

The two turned toward each other, that wide-eyed how-shall-we-respond look he'd seen before, then to Prosper again.

"First of all," May said, "they aren't really your uncles. Mert's your mother's cousin, and I don't even know what Fred is."

Prosper didn't know why that would exclude them from the women's world, and spooned the orange yolk from his egg. Now and then when he'd walked out with his father, he'd been taken into a diner or a garage to meet the two men, and those three had smoked a cigar together and talked of matters Prosper didn't understand, his father laughing with them and at the same time somehow shy and cautious, as though in their debt. He wondered now.

"They hang around down with that icehouse gang," May said. "You don't want to know."

But he did. Icehouse?

"They're not *bad*," Bea said, always ameliorative. "It's not that we don't *like* them. It's just."

"They have their uses," May said regally, and she and Bea laughed together.

Their place was too small to fit a wheelchair in, even if they could have afforded one, but May had a wheeled office chair, a model 404D, the Steno Deluxe, sent over from the business, and Prosper got good at navigating the space of the downstairs in it, moving quickly hand over hand from chair back to door frame to dresser like Tarzan sailing through the jungle on his vines. The women had to roll up and put away the rug, the beautiful Chinese rug, for him. Prosper only later understood how many such things they did, how many little costs they bore, all willingly paid. He had set them a problem, and they would solve it: for a time, they had to think up something new almost every day, and Prosper would try it, and at day's end they'd congratulate themselves and Prosper that *that* was done—Prosper had taken a bath and got out by himself, Prosper had been taken to the hospital for the sores on his feet, Prosper was going to go to school—and the next day face another.

They got him to school with the help of Mary Mack, who knocked one day at the door, appearing like the Marines (May said), face shining, having lost track of her client when he left the hospital—no one had told her! She invited May and Bea to share her astonishment at this, though they knew (and knew Miss Mack knew) that it was they themselves who had told no one that Prosper had got out—but well! Back again now, offering help, kidding Prosper (mute with bliss to be in her radiance again) about playing hooky. Yes of course he'd go to school. A few years back the progressives on the school board had passed a resolution, and the city an ordinance, stating that every child capable of being educated in the public schools ought to be, and accommodations must be made in the school, or at home for those unable to reach the school. And Miss Mack knew that the school to which Prosper would now be going had set up a special classroom that the cripples and wheelchair-bound children could reach. There was a sort of ramp, she said, such as wheelbarrows or hand trucks might use, and once inside there were no stairs to climb. Prosper had kept up with his lessons while in the hospital, hadn't he? Well his teachers would decide when he got there whether to advance him or keep him back. And how (May and Bea almost in unison asked) was he to get to and from this school? Miss Mack drew from her belted black leather satchel the papers for May or Bea to sign, Prosper's guardians as they now were or would become, so that Prosper could ride the special bus that would go around the district for the children who could not walk to school.

"I could walk," Prosper said with offhand certainty.

"It's a long way," said Mary Mack. She looked long into Prosper's eyes, and he looked into hers, deep dark blue and larger than seemed possible, somehow in his gazing absorbing her divinity unmediated. "Maybe you should save your strength."

"All right," Prosper said, unreleased.

"At first, anyway," said Mary Mack.

"All right," Prosper said.

So when September came, there Prosper would go, and what would come of that the women tried to imagine—how he would be regarded, whether kindly or disdainfully, and how he would get on included with a classful of children in his own case or maybe worse—but they couldn't imagine, really, and Fenix all that summer was dull or hostile, unresponsive, maybe jealous of the new child in the family.

Bea and May usually spent their week's vacation at a modest resort in the mountains, eating vegetarian meals and doing exercises under the instruction of a swami, but this year they saw that they'd have to be right there in their own hot house, which they hoped wasn't a sign of things to come for them. They played Hearts and cribbage and they listened to the radio and brought home books for Prosper from the library. Carefully, one of them on each side of him, they took walks around the block, returning in a sweat and feeling as though they'd walked every step of the way in his braces themselves. Once in the humid night May wept in Bea's arms, and couldn't say why: at the change in their lives that would be forever, at that poor child's losses, at his heartbreaking good cheer, at everything.

5

Sometime late in that summer, Prosper made a discovery: his mother and father were kept in the house, in the big closet under the stair. Curious and aimless in the hot afternoon, he'd started opening doors and peeking into drawers, learning the place, and this one last: that smaller-than-normal door, the door with the angular top, many a house he'd live in afterward would have one, and he'd always find them sinister. And in there in the dusty shadows, amid the boxes and a fur coat and a busted umbrella, stood or sat the great gray Hoover vacuum cleaner his mother had pushed and pulled all morning twice a week. It was the same one: there was the scar mended with thread where once the bag had caught on a protruding banister nail and torn. And close beside it, matrimonially close, his father's two leather sample cases, still shut up, buckled and strapped, just as they had been in the closet beneath the stair in his old home.

Prosper slid from his rolling chair to the floor and crept into the closet, just far enough so that he could snag one of the cases; he dragged it out, feeling as though it might have grabbed him instead and pulled him in. It was heavier than he would have thought, too heavy almost to carry, and his father had carried both, at least from cab to train station, station to hotel, up the stairs of businesses where he talked to prospects. Prosper knew about that. But somehow he had never known just what it was his father had sold. The story about selling, about carrying and talking and traveling, didn't include that; or if it had, it hadn't been anything he could speculate about, objects or matter only usable in the grown-up world, in business, none of his business though. He tugged at the straps, which had first to be pulled tighter in order to be released; when they were undone the catch on the top could be unsnapped, and then the case fell into two, all revealed. In the pockets and holders and clips were paints in lead tubes, and brushes in graduated sizes, beautiful pencils not yellow but emerald green, tucked into a looped belt like cartridges. In other compartments or layers, small pads and sheets of differing papers coarse to smooth. A case of pen nibs, all different, from hairstreak-fine to broad as chisels. Other pens whose use he couldn't grasp, elaborate heavy compasses, a dozen tools even more obscure. A thick catalog that showed all those things and also drafting tables, T squares, cyclostyle machines, airbrushes, gray pictures of gravely smiling men in bow ties using them.

Commercial Artist's Supplies was what he sold. The name of the company and his father's were on the cards tucked into a special holder at the case's top. Prosper could feel the raised lettering on the card under his finger, as though the words were made of black paint dribbled on with supernal precision. Cable COMARTSCO. The second case, when in a state of strange excitement he extracted and opened it too, contained more and different things, including three boxes of colored pencils of the kind Bea and May had given him, each full of pencils in more exquisitely graduated colors. For an instant he heard his father's voice.

He restored the contents as carefully as he could, shut them up, and pushed them back beneath the stair beside the Hoover. For a couple of days he said nothing, at once elated and oppressed by his discovery; but then, at dinner, he slyly turned the topic to his father and his work, those big cases he used to carry, what were those? And his aunts both jumped up at once, went to pull the cases out, glad for him, glad he had thought of them, glad he wanted to look into them, go ahead! Bea pulled out from one of the nested compartments a paper book called *Teach Yourself Commercial Art & Studio Skills,* and Prosper accepted it from her with a turn of his heart and a warmth in his throat he hadn't known before.

So the great cases went into his room. Bea and May said that the company'd asked for them back but Prosper's mother'd never got to it, and it seemed they'd sent an angry letter while she was in the hospital, and then they'd quietly gone out of business themselves. If Prosper wanted a T square and a board they'd have to find them elsewhere.

Meanwhile the women had to return to work, and it was just too hard to bear thinking of him all alone in the house, for he couldn't be a latchkey child, couldn't run to the park or hop on the streetcar to the natatorium (they were sure of that). So they asked around the neighborhood for someone who might be induced to come and visit him, play Parcheesi in the cool of the darkened house, draw and paint, sit on the porch and drink Coca-Cola; and because they were the persons they were they didn't think not to accept when a neighbor lady in pity assigned her daughter, a year and more older than Prosper, to do this service. And because Prosper was coming to be the person he was, he made no objection.

Her name was Elaine, dark and soft; strangely slow and languid she seemed to Prosper, her fingers moving more tentatively or cautiously to do any task than his would: he would watch fascinated as she opened a box of crackers or brought forward her skirt from behind her as she sat.

"What happened to you?" she asked when the grown-ups had all left them. He had got on his braces to meet her.

"I fell out of an airplane," Prosper said. He'd had no idea he would say that until he heard it. "I'll probably get better."

She seemed not to hear it anyway. She went on looking at the steel bars that came out from Prosper's pant legs and went underneath his shoes.

"Would you like a soda pop?" he asked. He couldn't perceive that she heard this either. Prosper, who was stared at a lot by different people in different ways, was learning methods of distracting their gaze, bringing it up to his face, even throwing it off him. Elaine's he seemed not to be able even to pull up. It wasn't one of the usual faces Prosper knew (but as yet had no name for, couldn't *say* he knew): it wasn't the cheerful I-see-nothing-out-of-the-way one, or the repelled-but-fascinated one, or the poor-animal-in-trouble one (head tilted, eyes big with pity). Elaine just looked, and went on looking. After a time she arose, in her unwilled way, and came to where he stood. He was unsure what she intended; should he step away? Was she headed for another room, the door out, did she mean to bean him? He'd never seen such an unknowable face. She stopped before him and squatted. He stood still. She lifted up the cuff of his trouser to see the shaft of the brace.

"How high up do they go?"

"Here." He touched his thigh. She looked up to where he touched, then at his face, and then, as though snapping out of something, she stood, turned, and walked away, and proposed a game, and said the African violets needed watering, and that she herself would be entering the eighth grade come September, and so went on talking for much of the day in a steady soft uncrossable stream.

The next day when she came he was sitting in his office chair. He hadn't been able to remember, when he woke, what she looked like, but now he could see that what made her face confusing was the way her eyebrows were made, lifting up from their outer edges toward the middle, as though she were perpetually asking a question.

"Why aren't you wearing those things?"

"The braces? They're hot. This is easier. Would you like a soda pop?"

She stood regarding him without responding, listening maybe to her own thoughts. Looking around in her slow absent-watchful way she saw his braces, propped against his bed in the parlor he occupied. She went in, and he followed on the chair. She squatted before the braces as she had before Prosper, and examined with her slow fingers the leather straps, the metal bars, the pad that covered his knee.

"Do they hurt?" she said.

"No. They make you sweat. You have to wear long socks. Stockinette."

"Stockinette," she said, as though she liked the word. "Are they hard to put on?"

"Not for me."

"Let me see."

"Okay," he said. Who would have thought someone would ask him that? But he didn't mind; it was about his only trick. He slid from the wheeled chair and to the floor. "I have to take my trousers off," he said.

Without getting up, Elaine turned herself around. Prosper worked off his pants where he sat, and took the long tubes of stockinette from the bed where he'd tossed them. Elaine, who had been peeking around to see, now turned, too fascinated not to. Prosper worked the long stockings up over his legs, then took one of the two frames, lifted his leg with his hands and fitted it inside. Then the other. He worked his feet into the Buster Browns that were attached at the bottoms. He wished it didn't take so long, he'd like to speed through it like characters in movie cartoons can do, a momentary blur of activity and it's done. He began the buckling, and Elaine came closer.

"Do they have to be tight?"

"Oh yes," he said. When his shoes were tied he said, "Now watch this." He reached out for a crutch, also propped there by the bed, rolled himself to his side, and with a hand on the floor pushed himself up, then pulled up farther on the crutch's crossbar till he was standing up. "See? Easy."

"You didn't put your pants on."

"Oh. I usually do." He laughed, but she didn't; once again she seemed to remember herself, rose and left the room, and when he had got the braces off and his pants on again he found her primly seated in the window seat with a magazine.

Since she evidently liked him better when his braces were on, he was careful to wear them for her visits, but it somehow didn't seem to win her, and he wanted to win her, trying various blandishments that she seemed to have little interest in, or scorned as childish. She was restless, bored, irritable, he knew it but couldn't fix it. On an afternoon hotter than any before, hottest in history but probably not as hot as tomorrow or the next day would be, she was staring at him in some dissatisfaction where he stood.

"Let's pretend," she said. "Let's pretend that it's me who needs them and you don't."

"What?"

"The braces. Let's pretend."

He didn't play let's-pretend any longer, and not only because he'd had no one to play with. Somehow that mode or way of being had been left behind, in the world before the hospital, where he was not now. "Why do you want to do that?"

"Let's just," she said.

Her unsad sadness. It was those strange eyebrows, maybe, surely.
"Okay," he said.

"Take them off."

"Okay."

Okay: so that's what they did, that day and each hot day after that:
she would sit on the floor of his room, take off her shoes and stockings,
push up her skirt, pull on the stockings he used, and buckle on his
braces. She was older than he but about the same height, and her legs
were not much longer than his. He buckled them for her at first but she
said he never did it tight enough. Then they sat together and played
Parcheesi or drew with the art supplies and ate crackers until she went
home. She never tried standing. He never learned what it was she
wanted from them, and she said nothing more, but when she wore
them she seemed at once content and turbulent, and within the circle of
her swarming feelings he felt that too. It all stopped one day when May
came home ill from work, and found Elaine with Prosper's braces on,
her skirt hiked up to her waist (she liked to look down at them often as
she read or played), and Prosper without his pants on (for he'd taken
them off to surrender the braces to her). May was generous about many
things, a taker of the Long View, but this fit nowhere in her picture of
life, and Elaine never came back again. Nothing was said to Prosper. A
week later, school started.

The bus that made its rounds through his part of town picking up the
students of the special health class arrived at the school building a little
after all the other students were beginning their classes—Prosper and
the others walking or rolling in could hear them reciting in unison
somewhere—and it returned for them just before three o'clock, was
awaiting them just beyond the ramp, engine running, when they were
dismissed: they'd begun climbing or being lifted aboard by the driver
and his husky helper even as the bell of the school exploded like a giant
alarm clock and the kids inside poured shrieking out. Some of those
aboard the bus looked out longingly at the games forming up on the
playground, one perhaps naming a child out there among the capture-
the-flag or pitch-penny gangs who had once said something pleasant to
him or to her; Prosper wouldn't do that. He was he, they were they.

Back home again he went to his room and took up his work where the day before he had left off.

He'd learned a lot from his book of Commercial Art and Studio Skills, and what of it he couldn't understand he made his own sense of. He used all the tools and the inks and the papers, the French Curve, the Mat Knife, but what he loved best were the Ruling Pens, which made the perfect even lines he saw in columns of type and bordering newspaper ads, squared at each end as though trimmed by scissors. He'd later learn that his method of using them was all his own—like a man who learns to play a guitar the wrong way around—but he got good at it. You turned a little dial atop the nib to narrow or broaden the stripe it scribed. He still never tried to make pictures, or copy nature, or draw faces. He created the letterheads of imaginary companies (ACME with beautiful winged A). But most of his time was spent producing, with great care and increasing realism, the documents—tax stamps, stock certificates, bank checks (he'd studied forms for these in sample books that May in puzzlement brought home for him)—of a nonexistent country. Once it had been a real place, he'd found its name in a ragged set of books on the shelf called the *People's Cyclopedia:* the Sabine Free State. At some past time it had been part of the territory of Louisiana. The Sabine Free State had been the home of the Redbone people, though no more, and no one knew where the Redbones who had once lived there had come from, or where they had gone. As he drew and lettered and crosshatched with precision he could see in his imagination the places and people of the Sabine Free State, the streets of the capital, the white-hatted men and white-dressed women like those in magazine pictures of hot places; the brown rivers and the cone of an extinct volcano, Bea's postcards of Mexico showed him those; the files of dark Redbone women bearing baskets of fruit on their heads. He saw all that, but what he drew were only the visas, permits, railroad shares, documents headed with the crest of the state: wings, and a badge, and a curling banner with the unintelligible motto that all such things seemed to have, *Ars Gratia Artis, E Pluribus Unum.* The motto of the Sabine Free State he took from what May and Bea had first spelled out on the Ouija board that guided their meditations: *Fenix Vigaron.*

Prosper went to the special class in the school for two years. Bea and
May gave him valuable advice on how to pay attention and please
those in authority without yielding up your Inner Self to them. He
was among the most able in that class, as he was among the least in
his old school, which somehow didn't seem to add up to an advantage, but it gave him a certain standing with the girls. In the boys'
toilet he learned what he would learn of the vocabulary employed in
what Bea called *the gutter*, trying to work out the meaning of each
new term without admitting he didn't have it down already, and falling for some common jokes (*'D you suck my dick if I washed it? No?
Dirty cocksucker!*). Then in the next year there was no city or state
money for it any longer, no money for anything, and certainly not for
a special health bus and a special class; tax revenues had evaporated
just as the welfare services were overwhelmed with desperate need,
more every day, husbands deserting families to go try to find work
somewhere and just disappearing, children living on coffee and crackers and pickles, pitiable older men in nice suits with upright bearing
and faces of suppressed dismay as though unable to believe they'd
come to ask the city for food and shelter. May saw her pay cut; there
was not a big call to furnish new offices. Bea's commission on per-
fumes and oils went down.

What would the two aunts do with him now? Miss Mack had
shaken her head wordlessly when Bea brought up the State School as a
possibility. But she did tell them (with some reluctance, it was easy to
see) about a Home in another part of town, and May one hot day,
without telling Bea, took a trolley out. Just to look at it. She'd never
been inside such a place, had only seen them in the movies or read
about them in novels, where orphans and crippled children were helped
by warmhearted baseball-playing priests, tough hurt boys who learned
and grew. The place itself when she reached it was smaller than she'd
expected, just a plain brick building amid old streets in a featureless
neighborhood. The first thing she noticed was that the windows were
barred: even the wide balconies that might have been nice places to sit
were fenced with wire barriers. Alarm made her tongue-tied, and she
asked the wrong questions of the torpid caretaker, and was refused a

look around, though she could hear a faint uproar. She'd have to make an application, she was told. Couldn't she just meet some of the children? Perhaps if she came on visiting day. Bea was feeling faint with sorrow, as though the walls were soaked with it. She seemed to smell cat piss, though there were no cats here.

She wandered, trying to peer down bleak corridors and into rooms. She got a glimpse of a line of girls being taken from a classroom, she thought, to somewhere else. The girls were dressed alike in gray jumpers washed a thousand times, their hair cut short, for lice maybe. Coldly strict as their teacher was she couldn't get them to march straight. So many different things were wrong with them May couldn't distinguish. One looked back at May, dull drawn face, wide-set eyes: a mongoloid, perhaps, but surely a soul, what would become of her.

May went home in the awful heat and never spoke of her trip. She convinced Bea it'd be all right, that Prosper was old enough to stay home alone; they'd get lessons from the school if they could, and do the best they could when they could.

By then Prosper was almost fourteen, and should have been going into high school, even if the actual grades he'd passed through didn't add up to that. The high school had never had provision for special cases like his; if he reached the eighth grade he was considered to have received as much benefit from education as he was ever likely to use—enough to get a job if he could hold one, and if he couldn't, more than he needed.

So he was on his own. With Bea and May he worked out a schedule, which May typed up at work—Prosper's name at the top of the sheet all in capitals, entrancing somehow. From eight to nine, he was to clean his room and as much of the rest of the house as he could manage; from nine to ten, physical exercise, as prescribed by the hospital, including stretching a big rubber band as far and in as many directions as he could. Ten till noon, reading and similar pursuits. Lunch, and so on. In the afternoon, practice his art skills; walk to the corner store if the weather was all right, carrying the string bag, and bring back necessities for dinner. May started instructing him in cooking, and within a few months he was regularly making dinner for them, macaroni, cutlets, potatoes with Lucky corned beef from a can, an apron around his middle and spoon in his hand. When they tired of his menus, May taught him something new out of the greasy and spine-broken cookbook.

Prosper thought getting on with his education would be a simple matter. The *People's Cyclopedia,* with many pearly illustrations that he liked to look at and even touch—the Holy Land, Thomas Edison in his laboratory, the Russian Fleet at Port Arthur, the *Three Graces* by Canova. He'd just start with volume I and read through to the end. The three naked Graces, holding one another in languid arms and touching as though comforting or merely enjoying one another, were in C, for *Canova,* the sculptor. Halfway through that first volume (*Bulbul, Bulgaria*) he gave up. There was a Bible on the same shelf, and since it at least was only one volume he decided to start on that instead. No one in his family had cared much about church, though Prosper'd been told to answer Protestant when asked what religion he was. There was supposed to be a minister among the ancestors on one side of the family, and at least one Jew on the other, and they seemed to cancel out, at once fulfilling the family's religious obligations and nullifying them. Prosper asked Bea, as he was beginning his new enterprise, if she believed in God.

"Of course I do," she said. She was cleaning the polish from her nails. "What do you take me for?"

"Jesus too?"

"Sure." She hadn't looked up from her nails. As an answer to his question this seemed definite but not definitive, and he couldn't think of another. He went on reading, turning the crinkly translucent pages, but grew increasingly mystified after the first familiar stories (familiar but not quite identical to the ones he knew or would have said he knew). He made his way through the rules of Deuteronomy, wondering if anyone had ever really followed them all and what kind of people those would be; and he came upon this:

When thou goest forth to war against thine enemies, and the LORD thy God hath delivered them into thine hands, and thou hast taken them captive, and seest among the captives a beautiful woman, and hast a desire unto her, that thou wouldest have her to thy wife; Then thou shalt bring her home to thine house, and she shall shave her head, and pare her nails; And she shall put the raiment of her captivity from off her, and shall remain in thine house, and bewail her father and her mother a full month: and after that thou shalt go in unto her, and be her husband, and she shall be thy wife. And it shall be, if thou have no delight in her, then thou shalt let her go whither she will; but thou shalt not sell her at all for money, thou shalt not make merchandise of her, because thou hast humbled her.

He was alone in the house, winter coming on and the lone lightbulb that May allowed to be lit dull and somehow melancholy in its inadequacy. Prosper thought: I wouldn't put her out. He'd explain the rule, that she had to shave her head and take off her clothes, but it wasn't *his* rule, just the rule. He supposed he couldn't tell her he was sorry about destroying her city and killing her people, since the LORD said to do it, and it had to be all right. But he wouldn't put her out, not if she was that beautiful to begin with. *I won't put you out,* he'd say to her. *You can stay as long as you want.* She'd have to and she'd want to, he was sure. She'd stay with him in his tent, naked inside with him, and she'd get over her grief.

He closed the perfumey-smelling Bible and went to get the first volume of the *Cyclopedia,* to look up C for *Canova.*

Meanwhile things just kept getting worse, although (as the President had said, standing in his top hat high up on the Capitol steps) the worst thing about it sometimes was just the fear, the fear that you'd lose your grip on the rung you'd got to and go down not only into poverty but also shame. The women worried for Prosper, how he'd ever make out, and they were right to worry, because the margin for him was thin, and in that time there were many whose thin margins, the thinnest of margins, just evaporated. It happened every day.

It might be that May and Bea conceived that Charlie Coutts would never want or need to use that telephone number that May'd given him, not that she was being insincere or hypocritical when she did so, it had just been one of those moments of sudden fellow-feeling that are forgotten about as soon as made. And she had forgotten it when the 'phone rang in the house and May tried to figure out who was on the line, which was hard because that person—it was Charlie's father—didn't have either of the women's names, which Charlie hadn't remembered, though he'd kept hold of the number.

When they'd straightened that out, Mr. Coutts said that Charlie
had been thinking of Prosper (he said "Proctor" at first) and had always
been grateful for how Prosper had befriended him in the hospital, and
wanted to ask if Prosper could come visit someday, at his convenience.
In a rush—maybe making up for her initial coldness to someone she'd
thought was a stranger or maybe a crank caller—May said sure, of
course, and even issued a counter-invitation, maybe Charlie could
come and visit at Prosper's house: an invitation Mr. Coutts quickly and
with what seemed profound gratitude accepted, somewhat surprising
May, who didn't try to take it back though. Charlie and his father lived
in a far part of town, and May—in for a penny, in for a pound—said
that Charlie was welcome to stay the night if that was more convenient; and she hung up in a state of apprehension and gratified benevolence.

Prosper felt a little the same. "Swell," he said when Bea told him.
"When's he coming?"

"Next Saturday," Bea said.

"Swell."

"Don't say *swell*, Prosper. It's so vulgar."

His father brought Charlie in an old heap of a car, which drove past
the house and then, as though becoming only slowly conscious of the
address it had passed, cycled back to park against the far curb. Charlie's father, in a windbreaker jacket and hat, cigarette between his lips,
got out and went around to the passenger side to get Charlie out. Bea,
May, and Prosper watched from the house. Prosper remembered the
hospital, more clearly than he had before, when Charlie's father lifted
him up with that careful love and both arms around him. He set him
down on the pavement. Then with a small grip in one hand and the
other on his son's shoulder to keep him steady, he aimed Charlie at the
house. The three inside watched him come toward them, Charlie
resembling a man walking under water, seeming to spoon the air with
lifted arms to help push his knees up against some invisible pressure,
uncertain feet falling where they had to. His father bent down and said
something to him around the cigarette, and Charlie hearing it laughed,
head wagging in glee.

They came out onto the porch to greet Charlie, his father guiding
though not aiding him up the stairs. Only when he'd seen the boy to

the top did he take off his hat and greet the ladies and Prosper. He was grateful for the invitation. Bea said that Charlie surely had grown, and certainly he looked to her both larger and more hazardous than she'd thought he'd be. May invited them both in, but Charlie's father with a quiet apology said he couldn't: he was starting a new job, Swing Shift at a plant, and didn't dare take a chance of being late. The women understood.

"Good-bye, son. Behave yourself."

"Byda."

"Don't do anything I wouldn't do."

Charlie liked that joke.

"Charlie!" Prosper said. "Come in and see my art supplies."

Charlie's father with a last touch on his son's shoulder turned to go, and May stepped down off the porch with him.

"Now, Mr. Coutts, is there anything at all we should know, I mean what is it we should, you know."

"Oh he's fine," said the man, discarding the remnant of his cigarette in the gutter. "He'll not give any trouble. You might tuck a big napkin in his shirt collar at dinner." He smiled at May. "I'll be back tomorrow morning."

Charlie'd gone into the house with a hand on Prosper's shoulder. Bea following after the two of them was made to think how large the world is, and how little of it we see most of the time. When Prosper'd got Charlie to his room and seated him on the bed, Bea put her head around the corner and with a motion drew Prosper out.

"Won't he need help?" she said. "You should offer him help."

"No, Aunt Bea. He doesn't need help. He can do everything fine. He just has to go slow."

"Well." Bea glanced back into the room where Charlie sat, rocking as though he heard a strange music, or as though now and then some small invisible being poked him. "If he needs any help you just call."

"All right."

"And you give him any help he needs."

"I will."

"Don't wait to be asked."

"I won't."

The women left the boys alone.

They looked over Prosper's art supplies, but Prosper, realizing they weren't much use to Charlie, shut them up again, and from the drawer where they were kept brought out games, cribbage, checkers, that he'd seen Charlie manage in the hospital. They talked about the hospital, and all that they had shared then, the bedpans, the crutch racing, Nurse Muscle Eenie—Charlie laughing as Prosper remembered him doing back then, laughter that seemed to run riot throughout him, tugging him this way and that so that Prosper watching him laughed harder too even as he tried to pull out of Charlie's orbit the game board or cup of coffee that Charlie's limbs threatened. Upstairs May and Bea listened to the hilarity and the banging of the braces and the furniture, taking turns rising up in alarm and starting off to go see, till pulled back by the other.

It actually fascinated Prosper how Charlie did things, as though he were badly adapted to do many common tasks but had figured out by long practice how to get them done. Once in the hospital a man had come to entertain the children, a small man in a dress suit with a little dog. The dog could do things you wouldn't think his paws and teeth could manage. While the man would pretend to be about to do a magic trick or juggle some balls, the little dog would run behind him and pull out the hidden scarves or cards from his pockets, nose open the secret drawers of trick boxes when the man wasn't looking, paw out the doves from the man's tall hat—he could do anything, so deft and alert to select the moment when the man's back was turned to spoil his tricks (though of course that *was* the trick), looking up with wide eyes as the man scolded him, then doing it again, so busy and satisfied and innocent. That's how it was watching Charlie sugar his coffee, or rub his chin questioningly, or mark his cribbage score with a pencil.

When long after dinner May called down the stairs to order them to turn off the radio and go to bed, Charlie went to the little grip his father had brought, worked open its catches, and pulled out a pair of gray cotton pajamas. He got into these, and Prosper into his, each using his own method and each making fun of the other for his contrivances. Prosper noted the knotted muscle in Charlie's rump and the big testicles too. In the bathroom they washed their faces and brushed their teeth, Prosper in his office chair and Charlie gripping the sink and wrestling with the brush as though it were a small animal that had got him. Laughing more, they climbed together into the bed, and Prosper pulled the string he had rigged up so he could shut off the light hanging from the ceiling.

"So good night," Prosper said.

"Ood nigh," said Charlie. "Own ledda bebbugs buy."

"Don't let the bedbugs bite. Okay, Charlie."

"Oh gay."

"Anything else you need?" May'd told him not to wait to be asked. "Anything else I can help you with?"

"Oh well," Charlie said, and began a series of twitches that might have been shy or apologetic, and his knees pushed the bedclothes sharply up. "I woont mine few could hep me yerp aw."

"What?"

Charlie was laughing, in embarrassment or maybe not—that's what this spiraling was. "I wool like you. To *hep* me. YERP AW."

Prosper thought a moment, and got it. "Charlie! What?"

"Cmaw," Charlie said sweetly. "Gme a *hand*."

Now they were both laughing, but Charlie didn't stop. It was apparent that he meant it, and asked it as a favor. He'd kicked away the coverlet, purposefully it now seemed. "Ow bowdid? Hey?"

"Well," Prosper said. "Well all right."

"Oh gay," said Charlie. He now became a mass of excited ungoverned activity from head to foot; Prosper had to help him get his bottoms down. Charlie's penis was already big, and bigger than Prosper had expected, bigger than his own, which had got up in sympathy, though Prosper kept his own pants on. It took a minute to figure how to grasp the thing from a point out in front rather than behind where he'd always been before, like trying to do something while looking only in a mirror, they struggled this way and that before they hit a rhythm, which Prosper now divined would be the hard part for Charlie when alone, especially as they got going and like a caught piglet Charlie's body underwent an alarming series of thrashes and wriggles at once urgent and random, Prosper pursuing him across the bed to keep at it. Charlie's noises were getting louder too, though it was clear he was trying to suppress them. His hand flew up, maybe trying to pitch in and help, and caught Prosper a smack in the ear so that Prosper too cried out. May from upstairs could be heard demanding quiet from the boys just as Prosper felt Charlie swell farther, and great lashings of stuff flew from him and across the bedsheets, Charlie nearly thrown off the bed onto the floor by his heavings.

"Okay?" Prosper whispered, after Charlie'd grown comparatively still.

"Oh gay," Charlie said. "Anks a bunch."

"You're welcome."

"Ooh nigh."

"Good night, Charlie."

Prosper telling the tale of those days to Vi in Henryville left out about Charlie Coutts. He didn't recount that early time with Elaine, either, for he didn't think these stories and what happened would count with her. He didn't really know why he was himself tempted to think that indeed they did count: couldn't have said what in them was part of that secret tissue that had no name, only instances. Can you say you've learned something if you don't know what it is you've learned?

Twice or three times more Charlie came to visit (*Prosper you can't let Charlie drink Coca-Cola in bed. He spills, and it leaves stains on the sheets. Brown stains. You hear?*) though somehow May and Bea hadn't the heart to organize a journey to Charlie's house, a failing they'd remember later with a little shame; and then once when Mr. Coutts came to pick up his son, a raw November day despite which the boys sat on the porch together (they were trying to memorize every make and model of car there was, outguessing each other and then arguing over which that one was, a Lincoln or a Packard), he announced that Charlie probably wouldn't be able to come back. Not anytime soon anyway.

May and Bea had come out to see him—they'd taken to the quiet man—and asked what had happened, they enjoyed Charlie's company, what was the matter? Well it was nothing about that; only Mr. Coutts had at length decided it was best if Charlie went to be taken care of in an institution, a school Mr. Coutts had learned about, in another city. A school or home for young people like himself. It was a charity, and there'd be no charge.

He sat down on the step beside his son.

"Plymouth Roadking," said Prosper.

"O," said Charlie. "Chrysle a-felow."

"No, nope son. Wasn't a Chrysler Airflow. It was the Plymouth."

Charlie roused, indignant, but said nothing more. No one said anything for a moment. Prosper knew about it already: Charlie'd told him. Far: that's all he knew. He'd get training there, but he didn't know what kind, or for what. Prosper tried to imagine him without his gentle father near him, and couldn't.

"Jobs the way they are, and his mother with other kids at home," Mr. Coutts said, and no more.

"Well we'll miss you, Charlie," said May. "We've got used to you."

Charlie smiled. "I'll sen you a poscar."

His father helped him stand, and they said good-byes all around. Prosper wanted to do something but couldn't think what it should be. He had given Charlie the only thing from his father's cases that Charlie could manage the use of: it was a thin paper book, *Drawing the Nude*. *I'll be pobular,* Charlie'd said, and tucked it in his shirt.

They got into the car and Mr. Coutts fixed Charlie's cap on his head. Charlie flung up a hand by way of a parting wave; to them on the porch it looked at once triumphant and desperate, but they knew it was just his muscles.

"He's just not made for this world," Bea said.

"Hmp," May said. "What's for sure is, this world's not made for him."

"Well, it's for the best, I'm sure," said Bea. "I'm sure it's the best thing."

"Oh hush, Bea," May said, and turned away, an awful catch in her throat that Prosper had never heard before. "For God's sake just hush."

6

Fenix Vigaron hadn't actually predicted it, but May later could look back over their conversations and see it figured there: just when things seemed like they were going to get a little better—and things had by then already got a lot better for some of us—May's office-supply business went quack. The owner, who'd kept it going through the worst years of the Depression by various impostures and financial shenanigans that caught up with him at last, shot himself in the private washroom behind his office. May was out of a job, with no prospect at her age of another. *Turn around, turn back,* said Fenix, and one hopeless night when Bea was washing May's hair, they both seemed to hit on the idea at the same moment.

What they always called the side room—maybe it had once been a sunporch or a summer kitchen but for as long as the two of them had owned the place it had gone unused except for boxes and things waiting to be fixed or thrown away—was about big enough and with work could be made into a cozy place. It had its own door to the alley, though nailed shut now. They'd have to invest most of their savings in plumbing and carpentry and supplies; they'd start with a single chair, or two. Bea already had a sort of following from the store, women who trusted her advice and might take a chance on her. May'd have a lot to learn, but she knew business and the keeping of books.

So the uncles were called again—May on the phone and Bea hovering nearby making urgent but ambiguous hand gestures that May waved off like pestering flies—and in turn Mert and Fred summoned from the dark pool of their connections a carpenter, a plumber, and a painter, each appearing without warning at dawn or dusk, needing instruction, slow mammals or needy and fearful, what debt were they working off? One a former chemist, another with a college degree, but it wasn't hard in those years to find such persons displaced from their rightful spots into whatever employment they could get. The women followed the for-sale ads in the paper and went to bankruptcy and going-out-of-business sales, conscious of the irony, and bought a big hair dryer and the sinks and mirrors and other things they needed, deciding after long thought not to acquire a used permanent-wave machine, a gorgon arrangement of electric rods and springs and wires such as you'd use to make the bride of Frankenstein, and anyway too prone to disastrous mishandling, as in a dozen comic movies. They'd offer waving and cutting, bleaching and dyeing, "consultations," and manicures, for the fashion now was for long long nails painted in the deepest reds, fire engine, blood, though toenails were still done in pale pinks or clear. Meanwhile May enrolled in a beauty school night class to get some basics, and in the rather squalid and hopeless studio, amid girls half her age she practiced pin waving and finger waving, the Straight Back (and variations), the Bias Wave, the Swirl, the Saucer Wave, the Sculpture Wave, the Windblown, and for the big night out, the Wet Mae Murray, a tricky finger wave that May mastered, making an effort out of fellow-feeling with poor Mae, the Hollywood castoff.

"You can teach this old dog new tricks," she said.

Prosper was a part of this plan, the other important part, it was the hope of solving two problems at once that had given Bea and May the energy to carry it out. He was eighteen; without any high school and his physical limitations, work at home was the best he could just now aim for ("just now" was Bea's addition to this judgment, the future ever unknowable but dimly bright to Bea). He'd been making something with his artwork, engrossing documents and signs that said CON-GRATULATIONS or WELCOME HOME or other things, lettering price cards for the butcher whose meat he bought; and of course he'd kept house for the absent women, a job that now didn't need doing.

So he'd go into business with them. He began by making the posters to be put up on the telephone poles around the neighborhood, and the little ad they placed after much thought in the evening paper—"Bring out your BEST and do it for LESS." He made their sign too—an old cupboard door lovingly enameled and varnished.

"May, look at this! This boy's a genius! So artistic!"

The Mayflower was the name they had chosen, arching over a somewhat emblematic flower and its visiting bee, a notion of Fenix Vigaron's. Beauty Salon with a dot between each letter and the next, elongating the phrase elegantly, and an arrow pointing down to the door in the alley, opened now and painted.

"Our shingle," May said and laughed. They hung it up on the house corner, and toasted it and themselves with a ruby glass of schnapps.

The shop began to do business, but only after a month or so of waiting, Bea and May dressed and ready every morning like hosts in that anxious hour when it seems no guests at all will show up. There were a couple of early mistakes, money refunded, free services offered in compensation and indignantly refused—Bea and May in the withering gaze of an enraged matron, Bea offering soothe and May ready to give the old bat an earful but smiling on. Bea's skills and generous approbation brought women back and back, and others were drawn in by May's hints of her connections beyond this plane of existence (she tried hard not to make too much of this, but the stories she heard as women soaked their nails in soapy water or sat beneath the penitential dryer were too intriguing not to report to her spirit guide; May delivered Fenix's gnomic responses to the women but refused to explicate them, which only made May seem the more privy to secret wisdom). Things got pretty busy.

"Prosper," Bea said to him as she cleaned the shop at day's end.

"Yes." He looked up from the old copy of *The Sunny Side* he was reading. *The Sunny Side* was the official publication of the American Optimists Association. Bea took the magazine, read it faithfully, and they piled old copies here for clients. Bea was an Optimist.

"We're thinking," Bea said, "that you can be more help in the shop."

"Sure," Prosper said. He closed the picture-less little magazine. The motto of the AOA, printed beneath the title, was *Every day, in every way, I'm getting better and better.* Émile Coué.

"There's things you can't do," Bea said, standing tiptoe to lower and lock the transom. "But also things you can."

"Sure," said Prosper. He straightened up, ready for his orders. What could he do? Well, he could answer the phone and keep the appointments book, he could greet the customers as they arrived, keep things orderly, just anything. Maybe—who knew—he could learn a bit of the business, washing hair or similar. Lots of men did such work, the best paid were men in fact, she could tell him.

"But now I have to tell you," Bea said, tidying and fussing with her back to him for so long that Prosper understood it was easier to say her piece without facing him. "You'll have to look nice. A nice clean shirt and a tie. You'll have to shave, you know, every day, and maybe a little talcum. Tooth powder. I know the bath's not easy for you, but." Now at last she did turn to him, beaming. "We'll be so proud to have you! Really!"

He could only beam back. He was possessed by the ticklish feeling of having been seen, of understanding that he could be seen by others, who passed certain judgments or came to certain opinions about him because they saw not the inside of himself that he saw but the outside, where the face he couldn't see and the smells of himself and the smuts and the wrinkles on him (that he inside could always account for or discount) came first, first and foremost. He remembered his father at the nightly labor of polishing his narrow shoes, instructing Prosper that one day he'd know how important it was, and why. Bring out your best.

"All right," he said.

From that day forward he did take an interest in himself, studying the image in the mirror, not only the plastered hair and knotted tie (the knot his own invention, as there was no one to instruct him in the four-in-hand) but also the odd attraction in his own green eyes, a question with no answer passing back and forth from him to it. *Every day, in every way, I'm getting better and better,* he'd say softly. Bea was astonished at the change, his going from indifference to punctilious attention, but it was only that he hadn't known, no one had explained to him you could take yourself in hand this way, as though you were a pot to be polished or a garden to be weeded.

He delighted in the shop, the women who came and went; he greeted each by name and made some remark pertinent to her, asked about her poodle or her daughter in business school or her ailing husband. They lost one or two customers repelled by Prosper's clattering around the shop still painfully bent, but he won the loyalty of others. His lacks and inabilities made them want to mother him, no surprise really, especially when they learned he had no real mother, was actually an Orphan: but the same lacks and inabilities somehow allowed them to be themselves in his presence, as they were in the shop with May and Bea but weren't with other men (he saw how they could change when, as now and then happened, a husband poked his head into the shop to pick one of them up—they'd switch in a moment to a guarded, practiced manner, even if it was a seemingly childish or dizzy one. And only he knew). He listened to their stories just as Bea and May did, and listened to the wisdom his aunts dispensed. He saw tears, more than once; overheard a shocking cynicism too. *He gets nothing from me in that bed but once a month. And he'd better make it worth my while, I'm telling you.*

He supplemented what he learned with his reading, after May began stocking old copies of *True Story* magazine she got from a younger cousin. When the shop was quiet and his tasks done, Prosper sat by the extension phone and read them. *I Married a Dictator. Aren't there limits to what a woman will stand, even for such a mad infatuation as hers?* The big pulp pages were a cyclopedia of female life, from which he learned of the whelming strength of women's fears and desires, the immensity of their sacrifices, the crimes they were capable of. They ran away from tyrannical preacher fathers, abased themselves in dime-a-dance halls and speakeasies, took awful vengeance on betraying lovers or pertinacious rivals, and always despite repression and abuse their honest need and goodness shone through. They went out on their own when Father died and the pension stopped, they worked hard amid dangers and pestering men, they fell for one night of passion with a man who seemed so clean and kind, only to find he's fronting for a sex exchange club! They escaped, they hid out, they made their own way, they met a man not like other men, they found love or at least wisdom. Sadder but wiser, or happy at last. He learned a lot from the ads too, about the clever counterfeits of underwear and makeup, and also the unnameable ills and pains that perhaps his mother had suffered, that any woman might and men never did. *For those special women's hygiene needs—be SURE with ZONITOR,* whatever that was, the woman's lined brow and worried eyes erased and smooth again.

The men in the stories were good but simple, or they were ignoble clods, or if they were smart they were only smart about cheating and lying; unlike the women they had desires and schemes and pride and even sturdy sense but no insides. No wonder the women lost them or lost faith in them or settled for them when they knew in their hearts it was wrong. *If she confided EVERYTHING in him, would he still love her? How could she be sure?* It seemed that the way to win the esteem of women was to become as like one as he could: as trusting, as unsoiled deep down, as wholehearted.

"Ha," Vi said to Prosper in Henryville. "I don't know how you could think that way about women. You were around them so much. Anybody who's around them that much'd have to find out pretty soon they're no better than men in most ways, and some ways worse."

"I don't know," Prosper said. "I just preferred them."

Vi shook her head over him. "It was those nice old Lizzies you lived with," she said. "You got the wrong idea."

"That's what my uncles thought," Prosper said.

"Prosper," said May to him one evening when the shop had closed, "it seems to me *your* hair's getting a little shaggy. Maybe it's time to give you a trim."

"Really?" said Prosper.

When he was a boy Bea and May had gone with him once to the barbershop down on the avenue, and at the door had sent him inside with two bits in his hand, but the vast glossy chairs and the row of white-coated unwelcoming men had defeated him—he'd have to ask for help to get into a chair, and then to get down again, and the barbers seemed unlikely to offer that help, though since he didn't dare to ask, he'd never know: anyway he turned around and came back out again, and went home with Bea and May, and they'd made do thereafter with scissors.

Now, though, they had a little more expertise.

"Maybe," Bea said, teasing, her hand pushing Prosper's hair this way and that, as though he were any client, "maybe you need a little something. You're a good-looking fellow, you know. You could look better."

Prosper laughed, embarrassed and alert, pleased too.

"Sure," May said. "Why not. Just a little soft wave. You know, like Rudy Vallee. Or who's that English fellow, Leslie Howard." With a motion of her hand she indicated that nice shy way his blond curls fell over his forehead, the way he pushed them back and they fell again. "Sure. Bea, fire up the dryer."

They wrapped a towel around him, laid his head back in the basin, and when the water was warm May washed his hair, delightful submission-inducing sensation of her strong fingers in his scalp. The two women argued over which of them would do the cut and wave, and finally took turns, each criticizing the other's work and laughing at Prosper's fatuous and ceaseless grin. They had him all pinned and ready to be put under the great bonnet of the dryer when there was a loud rap at the door, more like the cops than any belated client; they all started.

Parting the little curtain that hung over the window of the door, May murmured "Oh my stars," and opened the door. Mert came in, more as though exiting a familiar house and stepping into a cold and dangerous street than the reverse. "Hi, May, hi, I," he said, and stopped, catching sight of Prosper. Fred, coming in behind him, looked in over his shoulder.

"Hi, Uncle Mert," Prosper said.

"Jeez, May, what the hell," Mert said.

"Now, Mert," Bea said.

"What are you doing to this boy?"

"We're making him look nice. Anybody can look nice."

"Almost anybody," May said coldly, narrowing her eyes at Mert.

"Man oh man," said grinning Fred. "Will you get a load of this."

"Shut up," Mert said without ceasing to study Prosper. "This is just what I was afraid of. You two trying to raise a man."

"You button your lip," May said. She crossed her arms before her. "As if you could have done it."

"Well just look at him," Mert said. "Jeez." He came closer to where Prosper sat unmoving, still grinning like Joe E. Brown but now from a different impulse. "Just because he's a cripple he don't have to be a sissy."

"And where've you been the last seven years?" May said. Her foot was tapping the floor, her arms still crossed.

"Well starting now," Mert said. "He just needs a chance."

"Well then," Bea said gently, "you might start by saying hello." And Prosper saw his uncle's face suffused with a dramatic blush that rose from thick neck to forehead, the first adult he'd ever seen so taken, which was a thing of great interest; and then he put a big hand out to Prosper, who had to fumble his own right hand from under the towel to take it.

"Anyway we ought to finish up," Bea said. "Before those pins come loose."

The icehouse, where the disreputables that Bea and May had refused to describe to Prosper gathered, was over on the West Side, past the railroad tracks and in fact in another township, which made an important legal difference, even though no one much remembered the fact or even the name of that vanished village. It was close enough to what had once upon a time been a lake in the woods that ice could be cut and sledded there easily. Now the ice was made on the spot in a long shed where the big Westinghouse electric engines ran the belts of an ammonia condenser, but it was stored, covered in straw, down in the same old brick underground, breathing cold breath like a cave's mouth out to the office and the street. Since the way down into it had been built when oxen were used to slide the ice in and out in great blocks, it went sloping at a shallow angle: Prosper loved to walk down that way into the cool silence.

The front offices where Mert and Fred ran the ice business, and sold coal and fuel oil as well when and if they could spare the time from other enterprises, were a rich habitation—tin ceilings darkened with cigar smoke, girlie calendars, spiked orders growing yellow with age, freshly cracked decks of cards, ringing phones Mert talked into two at a time even while calling for Fred to deal with this or that matter. Whatever matter it was that Mert and Fred had come to talk to May and Bea about had gone no further that night; the men went away with a mission, to take (as Mert said) the boy in hand, and teach him a few things; and Prosper's world widened. Later on he'd think that May and

Bea must have felt abandoned by him, and must have resented if not hated it that he'd taken up with the icehouse gang, and he'd feel shame, but not then: too much that was new and gratifying came his way, and more lay just beyond envisioning. He started smoking, not Mert's Dutch Masters or Muniemakers but the more fastidious cigarette, though he found it hard to smoke and walk at the same time, and eventually mostly gave it up; he grew a mustache, a thin dark line above his lip like Ronald Colman's. The uncles gave him instruction in the arts of shaking hands and looking a man in the eye, what honor required you to do and what (they thought) it didn't, what was owed to friends and how to look out for Number One at the same time. They made over his clothes: dressed him not as they themselves dressed, though they got a tailor to make him a good suit, but as the young blades nowadays dressed: sport coats of houndstooth or herringbone collared like shirts rather than lapelled, pastel shirts worn with hand-painted silk foulards or without a tie, long collar points laid over the jacket. Trousers richly pleated and draped—Prosper's braces disappeared beneath them rather than poking everywhere through the fabric like a bony beast's joints. He studied himself in the mirror, considering how his new pale wide fedora should lie, back like Bing's or Hoagy's, or forward and nearly hiding an eye, mystery man or secret agent, pinch the front indents to lift it to a lady. Not much could be done with his shoes, to which the braces were bolted across the instep, but no reason he couldn't wear silk socks in argyle patterns or clocked with roses; Prosper, lifting the knees of his cheviot bags to sit, could glimpse them, pretty secrets revealed.

They kidded him too about what else they might do for him, take him out to the suburbs to a certain place, or downtown to one, get his cherry picked or his ashes hauled, saying it maybe only to laugh at the face he made—wide-eyed, that grin he was given to that they couldn't wipe. That was just joking, but Fred, late one night with half a bottle gone between them, gave Prosper a lot of corrective information he'd maybe soon need to know—Fred had ascertained, interested in the topic, that Prosper's weakness only reached a ways above his knees, so though it was maybe unlikely for someone like him, the Scout's motto was Be Prepared. But how, Prosper asked—hilariously muzzy-mouthed, and not sure what had brought this forth—how, when his own part rose at that specific angle so purposefully, was he supposed to get it into a girl, whose slot or cleft (he was thinking of Canova, of Mary Wilma) ran, well, sort of the other way or seemed to, crosswise, opening inward and running through toward the back? Didn't it? So how was he supposed to, was he supposed to bend, or? No no no, Fred said, you got it wrong, the thing you *see* when you look at her, the slot or slit there, that ain't the thing at all, no kid, that's just what shows. The thing you need's down underneath, see—and here Fred lifted his own big knees and thighs to his chest to illustrate, poking at a spot amid the creases of his trousers. There, just ahead of the other hole, and it runs up up up, just right, trust Mother Nature, she ain't going to make it hard to get into. You got that? You need another drink?

He learned just as much, or at least heard as much and remembered it, listening to his uncles talk during the day at business as he sat at a desk they'd rigged for him and did work they thought up for him.

"You speak to that woman on Wentworth?" Mert said. "The new tenant, the bakery?"

"Funny story," Fred said grinning. "Yeah, I talked to her. Single woman. She was real jittery about the health department inspector coming. I says, It's nothing. You wait for him to make his inspection, be nice, keep a ten in your hand. He might find a couple things, so you say—I told her—you say Well all that's going to be hard to fix, isn't there some other way we can handle this? And he might say no, or he might say Well, maybe, and you say Oh swell, and you shake hands, and the ten passes. Okay?"

Mert pushed back in his swivel chair, listening, already grinning as though he expected what would come next.

"So she had the inspection, and I asked her how did it go, and she says not so good. I ask her, did she do what I said? What did she tell him? And turns out what she said was, Well this is going to be expensive, *isn't there something I can do for you?* Jesus, she says it took her a half hour to get rid of the guy after that, and he was so pissed off he wouldn't take her ten."

"Send her over to Bill and Eddy," Mert said. "They'll fix it for her." Bill and Eddy, attorneys-at-law, did a certain amount of work for the icehouse gang; Mert often got his own stories from meetings with the two.

"Attorney Bill," he told them with mock gravity, "defending a man charged with verbally molesting a woman. So Bill's known this fellow a while, he's not surprised. Tells me how he'll be in a tavern at the bar with him, they see a nice skirt go by outside; this fellow pops out, has a few words with the woman, she turns away, he comes back in. Did he know her? Nah—just liked her looks. So what did he say to her? He asked her if she'd like to have a lay with him. She said no. Bill tells me he does that a lot. Always nice and polite, and a tip of the hat for a No. I said no wonder he's got in trouble—he must get his face slapped a lot at least. Oh, Bill says, he does—and he gets laid a lot too."

"So this time he asked the wrong dame," said Fred. He put his hand by his mouth: "Call for Bill and Eddy."

"Turns out there was a beat cop twirling his nightstick just about within earshot. Never mind. They'll get him out of it. Told me the lady's already looking sorry she brought the charges. Who knows, maybe this guy'll get her in the end."

The firm of Bill and Eddy (it was George Bill and Eustace Eddy, Prosper would learn in time) set up the papers that created and dissolved a number of enterprises operated out of the icehouse—Prosper's first job there was making up stationery for a warehousing and fulfilment business they'd begun. The uncles had also got into the vending machine business, which besides a string of Vendorlators dispensing candy and smokes and Pepsi-Cola around the West Side included a few semilegal "payout" pinball machines as well. Prosper was sent out on the truck that filled and serviced the machines. Mostly it was his job to sit in the big doorless truck and see that nobody stole the cartons of cigarettes and boxes of Collie bars and Zagnuts. Now and then he was allowed out to have a coffee in a diner while Roy the serviceman broke open the big machines to show their complex insides, the valves and springs and levers, to oil them and refill the long slots.

At Honey and Joe's Diner the cigarette machine was on the fritz, and Roy settled in to work. Prosper stood at the counter (easier than seating himself on the roll-around stools) and asked the redheaded woman for a coffee. It was midafternoon, the place was empty. He'd watched her watching him as he came in, how he took his stand, reached for a dime for the mug of pale liquid. She waved away his money.

"Mind if I smoke?" he asked.

She came to push a glass ashtray to where he sat.

"Where's Joe?" Prosper asked, and she leaned in confidentially to him.

"There's no Joe," she said. "There was, but no more."

"Just Honey," he said. An odd silence fell that he was conscious of having caused. He drew out a smoke and a match, which he lit with a snap of his thumbnail. She smiled and moved away.

"All done here," Roy said and clapped shut the steel machine.

"Red hair," Fred said to Prosper, back at the icehouse. "That your type? Hot tempered, they say."

"Fighters," Mert said. "She and Joe used to go at it hammer and tongs."

"Not Prosper," Fred said. "He's a lover not a fighter. She's out of your league, my boy."

Fred thought that any single man constituted as Prosper was needed two things: he needed a *line* he could use to break the ice and then go on with, and he needed a *type* that he was interested in so he could simplify the chase. Fred's own type depended on blond curls, chubby cheeks, and a *poitrine* approaching Mae West's; his line started off with *Scuse me, but do you happen to have a cousin named Carruthers? No? Gosh my mistake. So anyways tell me* . . . Prosper though could not tell if he had a type, and Fred's attempts to delimit the field weren't convincing to him. As for a line, he hardly needed an icebreaker—he found himself looked at plenty and had only to say hello, and then keep the starer from rushing off embarrassed. Beyond that he thought he now knew what to do, though not yet when to do it.

That cigarette machine at Honey and Joe's seemed to malfunction with surprising regularity, a lemon maybe, though when Fred said they ought to pull it and get it replaced, Roy said oh he'd get it going. Roy's difficulties weren't with machines but numbers, he hadn't a head for them, and if Prosper was willing to tot up his figures and fill in his book, Roy was happy to return him to the little diner now and then, and go read the paper in the truck.

"So does that hurt much?" Honey asked Prosper gently. It was May, and the air was full of the tiny blown green buds of some opening tree, even the floor of Honey and Joe's was littered with them. She picked one from Prosper's shoulder.

"Doesn't hurt a bit," Prosper said. "The other way around. I can't feel much."

"Oh."

"I mean from the knees down."

"Oh."

He cleaned up the last of the plate of goulash she'd put in front of him. She had a way of looking at him that reminded him of the way the women looked at themselves in the Mayflower's mirrors: a kind of dreamy questioning. He didn't yet know how to interpret it, but he was coming to notice it. Somehow a look to the outside and the inside at once. No man ever had it, not that he'd seen.

"So you get around good," she said, as though weighing his case.

"Oh sure."

She considered him or herself some more. Her hair was not only deep red, a color for an animal's fur more than a woman's hair, it was thick, tense, it strove to burst from her hairnet: it was as though he could feel it. She bent and pulled from under the counter a bottle of whiskey, put down a glass before him with a bang, and poured a shot for him. He took a taste, then a swallow.

"So, Honey," he said then. "Can I ask you a question?"

Honey lived behind the diner, through a door in the back. She sent Prosper to turn over the sign in the door that told people the diner was OPEN or CLOSED. It was now CLOSED. He clicked the switch that turned off the neon sign above the door (DINER), and its red glow faded. He opened the door and waved to Roy, go on, good-bye, see you later; Roy didn't ask him how he'd get back to the icehouse or downtown, just shrugged and rolled the toothpick he was never without from one side of his grin to the other and started the truck.

"Now we're getting someplace," Vi Harbison said to Prosper in Henryville. "This is good."

"Okay," Prosper said.

"So was she a natural redhead?"

"What?"

"You know. You found out, I'm guessing."

"Oh," Prosper said.

What Honey'd learned about Prosper was that he lived with two old never-married aunts, had never gone to high school or taken a girl out on a date or been to a dance. That interested her. Not that she hadn't known some wallflowers and some deadwood, oh she had, but Prosper wasn't that. He'd grown to be good-looking—calm light wide-spaced eyes; teeth white and even, never a toothache; fine hands like a glove model's. Visible beneath the silk shirt he wore were the broad shoulders and back he'd built by using them to walk. All that contrasting so strangely with the sway back and the legs that had not grown as the rest of him had. It didn't assort: man and boy, weak and strong. Honey liked it: it was the taste of tart and sweet together, the sensation of hot and cold, it made you think. She mightn't have liked it though if he hadn't been so open and ardent and willing—ignorant as a puppy, but his grip strong and oddly sure. After they'd gone through the rubbers Joe'd left behind he still wouldn't quit, not until late in the night when she pushed him away laughing, leave me alone, I have to start the range in about four hours, who taught you that anyway?

But nobody had. He didn't tell her she was the first woman he'd been with, but he didn't need to.

"Mind if I stay till later? I'm afraid I can't get home from here. Not in the middle of the night."

"Hell yes I mind. Think I want you stumbling out of here into my breakfast crowd? How'd that look?"

"Well."

She touched him gently, not quite sorry for him. "You got a dollar? Go into the front and use the phone. Call a cab. The number's right there."

She rolled away and pretended to sleep, thinking he wouldn't want her to watch him put on his equipment; he did it sitting on the floor (she could hear it) and then apparently hoisted himself upright on his crutches. Then she was sorry she hadn't watched, just to see. Then she slept, suddenly and profoundly.

Aglow, as though he could find his way in the dark by his own light, Prosper went out of the little rooms where she lived, wanting to touch everything he saw or sensed there, the harsh fabric of the armchair, the cold of the mirror, ashy weightless lace of the curtains through which the streetlight shone. Careful of the rag rug at the doorway. His arms were trembly from his exertions, who knew they'd have so much work to do, he laughed aloud as though joy bubbled up beneath his heart and out his throat. Long afterward in another city he'd share a reefer with a woman and only then feel again this wondrous hilarity. He did it, he'd done it, he was made now of a different and better stuff and ever after would be, he hadn't known that would be so and now he did. Ever after.

In the altogether transformed night, its odors sweet in the liquid air, silence of the city, he leaned against the lamppost to wait. He said to himself *I will always remember this night and this moment,* and he would, though not always with the rich First Communion solemnity he felt then, felt until the laughter rose again.

The cab was tiger yellow in the dawn, the rear door wide and the backseat generous, excellent. The scraggy elder driving it asked Where to, and Prosper caught him grinning in the rearview. Grinning at him.

"Takin' French lessons, huh, kid?"

"What?" Prosper at first thought the driver had mistaken him maybe for someone he knew. French lessons?

"I said *taking French lessons?*" the old fellow said more distinctly.

"I don't know what you mean," Prosper said, leaning forward.

"I mean, you been eatin' pussy?" the driver practically shouted. "Be surprised if you hadn't! Ha! Whew! Better wash up before you get home to Mom! My advice!"

Prosper got it then, and almost lifted his hands to his face to smell the smell still on them and on his face and mustache, but didn't, retired to the back of the seat in silence as the driver laughed.

French lessons. Because why, something about the French? He'd heard it called French kissing, that kiss with tongues entwined, imagine what his mother with her fear of germs would have thought of that.

How had he even thought of doing it, eating or virtually eating it, where had he got the idea, apparently not his alone anyway, so usual that even this guy could know it and joke about it. Did it just happen to everyone, he guessed it must, that you discovered that certain body parts you'd known and used in one way had a set of other functions and uses you hadn't been told about, unexpected but just as important and constant—mouths and tongues for more than tasting and eating, hands for using and manipulating, the hidden excreting parts able and even *meant* to go together with the other workaday parts, you might not think so but it turned out to be so and you somehow knew to use them so even if you hadn't thought of it before—couldn't have thought of it, it was so unlikely. Like those paperback novels where you read one story going one way and then turn the book over and upside down to read another going the other way: as you read you might finger open the pages that you'd discover later and see them upside down and backward but they wouldn't be when you went to read them. You'd just dive in. And he had, and she had known why he would want to and why she would want him to, even if at first she refused him.

And the sounds they'd made too, that *she*'d made, sounds borrowed from the other side, where they meant a different thing—Bea's coos as she handled a length of silk velvet, May's high whimper at the sight of a dead cat in the street, Mert's grunts of satisfaction at stool, or Fred's as he lifted a full shot of rye to his mouth, the same.

So he knew, and he would go on knowing that this was possible, knowing also that everybody else or almost everybody else (Bea and May, surely not, but how could you be sure?) knew it for a thing to do, a thing that could be done and was done. A thing you could practice even, as the grunting discus flinger or fungo slugger practices, driven to enact it over and over. As he would seek to do thereafter whenever and wherever he was welcome. He'd follow that Little Man in his boat up dark rivers into the interior, that limbless eyeless ongoing Little Man, parting the dense vegetation and hearing cries as of great birds, nearly forgetting over time how weird a thing it was, really.

Don't stop they'd say, an urgent whisper, or a cold command; a warning or plea, bashful or imperious.

Don't stop Vi said to him in Henryville, and amid her yearning thrashing struggle toward what she wanted to reach. Prosper had to work not to be thrown off and uncoupled, like a caboose at the end of a train making too much steam on a twisty roadbed, whipsnaked and banging the track. All that kept him connected and at work was her hands in his hair and his on her flexing haunches. Until up ahead some kind of derailment began, unstoppable: first the crying plunging engine escaped, gone wild and askew, and then one by one the cars, piling happily into one another, then all into stillness, silence, seethe.

Oh they said after a time softly, *oh:* and *Um* and *Haw. Ho*, he said, *huho*.

7

War and the sex urge go together," Pancho Notzing said.
"Is that so," Prosper inquired.

He and Pancho and Vi, with Sal Mass on Al's lap in the back, had taken the car down to the Wentz Pool on the west side of town, a famous amenity built by another of Ponca City's brief flaring of oil millionaires. It had just opened for the season. Pancho took a stately dip in an ancient bathing costume that drew almost as much attention as Al and Sal in theirs. Now Prosper watched Vi Harbison stretch out on a chaise, face up into the sun.

"It is certainly so," Pancho said. He had draped a towel around his throat and was performing a series of physical-culture exercises that didn't seem to inhibit his speaking one bit. "I know it from the last war. The Girl Problem."

"Soldiers and girls." Prosper knew that Pancho had three nieces, a great trial to him, restless and wild, entranced with men in uniform, *khaki-wacky* as the term was. At least they'd not be rounded up and treated as criminals and sinners like the poor girls of the last war, for which Pancho was grateful. Still he worried.

"It's the men themselves who are the problem," he said. "If there is a problem."

"Well sure," Prosper said. "If you think maybe you won't be alive next month or next spring. Sure."

"Not only that, not only that," Pancho said. He ceased his Macfadden program. "A lot of the women in the plant, in that town, they've nothing to fear—they aren't facing death on the battlefield. But I guarantee there's no end of intrigue going on there. Married or not."

"You think so?"

"I'm sure so."

Prosper didn't tell him that this week Anna Bandanna was issuing a subtle warning about VD—"Keep clean for that man who's far away." Not that he thought Pancho was being censorious. Intrigue, by which he meant something like hanky-panky, was a Passion that needed to be met, like any other. In the Harmonious City there would be young women in every job, doing every task their passional nature suited them to. Old and young, working alongside men, many different men in the course of a day. Intrigue. Women who were Butterflies, in Pancho's terminology, and never settled on a partner; others with more than one man for whom they cared deeply; others with but one lover for life. Pancho thought a woman who could and would bring happiness to dozens or hundreds of men did a wrong to herself as well as to those dozens if she kept herself for only one.

"I'd agree," said Prosper. "I believe I would."

"Not necessarily in the present instance, though?" Pancho lifted his chin in the direction of Vi, who just then rolled onto her stomach. Vi was an *object lesson* of the general principle that Pancho'd stated, in answer to a question of Prosper's about Vi, a question actually not meant to be answered (*Isn't she something?*). Vi's own bathing suit was the modern kind, made of a fabric Pancho could name, whose price he knew: a fabric that clung and stretched remarkably.

"Well. I don't have a jealous nature, Pancho. It's a thing I've learned about myself."

"And when did you learn this? It's an important insight."

Prosper was still in shirt and pants. He couldn't swim, and since he couldn't, he chose not to disrobe, though Vi'd urged him try it out, take a paddle, she'd help. "It wouldn't do me a lot of good," he said. "Making claims on someone."

"Ah." Pancho sat, regarded the hot blue sky. The uproar of children and youngsters stirring the pool like a seething pot was pleasant. "I think I see what you mean. In a sense you don't have the standing."

Prosper thought about that, wondering if it was what he'd meant. Not have the *standing*. Did Pancho mean that he couldn't be expected to fight, so his claim could be ignored? Say if he went up against a fellow like Larry the shop steward, though he couldn't imagine himself and Larry at odds over a woman. Well maybe in such a circumstance he *wouldn't* fight and maybe for the reasons Pancho'd think, and maybe not. He lit a cigarette, the match's flame too pale to see. At the pool's edge, Sal and Al were doing a shuffle-off-to-Buffalo from their old act as the crowd cheered.

"I'm a lover not a fighter," Prosper said.

When the draft began in 1940 Prosper was twenty-one; though his uncles (and his aunts too) said there was no call for it, Prosper went downtown to present himself to the Selective Service board to be registered with all the other men aged twenty-one to thirty-five, a huge mob of them as it happened, milling around the doors of city hall, laughing or patient or annoyed at the imposition. More than one looked Prosper over in some amalgam of expression that combined contempt and amusement and maybe even envy (he'd safely sit out any war), though Prosper looked away from such faces before he could really decide what attitude they put forth. A couple of young men, definitely amused, gave him a lift up the stairs, each holding an elbow, and set him down within, and when it was his turn at the long table where harried men filled out forms, those two and others waited to see what disposition would be made of him.

"Polio?" the man he had come up before asked.

"No," said Prosper. "Something different."

"Tabes dorsalis?"

"Um," said Prosper. "I can't tell you in a word."

"Permanent condition?"

"Seems so."

The man had no business asking these questions anyway, he was just curious, registering for the draft wasn't determinative of your status—the men had to explain that over and over, your draft status would only be determined when you were called for a physical. Prosper took his registration card (not the sort of document he'd made for the Sabine Free State, too crude and inelegant) and went away hearing laughter, not necessarily unkind, the same laughter that we laughed after the secretary of war picked the first draft numbers out of a huge glass bowl and the President read them out on the radio, and it was learned that the second number he read belonged to "a one-armed Negro banjo-picker," a sure IV-F man like Prosper.

Through that year and the next Prosper worked for the uncles and for Bea and May, and went to the tavern and the pictures and the ball game when he could, and polished his commercial art and studio skills; and now and then, rarely but not never, in circumstances that always seemed new and not like any of the others before, he'd get a Yes to his question. He came to think that George Bill's client hadn't actually just walked up to any pretty woman he saw and lifted his hat: he must have had some sort of Sixth Sense (Bea's name for how we perceive what we should be unable to perceive) as to how his proposal might be taken. Prosper kept working on his own Sixth Sense, with instructions taken out of *The Sunny Side* for *envisioning a desired state of affairs* and *believing in your deep perceptions,* and also with information he drew out of *True Story.* He made some atrocious mistakes, painful for him and her—horror and affront suffusing her face as he tried to retreat in confusion—but no one actually smacked him; maybe his crutches acted as eyeglasses did or were supposed to do, and kept at least the honorable ones from lashing out. He was a *masher,* one girl cried at him: *And you think anybody'd look twice at YOU?* He had refutations for both these charges but he didn't make them, because his rule was never to pursue or pester anyone who turned him down, which is what a masher did.

Anyway he mostly didn't approach women in the street, partly because he wasn't in the street himself that much, partly because he'd have had a hard time catching up with them: a woman in the street with a cripple in pursuit might have all kinds of thoughts but they weren't likely to be favorable. Those women who responded favorably, or at least smiled indulgently, he'd usually known for a time before putting his question; and it was likely (this never rose by itself into his consciousness, but he would see it was likely when at length Pancho and then Vi pointed it out to him) that the women who said Yes had already decided on Yes well before there was anything to say Yes to: maybe even before Prosper decided to ask.

"It's the one thing women can't do," Vi explained to him by the now-empty pool, its water soft and still as evening came. "They can answer, but they can't ask." She'd donned dark glasses; he thought she looked like a star.

"But you asked," he said.

"Shut up," said Vi.

The danger he'd seen—the danger he felt himself always in those days to be in—wasn't that he'd get turned down; it was that he might see something in one, suddenly, in a moment, something small and seemingly inconsequential—nothing more than the moist glitter in an eye corner, a momentary look of wild uncertainty, the tender hollow of a neck—that would cause him to commit entirely to one pursuit, never look back. He thought it could; he felt the tug once a week, once a day in some weeks, but (it was like robbery, and yet like relief too) those women didn't remain as he first perceived them: they shifted into something or someone else as quickly as they had taken hold of him, or they didn't stand still for the hook to set, they moved on and away, and (he supposed) maybe always would, his life flitting away with them around that corner, up in that elevator, into that shop. What he expected in fear (he thought of it as fear) didn't actually happen until he met Elaine again, after the war started.

We wouldn't always remember, later on, how many of us didn't expect a big war, how little we wanted one, how we felt we owed nobody anything on that score. President Roosevelt wanted to get us into it, we thought, but he wanted us to do a lot of things: he sometimes seemed like a wonderful fighting dad we wanted to please but didn't always want to mind. He wanted us to care about the displaced persons in foreign lands. He wanted us to give our dimes to charity to help him stop infantile paralysis too, and we did if we could, poor man.

"It is glorious to have one's birthday associated with a work like this," he told us over the radio in that big warm voice. "One touch of nature makes the whole world kin."

"What's that mean?" Fred asked. He and Prosper stood at the bar, looking upward at the big varnished box—Prosper wondered why

FOUR FREEDOMS / 181

people do that, stare at a radio from which somebody's speaking. It was the night of the President's Birthday Ball, 1941, and a lot of dance bands were playing for a lot of city big shots and socialites who'd given money for infantile paralysis. There were balls all around the country, the excited announcer said, and the President was speaking to all of them over a special national hookup.

"In sending a dime," the President said, "and in dancing that others may walk, we the people are striking a powerful blow in defense of American freedom and human decency."

In those days you let talk like that go by without thinking very much about it, everything was a blow for freedom, but Prosper said, "Hear that? You gotta dance, so I can walk."

"Sure," Mert said. "Rex here'll dance. Come on, Rex."

Mert had adopted a little dog, one of the eager lean big-eyed kind with clicking toenails at the end of his breakable-looking legs (that's how Prosper felt about him). Mert was teaching him tricks. He lifted Rex up by his front paws and they danced to "I'm in the Mood for Love" like a hippo with a weasel.

"Keep it up," Fred called out. "No effect so far."

"We," said the President. "We believe in and insist on the right of the helpless, the right of the weak, and the right of the crippled every-where to play their part in life—and survive."

Prosper (who'd not get a cent from those dimes, they were for the polios alone, though his uncles believed he could probably pass for one at need) stood propped at the bar, listening some to the President, laughing some at Rex, mostly considering his drink and waiting, for nothing and everything, and feeling in danger of getting the blues. The next time he heard the President speak he was telling us that the Japa-nese Empire had attacked Hawaii, so like it or not, whether we were for it or not, we were at war. That's what Prosper, without knowing it, had been awaiting, everything and nothing: and yet for him, for a long while, just as many things remained the same as changed.

"So take a look at this," Mert said. From within his jacket he extracted a folded paper wallet, its cover decorated with a rampant eagle astride a stars-and-stripes shield or badge. The badge shape was one Prosper loved to look at and create. GAS RATION BOOK it said, and on the other side (the *recto* Prosper knew to call it) it said DRIVE UNDER 35! and COMPLIMENTS OF YOUR LOCAL TEXACO SERVICE STATION. From within this folder, Mert drew out a little pamphlet printed in red. Another badge shape urged the bearer to BUY WAR BONDS. It was his gasoline ration stamp book, an A, the lowest rating—four gallons a week now, probably not even that much in the months and years to come.

"Okay," Prosper said.

"Here's the question," Mert said. "With the stuff around here—the stuff we got for you, your own stuff, the stuff, the Ditto machine there, the inks—would it be possible—theoretically—to make one of these?"

"Make the B or the C," Fred put in. "Twice the gas."

Prosper eyed the thing, felt the paper, studied the letters and type. He knew the rule, that you couldn't use the stamps without the book— stamps torn from the book were invalid. You'd have to make the whole book.

"Don't worry about that," Mert said. "We can make just the stamps, sell them to the gas stations. The gas stations sell them to the customers, then take 'em right back and give 'em the gas, and turn in the stamps to the government."

"Easy as pie," said Fred.

"The book's a different matter," Mert said. "If we can make the whole book we can sell it and clean up. Cut out the middle man."

Prosper was still holding the book. PUNISHMENTS AS HIGH AS TEN YEARS' IMPRISONMENT OR $10,000 FINE OR BOTH MAY BE IMPOSED BY UNITED STATES STATUTES FOR THE VIOLATION THEREOF.

"I can get twenty bucks a book," Mert said.

"But you shouldn't," Prosper said, not knowing he would till he did.

"It won't be many," Mert said. "A few."

"There's a war on," Prosper said. "It's not right."

"Listen," Mert said. He took hold of Prosper's shoulders. "Here's the real skinny, all right? There's plenty of gas in Texas. We ain't going to run out. You know why they ration it? So people don't use their tires. It's the rubber they don't have. The Japs got all the rubber now. See? Don't give people gas, they can't use their tires, they don't waste rubber. See?"

"It's a good idea," Fred said. "The stamps. The books too. It'll work."

"You think I'm not behind the war effort?" Mert asked Prosper. "Is that it? You know I fought for this country? Same as your dad. I can show you my medals. Good Conduct."

"Ha ha," said Fred.

"It's not that," Prosper said.

"You don't think you can do it? That's what I need to know."

"I don't know. Maybe. But I don't want to."

Mert turned away to gaze out the somewhat clouded window of the office (he liked it clouded) and put his fists on his hips. "Hell of a note," he said, sounding wounded. "Well. Hell with it. Let's knock off for the day."

More or less in silence, they closed the office: called out good nights and instructions to the night people, rang up the ice shed on the house telephone (Mert cranking the magneto with what seemed fury to Prosper) and told them the office was locking up, finally turning the sign in the glass of the door from OPEN to CLOSED.

Not much was said during the ride back to downtown. Finally Mert threw his arm over the seat and looked back at Prosper. "You can have it your way, son," he said. "But I'll just tell you something. There might not be any other work for you around the place. If you can't do this."

Stony-faced. Prosper tried to cast his own face in stone.

"Just think about it," Fred said into the rearview mirror.

"He's thought about it," Mert said, still regarding Prosper. "So where can we drop you?"

"Um." He didn't want to go back to the Mayflower Beauty Salon, but he didn't want to be too far from home either. "Drop me at the Paramount," he said.

"Going to the movies?" Mert said. "Man of leisure?"

That required a dignified silence.

"What's playing?" Fred asked.

"Dunno."

They turned on Main. The theater was a ways from Bea and May's, but Prosper'd done it before. Late on a winter afternoon and no one much going in. Fred let the car idle there—no one would be doing much of that from then on. The marquee advertised *No Room at the Inn* along with *The Invisible Agent*, newsreels and Selected Short Subjects.

"You're a good kid, Prosper," Mert said. He pulled out a money clip and plucked a couple of bills from it, then one more. "You do what you think you got to."

Prosper shook Mert's hand, then reached over and shook Fred's. He got out of the car with the usual clatter of braces and crutches. Hadn't they themselves, his uncles, taught him what Honor required? Wasn't it this? And what the heck was he going to do now to make money?

The second feature was just beginning when he entered into that soothing darkness, violet hued, lit by the shifting scenes bright and dim. He paused at the top of the long flight of broad steps—easy enough to manage but not if you couldn't see them; the usher, silhouetted against the huge heads on the screen, was showing someone to a seat, momentary ghost of a flashlight pointed discreetly downward. Prosper waited for him to come back up and light his way.

But it wasn't a him—it was an *usherette*, as they were called, women and girls taking the jobs of drafted boys, solemn in her big dark uniform. Tumble of black curls beneath her cap. She turned on the dim flashlight and was about to walk him down when he stepped forward, Swing Gait, and she halted: then, surely a breach of the usher's code, she lifted the light right up to his face.

"Prosper?" she whispered.

Blinded, he still knew whose voice he'd heard. The soft dry burr of it. She lowered the lamp, but he stood dazzled. She touched his arm and turned him away from the screen and back out toward the foyer.

"Prosper," she said again when they were in the light.

"Hi, Elaine."

"Are you okay?"

"I'm fine."

She gazed upon him. "I haven't seen you."

"I'm around. The same place."

"I moved out," she said. "Things happened. I have a room."

"Okay."

"Who did that to your hair?"

"What? Oh."

That face, the eyebrows lifting in a worried query that she seemed already to know the sad answer to—Is it mortal? Will we never return? Is all lost?—when she wasn't actually asking anything and

FOUR FREEDOMS / 185

wasn't sad. "Listen," she said. "I get off in an hour. Sit in the back. I'll see you then."

As though they'd agreed to this a long time ago. That was the sign, he was as yet unused to noticing it but he was learning: that sensation that the future has already happened and is only bringing itself about in staging these present moments.

He went back in and sat down. He lit a cigarette, after determining that a little ashtray was attached to the seat in front of him: one thing hard for him was stamping out a burning end from a seated position. The picture was well under way now. The grandson of the original Invisible Man had inherited his grandfather's secret formula, and the Nazis and the Japs were teamed up to steal it. The Invisible Agent pesters and pulls funny tricks on the bad guys; the audience watched in silence. It occurred to Prosper that the Agent must be damn cold—only without his clothes was he altogether invisible.

Elaine went past the row where he sat, a woman and a man in tow.

An invisible woman, that would be an idea for a picture. Naked, and you'd know it, but you'd see nothing.

He thought of Elaine, in his braces, on the floor of his aunts' house. Exchange of selves, his for hers, why would she have wanted that? And why his? However many eyes there were on him every day as he did this or that, walked a block, took a stool in a diner, went through a door, he often felt himself to be invisible. Like the Invisible Agent: people could see the suit and hat and gloves, and nothing of what was inside them. No matter that they stared.

He felt her slide into the seat behind him. "I'm off," she whispered, leaning over. "Come with me. I have to change."

Making as little noise as he could, he stood and left the row to follow her; the few in adjoining rows glancing up with interest, maybe one or two thinking he was being expelled, no cripples allowed. He went after her into the foyer and around to the far side and through a door that seemed to be just part of the wall. It opened to a hot shabby corridor lit by bare bulbs. Dim hollow voices of the picture could be heard. *I pity the Devil when you Nazis start arriving in bunches!*

"Here," she said.

It was a dressing room, a couple of blank lockers, a sink, a clothes rack of pipe where uniforms hung. Steam hissed from the radiator. She turned her back to him to take out the stud from her collar, then pulled the whole celluloid shirtfront with collar and tie attached out from her uniform jacket and tossed it down on a bench.

"Elaine," he said, and she turned to him; he could see that she'd worn nothing beneath the dickie, too hot maybe. As though he'd said much more than her name she came to him, and he knew it was time to put his arms around her, but that was hard; propping himself with one crutch he wrapped her in the other arm, still holding its crutch. She somehow melted into him anyway, partly supporting him, breasts soft against him. Then she seemed not to know what came next, forgetting or unable to predict, and she drew away, undoing the frogs of her uniform coat.

"Turn around," she said, and he did; when after a time he turned back he found she had put on a shirtwaist dress, was barelegged in white anklets, and he felt a piercing loss. She put on a dark thick coat and a shapeless hat. "We'll go out the back."

She took him out around the back of the stage, and for a moment Prosper could see that the great screen was actually translucent, and the picture of two lovers projected on the front shone through to be seen, reversed, by no one.

They came out into the alley, scaring a lean cat from a garbage pail. She lived many blocks away, in the opposite direction from Bea and May's. They didn't speak much as they walked, just enough so as not to appear strange to each other marching in urgent silence toward whatever it was, but what little from their shared past they might have spoken about ought not to be said now: that was obvious to both of them.

"So what happens to the Jap? In that picture."

"He commits Harry Carey."

"Oh."

Though the cold air burned his throat, he was wet with sweat beneath his coat by the time she said "Here." The place was heartsinkingly tall, a long pile of stairs with steeper than normal risers that climbed as though up a castle wall to a front door high above. He despaired. But Elaine then took him through a side gate (BEWARE OF THE DOG) and around to the back, a short winter-dry yard where an umbrella clothesline leaned like a blasted tree, and into a door. "Up," she said softly. "Don't be loud."

It was only a half-flight, though the banister was flimsy and the steps mismatched. How her room was fitted onto or into the house in front never came clear to him, though he tried later to draw a plan. The door at the top of the stairs led into a minute kitchen no bigger than a closet, and that to a bedroom. Elaine pulled a chain that lit a green-shaded lamp above the dark bed.

She turned to him then. He was breathing hard from exertion, and she seemed to be also, her mouth a little open and her face lifted to his. Her eyes huge and certain. He would come to learn—he was learning already—that these moments, different as each one was from all the others, were all more like one another than they were like any in the rest of his life: they were like the moment in some movies when a scene changes in an instant from black and white into color, and everything is the same but now this picture has become one of those rare ones that are colored, it joins that richer life, and for a time you live in it, until the gray real world comes back again.

Night. Negotiating in the dark the way out of her room and down the half flight of treacherous stairs holding the splintery banister, knowing there were things—tools, trash, boxes, a cat—he couldn't see. He bumped at length into the door outward, and pushed it open (beware of that dog) and made it out to the street. He saw at the block's end the cigar store right where he remembered it being, where there would be a telephone. Mert's bills in his pocket, enough for a while, but not for taxis every day. He felt a sudden anguish, he wanted to turn back now and climb those stairs again, there was something left undone there or not completed, it twisted within him painfully in the direction of her room even as he pushed himself down the block: something he'd never felt before, and seeming to be installed deeply now.

Why was she the way she was? Women with their clothes on could be utterly unlike themselves when they were without them, even those who were unwilling to take all or even most of them off, who made him paw through the folds of fabric like an actor fumbling through a stage curtain to come out and say something important. But none so far had been as different as Elaine. She'd lain still as he unbuttoned her buttons and his, mewing a little softly, a mewing that grew stronger when he'd got her last garments off, hard to do with no help at all. She lay still and naked then making that sound, as though something dreadful were about to happen to her that she was powerless to resist; she closed her eyes while he unbuckled his braces, she covered her eyes even for a moment with her hands, and then remained still, tense as a strung wire, while he attended to her. He tried to speak, tell her they had to be you know careful, but she wouldn't listen, drew him over atop her, parting her legs and pressing him down. But once he had gone in—swallowed up almost by the enveloping hot wetness—she held him still so he wouldn't move, made sounds of protest if he tried, almost as though he hurt her, and herself lay unmoving too except for small tremors that racked her, seemingly unwanted. He almost whispered *Hey what the heck Elaine* to make her behave in some more familiar way but actually could say nothing, and after what seemed a very long time she lifted her legs and circled him tightly; she murmured something as though to herself, a word or two, and he felt a sudden sensation of being grabbed or enveloped from within as by a hand. It was so startling and unlikely that he nearly withdrew, and did cry out, and so did she, even as he was held and ejaculating. And at that she began pushing him out and away, gently and then more forcefully; when he was separated she rolled over so that she faced away from him, and pulled the coverlet over herself.

Elaine? he'd said.

All right, she'd said, not turning back. Go away now, she'd said. I'll see you maybe at the theater tomorrow.

So.

He guessed that if she'd got herself knocked up today he'd have to marry her. The cab he called rolled up to the door of the cigar store where he stood next to a dour wooden Indian, and Prosper checked to see if it was driven by that same old fool who'd once mocked him, but of course it wasn't. He'd marry her and somehow they'd live, maybe in that tiny room. For an instant he knew it would be so and that he wanted nothing more, and how could that be? How could it?

8

Without his uncles' wages and the odd bill they'd slip him for this or that service, Prosper was back in the Mayflower, but May and Bea couldn't give him the money he needed if he was going to be seeing Elaine: though she seemed to want nothing from him, that only made him think she really did. So he went to work for The Light in the Woods. They needed people. He didn't have much of a choice. At least it appeared he wouldn't have to support a wife and child: after an uneasy week (he was uneasy, she seemed somehow bleakly indifferent) he knew that.

The Light in the Woods (Prosper'd first heard about it from Mary Mack, and then from the teacher of his special class at school) had for years been giving work to people with impairments who couldn't compete for jobs with other workers. They were blind or almost blind, they were deaf or crippled or untrainable, they were spastics or aged alkies with tremors. They were put to work making simple things like coco matting or brushes, or they picked up and refurbished discarded clothing or toys or furniture for resale, packed boxes or did contract labor assembling things for local factories—anything that almost anybody could do but nobody could make a living doing. For years The Light in the Woods had been losing work: in the Depression, standards had changed about what jobs an able-bodied person would willingly do.

Supported by charitable giving, they'd kept their workers on through those years, guaranteeing them their fifty cents a day even when there wasn't much to do. Now business was booming again: there were suddenly lots of jobs that nobody would do who could do anything else. A new age of junk had dawned; shortages of materials for war industries meant we were constantly urged to save them, bring them to collection centers for reuse and reclamation—rubber and scrap metal and fats and tin cans (wash off the labels, cut off both ends and smash them flat). Old silk stockings could be made into parachutes; new ones soon became unavailable. Use it up, wear it out, make it do, do without. In Prosper's city the collection and sorting of discards and donated matter was contracted out to The Light in the Woods, and the outfit opened a larger warehouse in the industrial district to handle it all. When Prosper made the trip downtown to the War Mobilization Employment Office, that's where he was sent. All he had to do was sign up for the special bus service that The Light in the Woods had arranged to circle the city and bring in their people who couldn't get there on their own.

A special bus. A special card allowing him to ride it. A right to survive.

Prosper put down Elaine's address as the one he'd need to be picked up at. That seemed like killing a couple of birds with one stone, though when he told her, her face didn't seem to agree that it was birds he'd killed.

"I can get them to come to my house instead," he said.

"No it's fine."

"I mean if you."

"It's fine."

"I'll be gone early. The bus'll stop at the corner. It'll still be dark. No one'll notice."

"All right."

Was she displeased? He thought he knew by now something of what women wanted or needed, what pleased them or most of them, but somehow with her he could never tell, and suspected he hadn't done enough, or done the right thing; it irritated him inside in a way he'd never known before. He knew women often liked to tell their stories, their True Stories, and he'd have liked to hear her story, why she was here in this place, what had become of her in the time since they'd sat together on the floor of his room. But no. When he asked about her life her wary gaze began to move away, as though bad things drew close around her at the question, and might come closer if she answered. What's it matter, she'd say. What's it to you. The worst was how it made him work all the harder to ease that dissatisfaction, to draw down her questioning black brows, to still the turmoil that he sensed in her being—that he even touched, he thought, when he was within her: when she lay without moving, always, never letting him move either, clutching at his arms to keep him still. Until her brief spasm came or didn't. Then she was done. Nor would she permit anything French, not lessons or anything else. Don't, she'd say, we shouldn't, that's only for married people. Sometimes afterward she was calm for a time and they'd lie beneath the blankets and swap silly jokes, or she'd rise and in her ratty plaid robe she'd cook them an egg or boil coffee and they'd sit at the table together in companionable silence.

He could only visit her after night had fallen (he never saw the people in the house to which her rooms were attached, almost didn't believe there were any there, never more than one window dimly alight when he came up the street). He'd awaken before dawn—for some reason The Light in the Woods started work at an early hour, maybe only to make their difference from a real business obvious—and put his braces on and dress, wanting to creep back into the bed beside the unmoving dark lump of her; drink a cup of cold coffee from the night before, take the lunch he'd made, and go out into the winter darkness and to the corner to await the bus. Then stand for a few hours at the clothes tables in the eternal odor of mothballs and moldered wool and sort the useless from the reclaimable, noting the missing buttons, the stain (blood?), the decayed lining or detached sleeve, thinking of the lives of these men and women and children, Fauntleroy suits of possibly dead boys, wedding dresses of disappointed brides, chalk-striped suits of bank tellers now in prison. *The More You Sort the More You Earn.*

Salvageable things went on the cart to Repairs. Silks were reserved for government reclaiming, whether women's negligees or men's fine monogrammed shirts. Foundation garments contained rubber, wave them aloft for laughs. Furs, no matter how moth-eaten, were set aside, for they would be cut up to line the vests of merchant marine sailors;

Prosper caught in them the faint remains of perfume from their long-ago wearers, strangely persistent, and thought of men standing watch on night ships smelling it too, shamingly intimate and evocative.

In addition to all the stuff coming in on the trucks to be sorted and fixed, The Light in the Woods had contracted with local war industries to do jobs that could be done off-site. The airplane factory sent them barrels of floor sweepings, from which dropped bolts and rivets could be extracted and returned to the works; a number of blind people sat along one table onto which the contents of these barrels were emptied, feeling through the sweepings and finding the rivets; after a short time they were able to distinguish each of the several sizes of rivets in the mix and distribute them to separate containers. One was a young woman whose blind eyes were pale and a little crossed, who smiled slightly and continuously at nothing, her head lifted—why should she look down? But it made her appear strangely joyful or alight, and Prosper watched her when he could, guiltily enjoying the fact that she couldn't tell he looked.

In the late winter afternoon the bus went back, circling the poorer parts of town, stopping to let off one after another, the driver getting out to set a wooden step before the door when needed, careful now, take your time. The Sad Sacks, Prosper called them to Elaine, not to seem one of them himself. She made him confess what The Light in the Woods was paying him, though he tried to put her off. She made no reply when he told her.

Neither Bea nor May would ask him where he spent his nights now—at least no more than to ascertain he was all right and needed nothing they had between them to give; he was a grown man now, and doing the things they imagined grown men did, though when either of them began a sentence of speculation about just what that might be, the other cut her off, not wanting to think about it. He seemed not to be at Mert's beck and call anyway, and that was a good sign. Bea had volunteered to be a local War Council block leader, wearing a cute cap with a Civilian Defense badge on it and going around her block, handing out pamphlets about reclaiming tin and rubber or growing a Victory Garden and preserving more food. Bea could talk to anybody.

May missed Prosper's company more. To her great sadness Fenix Vigaron had gone away. She'd informed May that the sudden vast increase in souls coming across to her side was upsetting the economy of heaven as nothing had before or since. So many people all over the world dying such terrible deaths all at once, arriving so sore and shaken and unprepared, strained the resources of solace and succor that even infinite Love could provide. Fenix's work was with them now: she blessed May and wished her well (the child had become, even as many living persons seemed to become, strangely nicer and warmer in the emergency) and promised that someday when the docks weren't so crowded with the lost and vastated she'd return to May's board and her glass and candle; she expected, though, that it would get worse before it got better.

So it was change in all they saw and did, for them as for everyone: but still the two women were shocked when Prosper told them he was leaving town to find a job that paid something and, also, to do his part: he thought there was a part he could do, and he was going to do it. Out west anybody sitting on a park bench would be approached within an hour by three people with offers of work. Bea and May could hardly answer: couldn't say no, of course, but like any parents who've raised a crippled child, it was going to be hard for them, war or no war, to see their boy go off: as hard and fearsome (though they'd never say it) as for any mother seeing off her soldier boy.

He'd quit at The Light in the Woods a week before. Ever since he began working there he'd been growing angrier, not a feeling he'd felt very often, somehow new to him, as new as what Elaine made him feel, and actually not different. Then on a Monday morning not long after the Sad Sacks had begun their work he'd flung aside the chesterfield overcoat with mangy collar he'd been assessing, and (hardly knowing he was about to) he turned himself toward the desk where the area supervisor, Mr. Fenniman, oversaw them all with his one good eye and did his paperwork. Like Oliver Twist in the picture with his milk bowl, he walked up past the eyes of the silent workers to the front table. The boss took no notice of his standing there.

"Mr. Fenniman," Prosper said. "There's a matter I'd like to discuss with you."

"You may discuss anything you like with me, Prosper." He continued to sort his papers, invoices and orders it appeared, but glanced up to hand Prosper a brief encouraging smile.

"It's about the, well the compensation provided here at the Light, as over against the money that's coming in." Mr. Fenniman put down the papers now, looked up, no smile. "Mr. Fenniman, I just don't think I'm getting my share of the gravy."

Mr. Fenniman considered him. "Well now, Prosper, I believe you're making good money since the work here expanded."

"Not compared to what the factories are paying."

"You're not at a factory, Prosper, are you?"

"I could be."

Mr. Fenniman's smile returned, but chilly. "I think you are making an all right wage as a proportion of any able worker's. All things considered."

Now everyone was listening, at least everyone who could hear, though many went on sorting rivets or tossing clothes as busily as ever.

"I'm thinking I'll go up and get myself one of those jobs," Prosper said. "Who's to say I can't."

"I'm to say. You don't even know what you're talking about. The war industries of this city have contracted with The Light in the Woods to do work for them. We are grateful for the opportunity to do our part." His good eye traveled over the benches, and some—not all—looked back down at their work.

"Well tell me this, then, Mr. Fenniman," Prosper said, shifting his stance, hard job standing tall after a time. "Just how much are you taking out of what those companies are paying for our work?"

"You are an ungrateful wretch."

"Just a question. For instance I know that the airplane company down there is paying fifty-sixty cents an hour. An *hour.*"

A motion passed over the people working within earshot, a wave of awe or restiveness. Some of them knew this fact very well, some were just learning it.

"To able-bodied workers," Mr. Fenniman said. "Not to the likes of you." He stared around himself a little wildly, as though he wished he could take that back, at the same time daring those who now looked frankly at him to take offense.

"Well we'll see," Prosper said. "For I am giving my notice."

Mr. Fenniman's shoulders sagged. "Now, son, don't be foolish. Go take your place and"—he lifted a weary hand—"the more you sort the more you earn."

"I'm *quitting*." He spoke gently now, as though he'd made the point a thousand times and was prepared to make it a thousand more.

"Son. The bus won't even be here till five. You can't quit. You can't get home."

Now even Prosper could feel the eyes and ears of the Sad Sacks on him. "I believe I can," he said. "I believe I can." He turned himself around.

"You go out that door, Prosper, don't you *dare* try to come back through. Ever."

Prosper, aflame within, wanted something more to say, some final, utter thing, like in the movies. He thought of turning to the others and saying "Anybody else had enough?" And if it were a movie, first one and then another and more and more would rise up, the fearful transformed, the oldsters with jaws set, the young alive at last. But what if no one did? And if they did get up and follow him, a mass of them, crippled and sightless and feeble, what would he do with them? He said nothing, went without hurry to the coatrack; he lifted his woolen scarf (taken from the tables) and laid it around his neck, and then his wonderful houndstooth jacket. He clipped it with his hand to the crosspiece of his crutch, not wanting to try struggling into it with everyone looking on. He pushed out the doors of The Light in the Woods and, holding the banister, he let himself down, hop, then hop, till he came to the street. His heart was still hot. He supposed they might be watching through the big windows, and he thought he might toss them a finger, but with the crutches and holding the jacket it was inconvenient, and actually he felt no ill will toward them, not even toward Mr. Fenniman, who wasn't the big boss and had formerly been kind to him.

The bus stop, as it happened, was right in front of The Light in the Woods, but Prosper couldn't feature standing there for however long, peering down the street to see if the thing was coming, then negotiating the steps up to get into it in view of the Sad Sacks and maybe failing. Or refused service—it'd been made clear to him on other occasions that was the driver's right. So he set off down to wherever the next stop was, not clear what the bus's route was or how close it would get him toward home. At least he had a dime in his pocket. As he went the workers heading for the airplane plant were beginning to throng the street, lunch boxes in hand and badges on their coats, he recognized them. He thought maybe he would just go and see if the plant would take him after all; but when the crowded bus lurched to a stop where he stood with the others, and he struggled to get aboard, holding everyone up and feeling for the first time profoundly embarrassed by his damn legs and back, he knew he wouldn't; and he knew what he'd do instead.

Go ahead and look, he thought, himself looking at no one there. Go ahead, go make your money, go fight your war. If I have to look out for Number One, I'll look out for Number One. You don't need me, I don't need you. A blond woman going out the back door glanced at him with something that looked like pity or reproach, and a furious shame possessed him.

"You go down Main?" he called to the driver. The bus was nearly empty now, with the industrial area behind.

"What?"

"I said. Do you. Go down. Main."

"I cross Main."

"Can I get out there?"

"It's not a stop."

"Can you just stop there? For a minute."

No answer, dumb lump. When they reached Main he stopped and opened the doors and gazed, indifferent, out his window as Prosper made it out, his feet landing on the pavement with a thump he felt up into his buttocks. It was a few long blocks down to the house where Elaine lived. He needed to tell her, needed to recount to her what he'd done and what he'd said, the reasons he'd been in the right, yet afraid she'd reject his words and his action, why was it always so with her, that he could be both sure he was right and afraid?

"Well that's it," Elaine said. He'd wakened her, she had the night shift tonight. She took his side even before he finished telling her, was instantly madder than he was. "Those, those. That's enough. We don't have to, we don't have to stand for that." She roamed her tiny space like a tiger, looking at nothing there, wrapped in her plaid robe, her feet bare. "We'll get out of here. We'll go out west. That's where the jobs are, everybody says, sixty cents an hour, closed shops, they can't push you around."

"I'll get money," Prosper said. "I know I can."

"You get money," she said, coming to look furiously into his face.

"I've got a little. I'm sick of that theater. I'm sick of this town. We'll go together."

All decided, no questions, whatever stood in the way of it of no account, not her family or his, not his handicap, not distance or fear or difficulty. Her rageful resolve had caught fire from his like a hot candlewick catching fire from a lit candle brought close. She wrapped his scarf around his throat as though arming him.

"Tell me you love me," she said, hands pulling tight the scarf. The last thing necessary.

"I love you, Elaine."

She said nothing in return.

From the cigar store Prosper called the icehouse. A new voice answered, female, blond (how could he tell?). When Mert came to the phone Prosper said he'd been thinking and that if they still needed that job done they'd talked about, he would probably be able to do it. If the money was good.

"The money's good," Mert said.

"So when, where will I."

"Where are you now?"

Prosper named the streets.

"Wait there," Mert said. "Fred'll pick you up."

It wasn't hard to do. The coupons themselves were crude things. The Ditto machine in the icehouse office could be adapted to print in red instead of its usual purple. Prosper went with Fred to a warehouse in the city filled with paper, paper in high stacks, newsprint in rolls, discount paper in fallen slides like avalanches. Fred distracted the salesman while Prosper took a sheet of stamps from his pocket and sought for a paper like it. The big investment was in spirit masters for the machine; Prosper spoiled several before he perfected a way to make a sheetful of stamps rather than a single one. As he drew he had to press hard enough to transfer the colored wax on the bottom sheet of the two-ply master to the back of the sheet he was drawing on, like the wrong-way writing that a piece of carbon paper puts on your typed sheet if you insert the carbon backward. Then he separated the two sheets of the master and fastened the top sheet to the drum of the Ditto.

As he turned the handle of the drum, a solvent with the intoxicating smell of some sublime liquor was washed over the sheets of paper drawn in to be printed; the solvent would dissolve just enough of the colored wax on the master to transfer the backward image right-way-around to the paper. It worked. Mert said it wouldn't fool everybody for long but it'd fool anybody long enough.

How to perforate the printed sheets was a different problem, not put to Prosper; Mert knew a guy. Prosper's problem was that the original could only print fifty copies or so before it grew dim, and he'd have to start a new master.

The C book cover was easier; it was just like making documents for the Sabine Free State. He drew down the lamp over his desk at May and Bea's and worked with a magnifying glass, reproducing by hand every letter and line of type with his pens and India ink, the red bits in red. Eagle, badge, warning of jail time. He could do two a day, and got three dollars apiece; the money piled up. He had finished his first one of the day, stapled it to the coupons, all ready but the signature, when the doorbell rang.

It was Elaine.

"Here," she said. She handed him a shapeless lump of brown canvas. "Let's go."

It was her idea: he'd said he had no way to carry a suitcase and walk at the same time, and after she'd thought about this for a day she'd said that he could carry a knapsack on his back, like hikers and soldiers, she'd just seen one in a movie and then realized she knew where to get one, the Army and Navy Store just then replete with stuff from previous war eras as useless now as flintlocks and sabers. She'd bring him one. Here it was. It was time.

Last thing, just before he slung the lumpy kit bag over his shoulders, filled with his clothes and belongings gathered somewhat at random, he picked up the fresh C ration book and put it into an inside pocket of his jacket. And Elaine fixed his hat on his head. The El stop was twenty blocks away.

"So she left you standing there?" Vi Harbison asked Prosper in Henryville.
They were upright now and dressed, Vi ready for the Swing Shift, she

was doing double. Pancho Notzing in the parlor listening to the radio in a straightback chair as though in church. He knew this part of Prosper's story.

"We got there and I couldn't get up the stairs," Prosper said. "I guess we hadn't thought of that. I mean I think *I'd* thought of it, but."

"What did she say? 'So long, sucker'?"

"She didn't say anything. I said I'd go around and look to see if there was another way up. I don't know what I was thinking." He could remember her face when he'd said this to her, as though now everything that her face had always seemed to express and yet maybe didn't—the questions with bad answers, the dissatisfaction—it did express now for real. "When I came back to tell her, she was gone."

"She took that train."

Prosper said nothing.

"So that didn't change your mind about women?"

"How do you mean?"

"I mean liking them better. Thinking they're better. After she did that to you, leaving you flat. Did it?"

"Well I guess not," he said, actually never having wondered this before, or considered that it should have changed his mind; maybe it should have. "I guess she had her reasons. I mean it wasn't going to be easy."

Vi regarded him in what seemed to Prosper a kind of tender disgust, the look you might give a bad puppy.

"I thought," he said, "that she'd given up on me, but that if I could go out there and find her I could show her she didn't need to. That she shouldn't have."

"But you came here instead."

"Well, yes, in the end."

"You know what I think?" Vi said. "I think your heart got broken. Right then on that day."

"Really?"

"Yes. And you know, when your heart gets broken it can't feel the same way afterward."

"Oh?"

She put her elbows on the oilcloth to look into Prosper's eyes. Outside the window, troops of people were passing, headed for work, marching together, some yellow bicycles moving faster than the crowd. "I think that after your heart is broken you maybe still want to have love affairs. Still want to make love, still want to marry even. But people don't stir your heart the same."

"Oh."

"Your heart," she said, touching her own. "It can't be heated up the same as before."

"That's not good, I guess."

"Depends," Vi said. "It can keep you from being hurt again. It can keep you from being jealous. 'Cause you don't care so much."

"Oh."

"You don't get that stab to the heart," Vi said.

"Oh."

"For instance me," Vi said. "It doesn't make me jealous that you're two-timing me with that blonde."

"What?"

"Your new friend. The one you knew back home."

"I didn't know her. Who?"

"The one with the little boy. She likes ice-cream sodas." Vi sang: *"The prettiest girl. I ever saw. Was sippin' soda. Through a straw . . ."*

"Oh ho," Prosper said, as though just remembering. "Oh no. No. That's nothing. She's married. I just knew her back home. Or actually I didn't know her."

"You," said Vi, aiming a finger at him like a gun, "are a terrible liar. But it doesn't matter. Like I just said. Who cares? If you don't care I don't. And you don't."

Prosper sat hands folded on the table that separated them. Caught out so unexpectedly, he'd got distracted; there was a thread there in Vi's story he'd intended to follow, now he'd dropped it, what was it? Oh yes.

"Who broke your heart, Vi?" he asked.

She stuffed her hands in her overall pockets. "Maybe I'll tell you sometime," she said. "I'm going to work."

9

It had been a Wednesday night a couple of weeks before when Prosper Olander and Pancho Notzing went into Ponca City to see a movie and pick up some sundries (as Prosper said). Pancho drove, the seats filled with Teenie Weenies out to do the town, insofar as it could be done, not something Pancho cared to do, and they'd have to make their own way home. He let them out by the Poncan, a Spanish-style picture palace on Grand Avenue and the best in town, and went to park the car; he joined Prosper at the ticket booth, and they reached doors just as a black man in a bow tie holding the hand of a small girl in lace and ribbons did too. Pancho opened the door to let them pass in, and followed. Prosper went in after, and a local gent too, coatless in a skimmer, his eyes narrowed.

"I wouldn't open a grave for one of them," the fellow muttered, not exactly to Prosper; it took Prosper a minute to put together what the man had seen, and what he meant by what he'd said—the black man and his daughter, Pancho opening the door for them. Open a grave? Had the fellow had that remark ready, or was it just now he'd thought of it? It didn't ask for a response, and he made none; the white man lingered in the lobby, eyes fixed on the black man's back as he mounted the stairs to the balcony: for once Prosper felt ignored.

The theater was Cooled by Refrigeration, not necessary on this spring night. A few steps to negotiate, hold up the crowd briefly, and then in. Prosper (as he always would in movie theaters) thought of Elaine, her uniform jacket, breasts bare beneath it. The picture showing was *The Human Comedy,* with selected short subjects and a newsreel. That was what Pancho'd come for, though he chiefly got from it cues for his own pointedly expressed opinions, which earned him a lot of shushing. Next week the bill changed: *Cabin in the Sky.*

Just as the picture, rather dull and uneventful, wrapped up, Prosper whispered to Pancho that he'd meet him as agreed, and got up to go. Crowds in aisles always made him anxious, chance of a stray foot accidentally kicking his props away.

Cuzalina's pharmacy ("Save When You're Sick") was a few blocks away, and open late that year, serving the oil crews as well as the round-the-clock workers at the *Pax* plant who lived in town or who poured in after every shift to get what couldn't be got out in Henryville, where the clinics dispensed pills and hernia trusses and Mercurochrome but not all the other things a person needed and could find in any real drugstore: razor blades and Brylcreem and hairnets and lipstick, Ipana toothpaste in its tube of ivory-yellow, the repellent color of bad teeth. And more. At ten o'clock there was a line that snaked around the displays to reach the counter where the clerk seemed to be in no great hurry. A couple of people let Prosper advance, and called on others ahead to let him by, which Prosper wished they wouldn't do: how often had he told people that it was no trouble for him to just stand, cost him no more than it did them. He reached the counter and stood a moment, pressed from behind by the many others. The clerk finally raised his eyebrows, let's go.

"I would like to buy some rubbers," Prosper said in what even he could hear was a weirdly solemn murmur.

"Some what?"

"I would like," Prosper said, a bit more brightly, "a package of rubbers. Condoms."

The clerk looked him over. "And who sent you to buy them?"

"No one sent me."

"Well then . . ."

"I need them for myself."

A kind of delighted satisfaction settled over the fellow's face, as though he'd just got a small gift of a kind he liked but hadn't expected.

It was one of those big faces with a set of features tightly bunched in the middle, seeming too small for it. "Well now. You know the use of this product?"

"I believe I do," Prosper said. The line behind him had got longer and drawn tighter: he could sense it without turning to look. He propped himself up a little straighter. "Why do you ask?"

"This product is sold for the prevention of disease only. Were you aware of that?"

Prosper said nothing. The man's smile had steadied, confirmed. "Aha," he said. "So you wouldn't be able to certify that use. As a purchaser."

Prosper said nothing again. As though he'd hoped for more, the clerk said grudgingly, "Well what brand would you like to purchase?" He bent closer to Prosper and spoke lower. "Skins or rubbers? I believe you said rubbers."

"Yes."

"Choice is yours. We have Sheik. Mermaid. Silver Glow. Lucky. Co-ed. Merry Widow."

"Lucky."

The man shrugged, as though to say that it was up to Prosper but maybe he should think again. "How many?"

"A dozen."

"A *dozen?*" said the clerk, his little eyes widening—this was almost too wonderful, but Prosper again would say nothing back, he'd placed his order. "Well as it happens we don't have 'm by the dozen. We have 'm in tins of three. Sorry. You want *four of those?*"

"Will you serve that customer?" said a voice from behind Prosper. "Let's get this show on the road."

"Two," said Prosper humbly, though it meant he'd have to come back soon, maybe, probably. "Two tins."

The clerk pulled open a drawer beneath the counter, rummaged in it for a moment, and extracted a tin, which he tossed into the air with one hand and caught with the other; then one more. "A couple of the Lucky," he said, not quietly, proffering the two as though he'd conjured them, and just out of Prosper's reach. "One-fifty."

Prosper, leaning on the counter, slipped his right crutch into his left hand and reached out for the little square tins; he put them into his trouser pocket, took money from his jacket, and paid; swapped back his right crutch into his right hand. Then—he'd been imagining the moment, in a vague state of alarm, for the last few minutes—he turned himself toward the line behind, chose a face (rapt indifference, Sphinx-like) and started out, suffering their inspection but also feeling a deep warm glee as the tins in his pocket bounced against his hip.

Larry the shop steward was among those on line. "Lucky," he said as though to no one when Prosper passed. "Lucky if they don't bust."

Pancho said he'd parked down by the railroad station, and Prosper was passing beneath the vast bulk of the flour mill and grain elevators as the last of the midnight train's passengers were dispersing from the double doors of the station. The Atchison, Topeka and Santa Fe ran specials almost daily in that time, so many people coming in to get work, so many government people come to look over the advancing aircraft. The taxis waiting along Oklahoma charged seven cents a mile, it had been a nickel before the war but a cabbie's life was hard these days—gas, tires, maintenance on the decaying cars—and everybody seemed to have the money and didn't mind the surcharge. As Prosper neared the station, which was too small for the traffic that passed through it, he noticed a woman with a child, a boy who clung to her skirt. He picked her out, maybe because she alone was still and some-how entranced or bewildered while everybody else was in motion—the way, in the movie he'd just watched, the girl who would be the heroine of the story could be picked out from the crowd around her when she was first seen: alight and glowing, sharply drawn while the others moving around her were dim and unclear.

Also she seemed to be in trouble.

Prosper stopped before her. Ought, he knew, to lift his hat, but that gesture always caused more attention than he intended to draw. "Evening," he said.

She nodded warily. Prosper knew he could alarm some people, though he never knew which people.

"You need any directions? Can I get you a taxi?"

"Well," she said. "Do you know if they go out to the airplane factory?"

"Oh yes, ma'am, they do. They'd love to take you out there. It'll cost you almost a buck."

"Oh dear."

Her little boy had detached himself from her and was looking at Prosper's crutches with interest: Prosper could tell. Kids liked to watch somebody walk in a new way, liked to ask why he had them, though their parents shushed them and pulled them away. He remembered one boy telling his mother *Mommy get me those*, as though they were a new kind of pogo stick. He took a step toward the boy, who smiled but retreated.

"Hello little fella," he said. The boy's mother looked down at him, as though just then discovering him there. "What's your name?"

The kid didn't answer, and Mom seemed not to want to volunteer one. "His daddy's working out there, at the plant," she said, still regarding the boy, as though it was he who needed the information. She was a rose-gold blonde, one of those whose skin seems to have taken its shade from her hair, her brows fading almost into invisibility against it. For a second they stood looking, her at the boy, the boy wide-eyed at Prosper, Prosper at her.

"Was he coming out to meet you?"

"No," she said. "He doesn't know we've come."

"Oh. Aha. Surprise visit?"

"Well."

"What shop's he work in? Does he live in Henryville?"

"Where's that?" she asked in something like despair, as though suddenly envisioning more journeying. She looked all in.

"Just the town around the plant. The new houses. Do you have an address?"

She didn't answer, as though to let him guess she knew nothing at all and would have no answer to any further question. She watched Prosper shift his weight. "I'm sorry," she said. "Are you . . ."

"I'm fine," he said. "Listen. If you're going out to find him, you could come with me. My friend's got a car. There's room for you two. We work out there, maybe we can give you some help finding him."

"Oh gosh. Oh that's so nice."

"This way," he said, and took a few steps under their gaze, the kid still smiling, interested. "Or no wait. You'd have to lug the bags. Sorry."

"No, oh no it's fine," she said, reaching for what looked like a one-ton strapped leather suitcase.

"No wait here," Prosper said. "I'm to meet him right around the corner. Wait here and I'll go get him and we'll drive around. Okay? Just wait here."

He had just turned to set off when a wheezy *beebeep* behind him turned him back. Pancho pulled up to the curb, himself beeped at by the affronted cab behind. Prosper guided his new finds to the car with one hand. "How's that for luck," he said. Pancho pulled the brake and leapt out to help with the bag, and got the mother and child stowed in the backseat. Prosper went around and performed his get-in-the-car act, talking away. "So how far you two come? Where'd you start out from?"

She named the place, Prosper astonished to hear the name of his own northern city. They had to compare neighborhoods then, families, schools, finding no connection.

Pancho leaned over the seat, proffered his hand and gave his name, and Prosper's.

"Constance," she said in reply. "Connie. This my son Adolph."

"Well," Pancho said, as if in commendation. "Well let's get going."

"This is a good thing," Prosper said, grinning proudly as the car rolled off. "This is a very good thing."

Within minutes they were outside the town and in utter darkness, stars scattered overhead. Connie Wrobleski tasted something thick and sweetish in the air they moved through. Crude oil, said the little man at the wheel: you'll get used to it. He pointed a thumb back toward where they'd come from, and Connie saw the far-off glitter of lights and a flare like a titanic match burning. It had turned to warm spring, nearly summer, as she'd gone south; she opened her coat. The crippled man smiled back at her as though glad for her. And then—Connie at first thought it was dawn rising, though it couldn't be that late—the great glow of the *Pax* plant and hangars put out the western stars.

Three days before she'd set out with these bags and Adolph, nearly two years old, her good suit on but flats because she knew what lay ahead. She couldn't face the Elevated with the bags and Adolph, and her purse felt heavy with money from the war job she'd had, so she called a cab.

"Leaving home?" the taxi driver said, loading the bags in the trunk—greasy Mediterranean type Connie had always mistrusted—and in a sudden rush of careless energy she said "None of your business," smiled, and slammed the door with a satisfying thud; and they went to the station in silence.

The station was packed, like the first day of a giveaway at the department store, Connie had known it would be, the newspaper was full of stories, people in motion. The noise of all of them as she came in holding Adolph's hand seemed to rise up toward the ceiling and rain back down on them, the voices, the announcements over the loudspeakers, the click of heels. The station was a new one, built only a few years ago by the WPA; over the doors were stern blocky stone eagles, and above the row of ticket windows where people patient or impatient worked out their trips or made demands or pleas, there ran a broad paneled painting, the history of the city and the region done in forms of travel: Indians with those things they drag, not trapezes, and pigtailed men with oxcarts, larky boatmen on canal boats, a stagecoach and an old puffer-belly locomotive, all of it pressed up together in the picture as though it had happened all at once, as crowded with contrary people pushing and tugging as the station below it. Around her as she moved slowly forward men were working the line, offering Pullman tickets to the South, where Connie was headed; they were asking ten or twenty dollars above the standard price for these tickets, which were (they said) all sold out at the window. Everybody wanted to go south now, old people to Florida, women to the training camps where their men were stationed. Right by the ticket window as Connie reached it was a sign that said IS THIS TRIP NECESSARY? in stark black letters. Like an old aunt or nun, the government making sure you weren't doing anything just for fun, and she wasn't, if the government were to ask her she could say Yes this trip is necessary.

"Ponca City, Oklahoma," she said, or cried aloud in the din. "Coach class. Myself and a baby, is all. One way."

PART THREE

1

The week after Christmas Bunce Wrobleski came home from the Bull aircraft plant with newspapers that were full of ads for workers with skills like his—ads for workers of any kind, actually, columns and columns of them after the deserts of last decade's employment pages, jobs in this city and jobs far away. Situations Available. Bunce wanted a new situation. Well, that was pretty obvious. He stood in the lamplight at midnight (couldn't even get off Swing Shift at this damn plant, he'd said), a Lucky dangling from his plump sweet lower lip, his collar turned up and his cap still on at a rakish angle with its bill sharply curled, its buttons on it—his union button, Blue Team button, plant admission button with his picture on it wearing the same cap the button was pinned to; and Connie'd thought, What a beautiful man, as she never could help thinking, despite that foxy or wolfish cunning that was sometimes in his lashy eyes, as it was then. He pulled off the cap and tossed it and tousled his thick hair. The job listing he had shown her was in an aircraft plant miles away.

The rule now was that if a man quit his war-work job to go look for something better, or if he took some job that wasn't war work, then his deferment could end, even fathers wouldn't be exempt for long. Basically he was tied to his job. That was the rule. He was the same as a soldier, in a way; no different. At the kitchen table he had laid it out for Connie, moving the salt and pepper shakers and the ashtray gently around the oilcloth in relation to one another, as though they were the elements of the contract he had accepted. Constance watched his broken-nailed hands as he explained. His eyes weren't meeting hers. The salt and pepper shakers were little bisque figures of a hen and a rooster; the rooster was the pepper.

But—Bunce explained, moving away the ashtray, opening a path for the rooster across the flowery field of the oilcloth—but if you could locate a different job in some other war industry plant, a job that was rated higher than the one you had, and you had the qualifications for it, then you could quit the one and be in no danger from the draft if you went and took the other. The job he had here was no good. He could do better.

"You know why I got stuck here," he said, and only now did he raise his eyes to Connie—she being the other piece of the rebus, she and Adolph asleep in the next room. Sure she knew, and she wasn't going to look down or away from him. He could have used a safe that night in the back of the Plymouth and they wouldn't be stuck, but then there'd be no Adolph either, and she wasn't going to think that would be a good thing.

For a time after Bunce went across the country to the new job, a kind of stasis settled over her; it was like waiting for him to get home from the shift but it went on all day long, and was there at night when Adolph woke her, the sensation of Bunce not there and nothing to do or to be until he came in, which he wasn't going to do. She was careful to keep herself up, for no one. She put on her makeup and a pair of the nylons that Bunce had bought from a guy who suddenly had a lot of pairs. She went to the hairdresser and with a ration stamp got her bangs curled high on her head and the length in back curled too like the bottom of a waterfall striking its pool. She did all that and at the same time felt a strange temptation, a yen or tug, not to do it, to stop altogether and live in the house and the bed the way Adolph did, without caring or thinking.

For a few weeks the postal orders came regularly from Bunce, for different amounts, sometimes more, sometimes less. Then a week went by without one: it was like the sudden stopping of her heart, when it takes that gulp of nothing, then rolls over somehow and starts again, thumping hard and fast for a moment as though to catch up. Just that same way a postal order came the next week, bigger than ever. But then weeks started to pass without them.

She wrote a postcard to Bunce at the last address she had for him and heard nothing for a while; then a letter came, with some bills folded small and tucked into the small sheets, a five, two tens, some ones.

Honey I'm sorry I didn't send more lately but you can't believe how expensive it is out here Food costs more and every cheap diner charges fifty cents for a plate of stew The rents are worse when you can even get a place I was rooming with some fellows and we got into a wrangle I'm sorry to say and I had to leave I am doing all right now but they aren't going to forward mail if you wrote any, they never do from rooming houses. I hope to come home for a while soon with any luck but you know how the trains are. Kiss my boy for me.

So that was the rent for the month plus the five she was shy for last month, and some food money, which wasn't so cheap here either in spite of all the controls they talked about. The next three weeks went by with nothing from Bunce.

Connie Wrobleski was twenty years old and hadn't ever faced the prospect of nothing, no support, no surrounding provider. Kids she knew at school had to drop out because their fathers lost their jobs, but she hadn't worried because her father was a bus driver for the city and the union was good. Not even finding out she was pregnant had felt like facing nothing, because Bunce (after he had banged on the steering wheel of the Plymouth so long and hard she thought it would break, making a noise behind his clenched teeth like a bad dog) promised her it was okay and he'd never leave her, he wasn't that kind of guy. And anyway so many of the girls in her class at Holy Name were in the same condition by the night of the Senior Ball, some of them showing already and proudly wearing their rings even though the Father Superintendent said they were forbidden to—well if all of them were in the same boat, and if Bunce was going to be good and already had a good job, then it felt more like the good scary beginning of something larger than she had ever known, something that would just go on and on and show her what it was as it happened, like that scene in movies where at the start you fly over hills and down roads and up to a house in a town and through a door that opens as you come to it and into the kitchen where a family is in the middle of their lives. This, though— the drying up of those letters, the little flight of them failing—this felt like having and knowing nothing at all. Adolph looked up at her and she down into the huge pools of his eyes, and he was sure of more than she was.

Late on the last Saturday of the month—suddenly remembering the task with a grip to her heart—Connie got Adolph wrapped in the red-and-white woolens and cap her mother had knitted for him, and lifted him into the huge blue-black baby carriage for which he was already too big, and from which he seemed likely to fling himself out like a movie gangster from a speeding sedan. She walked the carriage backward down the steep steps before her house (Adolph laughing at every bump). The house was a double one, each half the mirror image of the other, to which it was joined like a Siamese twin, two apart-ments per house. She turned rightward up the street. Leftward went down under the viaduct and past the millworkers' houses and the coal and ice dealer's to where you caught a bus that went along the train yards out to where the Bull plant was, the great brick buildings marked with big numbers, Number 3 where Bunce had worked. Rightward the street went up for a while, the heavy carriage bouncing sedately over the seams in the sidewalk, past the blackened and forbidding Methodist church and then down, past the IGA and into a neighbor-hood of single houses, to cross the avenue where the brown-brick grammar school stood on its pillow of earth. On this day the ration books for the month were given out there. You went around back, where in the playground kids were dangling from the jungle gym wait-ing for their mothers; Connie could feel their cold skinned knees and barked knuckles—Bunce always said that imagining pain and discom-fort was worse for her than the real thing when it came, which it almost never did.

She went in the back door to the strangeness of an empty echoey school smelling of kids and old lunches, to the cafeteria where the volunteers were handing out booklets and checking names. Most of the volunteers were teachers at the school, and since Connie didn't have a child at the school they didn't know her. She carried Adolph in her arms, he was scared to get down and walk, and of course all the women wanted a look at him and smiled and asked Connie what his name was.

"Adolph?" said a man behind her in line. "There's a heck of a name to lay on a kid."

"It's his grandfather's name," Connie said, looking straight ahead, thinking maybe that made it worse.

"Is he a German?"

"It's a fine name," said the woman behind the scarred table. A wooden box filled with stamp books was beside her.

"It was a fine name a couple of years ago," Connie said. "When he got it."

"Well sure. Like Adolphe Menjou." Connie handed her the ragged and empty remains of the old book—you couldn't get a new one without handing in the old—and was given her book of rough gray paper and a sheet of printed reminders and notices for the month, which she would sit down later and try to master.

At the door where the people who had been given their books went out, a man in a sleeveless sweater and a bedraggled bow tie stood by a folding table. A sandwich board was open beside it. It showed four women's faces in profile, almost identical but receding into the distance; their eyes were lifted toward the horizon or the sky, and their hair was rolled in fat curls like Connie's. A wide red band ran across the middle of the picture as though someone had rushed up and slapped it on. It said AMERICAN WOMEN—THEY CAN DO IT!

Connie had seen this poster and other posters like it before, in the movies and in the papers, the newsreel stories about women trooping off to work in their overalls and bandannas, moving huge machines and handling tools with big smiles on their faces and then touching up their makeup after work with a different kind of smile. But just then on that Saturday the picture struck her as somehow *about her* in a way the others before had not. The man in the bow tie looked at her, smiling in an appraising sort of way, but she felt no constraint at his look, his hands were clasped harmlessly behind him like a minister or a floorwalker, someone ready to do you good.

"Hello," she said. She let Adolph slip from her and settle to the ground, where with great care he crept under the tentlike sandwich board and sat, hands on his knees.

"Cute little fella," the man said. "His dad in the service?"

Connie raised her eyes to him but said nothing, not evasive though, feeling her face to be like the faces of the women in the poster, frank and farsighted and at the same time containing a secret about themselves.

"Best thing you could do for him is go down to city hall and fill out an application for work," he said then, raising a definite forefinger. "Everybody can help."

"I couldn't, because of," Connie said, and reached a hand toward Adolph.

"Lot of girls think that," the man said. "They find a way." He picked up one each of the papers in piles on the table and gave them to her. "You go on down. You'll see. Everybody can do something. City hall. There's a poster just outside, tells you what to do next. You just go on from there."

In the apartment again Connie turned on all the lights to banish the growing dark. They seemed pale and ineffectual for a long time until the dark came fully down and they grew strong and yellow and warm. Bunce hated to have more than just the one bulb burning you needed to see what you were doing at the moment; when he was with her she hadn't minded the little pools of light and the dark rooms around, but now she did.

"Okay, honey?" she said to Adolph, who sat on the little painted potty chair in the bathroom, pants down and waiting, hands clasped together before him like a little old man or a schoolmarm. "Can you push?" She grunted for him, give him the idea, and he watched her with interest but wouldn't imitate. Sometimes she wondered if he was all there, Adolph. So mild and good and quiet. His eyes now searching her face, untroubled and interested. "Okay, you sit a while and see. Okay?"

She went out into the kitchen, stepping backward so that he could see she was still there, still smiling. Then she sat at the table with her book of stamps and the announcements that had been given out with it.

G, H and J blue stamps, worth a total of forty-eight points a person, become valid tomorrow, January 24, and are good throughout the month of February. D, E and F blue stamps, in use since December 25, expire January 31. Thus there will be an overlap period of one week in which all six stamps will be valid. These stamps cover canned, bottled and frozen fruits and vegetables and their juices, dry beans, peas, lentils, etc., and processed foods such as soups, baby foods, baked beans, catsup and chili sauce.

A bottle of ketchup cost a whopping fifteen points and Bunce couldn't live without it. Connie got more points than she could use, now that it was just her and Adolph. Dolph. Adi. Addo. There just wasn't a nickname. Her father-in-law was called Buster by everyone and always had been.

She had plenty of stamps but not a lot of money. Her purse, soft and with a crossbones catch like a miniature carpetbag, hung inside her handbag, attached by a ribbon—meant to keep it from getting lost, she guessed, unless the whole bag was. She emptied it on the table, the coins clinking and rolling away merrily on the oilcloth till she caught them. There weren't many bills, and only a couple of tens in the tin candy box on the top shelf.

When Bunce got into the union her father had solemnly taken his shoulder and Connie's and said that he was glad, glad to know now they would never be in want. Want: never to want for anything. *Freedom from Want* was one of the Four Freedoms the President had said everyone should have, the whole world. The pale ghost children in newsreels, refugees, eating their bowls of soup but still alert and afraid. She turned back to the bathroom. If Adolph inclined his head he could see her in the kitchen, and she could see his little blond head around the door's corner.

"Okay? Anything coming?"

He smiled as though at a joke.

There just wasn't a way to be sure enough money would be coming in, no way to guarantee it. Every week there might be or there might not. And every week that there wasn't would press you further down till you had gone too far to come back. Of course they weren't going to starve, her parents and Bunce's wouldn't let that happen, but that didn't make her feel safe. She thought that now maybe she wouldn't ever feel safe again in the way that she once had, and that this moment of understanding had lain deep within the whole life she had led, at home and in school and in church, in the movie theater, with the Sodality girls, in the Plymouth and the big lumpy bed with Bunce. She had never been safe at all, and she hadn't known it, and now she did.

"Ine done, Mommy."

"Okay, sweet. That was a good try." He pulled up his pants as he walked, a cute trick he wouldn't be able to do so well forever, like a guy hurrying out of a girl's room before he was caught with her.

City hall, that's where the man had said to go. Where she'd got her marriage license, never having been in it before, the tall corridors lined with gold-numbered wooden doors. A poster outside, to tell you what to do.

Freedom from Fear. That was another of the four.

On Tuesday (it took a couple of days to make a decision, and she made it only on the grounds that going downtown and inquiring committed her to nothing) Connie lined up in the corridor outside the doors of the United States Employment Agency with a crowd mostly female and of all ages, far too many to fit into the little waiting room (Connie could glimpse into it, crowded with people, when the secretary opened the door to let someone out or call someone in). She'd taken a long time to dress, not knowing what would look right for someone applying to work in a factory, where she imagined the jobs would mostly be, and then—annoyed at herself for trying to make people think she was who they wanted, when she didn't know if she even wanted them to think so—she put on a tartan skirt, a sweater, flats but with a pair of Bunce's stockings, her old cloth coat, and a beret. She thought she looked like anybody.

"Just don't tell them you can type," said an older woman behind her to a friend, a pale and ill-looking blonde. "If they know you can type you'll be typing till Tojo's dead."

The blonde said nothing. Connie thought the girl was planning to say that she typed, and Connie wished she could too. She'd taken

Modern Homemaking instead of typing. In a magazine story she'd recently looked at, jobs in factories were compared to housework. Running a drill press, it said, was no different from operating a mangle. Washing engine parts in chemicals was like washing dishes—gray-haired women were shown doing it, rubber gloves on their hands, smiling, unafraid.

A crowd of people, hands full of forms, were let out from the employment office. Connie was in the next group called in. In the office she got into one of the lines before the counter. All around in every seat and leaning against the wall women and some men too filled out the same forms. The room smelled of unemptied ashtrays and overheated people. The woman at the counter, astonishingly placid amid all this, with two pencils stuck in her bun, gave Connie a form, even while she answered what even Connie could tell were stupid questions from applicants and form fillers. It seemed to Connie that women like this, with gray buns and patient smiles, were really conducting the life of the nation while the generals and the statesmen busied themselves with their important things.

The form was easy to fill out. All the answers were No. Typing? Shorthand? Experience with Hollerith card sorter? PBX? Chauffeur's license? She assumed that if she didn't understand a question she could answer No or None. Physical handicap? Color-blind? Hard of hearing? College degree? Own car? Married? She almost checked No for that too, going rapidly down the row of boxes.

The lady with the gray bun seemed delighted with her application. "Unskilled," she said, as though it were to Connie's credit. And then, oblivious of the mob beating against her counter like waves on a rock face, she engaged Connie in a conversation about where she could work, what sort of work it would be ("dirty work, sometimes really dirty," and she brushed imaginary or symbolic dirt from her own hands). They talked about Adolph, about what shift Connie might be able to take, part-time, full-time. Connie could see, through the Venetian blinds, the men on telephones in the back office, checking long banners of paper; as soon as they hung up one phone they picked up another. "There," the woman said, writing words on a card. "Right near by you. You g'down there tomorrow, eight A.M., and they'll do the intake."

Her kindly attention had already slipped away from Connie. Connie took the card, thinking that she didn't know exactly when she'd agreed to do this, and was elbowed gently out of the way by the typist and her friend. Not until she was back out in the day did she realize where she'd been sent: to the same factory that was building Bull fighter planes, where Bunce had worked before he left.

Wednesday was colder. Connie's mother had come the day before, a little doubtful, speaking in the small voice that Connie knew meant she didn't approve—or rather didn't know whether to approve or not, but thought not. Like the annuity her husband had invested his money in, or Eleanor Roosevelt's gadding, or Connie's first pair of saddle shoes. Anyway she was glad to see her grandson, and Adolph gave her the wholehearted face of wondering joy—how could you resist it? Connie already had her coat on and was tying her kerchief under her chin. She wore a pair of slacks (the working women in the newsreels all wore them, Connie didn't have to explain) and those same saddle shoes, their white parts scuffed and dingy.

"There's a can of tomato soup," she said to her mother. For a moment she couldn't find the card given to her the day before, no here it was in the coat's inside pocket. "And some Velveeta cheese you can put in it." Her mother said nothing, and would do as she saw fit, but Connie needed to show her that she'd thought about this and was prepared. She hugged Adolph with a strange sudden passion, as though it might be a long time till she returned, and went out and down the steep steps into the unwelcoming day. She turned left not right at the sidewalk. In this direction there had never been anything of much use to her. The sidewalk tilted downward, its squares cracked and buckled, and in a few blocks Connie passed under the black railroad viaduct that crossed all that industrial bottom. A train was chugging toward the crossing over her head—she'd heard its approaching wail as she left her house—and just as Connie walked under, it did cross, thudding and still screaming. The damp sky turned away the ashy yellow smoke, the hollow of earth drew it down and it covered Connie like a dropped curtain, bitter and stinging; for a moment she couldn't see anything at all, but then she parted the curtain and came out on the other side; the train had passed. Farther on was the green wooden shelter where the bus stopped.

Why should she feel ashamed, when no one knew or could guess she was here not because she wanted to help and be a good person but because she was afraid—more afraid of not having enough than she was afraid to go farther on, on this side where she had not before belonged? The shelter, and the bus when it came, was full of women and men talking and complaining and kidding one another, and some others like her seemingly here for the first time and looking around themselves boldly or uncertainly, peach-faced teenagers too skinny to be soldiers, women her mother's age, one in a fox fur piece. Together. Connie clung to the enameled pole, rocked with all of them.

At a farther stop a problem of some kind arose—Connie in the dense middle of the bus couldn't see it directly, only hear the exchange between the driver and someone having trouble getting on. Listen mister I am under no obligation. Reserve the right I mean. Other voices entered in, either taking the driver's side that whoever it was couldn't be accommodated, or arguing with the driver and the others to let the guy on, give him a hand for Chrissake, what's it to ya, let's get this wagon rolling. One of the voices must have been the fellow trying to get on, but Connie couldn't tell which. Then she could see a couple of people had joined in to help him despite the driver and the others, and a long crutch was handed up and then another, and after them a lanky body, a man in a fedora and a houndstooth jacket. He was lifted up into the bus like someone pulled from a well, looking startled and wary and maybe grateful, while the complainers still went on about moving along, voices from Connie's back of the bus calling out impatiently now also. The gears of the bus ground horribly. Everybody seemed to have an opinion about the matter, but nobody spoke to the young man himself as far as she could tell; she could see his hat bobbing a little between some of their heads.

At the various plant and shop gates the workers got off—Connie could see, out the rear window, another bus just behind hers, carrying more—until the Bull plant was reached. Once, Connie had brought Bunce his lunch pail here when he'd forgot it, and he'd told her never to come again. There was an aluminum model of the Bull fighter plane in front, looking unlikely or imaginary, but the buildings of the plant

222 / JOHN CROWLEY

behind were just factory buildings, three big brick buildings that had once made something else and were now combined. 1. 2. 3. Connie got out the rear door with some others; she glanced back once at the crippled man now seated and holding his crutches by the middle hand-bar, like a man holding a trombone. She could see his back was severely swayed.

"If that was me I'd kill myself," a man walking beside her said. He was hatless and wore a badge like Bunce's pinned to his jacket. Connie said nothing; she shrank from people who offered opinions like that out loud in public to no one. The man had a black dead look, as though he might just kill himself anyway. They all walked toward the gates of Number 3, just then sliding open on their tracks.

She did no work that day, but still she was there the whole of the shift. With the other new employees she was set on a broad yellow stripe painted on the concrete floor and already flaking away, and told to follow it to the different places she needed to go. Far off the huge nameless noises of the plant could be heard. She hadn't thought she'd just arrive and take her place in line and begin doing one of the things shown in the magazines, but she hadn't had a different picture of what would happen either. The first place the yellow stripe led to was a long room with a paper sign on the door that said Induction. Inside were a number of booths and stations labeled with arrows to show you how to proceed. At Requisition she handed in her card from the government employment agency but had to go through the same information again, with variations, as the clerk filled in things without lifting his eyes; he handed her forms and asked, still not looking up, if she had any questions, and after a moment of being unable to produce a thought of any kind she said no. Then at the next station she had to show her birth certificate, and here it is, with two infant footprints, but it's the wrong thing—this is a hospital notice of live birth and not a legal birth certificate like the others have, an engrossed document with seals. The clerk shrugged wearily. Connie thought of offering her grown-up feet for comparison, but the clerk just handed it back to her without looking up and pointed the way to the next booth. She folded up the little feet. The Clock Clerk (that's who the sign said the next person was) gave her an employee number and a time card and told her how to use it. Her starting rate of pay was fifty cents an hour for base-rate production and a bonus prorated on work done above the base. Any questions? Connie said no. Probably it would all be obvious what to do and how to do it if she actually started. Behind her the line of new employees shuffled forward. She had her fingerprints taken, by a man who grasped her fingers and thumbs like tools, pressed them firmly on the somehow loathsome leaking purple pad and rolled them expertly onto the spaces on a paper form. Her employee number was written on the top. Herself and none other. She was photographed, asked curtly to take off her hat, no time to check her hair or choose an expression. Bunce had looked in his photograph like John Garfield in a picture they'd post outside a theater, he always looked splendid in pictures. Next she and a group of others were read the Espionage Act at a mile a minute. *By Order of the President of the United States.* Connie had already decided that she would figure out some way to tell them she couldn't do this, she'd made a mistake and couldn't come back, she was sorry sorry sorry. She would write a letter maybe. But meanwhile there was no way to turn back, she could only follow the yellow band with the others pressing behind her; she went down a strange-smelling hall to Physical Examinations. Just looking in at the door into the room, where screens had been set up to roughly divide the men from the women, she felt shamed and exposed and wondered why she'd ever thought she was brave enough to do this. What you imagine something is going to be like before you jump into it is never what it will be, it's just the feeling you have at the time, made into a picture, like that picture of the three women looking into the sky and the future.

She had a chest X-ray, the remarkably ugly and bewigged nurse pushing Connie into place before the glass of the machine and pulling her arms back, as though she meant to handcuff her; then she took Connie's blood pressure and murmured through a list of questions so fast Connie hardly had time to think of an answer. The nurse did the things they always did at physicals without explanation, learning facts they wouldn't or didn't have time to divulge. Nothing so bad as to keep her from working here: her form was stamped and the stamp signed across by the nurse, who capped her pen and was eyeing the next in line even as she handed the sheet to Connie to add to the others she had been given.

After that she was herded into a group cut out from the mass of applicants and sent with them into a room full of benches, where they were each seated before a big square magnifying glass in a frame. A tin box of tiny gears was under the glass. A man at the center of the room in a gray cloth coat waited till they were all seated, then started talking loudly and distinctly, telling them what they were to do. It was a Manual Dexterity and Visual Acuity Test. You were to Pick Up a Single Pinion with Thumb and Forefinger. Turn the Pinion Clockwise between the Two Fingers. Look to See if the Teeth of the Pinion are All of the Same Width. When you have Assessed the Pinion, place it either in the Left Box, Accepted, or the Right Box, Rejected. Work as Fast and Accurately as you Can. You have Five Minutes. He lifted his finger, pressed a button on the big watch he held, and said Begin. Just then a woman next to Connie piped up: Were the airplanes really going to use these little things if we-all accept them? The man smiled and laughed and said Goodness no, it was just a test, there were good ones and bad ones in the box and you just try to tell which are which, and everybody laughed a little and he raised his finger again and said Begin.

Connie picked up one of the little things with thumb and forefinger. It took a moment to adjust her vision to the hugely enlarged fingertips she saw, their uncared-for nails, she'd meant to give herself a manicure, and the toothed wheel; she moved it back and forth until it came clear. But as soon as it did she saw that one of the teeth was wider, or had a slight burr or something on it. She put it in the right box, and picked up another. Around her she was aware of the voices of the other applicants, complaining or marveling at the task, laughing when they dropped or fumbled the pinions, but almost immediately all the noise sank away and she picked up the pinions one after another; for a moment she doubted herself—would she really see a difference, and was it a big enough difference? But she felt the differences so distinctly—she always knew when she saw one—that she decided just to trust herself. Before the five minutes were up she had emptied her box, sorted left and right, and the man glanced up from his watch at her doubtfully or with a little smile that seemed to say Oh you think so? Then he said Stop. They were each to leave the proper form (pink) next to their work, which would be returned to them later. Then they were sent out a farther door as another group came in behind.

It was time for lunch.

She wasn't the only one whose husband had worked here, though almost

all the ones who spoke up said their husbands had been drafted or joined up, and that was the reason they applied. One said her husband would kill her if he found out. She needed the money, she said, and when no one responded to that, shrugged one shoulder and went back to her sandwich. Connie wanted to ask her more, since she had no idea what Bunce would think about her taking a job, though whenever she thought about telling him, or him finding out, a kind of dread came up under her heart. But he'd have to understand. He was a good man; everybody who knew him said so. And when that dread arose there was Adolph too, as in one of those dreams where you leave your child for a minute to do something, and that leads to something else, and you remember the kid finally but by then the whole world's changed and there's no way to get back to him.

She was thinking those things when her shoulder was touched, and she leapt slightly—it was easy to startle her, Bunce liked that about her, and was pleased that he knew it. The man behind her, stepping back at her response, was the one in the gray cloth coat who had given them the Manual Dexterity and Visual Acuity Test.

"Mind if I see your card?" he said.

She stood, picked up the pile of colored papers small and large she'd been collecting all day, and began looking through them. The man saw what he wanted and neatly two-fingered it out of the pile, looked at it back and front. "Mrs. Constance Wrobleski." He compared the card to the pink sheet he had.

"Yes." She had a sudden thought that he had discerned she wanted to get out without signing up for a job, and was here to send her home. No, how dumb.

"I wanted to ask," he said. "Have you ever done any work like this before? I mean like the little job you did there?" He pointed his head in the direction of the test room.

"Um no," Connie said.

"I don't mean a job, but for instance anything like retouching photos, or similar?"

Connie said nothing, not even sure what that was. She was getting a little restive at having to answer No to questions about what she could do or had done.

"Ever do fine needlework?"

"No. Never."

The man looked again at the sheet in his hand. "Well, I must say you have remarkable visual acuity. You scored near a hundred percent on that task. And you did it in near record time."

He looked up now and gave her a big smile, as though he had been conscious all along that he was being unsettling but that the joke was over. "Really?" she said.

"Yes." He grinned more broadly. "You surprise yourself?"

"Well I don't know. I mean I didn't think."

"All right, well listen now. We'd here like to encourage you to come and take another test or so. We think somebody like you could be of some real service. The tests'll take an hour or so, not more."

Connie regarded him in amazement, and said nothing.

"It might mean a better pay rate," the man said, as though in confidence.

"Okay," Connie said.

"You finished up your lunch?"

She looked back at the deflated bag, and at the women at the table, who had all turned to her, like the faces of girls at school when one of them was called out by a nun for some special purpose: was it good or bad? Good for them, bad for her? Or the opposite? "All done," Connie said. The man motioned to her place at the table, and Connie first thought he meant she ought to pick up her leavings, then saw he wanted her to take her coat and follow him, and she did.

Her revised pay rate would be sixty cents an hour, a sum she kept multiplying all the way home in various combinations, by the day, the minute, the week, the month. Above that base rate she would get a half a cent more for every ten pieces completed, and the man who put her through her tests (which included loading tiny ball bearings into a

wheel, moving through a series of meaningless tasks in the most efficient way, reading eye charts through elaborate goggles) said she was
sure to do well with that, and in not too long a time she would be
moving up into Quality Control and make just a little more, if she
chose to stay, which he hoped she would—nodding at her in an affir-
mative way that made it hard for her to resist nodding back. She was
amazed to find she was good at something she'd never known about
before, not good at a task or good at sticking to it or any of those
qualities, but good at it in herself, in her being, her body: eyes and fingers and senses. She tried to remember instances where she had used
those abilities without noticing them, in homemaking class, in making
birthday cards or Spiritual Bouquets, finding lost things, picking up
pins, but nothing struck her. Hand-Eye Coordination. That was the
talent really, plus the Visual Acuity. She had excellent visual acuity. She
said it out loud as she went up the hill under the viaduct toward her
street: excellent visual acuity. She looked steadily and intently to where
her own house was just then coming into view, and by somehow not
straining but relaxing—not pointing her vision toward the place but
opening her eyes to receive the incoming pictures—she could clearly
see someone standing on the porch. It was the woman in the top apartment of the right-hand house, a long-armed bony square-jawed woman
named Mrs. Freundlich. She had lived there with her grown son, who
for some reason had not been drafted for a long time; maybe he was
too fat, though that didn't seem to keep others out. When he finally did
get his notice and went away the mother was left; she seemed never to
come out of her apartment, and Connie would have felt sorry for her,
except that she seemed to forbid sympathy. She was standing on the
steps of the building, hands under her apron, a coat over it, seeming
lost in thought, maybe waiting for someone (the mailman?). Connie,
exalted somehow by her day at the Bull plant, waved and smiled at the
woman as she came closer, and got an idea at the same moment. It was
only a matter of thinking how to put it.

"How is your son, Mrs. Freundlich? How is he doing?"

"Got a postal card t'other day," the woman said, leaving it at that.

"Does that leave you a lot of time?" Connie asked. "Him not being
here, I mean?" A look of incomprehension grew across the old lady's
face, and Connie hurried on. She got through the basic proposal, and

said that she'd be making good money at the plant and could pay whatever Mrs. Freundlich thought was fair, to all of which Mrs. Freundlich listened without response, when she suddenly said, "Does he mind?"

Connie tried out a couple of possible meanings for this and then said "Oh sure. Yes. He's a good boy."

"I won't have him if he won't mind."

Connie almost told her to go talk to Adolph's grandmother, who was upstairs with him right now, but instead she just let the idea sink in a little; and after a strange silent moment Mrs. Freundlich seemed to collect herself and began to ask sensible questions and offer arrangements and even praised Connie brusquely for doing war work.

So that was done. What a piece of luck. Adolph would be right in the building, and her mother could go home. And Connie Wirobleski, without husband or child, would spend all day doing what? Something she had never done before. The world was no longer the same as it was: everyone said so.

2

For all the talk about her visual acuity and all that, the job Connie was given without explanation or apology was running a huge electric welder that formed U-shaped pieces of steel into frame parts, and mostly involved turning it on and off at the right times. She fed in the half-circle of steel, along with a steel cylinder, which was the sleeve for a driving pinion (that's what she was told it was), shut the machine door, and threw a switch to turn on the juice. At intervals she had to press big buttons to govern the process, but the machine had a revolving guard that prevented her pressing any but the right one at the right instant; as long as she could move her arm she couldn't go wrong. It seemed amazing, fearsome, to her, but the engineer who taught her about it treated it like it was an antique, a buggy, a cider press, smacking it with his hand now and then and talking to it or about it, *Come on old horse, aw now don't go doing that, y'old rattletrap.* When it seized up for one reason or another he had to come back, decouple the power cords, open the side panels, and do things she couldn't understand while she stood arms crossed nearby trying to look ready to help. Why was he so angry? She felt she had descended into another kind of world, where everything had grown huge, or she had grown small. Noises here were vast: there was a continuous ringing of metal, a sledge dropped onto steel flooring plates made a noise huger than she had known was possible just from somebody dropping something. The power cords that the annoyed engineer coupled and decoupled from the rank of outlets on the wall were thicker than her arm, the couplings like buckets, things unrelated to lamp cords or plugs or the twisted wires of electric fans—when he signaled her to pull the start-up switch again, the power seemed to hit the machine with a ringing blow, making it shudder.

The whole place was also dirty and messy, which surprised her. Piles of stuff in process covered with dust and overlaid with other stuff, as though somebody had bought the wrong things and just left them sitting. There was something wrong here: some people, like her supervisor, worked constantly, and others seemed not to work at all, they jawed and laughed, sorted through machine parts idly and knocked off for lunch before the horn sounded; far off amid the noise of machinery she could hear human rows too. Maybe it was always like this, factory work, as full of loose ends and cross-purposes as home, though she was surprised to think it was so; in the movies work always proceeded through the stages of production purposefully, white molten metal poured into rods, rods shaped into this or that, a product taking shape as farsighted men gave directions to great machines and the assembly line crawled forward. Had she learned better? Or was it just this place? Bunce always griped about it, said it was a shambles. She was sorry that in her part of the plant she didn't even see the airplanes taking shape; that was in another of the three buildings that were combined into the Bull works.

"It's crazy," a woman said to her in the lunchroom, lifting a sandwich to her mouth with hands not quite cleaned of metal dust, in her nails and the ridges of her knuckles. "They build the planes here but there's nowhere to fly 'em, you know, test 'em out. So when they're all built they take them apart, put the pieces on a train, and take 'em out to a field out there somewheres, and put the pieces together again to fly the things." She chewed, seeming delighted with the craziness of it. "I guess they know best."

Though the work itself didn't seem hard, it was continuous, unrelenting, in a way nothing she'd ever done before was; the only thing it resembled was the couple of days in the late summer when her dad went out to the country and bought bushel baskets of peaches, and she and her mother and her mother's and father's sisters all canned peaches, skinning and cutting and scalding the fruit, heating the huge black kettles, lowering the pale green Ball jars in their racks into the boiling water; then filling the jars, pouring the melted paraffin over each top to seal it, over and over, never done, her father carrying the filled jars to the basement, climbing up again, weary and persistent. Like that, but every day, endlessly, and without the steady accumulation of good things to eat in the sweet steam. At evening she made it to the bus and walked back up the hill feeling made out of sticks and stones, watching her building come into view with a longing so fervent it was as though she'd never make it.

"Was he good?" she asked Mrs. Freundlich, who seemed to watch from her window to see Connie approaching and was always there to throw open the door before she reached it, displaying Adolph ready to go.

"Well," Mrs. Freundlich said, looking down at Adolph as though trying to make a decision.

He was dressed and clean, in fact his little cheeks shone like a cartoon kid's, one of the Campbell's soup kids, and his hair was combed and wet on his head. He looked up at his mother with that huge happy but questioning look, and—unable to answer it—Connie swept him up, and he held tight to her, smelling of something like Florida water and his own good smell; and she thanked Mrs. Freundlich briefly and took him away, since she'd learned that the woman found it a chore to describe what she and Adolph had done all day. *It was all right* was about as explicit as she got. Connie wondered if she even spoke to him.

Holding him on her hip with one arm she fingered a letter from Bunce from her mailbox. She glimpsed Mrs. Freundlich, half-hidden behind her unclosed door, studying her through the door's window.

Honey, Well I have changed jobs again and am working for Van Damme Aero in their big plant here. The moneys better and the place is swell, all new built, the best of everything. They even have a bank right here in the plant! Mostly women work here I have to say they don't know much tho they would learn faster if somebody took an interest in them. They are ready for anything.

Say this is the place to be, out west, I doubt I'll be able to live in
that smoky old town again. Bye for now, Bunce.

There was a postal money order for twenty dollars in the envelope.
The postmark on the envelope said Ponca City, but the letters signify-
ing the state were smeared and there wasn't any return address on it.
You should always put that on, so that letters can find their way back
to you if they are misdirected. Always.

She folded the letter back up along the folds he had made and
thought she would quit her job. She felt certain she'd done something
to make him not want to come home, and all she could think of was
that she'd gone out and taken a job and not told him, and it was as
though her having done that had been somehow communicated to him
over the spaces between them, between here and the West, maybe in
the war news they all shared, no matter that it was crazy to think
that.

Why hadn't she pleaded with him to stay, back then when he had
decided to quit? She saw as though arrayed across the nation those
smiling willing women of the magazine covers and the newsreels,
marching to work to stand all day beside a helpful man, rising on tiptoe
to nail this or screw that, his hot eyes on her, cap lifted in admiration.

He wasn't coming back. He was just going to go on farther into the
war, and when it was over he would be where he was, he'd go on from
there rather than turning back.

That night she woke in the deep dark, startled out of sleep by her
own cry. Something she had dreamed or learned, she couldn't remember what. She thought of that letter from Bunce and all that it had left
unsaid, the thing that had been going on all along and that she hadn't
really known and now she did. She lay entirely still, feeling that she
was on the point of dissolution, that she would *fall to pieces*, not just
as a way of talking but actually: that what made up *her* would dissoci-
ate and shrivel away like ash. He would never come back. She knew it,
it had been what was going to happen from the beginning, like a dealt
hand of cards. If she could go back now to before he left, she'd hold
him tight and promise him anything.

Night went on unrelieved. She was aware of the ticking of the clock,
warning her with disinterested compassion of the time passing, that

before the light was full she would have to get up to get to work. She began a rosary: not wanting to move to get her beads from where they hung on the dresser mirror, afraid that if she moved she'd come apart somehow, she counted on her fingers. *Pray for us sinners now and at the hour of our deaths.* When the alarm went off at last it woke her, though she had no memory of having slept again.

The day after that was her day off, and she went to visit Bunce's par-ents, as she had promised Bunce she would do, to bring Adolph for them to see. She took a city bus to the station and the interurban to the neighborhood they lived in, in a square plain house covered in something meant to look like bricks. For some reason it was a hard house to be glad to go into—stern or forbidding—but once inside it was nice, and Bunce's parents were as warm as little stoves. Like her, Bunce was an only child.

"Oh my gosh, how he's *grown*! Dad, come see!"

Bunce's father had been a machinist too, but he'd been in an accident at work long before, bones crushed in the overturning of a mechanical bin, Connie had never been able to picture it exactly, though she could a little better now, the Bull plant seemed like it was made to cause awful accidents, she saw two or three nearly happen every day. He lived on a workmen's compensation pension and was in pain a lot, though rosy-cheeked and always smiling. He grabbed for his cane and got up with effort from his chair, though Connie tried to keep him there.

"Well hello, little fella," he said, tottering above Adolph. "Say you're doing a wonderful job with him, Connie, we're so proud of you, bearing up. If there's anything we can do, we wantcha to let us know."

She hadn't told them she was working, and she'd warned her mother not to tell them; her mother had anyway known not to.

They gathered around the table, and Mom Wrobleski put out a cake, which had an epic tale behind it to tell, how it had come to be, as every cake did that year—the sugar, the raisins, the eggs. They took turns holding Adolph and feeding him cake. Connie had dressed him in his little brown suit like a soldier's with the tie attached—Mom said he looked like Herbert Hoover, but Buster said John Bunny. And all the time the hollow of absence and guilt and fear opened and shrank, opened and shrank again inside Connie.

His parents too had had letters from Bunce, and they brought them out to read while the percolator burbled comically. His letters to them were more detailed, less jaunty. He described the work he did to his father; he complained more expansively to his mother, who shook her head in sympathy and made that noise with tongue and teeth that has no name. And he gave them, carefully and thoroughly, the addresses where they could write back to him. *Gosh I miss you old folks at home.*

"I had a letter just yesterday," Connie said. They turned toward her, leaned in even, smiling and eager. The cake-matter turned in her stomach. "Well he's doing fine," she said. The coffeepot burped powerfully, not only throwing coffee up into the little glass bulb at the top but also lifting the lid to emit a puff of steam; Adolph laughed and made the noise too, and they all laughed together. Connie could go on. "He's moved on to a new plant," she said. "Everything's wonderful there. It's all new. He just went. They needed people."

"I'll be," said Mom. "Where did you say?"

"Ponca City," Connie said. "Van Damme Aero."

Buster clambered from his chair, making noises, going from chair-back to chair-back to his own big mauve armchair with the antimacassars on the arms and back, where he spent most of his day. Beside it there was a maple magazine holder, and from it he pulled a big picture magazine. "Here," he said. "For gosh sakes it must be here."

They laid it on the table amid them. The cover showed a vast semi-circle that you could only tell was a building because workers were streaming into it, tiny figures, maybe one of them Bunce. Harsh sunlight cast their black shadows on the macadam. BUILDING THE GREAT WARBIRD IN INDIAN COUNTRY, it said.

Buster flipped through the pages, past the ads for whiskey and cleaners and radio tubes and life insurance, every one telling how they were helping win the war. "Here it is," Mom said.

In the great hangar the wingless bodies were lined up one behind the other, each one with its crowd of workers around it. Married couples worked on the factory floor together, it said: one couple were midgets. In another part of the plant drafting tables went on farther than you could make them out, men and some women too bent over them and the fluorescent strip lighting overhead matching their white tables. Women who carried messages through the vast spaces to the designers and engineers went on roller skates!

" 'The cafeteria is larger than a city block,' " Mom read. " 'Seventeen hundred people can be served at a time.' " You could see them, six lines of workers in their uniforms, trays in hand, passing the steam tables. Mom looked again among them for Bunce, but Buster said they would have taken these pictures long ago, before the boy got there, use your head. The white walls, gleaming as though wet, were all made of tile.

" 'Each worker receives a health code number and a card, listing job capability and description and any health conditions,' " Mom read. " 'Three clinics serve the plant, and a full hospital is being built in the city nearby.' Imagine." There was a picture of a large man in a double-breasted suit, meeting with a delegation of Indians: Henry Van Damme. The health cards were his idea. He'd even thought of having a psychologist in the clinics. For instance to talk to, if someone lost someone in the war.

"Oh look," said Mom. A picture showed the nursery: you seemed to be looking in through wide high plate-glass windows at a bright indoors. In playrooms protected from plant traffic trained nurses cared for workers' children, hundreds of them, Mexican, Indian, black and white children all together. Cost was seventy-five cents a day, a dollar and a quarter for two kids. "Why that's not more than I—" Connie said, then stopped, but she hadn't been heard or understood. "Oh precious," she said: a boy in rompers, a smiling nurse bent down to hear him. " 'Fresh fruits and vegetables are abundant, grown in the huge Victory Gardens in surrounding fields.' "

They each turned the magazine to themselves to look, and passed it on. The sweep of the corn rows was like the curving sweep of the windowed nursery wall, like the sweep of the drafting tables under their banks of lights. They read every word. "If the world could be like this," Buster said.

When it was growing dark, Connie and his grandmother wrapped Adolph up again in his warm suit as he looked from one face to the other. Sometimes doing this Connie thought she could remember what it had been like to be handled this way, by big loving smiling people who did everything for you.

It was so clear outside you could see stars, though the sky was pale and green at the horizon, the thin bare trees and the buildings and the metal trellis of the overpass as though drawn in ink with fearful precision. Adolph lay against her, put to sleep by her motion. Bunce had said that ages ago, when we all were living in the woods, you had to keep quiet as you traveled so the wolves and such wouldn't hear you, which means it's natural that babies would fall asleep when their mothers walk. It makes sense.

You have to fight for him. Your man. She heard herself say it to herself. You have to not let him go, you have to fight, you can fight and you have to. The hard heels of her shoes struck the pavement. You have to go and fight for your man. It was part of what you had to do, and she knew she would.

The next day at the plant it was evident that something big was wrong. Lines had stopped moving that were always going when she got there; some of the ever-present racket was stilled, which made the place seem somehow bigger, empty and expectant. Before noon Connie ran out of parts to shape, and the little electric truck didn't roll by with more. Sometimes that had happened before, but she'd never had to wait more than a few minutes before it came, driven too fast by the man with one built-up shoe on his short leg. Connie looked around for the supervisor, but he wasn't where he usually was. There was nothing to do but stand by her machine, ready to go. She felt conspicuous even though no one was looking her way, except the man at the next machine whom she distrusted, who left his place with a foxy grin her way, took a seat on some boxes and lit a forbidden smoke.

Just then the noon horn sounded, though it wasn't nearly lunchtime. Everyone stopped working; some people downed tools and drifted toward the lunchroom and then came back again. Connie saw coming down the line a number of men, her own supervisor and some others in shirtsleeves, and three or four men grim-faced in overcoats and hats whom she had seen roving through the plant lately asking questions and making notes. They stopped at each station and said a few words to the workers and went on. The man next down from Connie listened and then tossed his cigarette to the floor and ground it with his heel in disgust.

"The plant's closing, sweetheart," said the man who reached her first. She could see that a badge was clipped to his lapel beneath the overcoat. "Everybody's going to be let go. Pack your gear and go down to payroll for severance."

She had no gear. He had moved on before she could speak. The union man, looking harried and put-upon—his wiry hair springing in exasperation from his temples—gave her a numbered chit and told her to hand it in with her time card. Connie opened her mouth to speak.

"Bankruptcy," said the union man. "Receivership. The jig's up. Go home. Apply tomorrow at the union office for unemployment compensation forms." One of the other men took his arm and drew him along. Workers were leaving their places and falling in behind them. The union man began walking backward like an usher at the movies, trying to answer questions. Connie could hear the big thuds of electric motors being shut down.

She followed the crowd. She thought it was a good thing that the union steward stood between the workers and the officers and managers who strode forward carrying their news; some of the people were angry and shouting, women were crying; some seemed unsurprised, they'd known it all along, mismanagement, big shots, profiteers. It felt like a march, a protest. At the juncture where you turned off to the cafeteria and the coatrooms and the exit, the crowd parted, some to go out and others, querulous or angry, still in pursuit of the closed-faced officers.

Connie turned back against the traffic.

She went, begging pardon, through the people and back down the now near-empty factory. A glimmer of dust that seemed to have been stirred up by the upheaval stood in the haloes of the big overhead lights. Connie went down the stairs and along the passage to the Number 3 building, where she had first been examined and tested. Once there— after a wrong turn into a wing of offices where more harried people were emptying file drawers and piling up folders, who looked up in suspicion to see her—she found the yellow line painted on the floor and followed it back toward the intake rooms. At first there seemed no one there at all, the nurse's station closed and the X-ray machine hooded in black, but in the room where tests were given she found the gray man in the gray cloth coat who had administered the Manual Dexterity and Visual Acuity Test. He was sitting on a table, a coffee mug beside him, swinging his legs like a child.

"Hello," she said.

He looked up, weary, maybe sad. She suddenly felt sorry for him.

"I wonder," she said. "If I could get back my test."

He said nothing; lifting his eyebrows seemed all he had the strength to do.

"I took a test when I came here. A month ago, or really five weeks. I . . . You said I did well. Visual Acuity. My name is Constance Wrobleski. I would like to have that test. Or a copy if you have one."

He seemed to remember, or maybe not, but he let himself down gingerly off the table—his socks fallen around his white ankles were dispiriting—and motioning to Connie to follow him he went back the way Connie had come. She wanted to say something, that she was sorry about the plant and the Bull, and would it be opening again later, and what would become of him now, but all these seemed like the wrong thing. At a turning he led her into those offices where she had earlier found herself by mistake. Now a woman had lowered her head onto her desk and apparently was weeping; no one paid attention to her, only kept on with what they were doing, which seemed at once pointless and urgent to Connie.

The man she followed was oblivious to all this, only went on stooped and purposeful as though this were a day like any other, moving along a rank of tall filing cabinets until he found the drawer he wanted; clicked its catch and slid it open on its greased tracks; fingered through the papers within, by their upstanding tabs; stopped, went back a few, and pulled out a paper, which he looked at up and down to make sure it was what he thought it was. It was a plain white form with the name of the test on it and her name and employee number. It listed the tests she'd taken, with a blue check next to each, and at the bottom a row of boxes to check, labeled Below Normal, Normal, Above Normal, Superior. Hers was checked in the Superior box.

"All yours," he said.

"You sure you don't need it?" she asked.

He laughed gently. "*I* certainly don't," he said. "You take that and go on. Find something else. You can help. You ought to."

It was after two by the time Connie got off one of the crowded buses

that were carrying away all the laid-off Bull workers. She'd been given ten days' severance pay but she hadn't worked long enough to get any unemployment compensation; there was, she was told, always welfare. The no-strike agreement the unions had all made with the government meant they wouldn't or couldn't stand up for the workers and get any better deal; things just had to go on as fast as they could, everybody dispersed to look for work elsewhere. Maybe the Bull works would be reorganized and reopen, maybe not, but you couldn't wait.

When she got to her building she realized that at this hour Mrs. Freundlich wouldn't be waiting for her with Adolph; she pressed the electric doorbell, but it didn't seem to be working, and she opened the door and went up. Just as she reached the apartment door it was flung open, Mrs. Freundlich red-faced and with an expression Connie couldn't name, shock or fear or guilt or.

"I'm off early," Connie said. She didn't feel like explaining. "I'll take Adolph now, all right?"

The woman glanced behind herself, as though she'd heard something that way. And back at Connie.

"You'll get the whole day's pay," Connie said.

Mrs. Freundlich turned from the door and marched away with a heavy tread that Connie realized she'd often heard without knowing what it was. She followed, across the worn Turkey carpet and the hulking mahogany table and sideboard—who brought such stuff into an apartment?—and into a bedroom. Adolph wasn't there, but on the steam radiator a pair of his pants was laid to dry.

"Oh dear," said Connie. "Oh no."

Without a word—she hadn't spoken one yet—Mrs. Freundlich opened the closet door. At first Connie couldn't see into the dark space, or was so unready for what was in there that she misread it. Adolph. Adolph had been put there, in the dark, amid the old lady's coats and dresses and shoes, on a little stool, and shut in. He looked like a culprit, eyes wide, holding his hands together as he did when he was frightened.

"Wouldn't mind," said Mrs. Freundlich. "I warned him. Warned you too."

"Oh my God my baby!" Connie reached with both hands into the closet and lifted Adolph out. Now he was crying, crying *Mommy* into her ear in awful gladness and clinging hard around her neck. "How long has he been *in* there?" Connie said to Mrs. Freundlich. "How could you *do* that, how *could* you," she cried, even as she bore the child out of the bedroom and out of the apartment as though from a fire. "You *awful woman!*"

"Serves him right," said Mrs. Freundlich, tramping after her, still red-faced and defiant. "All's I can say."

Connie pushed past her and out the door.

"You'll want his trousers," the old woman called after her.

Back in her own kitchen Connie decided that the best thing to do was never to speak to Adolph about what had happened in that place, never, and just love her son and teach him he was a good good boy and he didn't need to be afraid of anybody or anything. She told him so now, even as she tried to get him to loosen his hold on her; she could feel his heart beating against her.

"You're a good boy," she said. "A good boy."

In another part of her heart and mind she was making calculations, counting money she had and money she could get. She kept thinking and counting while Adolph napped in the bed beside her—unwilling to let her go, his big blond head buried in her side. When he awoke and after he ate, Connie pulled out his potty from where it was kept behind the bathroom door.

"I don't want to, Mommy," he said, regarding it with something like alarm, its white basin, its decals of rabbit and kitty.

"It's okay," Connie said. "Just try."

He hung back. Connie at last knelt before him, bringing her face right before his. "Okay, honey," she said. "Listen. We have to go on a trip. You and me. Okay? On a train. Okay?"

"Okay."

"We're going to go find your daddy. Okay?"

"Okay."

It occurred to Connie that sons had to love their fathers, but that if you were two years old and had never lived a human life before, you might not think it was strange to have your father leave. You wouldn't think anything was strange; you wouldn't know. You'd know well enough what you wanted and what you didn't, though.

"So you have to learn," she said, holding his shoulders in her hands. "To go in the potty. So we can travel, ride on the train. Okay?"

Of this he was less sure. He said nothing.

"Two weeks," Connie said. It would take her that long to close up the apartment, tell her parents and Bunce's parents, a hot wave of shame and foreboding at that thought, but this first, nothing without this. She held up a V of fingers before him. "That's how long you have, till we leave. Okay?"

"Okay."

"Okay!"

He was laughing now, and she started to laugh too. It was true and it was urgent, but it was funny too. "Two. Weeks," she said again. "You bunny."

They stretched the rules at the Van Damme dormitory in Henryville to let her have a space, because no children were allowed; it didn't seem to Connie that it was the first time the women at the desk had stretched the rules, or that the rules were all that important to them. They only needed to know that Adolph was toilet trained, and Connie could say Yes. Not a single accident since far to the north on the Katy Line, too late a warning, too long a line at the smelly toilet. Actually he'd got used to facilities of several kinds—rows of station toilets with clanging steel doors, overused toilets like squalid privies in crowded coaches; old Negro porters helped him, soldiers too, hey give the little kid a break. Once in a train so filled with soldiers and sailors it was impossible to move, they'd passed him hand to hand over the heads of the passengers till the far end of the coach was reached—he'd been game even for that, seeming to get braver and more ready for things with every mile. Now and then he'd whined and wept, and once worked up a nice tantrum, as though the new self coming out hurt like teething: but Connie'd have worried for him if he hadn't had one at least.

So the dormitory people tucked a little roller cot into the room she was allotted, best they could do, and after she'd whispered a story into his ear about trains and planes and cars, he slept. Exhausted as she was, she couldn't: not even his soft automatic breathing could seduce her into sleep. The small room was meant for four, two bunk beds, their ticking-covered mattresses rolled up, only her bed made. Like the first girl in a summer-camp cabin. The sheets were rough and clean. For a moment she wanted not to wonder at any of it, or think of it, just lie and look and feel. She was nowhere she'd ever thought to be.

Those two men who'd given her a ride out here hadn't been able to think of a way to find Bunce: the plant and its processes went on around the clock, but offices where inessential paperwork was done closed sometimes, and the union office was closed too when they tried to call there from the desk of the dormitory.

That crippled fellow: looking around the dormitory lounge where the women sat or played cards or table tennis or just came and went. The expression on his face. Never been inside here, he'd said. Connie wanted to tell him to withdraw a bit; he looked like a kid in a toy store, watching the electric train go around. Maybe that's why she tugged his coat, made him turn to face her, thanked him and kissed his cheek with gratitude. She thought about him, his handicap, what that would be like. She thought of the first day she'd gone to work at the Bull plant. It had taken all her strength to act on what she'd known she had to do—to get here with Adolph—and she didn't know what she'd do now, or what would come of it. She slept.

That night a hundred miles and more to the north of Ponca City, Muriel

Gunderson headed out on the dirt road from town to Little Tom Field and the weather station there. Muriel was on rotation with three other FAA weather observers, and while two shared the day and evening shifts, Muriel would be all by herself on the 0000 to 0008 shift. The drive out to the station was twenty miles—she got extra stamps—and while she didn't mind the night she got lonely and fretful sometimes, so she brought her old dog Tootie along with her for the company.

She let herself into the weather station, a small gray building and a shed between the two hangars that Little Tom Field offered. A couple of Jennys and an old retired Kaydet were tied up by their noses out on the field. She lit the lights and checked the instrument array, the thermometer, the wet bulb, and then the anemometer, which was at the top of a pole on the roof. She had to climb up the outside stair and then up a staggered row of iron footholds, detach the machine, take it down into the station, and record the wind speed—not much at all this still night—and then climb back up the pole to replace it while Tootie barked at her from below. She was always nervous about climbing the pole, not because she was afraid of heights—she wasn't, and was glad she'd wiped the grin off the face of the chief observer when he first told her she'd have to climb it. No, she was afraid that if a rusted step broke off or was wet or icy and she fell, there'd be no one who'd know about it for hours, except Tootie, and he was no Rex the Wonder Dog who'd go for help. Tootie'd bark and bark and then quit while she just lay there and died.

She made coffee on the hot plate and plotted her observations on the weather map, the part of the job she liked the best. At 0002 she went out to the shed to launch the balloon. It was cold now and she pulled on gloves—the helium tanks could be icy to the touch and the connections could take a long time to get right, especially for a single observer on a night shift. The empty balloon was slick and sticky like peeled skin when you took it from the box and you had to get it unfolded right and connected to the tank, and then you had to inflate it enough to get it aloft but not so much that it would burst from the decreasing pressure before it reached the cloud ceiling, which was high tonight. Muriel had set up the theodolite on its tripod to track it as it rose. When the limp balloon had started filling and swelling and lifting itself—there were always jokes about what it reminded you of, you couldn't make them around the unmarried girls—Muriel prepared the little candle in a paper lantern that it would carry upward. During the day you could just track the balloon itself against the sky until it disappeared, but at night you needed that light. Muriel thought: better to light one candle than to curse the darkness. She thought that once on every night shift: better to light one candle than to curse the darkness. She got tired of herself, sometimes, alone.

This night she got the balloon off all right, it rose lightly and confidently, there was no wind to snatch it out of her hand (take her hand too and maybe herself upward with it) and the candle stayed lit, and Muriel followed it with the scope of the theodolite, racking it upward steadily, losing the little dot of light and finding it again. Until at last it came to the cloud layer and dimmed and was gone. It always seemed brave to her, that little flickerer, like the light of an old Columbus sailing ship going off into the unknown.

She clamped the theodolite and took the reading down. She was returning to the station to phone in her report—Little Tom Field was too little even to have a Teletype, it was just a few acres of prairie outlined in lights—when she began to feel something. Later she'd say "hear something," but in that first moment it seemed to be something she felt. Tootie felt it too, and barked at it, whatever or wherever it was.

Muriel was used to some strange weather. She'd been knocked over by a fireball rolling through the station, and ached for a week; when a downpour followed hard on a dust storm, she called in a report of "flying mud balls," which they didn't like but which she was just then seeing smack the windows as though thrown by bad boys. So what was this coming?

Not weather, no. A sound: now it was certainly a sound, a big sound aloft, and she could start to think it was likely an aircraft of some kind though no lights were visible yet. It sometimes happened that lost aircraft would come in to Little Tom Field, or planes would land that didn't like the weather—once even a DC-2, the pilot had wanted to fly under the cloud cover (he told her), but company rules wouldn't let him fly that low. There was a dit-da transmitter in the station that sent out a signal all the time, just an International Code "A" for identification, but you could ride in on it if you had to, a little footpath in the sky.

Bigger than a DC-2. The high cloud cover was shredding as she expected it to and a full moon overhead glowed through. Whatever it was came closer, the felt sound growing into an awful, awesome noise. It was coming in way too low for its size and coming in fast. She felt like running away, but which way? Then there it was, good Christ, blotting out a huge swath of sky, its running lights out but streams of flame trailing out behind its wings. She'd never seen anything that big aloft. It lowered itself toward the field, which was almost smaller than itself, and it seemed just then to realize how hopeless a hope it was, this field it had come upon in its troubles, and it leveled off, not rising though but skimming between the earth and the clouds. It had *six engines* she could now see, and three of them were on fire and two of the other props were revolving in a halting hopeless way and they were all attached to the wrong side of the wing. It was passing overhead, lit by the field's lights, vast belly passing right over her and causing her, foolishly, to duck.

What was it, was this prairie under attack from some new Jap or German war machine we'd brought down? It had gone beyond the field's lights, but she could still feel its roar and still see, like the candle of the weather balloon, the sparkle of the fires coming from those engines. Out there where it went there were only low hills and woods. She waited, looking into that darkness, almost knowing what she would see, and yet seized with a huge shudder when not two minutes later she saw it, a bloom of flame-light that reflected from the clouds; then the dull thunder following after. Muriel was already headed for the shack and the telephone.

At about the same hour by the clock (though two hours later by the sun) Henry Van Damme was awakened in his bedroom that looked out to the Pacific over the city. It was his brother, who alone knew this telephone number. The silken body beside Henry in the wide bed stirred also at the sound, and Henry got up, bringing the phone with him on its long cord, and pulled on a dressing gown while he listened.

"I'm securing the site," Julius said. "The weather observer who saw it asked if it was an enemy bomber, she'd never seen the like."

"Crew?" Henry asked.

"Lost. Ship had lost power and they were too low to ditch when the fires started."

"Oh dear."

"It's the cylinder heads overheating," Julius said. "The cowl flaps need to be shortened. Ship was on its way to the coast for the modifications."

"Won't be enough," Henry said. "My guess."

Julius said nothing. They both knew the problem: that the B-30 was being designed, prototyped, tested, debugged, retested, built, and deployed all at the same time, and by ten or fifteen different companies, suppliers, builders, their old competitors, the government. How could it not keep going wrong in little ways, little ways that added up to big ways.

"Get everybody together as soon as we can," Henry said, though of course Julius would have already begun doing that.

"We'll ground the ships that are coming off the line now," Julius said. "Till we know what modifications work."

On the bejeweled map of the city outside Henry's wide plate-glass windows, lines of light like airstrips, not so bright as before the war, ran toward the sea, yellow, bluish, white. In the dark room a clock glowed, and beside its face a little window showed the date, white tiles that turned every twenty-four hours with a soft clack. The fourteenth of April 1944. No one would forget it.

"I'll call the families," Henry said. "Get me the names."

In the morning Connie and her son got breakfast in the dorm cafeteria, the women gathering around to see a child and touch him and marvel at him spooning oatmeal into his mouth with a big spoon. The desk found out where Bunce was, a house in Henryville, not far they said, and the shop roster said he was on the Swing Shift, so he might be there now.

Now.

The address they gave her didn't seem even to look like one—8-19-N? What did it mean? But they pointed her the way and she set out into the little town, vanishing and gray in the morning light, down the wide street (wasn't it too wide, and the houses too low, she thought for a minute it wasn't real, like those fake towns you heard were built above factories to hide them from bombers). Adolph walked a little, then had to be picked up and carried. Day came on, sweet and cool, the gray burned off, the town was real, people came out of some houses and waved to her and smiled. Each of the houses bore a number like the one written on her paper. At last she came upon a woman watering a window box of geraniums with a coffeepot and hailed her.

"Howdy," the woman answered. Connie didn't think people who weren't in the movies or in radio comedies really said Howdy, but the woman seemed to mean it. She had a huge paper or silk geranium, or maybe it was a rose, in her curled hair.

"Oh sure," she said when Connie showed her paper. "That's number eight on block nineteen of N Street. This-here's J Street, block fifteen, so y'all's got four blocks to go down and K, L, M, to go over, left. All right?"

"Yes, all right, thanks." They regarded each other for a moment. "Pretty flowers."

The woman touched the one in her hair, and turned back to her watering. For some reason Connie found her unsettling, her good cheer, her strange speech, her being at home here. She kept on, feeling excluded. When she approached the right block, Adolph had grown insupportably heavy, like baby Jesus in the Saint Christopher story, and her armpits were damp. That would be it. No it wasn't: a small plump woman, a bottle blonde, just then came out of it, turned to wave good-bye to someone inside, then closed the door behind her and set out, smiling and pulling straight her girdle. Was it across the street? Odd numbers on one side, even on the other. The last house was 9. His was 8. Connie went on to the next block. Some blocks had no number or letter signs, never put up or fallen off.

"Mommy."

"Yes, bunny."

"Mommy I'm hot."

"Okay, hon."

She turned back. The houses were so identical. It must be that one, but wasn't that the one the blond woman had come out of? Now she wasn't sure. But it had to be it. She went up the path, just a couple of feet, and knocked at the door, thinking nothing now but that she wanted to be somewhere inside where she could put Adolph down, and almost instantly, as though he'd been standing just behind it, Bunce opened it.

"Hello," she said.

He said nothing. He was in his underwear, a singlet and wrinkled shorts. Just seeing him a torrent of warm gratitude filled her, her son grew lighter, she knew she'd done the right thing, it'd been hard and she'd never been sure and now she was. "Here's Adolph," she said.

"Connie, what the hell." He looked from her to his son as though trying to remember them and then suddenly remembering. A great grin broke over his face, he took the boy from her and lifted him high. Adolph squealed in delight at Bunce's delight and at the heave Bunce had given him, but looked away, toward nothing or for something. His father lifting him in his big hands, his hands.

"I didn't write to tell you," she said. "I thought you'd tell me not to come."

There was almost nothing in the house, an unmade bed, a kitchen table and chairs, another smaller bare bed in another room; a new refrigerator; a big bamboo chair, with a floor lamp beside it; and some kind of box or crate with rope handles used for a table, covered with stuff, an apple core, a root beer bottle, papers and comic books. Bunce liked comic books.

"Why would I tell you not to come?" He wasn't looking at her but at Adolph, who was trying to balance standing on Bunce's thighs where he sat in the bamboo chair. Their eyes were locked together, as though a current passed between them. "Who wouldn't want a visit from his wife? His son?"

Connie sat on a straight-backed kitchen chair. She hadn't taken her coat off. "Well, I guess," she said. "Sure."

"Daddy," said Bunce. "Daddy. Say Daddy."

Adolph laughed in that funny way he had, as though he didn't actually believe you, but he said nothing.

"So how," Bunce said. "How'd you, I mean, the train and all. I mean I've sent you what I could."

"I bought the tickets. One way."

Bunce still smiling turned to her. "With what?"

"I had the money." This had gone a way she'd known she'd have to go, but faster than she'd been ready for. "Well," she said again. "You won't believe it. I got a job."

Now Bunce pulled Adolph's exploring hands away from his face. "A job? Connie."

"You know everybody's working now. I thought I could help."

"Did you ask me whether I thought you ought to get a job? Did you even tell me you had this in mind?"

He'd put Adolph down and stood, looming over her a little. She knew better than to answer right off, that these weren't actual questions but statements to be listened to without expression.

"Jesus, Connie. What the hell."

"Bunce," she cautioned him in a whisper, pointing to Adolph. He turned away from both of them and seemed suddenly to realize he wasn't dressed. He went into the bedroom and from the floor picked up a pair of trousers and began furiously pulling them on. Why was this house such a mess? He hated mess.

"So where was this job?" he said. "By the way."

"Well that's the crazy part," Connie said, willing a big smile. "It was at the Bull plant. That's where I was sent. How do you like that."

So that was said, and he didn't blow up, just went into the bathroom and stood for a minute looking in the little mirror over the sink, then turned on both faucets, cupped his hands, splashed water on his face and neck, and took a towel from a hook to rub himself. Then he stood looking into the mirror a long time.

"You know you made a liar out of me, Connie?" he said.

"What?" she said, feeling a stab of panic.

"Maybe a criminal too," he said, still looking only in the mirror. "My draft registration. It says I do necessary war work, *and* that I'm the sole support of my family." He turned to her at last. "You think of that?"

"Well you could have maybe changed it," she said softly.

"Sure. And lost my deferment maybe too," he said. He tossed away the towel. "Okay. You're gonna quit."

"I don't need to quit," she said. "That's the next crazy part. They went out of business."

"What?"

"The whole plant. There were marshals and everything. They threw us all out."

"What the heck. Where was the union? They can't do that."

Connie explained what she'd seen, what she knew, what the papers had said, hadn't he seen it in the papers? Hadn't his mom and Buster told him?

"Goddam profiteers," Bunce said. "Serves them right." He aimed this darkly right at Connie, as though she were one of them, or it was her fault. Then, in sudden realization that time had gone on while she'd unfolded these things before him, he said to no one or to himself: "Man I've got to go, got to get to work."

"I couldn't figure out why," Connie said.

"Why what? Why they closed? Cause they're dopes. Crooks. Just out to take from the working man."

"No, but why? What did they do so badly?"

"What's it have to do with you? You don't have to worry about that stuff."

Connie lowered her eyes, catching up with herself. "I was just wondering," she said.

"So it doesn't matter anymore," he said, and came to kneel by her chair, where Adolph stood to look up at her. "That's good."

"So I came," she said.

"Uh."

"I just wanted us to be together again. The three of us staying together."

He disengaged from their embrace. "Not here," he said.

"Well I just thought . . ."

"Connie. Our home's not here. When all this is over . . ."

"My mom's watching out for the apartment. It's all all right. I had the gas turned off and the electricity. She can send the furniture anytime, Railway Express, it won't cost that much. I have the money."

Maybe she shouldn't have said that last part. He'd risen away from her now with a look that made Adolph start to cry, she'd cry too if she didn't keep up her courage. Why'd she just blurt all that out?

"That's swell, Connie," he said, not loud. "That's just swell. You don't ask me a damn thing, you just decide we're not living in our *own damn house* anymore, that you're a *working girl,* that you— Shut up!" He shot that at Adolph, who only cried louder, and Bunce picked him up and held him.

"I read about this place here," she said. "It was at your mom's." Tears were leaking from her eyes, she tried to just keep on. "It seemed so wonderful. That you could help, that you could be a help and be useful, and still have a good life, a family life. You could have what you needed."

"You're going back," he said, his words soothing in sound for Adolph's sake but not in import.

"I saw the pictures of the nursery in the plant, and the part about the free clinics, the way everything was thought of." She thought of telling him about Mrs. Freundlich but stopped herself. She wiped her eyes with her wrists. "I just wanted to help."

Bunce holding Adolph put his hand in Connie's hair.

"Well you're not working here," he said, grinning as at an impossibility, but not actually amused. "Honey no."

"Oh Bunce."

He lifted her up and by the hand and led her to the broad bamboo chair. He sat, drawing both of them into his lap. "Connie," he said,

252 / JOHN CROWLEY

and stroked her cheek with the back of his hand. "Baby. You think I want to see you every day on that floor in a pair of trousers? What are we going to do, head out for work together every day with our toolboxes?"

"Women do. People do."

He pressed his face against her neck, his sweet lips. "Sure they work. Till they get enough money to get their fur coat. Then they quit. Or when their man comes home from overseas. You'll see them down tools right in the middle of the shift. 'My man's home, I'm done.' "

"Oh Bunce."

"You know when my dad was first hurt, Mom went to work, in that hotel kitchen. It almost killed Dad; it was worse than his back. Him sitting home and his wife working. My mom."

Just as he said that, Connie's eyes fell on a comic poking out from under the others on the box-table. The part of the cover she could see showed a woman, caped and booted in red, her arms extended the way flying heroes always held them and she never did when she flew in dreams. The woman was shooting straight down through the clouds, toward earth presumably, and toward the bottom of the book, where huge red letters spelled *MOM*.

"I gotta get to work," he said, lifting her.

She let him go and dress, watched him and talked with Adolph: See Daddy put on socks, put on boots and lace them up, put on his shirt and button it up to his neck, and his jacket. She wandered the little place, went into the bathroom, where Bunce's razor and brush and cup of soap stood on the back of the sink. He used a straight razor, liking the skill it took, proud of his skill with it. A comb there too, clogged with hair. Blond hair.

"Do you live here all alone?" she called to Bunce, and when he couldn't hear she came out with the comb in her hand and asked again.

"Of course not," he said. "Couldn't afford it. I have a fellow lives here, that's his room over there. Except he just got fired for some black market stuff, stealing from the company, and he's gone. Good riddance to bad rubbish."

He was done dressing, he was Bunce again, broad belt buckled and the long end tucked in, crushed cap on—he put it on Adolf, then back on himself as Adolph reached for the buttons on it.

"What'll I do?" Connie said. "Adolph's going to get hungry."

"There's milk in the icebox," Bunce said. "And here." From the table he picked up his brown pay envelope, two-fingered out the bills, a thick wad it seemed to her, and took a five to give her. "There's a bus that stops at the corner, that way. It goes out to the market. They'll tell you where. Go buy some food."

"Okay."

He took her in his arms. "So no more about working," he said. "You make a home for us."

"All right I'll try," she said—what else, in his arms, could she do?— and it wasn't as though she lied, or didn't mean it; it was as in Confession, when you had a Firm Purpose of Amendment in regard to something sinful (Bunce, the back seat of the Plymouth) and meant it with all your might even as you heard yourself dissent deep inside, a you that you knew you'd listen to, the you on whose side you always really were. The priest called that a Mental Reservation.

"Good," he said. "I love you, Connie."

"Oh God I love you too Bunce, so much." So rarely could he say it to her with that kind of plain sincerity that it swept her hotly to hear it, and she assented within herself, she'd do what he asked, all that he asked, with only the Mental Reservation because there was no help for that.

When he'd shut the door she looked around herself. She could clean up.

"Daddy," said Adolph, as you might say *A storm*.

"Daddy," Connie said, nodding. "Tell him that. Daddy."

She pushed the papers on the table into a pile, and the comic book with the red-clad heroine on it came out, and she saw she'd got it wrong. The girl—Mary Marvel, a windblown skirt and cascade of chestnut curls—was flying not down but up, through the clouds to blue sky beyond, and the real title of the book, now right side up, was *WOW*.

Toward the end of his shift, as he was making his way up the Assembly Building, Prosper caught sight of the woman from the train station, Connie, and her boy, walking slowly and both looking upward, as once he had done on first entering here. The boy was pointing up into the fantastic tangle of beams and struts filling the spaces overhead.

He reached where they stood and looked up with them. A crane car was now drifting with great slowness toward them, carrying an entire assembled wing section slung below and hanging in midair.

"Uh-oh," he said. "They've got it backward."

"Oh. Oh hi."

Connie looked where he looked: it made her heart sink toward her stomach to watch the wings proceed down the line. They weren't finished, they needed their final pieces on each end, she could see that, but they had their huge engines all installed, three on each side, and yes, she saw that they were on the wrong edge, they were on the behind edge not the leading edge where all airplanes have their engines.

"Oh gee," Prosper said. "This one'll never fly."

Was he joking? He had to be. Above the moving wing assembly she could see the crane operator, a woman. Maybe she'd made some dreadful . . . But no, of course not, all the dozens of men on the floor were look-

ing up too, whole teams ready to mount the rolling staircases and assist
the mating, which wasn't different in a way from affixing the wings crosswise on a little balsa-wood model, the notches precut to receive the tabs.
They'd surely see if anything wasn't right. She felt Prosper's hand on her
elbow—looking upward she hadn't seen him come so close as to touch
her—and he was smiling. "Nah. They told me the same thing when I
started," he said. "They're called pusher engines. They work fine. They
push instead of pulling. They told us how, but I couldn't repeat it."

Now the two parts were coming together, so slowly as to seem
unmoving. A team of men (and one tall woman) guided it down—they
seemed able to move it with a touch, vast as it was. The little people—
they seemed little now compared to it, its huge tires and struts and
expanses of silvery metal—swarmed up the ladders and made ready to
do whatever they had to do to link them.

Connie walked on. She'd begun to see, in that moment, as though
through the confusing reflection of thousands of overhead bars of light
on shiny identical parts, how it was meant to work, how it *did* work.
Behind the plane another middle part stood, and another crane now
turned the corner bringing in another pair of wings to be rested on it.

Who thought of this? she wondered. How long did it take to think
of? Did people just know that's the way big airplanes had to be built, or
was it a new plan just for these? Did they argue about it, work it all out,
come to an agreement? If it didn't work, and it was you who'd thought
of it and convinced the others, what happened to you? Did you lose
your job and have to go away in shame? Or did they spread the blame
around, and just set to work to do better? Nobody'd ever explained any
of this to her. Maybe everybody knew about it, maybe it was so univer-
sally known that nobody thought they needed to explain it to her. She
bet not, though. She bet almost nobody knew it, not all these women
and men working away, the shop stewards and the engineers unrolling
their blueprints, toolshops dispensing tools, she bet none of them knew
any more than she did. She wondered if they'd even wondered. If *she*
had, they must have, mustn't they? Some of them at least. A few.

She became aware of Adolph tugging at her slacks. Somehow the
place didn't alarm or terrify him, maybe it was just too huge to be perceived, out of his ken.

"Yes, hon."

He tugged again, she was to get it. "Tired and hungry," she said to Prosper. "We came to see where his daddy works." She showed him the VISITOR pass she'd been given.

"Well say," he said. "Maybe he'd like an ice cream. There's a milk bar just down in the far corner there, off the floor."

"Really. Well, that's nice. We'll do that."

"I'm just off," Prosper said. "I could use a soda too. Mind if I . . ."

"No no," Connie said. She looked down at Adolph. "Okeydokey?" she said.

The milk bar was a long space with the wide plate-glass windows that were everywhere here, as though no one should be hidden from anyone else, the common job proceeding in your sight even if you weren't doing it, and if you were, showing you what you could do next, relax and enjoy. It was sort of self-service, you stood in line and ordered from a long menu, then moved away to be given what you'd ordered. The whole place was painted in pink, pale brown, and yellow, like Neapolitan ice cream.

"Oh gee I forgot, I didn't bring any money," Connie said. "Oh I'm so sorry." They were already far up the line, and Adolph, who knew where he was now, was reaching symbolically toward the treats being handed out. What had she thought, that this was a date?

"I think I've got some," Prosper said. "A little."

"Oh no," she said. "No no."

"Sure." Balancing on each crutch in turn, he rooted in his right then his left pocket. He held out the coins he'd found to her in his palm, and she counted them with a forefinger. Not much.

"It's all right," she said. "I mean I don't really need."

"No come on," he said. "An ice cream for, for Adolph, and why don't we split an ice-cream soda? Would that be all right?"

"Well." He was so, what, so willing, no standing on pride, it made her smile. "All right."

"Double chocolate?"

"All right."

She got Adolph's ice cream; she was making for a booth when she looked back—Prosper still stood at the counter and the soda was before him and Connie realized he'd have a hard time carrying it away, maybe couldn't at all, had he always had someone to help? He must need it. Like Adolph. But never really growing all the way up.

She got the soda and they sat; Adolph dug into the ice cream and Connie and Prosper de-papered their straws and plunged them into the dark foaming soda together; took a suck; raised their eyes to meet. Like a kid's first date, she thought, like one in the movies anyway.

It was that scene, displayed by the picture windows, that Vi Harbison saw, just knocking off then too. Stopped even to observe for a bit, occluded by the crowd passing outward around her: how absorbed they were, spooning, sucking, speaking, smiling. Ain't that grand, she thought, and she really thought it was; almost laughed a hot dangerous laugh at the pleasure it gave her, well well well.

They weren't quite done, still sucking noisily at the bottom of the glass in its silvery holder, when Bunce came by. In the great seamless transition from shift to shift nearly everyone going out passed these windows, this place, which is why it was where it was.

He banged in through the glass doors and was beside Connie's booth before she knew he'd come in.

"What are you doing, Connie?"

He shot one look at Prosper and no more, inviting no remark.

"Bunce."

"Are you trying to make a monkey out of me?" He lifted Adolph from his seat, who began to complain, not done yet. "Come on."

Connie glanced once at Prosper, who'd neither moved nor spoken, whose face was attempting to express nothing but a pleasant detachment, and rose to follow Bunce out.

"So what the hell's all that?" Bunce said, still a step ahead of her.

"I came to visit. To see if I could find you, see where you worked." She showed him her pass.

"And you found that guy instead." He flicked one look her way, then fiercely on ahead again. "You don't know what it's like around here," he said. "The men around here."

She caught up with him, took his arm.

"Bunce," she said with soft urgency. "Just look at him."

Prosper was gathering himself now to leave the table, and Bunce stopped, looked back to see him manipulate his crutches, swing his inert legs away from the table, steady himself, and attempt to rise; fail; try again, and succeed. Then set off.

"Yeah well," Bunce said.

258 / JOHN CROWLEY

"I was being nice."

"Yeah." He looked down at her. "Yeah well. Be careful too."

She took his arm. Adolph was still held in his other arm. She wanted to look back too, and see how Prosper had managed in the milk bar, if he'd got out all right, but that only made her cling tighter to her husband. "So you'll be home for dinner," she said. "I'll make a Swiss steak."

"I can't come home. I'll be back late."

"Why? Where are you going? Do you have overtime?"

"No."

"Then what—"

"Nothing."

"Well what—"

"Connie, you don't ask me!" He shifted Adolph violently in his grip. "Connie you just come down here, you bust right into my life here without asking, and you . . . Just listen when I tell you. I'll be back later."

She said nothing more, marched along beside him, didn't shrug away his arm when again he took hers. She'd come so far. She'd come to fight for him, and she knew what that meant, it meant actually *not* fighting. She knew what happened to the desperate weepers and beggars, the cold schemers and the furious hair-pullers, they never won and she wasn't going to be one of them. You just kept your head high. You waited and you saw it through and stayed ready and kept your head high. The only way you could lose was if you stopped wanting to win.

In that month a directive came down from the front office, ultimately from the War Department, that all men with deferments had to report to their local draft boards to be reassessed. Rollo Stallworthy told the men on his team that this did not, repeat not, mean that anyone was necessarily going to lose his deferment. Just Our Government at Work, he said: they want to make sure they're using every available person to maximum gain. Most of the men at Van Damme had registered at draft boards far away, so arrangements were made to bus the men to the capital, rather than burden the local Ponca City board and cause delays in getting back to work. Chits were handed out.

Prosper's draft status was ambiguous. He'd gone down that first time to register, before the war began. Then somehow the notice to report for his physical never came, or had been missed. (Actually Bea had discarded it, supposing the army must know better and it had come in error.) Then he'd worked at The Light in the Woods, and all the workers there who weren't already iv-F got a provisional deferment, till they quit or were otherwise let go; then he'd left town. So he signed up to be sent with the others, in order to be finally rejected. On a morning growing fearsomely hot, he mounted a bus with the skilled machinists, tool-and-die men, draftsmen, engineers, farm laborers, Indians, and fathers in war work (fatherhood alone wasn't enough now), and took an empty seat. A school trip hilarity prevailed on the bus as it set out, except among a few men who found the exercise a waste of time (the unions were arguing with Van Damme Aero as to whether the men would be paid for this jaunt) or who actively feared losing their status: not every floor sweeper or lightbulb changer or pharmacist's helper in the vast complex was "a man necessary to national defense" and might see his cozy iii-A rating evaporate. We didn't all want to be heroes.

The bus had turned out onto the highway, a hot breeze coming in the window, when someone changing his spot sat down next to Prosper. Momentarily, Prosper tasted chocolate ice cream. It was Connie's husband. Bunce.

Prosper moved his crutches out of the way and gave Bunce a nod; Bunce thumbed the bill of his cap in minimal greeting. He neither spoke nor smiled, and turned away. Neither of them remarked on Bunce's having shifted seats. Bunce pulled from his denim coat pocket a toothpick, and chewed delicately. Prosper felt sweat gather on his neck and sides.

"So this is stupid," Bunce said at last, but not as though to Prosper. "I've got a war job, I've got a family dependent on me." He turned then to point a look at Prosper. "You know? A family."

Prosper made small sympathetic facial movements, what're you gonna do. They rode in silence a time, looking forward, till Bunce, still unsmiling, began to regard Prosper more deliberately, as though he were a thing that deserved study. Prosper had been the object of hostile scrutiny before, though not often so close to him. He thought of Larry's instructions, how to win a fight, or not lose one.

"So that's tough," Bunce said. He made a gesture toward Prosper's body.

Prosper made a different face.

"What's the toughest thing?" Bunce said. "I mean, living that way."

Prosper cast his eyes upward thoughtfully, as though considering possibilities. "Well I think," he said, "the toughest thing is drying my ass after I get out of the bath."

Not the shadow of a smile from Bunce. That line always got a laugh.

Bunce withdrew the toothpick. "I think I'm asking a serious question."

"Do you mean," Prosper said, "not having the chance for a wife and kids, a family I mean, such as yours?"

Bunce made no response.

"Well yes," Prosper said. "Yes, I'd have to say. Not having that. That's hard."

"I knew this guy," Bunce said. "He used to go around the bars and the Legion hall. He had no legs. He rolled on a little truck, with these wooden blocks on his hands to push with. He made candies, and sold them. Always smiling."

Prosper smiled. Bunce didn't.

"Funny thing was," Bunce said, "if you saw him in his own neighborhood, not making his rounds. I did once. He had a couple of, I guess, wooden legs. And two canes. He was dressed in a suit. He looked fine."

"Oho," said Prosper, not wanting to seem too familiar with this dodge.

"He had a wife," Bunce said.

"He did. Well."

"Not bad looking, either."

"How do you like that."

The bus swung around a sharp right, entering the streets of the capital. Bunce fell heavily against Prosper somehow without taking his eyes from him. Then he climbed out of the seat. "Do yourself a good turn," he said. "Stay away from my family."

5

On a Friday night the Teenie Weenies bused or drove into Ponca City to watch Vi play fast-pitch softball with the Moths under the lights. The little stadium had been built by the oil company, but the new lights were Van Damme's gift to Ponca City. The game was an exhibition game against the Traveling Ladies, a touring pro club, to promote war bonds.

"Now how are *women* gonna play this g-g-g-game," Al said, imitating Porky Pig, "when among the l-l-l-lot of them they haven't got a single b-b-b-b—"

"Shut up, Al," said Sal.

Sal and Al had come with Prosper. The park was packed, and all the lower bleachers full. Sal and Al liked to get a seat in the lowest row so they didn't have to stand on their seats like nine-year-olds just to see. But not today. The steps were okay for climbing, and they went high up, passing as they went Bunce, Connie, and their son, primly in a row, Bunce for once without his cap. Prosper made himself seem too preoccupied with going upward to acknowledge her or him or them, and they looked out at the warm-ups on the field.

The Traveling Ladies were show-offs, in their striped schoolgirl skirts and knee-high socks, hats like Gay '90s ballplayers with a fuzzy button on the top; but they played hard. They played hard and made it look easy, making fancy catches for no reason, setting up nick-of-time plays on purpose—you could catch them at it if you watched closely. Whenever they cleared the bases they tossed the ball round the horn with a little individual spin or jump or bend for each of the infielders, the third baseman always pretending not to notice and waving to the crowd up until the last moment, when she turned and snagged the ball backhand and laughed. When they got well ahead they'd sometimes pretend to be checking their makeup in little hand mirrors or exchanging gossip with the first base coach and let a ball go by them and a runner make a base she shouldn't have—as though they were acting in a movie about girl baseball players as much as actually being them. The crowd loved it.

But Vi and the Moths played hard too, a little grim in the face of all the funning, but Vi as good as anything the Ladies could show, her fiery fastball taking their best sticks by surprise. Most softball pitchers change their stance when they change their pitch—this way for a fastball, that way for a slider—but Dad had taught Vi to stand always the same, give nothing away, her body preternaturally still just before she wound up and fired. And unlike most pitchers who just stoop a bit when they throw, as though they were pitching horseshoes, Vi's knuckles nearly scraped the ground, the big pill floating and dropping trickily or slamming into the catcher's glove.

Prosper's difficulty in ballparks was that he missed most of the exciting plays, when all around him the spectators rose to their feet to see the ball sail over the fence or the fielder make the catch, or just in spontaneous delight or astonishment or outrage. He couldn't get up fast enough and would finally be standing by the time everybody else had cooled off and sat down again. He liked a so-so game. This wasn't that. This night he also wanted a clear sight of Connie and Bunce and the boy with the unfortunate name, just down there between the heads and hats. What he saw, as an inconclusive inning was drawing to an end, was a blond woman, one he knew and had himself swapped wisecracks with, slip into their row and seat herself beside Bunce. Connie on his other side. It seemed to Prosper that the blonde—was her name Frances?—actually leaned around Bunce to greet Connie, which seemed to take a lot of crust. Prosper couldn't help but feel for Bunce in between them.

Just then, the Ladies' right fielder, with a three-and-two count on her, backed off a high inside pitch, and then came running out at Vi, bat in hand, yelling that she'd been aimed at; then she turned on the umpire who called after her, denouncing him in fury as the spectators variously booed and cheered. The ump threatened to toss her out of the game. She stuck out her tongue at him, a dame after all, and at that the ump did order her out, or tried to—the Ladies instantly came off the bench in a crowd, yelling and gesturing; when they made for Vi on the mound, the Moths rushed the infield. A fine rhubarb, everyone pushing and shoving and those girlie skirts flying while the men rose and roared. It was hard not to believe they'd got into it on purpose just for the fun of it; certainly Vi, alone and superb on the mound, chewing bubble gum and waiting for the dust to settle, seemed to think so.

Prosper had seen nothing much but backs and behinds, but when the view cleared again he saw in some alarm that Connie, Adolph in tow, was mounting the steps toward where he sat, and even from that distance Prosper could see grim resolve in her face, or maybe fury. By the time she reached his pew she was smiling theatrically, not for his sake he knew, and indicated she'd like the seat next to him, yes that one, if Sal would scoot down a bit, yes thanks, Prosper turned his knees outward so she and Adolph could work their way past him. She sat. She still said nothing, only looked on him with a blind beatific gaze.

"Hi there," he said.

She seemed not to notice that Adolph was tugging her arm, trying to be released from her ferocious grip.

Play resumed, the apologetic Lady fielder kept in the game, Vi scrunching her shoulders, gloving the ball, warming up.

"So," Connie said icily. "Who are you rooting for?"

"Well, the Moths," said Prosper. "Of course."

"Well, sure."

"But the Ladies are, well."

"Yes, they sure are. They sure know their stuff." The smile unchanged, as though it was going to last forever.

He thought it would be best to face front, not engage in eye-play, no matter how innocent. His pose was that she'd happened to desire to change her seat, for reasons he couldn't be expected to know, and happened to choose the one next to him, ditto. How much of this his face and body expressed to distant onlookers he couldn't be sure. "Though actually, I guess," he said to the air. "I guess I'd hope they both could win."

"Well that's dumb," she said. "They can't both."

"I know."

"It's stupid."

He chanced a glance in her direction. The smile was gone. "Maybe better say," he said, "I don't want either of them to lose."

Vi gave up a big hit then, and once again Prosper lost sight of the field, though Connie was up as fast as anyone. When they sat, Bunce and Francine—that was her name—down the bleachers were revealed, and it was apparent her arm was in his, and just then she laid her head on his shoulder. At that, Bunce's head swiveled a bit to the rear, as though tempted to look back up toward Connie, then changed its mind and swiveled back.

"God damn it," said Connie.

"Hey," Prosper said softly. "It's okay." But Connie had got up again, and lifted unsurprised Adolph to her hip, and begun pushing out of the row. Prosper held up a hand to forestall her, gathering his crutches and preparing to stand, as there was no way she could climb over him without everybody losing their dignity, which he thought mattered.

"Now listen, Connie, you're not, you're not gonna . . ."

"I'm just getting out of here. I'm sorry."

"Well hold your horses." He wasn't sure she wasn't going to go down and black his eye, or hers, kid or no kid, and he had a feeling that the vengeance for that would be wreaked on him, not Connie. He'd got up from his seat and stepped into the aisle, Connie after him, and as he turned to get out of the way downward, the tip of his right crutch landed on something, a candy wrapper maybe, something slick that slid away, turning him halfway around; in putting out his left crutch in haste to stabilize himself, he overshot the step and put it into air—it went down to the next step, and he knew he was falling, stiff-legged, face forward and one arm behind. The steps were concrete, as he'd already noticed; he actually had a moment to consider this as they rushed up toward him and a high shriek filled his ears, not because of something happening on the field—out, home run, grandstand play—but for his own disaster. Then for a while he knew nothing at all.

"You look bad," Vi said. "Very bad."

"It's just my face," Prosper said. The scabs had hardened around his chin and cheek, and the bruises at his nose, spreading under his left eye, were the colors of a sinister sundown. Plaster bandage across his forehead. He lay in his bed on Z Street, where Vi the morning after the game had gone to find him. "I'm all right otherwise. Except for the wrist."

He held it up to her, rigid in its wad of windings. He'd "come to" pretty quickly, though he had little memory now of what had happened before the stretcher that the ambulance men rolled him onto was lifted to slide into the little brown van with its flashing red light. A small crowd gathered there at the ballpark entrance to see him off.

"I can't walk," he said. "Not for a week or so. Not broken though. Just a sprain." He didn't describe the bruises up and down his thighs from the contact of the stone steps with the metal that encased them. By the bed he lay in, which Pancho had pulled out into the sitting room for him, was the wheelchair the clinic had furnished him with, an old model with a wicker seat and wooden arms. It wouldn't fit into the bathroom; getting out of it and then up onto the john with only one hand working was a process. Of course when he was without his braces he always sat on the pot, like a girl. He kept all that to himself.

"I heard at the shop they were making you a new pair of crutches."

"So they said." He tried a smile. "They're good fellows. It's kind."

"People like to help."

"I'll be up and around before they're done."

"Well you might still use this chair, though. Easier for getting to work, maybe. Or church. You know."

"Oh. Well I wouldn't want to use it in the street."

"Why not?"

"Oh I don't know." He knew: lame but upright was one thing, but in a wheelchair he knew how he'd be regarded. Even by Vi herself, maybe, at first sight anyway, and that would be the only sight he'd likely get. "So who won the game?"

"They did. Ten-six." She looked at him long and somehow appreciatively. "I'm not ashamed. We came off better than you did."

"Hum." With his elbows he hoisted himself up a little on the bed, bandaged wrist held up.

"Was this the worst one ever?" Vi'd seen him go down once before, not badly.

"Just about. I fell a lot when I was a kid. I got used to it. But the older I got the farther my head got from the floor. It's a long way down these days."

"The way you do it," Vi said. With her forearm she illustrated his headlong fall, like a felled tree. "Anyway," she said. "That was my last game."

"What," said Prosper. "Season's just starting."

"I'm quitting, Prosper," she said. "Not the team. Van Damme. I'm done."

"What do you mean?" A coldness began to grow in him, starting from way down in, below any physical part of him. "What's that supposed to mean?"

"I'm quitting means I'm quitting," she said. For a moment her eyes left his, and then returned, frank and warm.

"You're not leaving," he said.

"Well I'm not staying here if I'm not working." She put a hand on him. "Listen, this is really amazing. There was a woman I met when I first left home. Maybe you remember—I told you—I think I did . . ."

"The one in the truck."

"Yes! You know I've never stopped thinking about her, I don't know why. Maybe because she was the first, the first war worker I met. I don't know. But anyway guess what."

"What."

"She found out I work here, and she came to see me."

"Okay," Prosper said, his apprehension unrelieved. "Good."

"Guess how she found me."

"Stop making me guess, Vi." That coldness was growing, going farther up, it was nothing he'd known before and at the same time he knew it.

"She saw that big magazine article that Horse wrote about the team. She knew right away."

"Oho."

"And so. We've been talking. She quit the place she was working, driving trucks, and we're going up north together. Up to my daddy's place. We're going to get it going again. We've decided."

Her eyes looked down away again, as though they knew how much they shone and were a little shy about it, but they came back, alight, ablaze. "You want to meet her?"

"Sure. Sometime."

"She's outside now. Her name's Shirley." She rose, holding out a hand at him that meant Stay there, which was ridiculous, and she laughed at herself, but Prosper didn't laugh.

"Wait, Vi."

"Yes?"

"What about me?"

"What do you mean, what about you? You're not aiming to come be a cowboy, are you?" When he said nothing, she stopped. "Do you mean," she asked, "you and me?"

He didn't need to answer that. She came back and sat on the edge of the bed. She took his shoulders in her long wise hands. "Prosper. You and me. That was good, that was such fun, it meant a lot. You're a fine man, the best kind. But now. It's got to be the way it is."

Prosper, looking up at her, thought for a horrified moment that he might weep, for the first time since childhood. "Is that what *he* said? Is that what he said to you, Vi, something like that? Is that the thing you're supposed to say?"

The door opened then, tentatively, at the same time as the person entering knocked on it. A dark blonde, large-mouthed and large-eyed, older than Vi and a bit stringy, but Prosper responded, his Sixth Sense alerted, which made the whole thing worse, as he wanted to say to Vi but could think of no reason to.

"This is Shirley," Vi said.

Shirley lifted a tentative hand to Prosper, not sure how welcome she was but smiling.

"Hi, come on in. Sorry I can't, you know."

She waved him still, talking with her hands, to Vi too, whose shoulder she patted.

"So you two," Prosper said, still uncertain of his self-control. "Going off to, to wherever it is. Where the buffalo roam."

"Yep," said Vi. "Back in the saddle again."

"Yep," Shirley said. "Rockin' to and fro."

They both laughed.

"The war's not over, you know, Vi," Prosper said, with something like reproach. "There's more to do."

"Oh sure," Vi said. "Yes. Well I'm going back into the cattle business. Those boys in the service will soon be eating my meat."

She leaned over him, and Shirley politely stepped back. "We've got to go," she said. "I'll write. We'll meet again." She leaned to kiss his cheek, and at the same time her hand slipped under the sheet and into the wide slit in his pajamas. She gave him a squeeze, gentle and firm. "So long, big fella," she said but looking at Prosper's eyes. "Keep yourself busy."

She was gone, he could hear her laughter and Shirley's as the door closed behind them.

He'd never felt so sorry for himself in his life.

He ought to be able to get up and pursue her, not let her go, and here he was stuck. He thought of scrambling into that damn chair and racing out the door, but there were two steps there he'd never get over, and if he did he'd never be able to get back in. Cry after her.

Sad Sack.

He still felt the squeeze she'd given him; and, as though it did too, his organ swelled. What he and Vi had done, no more of that now, all those things. He reached beneath the sheet as she had done, she for the last time. His bandaged hand useless even for this, he had to swap it to his left; tears now at last running one after the other toward his ears as he lay, his soft sorry sobs and the other sound mixing.

There was a knock on the door, which Vi had left ajar. Startled, he struggled to tuck himself away.

"Hi?" A woman's voice. Not Vi.

"Yes!" he cried.

Connie Wrobleski in white shorts and tennis shoes opened the door. She had a covered dish in her hands, her face was stricken with some wild feeling that looked to him like grief or maybe guilt, and her little boy peeped through her bare legs at him.

6

Vi Harbison thought it was odd how her heartbreak, like Prosper's, had started at the movies. Like the preachers used to say: Satan's machine for ruining young girls.

The theater in her town had closed in the bad years and only opened again when times got a little better; Vi graduated from high school that summer, aiming to go on to normal school—she'd got a scholarship. The theater was called the Odeon, and Vi knew why; she explained the name to the new manager, the day he came to take the padlock and chain off the double doors, and Vi happened to be passing: she watched him insert the key into the lock and turn it, and the fat gray thing fall in two in his hands. He was new in town.

"Odeon," she'd said. "It's Greek for 'a place for performances.'"

"Well you're pretty bright," he said. She couldn't judge his age—not old, unburned and unlined, but maybe that came from making a living in the dark: his eyes wide and soft, not like the men of this place, around here even the boys' eyes were always narrowed by the sun, corners puckered in crow's-feet. What made her speak to him that way, offer her bit of knowledge, she didn't know. He reached into the pocket of his pants and took out a handful of free passes.

"Bring all your friends," he said, giving them to her.

"I don't have this many," she said.

He laughed and with a forefinger pushed back his white hat. "You can use them all yourself," he said. "A year's worth of pictures."

She was there with her father and brothers the night it opened, everyone glad, they'd not known how much they'd missed it. A rootin' tootin' shoot-em-up, they delighted in it, laughing appreciatively at the unreal lives of movie cowboys. He'd got the place swept of its wind-driven dust and the broken chairs repaired and the chandelier rewired, but it was the same place, nothing much, just a hick-town picture show. She wanted to know why someone like him would want to come to this town that she only wanted to leave, and she thought that finding the answer to that was why she came in the middle of the day when almost nobody else did, when he ran the picture for her alone—that's what he said, selling her a ticket, then immediately ripping it in half and giving her the stub, which seemed unnecessary till he explained that those stubs he kept were how the distributors of the picture calculated how much he'd make at every showing. That two bits of yours has a nickel in it for me, he said.

Sometimes he'd come down from up where the picture was projected through a glass window, a cone of dusty shifting heaven-light, and sit beside her, still wearing his hat; he'd feed her Milk Duds and speak softly to her about the picture, tall pale women bantering with clever men, their jokes meaning more than one thing, spoken in a way that wasn't like anyone spoke anywhere, speech as finely made as their shimmering dresses.

"You could learn a lot from her," he whispered. "She could teach you a lot. Smart as you are."

Teach her what? She tried to soften and silken her voice, speak in those pear-shaped tones, say what shouldn't be said in a way that could be: and when she did it well—not blushing even—he'd smile at her in the same way that the dark-eyed male actors smiled down at their clever girls: as though he'd learned more than she'd said.

Because she was still a gangly half-made girl with bitten nails whose father ran a failing farm supply store, whose best friends were her brothers. He knew very well what she didn't know.

He lived at the hotel, paying his rent every day, a dollar a day, as though he'd not want to pay in advance for a room he might not have a use for. He had a bed in his little office at the theater too, a daybed he called it, a davenport she said, which made him laugh.

Daybed. Bed for day. Her mother told her that men only want one thing, that they are like beasts without thought or consideration; at the same time she told Vi that someday one would come who was good and kind and thoughtful and would love and care for her forever. The two things canceled out and left her with no counsel. The high school boys now headed out to farms and ranches or out of town hadn't much interested her, she'd moved among them as through a shoal of fish that parted to let her pass and then regrouped behind her. She was taller than most of them and played ball better. She liked their horses more than she liked them. She had no way of knowing if this man was like other men, if he had no consideration, or was good and thoughtful, she only knew she could make no objection to him, not even when he paused to see if she would: she could think of no reason to. He was more like a land she'd come into than someone to know or judge. She had no way to go back, but she didn't think of that: he told her not to, not to think about the future. It was the one thing he forbade. Anyway this country she'd come into was her too: she just hadn't known it could be so.

He told her he was sorry he couldn't take her to nice places or on moonlight drives, squire her around as she deserved, but he figured those brothers of hers wouldn't cotton to that, and she said he was right, they wouldn't; it was only because she'd started at the normal school on the hill that her time was her own now and none of their business. She didn't care: inside the picture palace (that's what he called it in his double way of speaking) they were alone with the moviegoers. He brought her up into the little insulated booth where the great rattling projectors burned away, hot as stoves, two of them because when the film on one ran out he turned on the other, where the next *reel* was already loaded and strung up, and seamlessly the picture changed from one to the other. He brought her to the little double-glass window in the wall where the picture could be watched, and showed her the marks that appear for an instant in the corner of the screen, that warned him the reels would need to be changed in five minutes, in three, in ten seconds, now: and she realized she'd seen those Xs and dots forever, and not understood them. Once, as she stood there to look out, he came behind her, drew up her skirt and gently eased down her pants, she lifted a leg so he could slip them off. She held herself against the padded wall, legs wide apart for him to enter, still watching through the window the great silvery faces come and go; sometimes the actors looked her way, speaking as though to her, troubled or threatening or surprised by joy, but without words, for she could hear nothing they said, could hear nothing at all but the uncaring projectors, and the people out there looking at the screen couldn't hear the sounds he and she made either: she knew they couldn't, and still she tried to be quiet as he rose up within her beyond what she'd thought possible. Five minutes till done, three minutes, ten seconds, now.

When winter came her mother began to worsen from whatever it was that she had, that ate her away from within. Her father could hardly speak of it; her brothers tried to go on acting in the same ways they had always done, belligerent or jaunty or uncaring, intent on their jobs or their games or their pecking order, and Vi could understand—it seemed not to be in them to rise to this, which didn't mean they weren't hurt inside: only she couldn't talk to them. She had only her man in the movie theater to talk to. He listened, too: calm and quiet and unafraid. Until (she could tell it) he could go no further. She knew she shouldn't hand him something he couldn't fix. She felt she cost him something just by being so hurt by it, so confused and hurt, herself: she had made herself less his, less what he wanted, she subtracted from herself some quality or value he deserved to have. Ever after she'd have to tell herself it wasn't for that reason—not for that reason alone, not mostly, not at all—that he'd moved away.

In the center of the proscenium of the old theater were plaster leaves and flowers surrounding two masks, one of them with wide mouth turned down in a frozen rictus of awful grief, the other in an even worse contortion of awful laughter. No picture showing: it was the middle of the morning but as eternally dark as ever here, the dim house lights on. He told her he was leaving town, selling up, heading out. The way he said it was more gentle but not otherwise so different from the way he'd say anything, any jaunt he'd propose, any scheme to make it big or see the world. She sat in the seat beside him in the grip of an awful fear, that there was a right thing she might say, one thing, that would make him retract what he'd told her and change him back into what he had been just before, but she didn't know what that right thing was and wouldn't ever know it.

"Why?" she said at last: the one word, one syllable, that she could manage without tears. She looked straight ahead.

"Couple of reasons," he said. "There's some gentlemen who've learned about my little enterprise here, people I knew a long time ago; they'd like to have a talk with me and I don't believe I want to start up that old acquaintance."

That was language from the movies. She had to believe it contained a truth about him. She thought of saying he could hide out at the ranch: but that was just more movie talk. She didn't know who he was: never had.

"And," he said. "Well, just time to move on. Never been happy long in one place." He turned to look at her, she could sense it but wouldn't turn herself. "Hadn't been for you, I'd have been gone a while ago."

She had to go, she had snatched these moments from her mother and her family, she'd told them lies that weren't going to last long, she had to leave and go out into the day. She got up and pushed past him like a moviegoer when the picture's reached the place where she came in. There was no one in the hot street or in the store, she could weep and cry aloud in an agony that was like (she'd learned the word in music class at the school) a *descant* on the cry of grief always in her then for her mother and herself.

When her mother was dead and buried, though, and he was still intent on leaving and had announced the closing of the theater, she made a spectacle of herself; she was seen banging on his door in the hotel and people talked and she ran from the house and her brothers knew where she was headed and followed her, pulling at her arms as though she were ten years old and in a tantrum, a madness possessing her that she would deny possessed her. She'd deny even to herself that she had to see him and then find herself looking up at the lighted window of his office at midnight not knowing how she'd got there. Her mother not a month in her grave.

She was waiting there loitering the day he came down from the office with a stack of file folders and a tin money-box that he put into that cream and gray convertible he had, and a small pistol too in a holster, belt wrapped around it, which he put in the glove compartment. Two alligator suitcases, a little shabby, were already in there. She could say nothing, a clear coldness all through her worse than the fiery oblivion. He nodded to her as though she were a dim acquaintance he had nothing against. When she didn't respond in any way, he held up the files to her.

"Like to invest in a picture palace? Steady income."

"Stop it," she said. "You stop it. I'll never go to the pictures again."

"Oh honey. You will. You'll see. Plenty of good pictures, always more in fact, brand-new, all-talking all-singing all-dancing. You'll see."

Everything he owned was in the car. He had to pass her to get to the driver's seat, and as he did he seemed to convince himself of something, and he turned back and took her and kissed her and touched her. Then he got in the car and started it. She could hear the gears engage and it moved away, leaving tracks in the dust of the road, not seeming to grow any smaller though as it went.

Three years passed.

The train blew its whistle for a grade crossing, and Shirley in the coach seat opposite hers awoke for a moment. "Hey," she said, and went back to sleep. Shirley'd been married and divorced, Vi didn't yet know the whole tale. Outside the train window the landscape was growing more familiar. Vi hadn't told Shirley about the picture show. It hadn't ever reopened.

She'd said to Prosper Olander that you can only get your heart broken once. She thought of it as like a horse's broken leg: after that they shoot you. Whatever you are afterward isn't as alive; you can't be burned, but you don't feel the fire. She'd said to Prosper that the woman who'd left him at the stairs to the train had broken his heart, as hers had been broken; but something about him made her think differently. It might be that his heart was cold from the beginning, because he was a cripple. Weak and twisted as his body was, he seemed unbreakable within, elastic, immune to whatever it was that pierced you and then was never after withdrawn. If it was so he was lucky, maybe, because how could he live otherwise? How could he risk it, falling for somebody, with that? Even the words "fall for" still induced in Vi a kind of panic, a vertigo that she'd once been sure she'd eventually pass beyond, and hadn't.

She wondered if she'd really been right about him and that married woman. She thought most likely yes, the way he'd responded when she'd brought it up. A married woman. With a kid, and a husband right there at the plant where you worked too. That just took the cake, in Vi's mind. Not that she herself hadn't ever. But surely it was different if you could do it with a cold heart: if you could, it would actually make you kinder, more careful, less likely to do stupid bad things, hang on, wreck everything the way maddened lovers in the movies did. She hadn't done any of that with her married man, hadn't thought to do it, she'd stayed cool.

A *cool* heart. Not cold; not hardened with cold. She didn't know if Prosper had a cool heart. She'd write, and maybe learn how it turned out.

O h my heavens look at you," Connie said. "Oh I'm so sorry."

"It's all right," Prosper said. "My own damn fault. Just not watching my step. So to speak."

She came in, pushed the door shut behind her, not taking her eyes from the ravages that she'd inflicted on him—that's what her face said. She put the dish in the kitchen and came to where he lay. He described his injuries, just as he had to Vi, and just as Vi had, she sat down on the bed's edge the better to study him, sat in fact perilously close to his legs, the third included, which was only just then starting to take it easy.

"I can help," she said. "I've got time. All the time in the world. I can run errands, I can get you things. Aspirins. Vaseline for the scabs."

"No no."

"I want to. I should."

"Okay thanks."

"My mother was a nurse."

"Oh."

She jumped up then, the bed bouncing painfully under Prosper, to take a magazine from Adolph, who'd found out how easily and sweetly it tore.

"Oh let him have it," said Prosper.

She turned to face him, still stricken. "He's joining up," she said.

"Who is? Joining up with what?"

"They said that he'd have to reestablish his deferment with the draft board because *his situation changed*. They said they thought it might be all right if he produced the documents, but he just said oh the heck with it, he's not going to, he's going to volunteer. He leaves in a week."

She was weeping now, not desperately but steadily, the way women can, he'd always marveled at it, the tears one by one tumbling out, hovering on the lashes, as though all on their own, while the weeper kept on making sense, sniffling now and then.

"He said his life was too damn complicated."

"Oh."

"That's what he said to me."

"Well, kind of in a way, I mean . . ."

"It's my fault," she said. "I drove him away."

"What's that supposed to mean?" Prosper said. He pulled his handkerchief from under his pillow and proffered it. She came and sat again on the bed.

"I should never have left my home," she said. "I should never have come down here. I should have stayed up there."

"Well," Prosper said. *True Story* was full of accounts from women who felt that they'd driven their man away, by withholding themselves, by not meeting his needs, by indulging in finery or jewels or frolicking. But you often wondered if they meant it, or really believed they deserved what they got for it.

"I mean shouldn't I have? Shouldn't I have just stayed home?"

"Keep the home fires burning," Prosper said, with what he hoped was sincere gravity, but Connie made a face and looked away, as though she knew better.

"Oh yes. So I'd stay home and light my little light in the window and he could just go wherever he pleased and do whatever he pleased." Her eyes, dry now, roamed in a rather scary way, unseeing, or seeing things and people not present. "Sure. Oh sure."

"No, well."

"That woman," Connie said.

"Oh Francine's okay," Prosper said. "She means no harm, she's . . ."

The glare she gave him stopped that line of thinking.

"So um," he said. "The army? That's what he's joining?"

She seemed to come to, grow conscious of what he'd said, its meaning for her. "Oh God," she said. "I ought to go. I have to go."

"You're not going back north now, are you?" She hadn't arisen from his bed.

"No. No."

"You'll take a job here maybe?" he said.

"I might," Connie said, as though Prosper might dispute this with her. "Otherwise I'd have to live on this allotment they give you. With my *son*." She looked toward Adolph, who, smiling, showed her the destruction he'd wrought.

"You'll do what you have to do," Prosper said.

"I'll do what I want," Connie said. She put her hand with grave gentleness on his cheek, looking into him with thrilling intensity. "I'm going to come again," she said. "I don't care, I'm going to come every day and help and see what you need until you're better and up and around again. It was my fault and *his* fault and I don't care what he thinks."

She patted his arm, stood, and went to the kitchen, discreetly tugging down the legs of her shorts. She picked up the dish she had put down there and held it up to him, tears again maybe glittering a little in her eyes, and gave him a big smile. "Tuna casserole," she said.

Vi never did write—too many things, too much life happening then— but years afterward, in a different world, she was sitting in a dentist's office and picked up a magazine called *Remember When,* and saw, amid the articles about bottle collectors and old crafts, a collection of memories about the Ponca City plant, with a photograph of all of the Associates going in on the day shift; most of the people who'd sent in anecdotes were unknown to her, but in one of the letters there was Prosper's name, amazing thing, and Vi thought she could guess who'd written it. She put the magazine in her bag; read it again later at night and thought of responding herself, even got out the typewriter, but in the end she wrote nothing. What had happened there couldn't be recovered, because too much was happening at the same time, and how could you express it all without wiping away all that had made it what it was—as this Connie W. person had done in her letter?

I have so many memories of the men and women who worked there at Van Damme Aero P.C. and when I look back it all comes so vividly into my mind, the good things and other things. "It was the best of times, it was the worst of times." I don't suppose that anyone who hadn't been there could imagine what it was really like—a lot different than you might think! The person I remember best was a fellow whose name was Prosper, though for the life of me I can't remember his last name. He was handicapped and walked with two crutches, or two canes I think; as I remember he worked in the print shop with an awful man who wrote press releases and harassed everyone. Well he had a lot to overcome (this Prosper I mean) but he was always so cheerful and optimistic and gave everyone who knew him a boost. He was a good friend to me after my husband went into the Army and I went to work there as an inspector. My shop number was 128. I guess I came to know him a little more intimately than anyone else there, and I still can't account in my mind for what made him the way he was, and how for all the trouble he'd had in his life he could take the trouble to make another person just feel all right inside.

8

Back then, Connie had wondered at Prosper too, just as Vi had: wondered at something that seemed so impervious in him, unbroken, undiscourageable. Lying beside his bare body in the spare bed in her house on N Street, Connie thought it was almost spooky: he was like one of those cheerful ghosts in the movies, who seem to have nothing left to lose, and only goodwill toward the living among whom they fade in and out, making things right.

He was no ghost though. She put her hand tentatively down where his had been, and also where he'd. A little sore there. She'd always been reluctant to touch it much, but he sure hadn't been, so why should she be? It was hers.

What made him so complacent about all that, sex, as though it was easy? He of all people. Surely he couldn't have been with many women, not so many that it would make him so—what was the word she wanted, so certain or steady, and yet so different from an actual ordinary man. She thought of Bunce. How different it was with him. Were there other different ways for men to be, other than those two? She'd probably never know. With Bunce it was sometimes more like a test, or a problem to be solved, only that was wrong because it wasn't something you did with your head. There seemed to be rules she didn't know, that Bunce thought she'd know; he'd grow tense and watchful when she did things wrong, sometimes if she did anything at all. Now and then his intense attention would remind her of his look when he played or practiced football and the whole of him was bent on doing the thing right, the unsmiling intent face and the funny leather hat that made it almost ridiculous if you weren't doing it but watching it: in the bed sometimes too—times when she felt like she *was* watching and not doing—it was, just a little, ridiculous, since he was naked except for his socks, and the big bobbing thing to be managed right.

She laughed or sobbed a little, and Prosper turned a little to touch her, laughing a little too, so she went quiet.

Bunce had told her that, for a man, every time you spent, you lost a little time off your life—she couldn't remember if he'd said a day or a month—and so every one cost him something, left him just a little weaker. And that's what it seemed like.

But oh not always. Not when, helpless and forgetful of all that at last, he'd just. And in those times it couldn't be said who carried who forward, whether he'd surrendered to her or she to him. Those times it seemed to go on forever even though it was only a few minutes, seemed to be forever in the way they said immortal souls live outside time. They became "one with"—Father Mulcahy said you could become *one with* Jesus our Savior, one with Mary our Mother. Connie didn't know what that would be like but she did know, in those moments with Bunce, what *one with* meant. She was one with him then. Oh Bunce.

Prosper stirred beside her, strange bones of his stranger body on her, and a dark grief unlike any she'd known arose like something she'd swallowed and couldn't expel.

"What is it?" Prosper asked her softly. "Huh?"

She wouldn't say. She wept, but he wouldn't just let her, cheerful himself and smiling, wanting to know, to make her feel better, as though nothing could really be the matter, hey come on, until she rose up and turned to him, face wet.

"What's up?" he said.

"What's up, what's *up*?" she cried at him. "I'm cheating on my husband! He's gone to be a soldier and he's gone for *one day* and I'm cheating on him! I'm cheating on him with a *cripple*!"

She plunged her face into the pillow and sobbed, as much so that she wouldn't think of what she'd just said as to mourn or keen. After a bit though she stopped. She wiped her face with the pillow slip and turned her face to him, to see how terribly angry he was. He was hard to read in the predawn, but he wasn't looking her way; his eyes cast down, diminished, maybe crushed.

"So," he said softly, and she waited. "So does that mean," not raising his eyes to her, "I mean, if you feel that way about it—well I can understand, but does that mean you don't want me to come back?"

Prosper hadn't, honestly hadn't, expected all of that to happen, uneasily glad as he was that it had, and sorry as he'd be if it had to stop. He'd only come to the house on N Street (identical to his own) to show that he was truly now up and about, on his own, good as new or at least as good as he had been before, due to her ministrations, and to bring her a bottle of wine, Italian Swiss Colony, that he'd asked Pancho to buy for him on his monthly trip to the wet state next door. He'd also wanted to show her his new aluminum crutches, though he knew better than to carry on about them, people found it off-putting and after all they weren't (though they might seem so to him) a new sport-model car or a Buck Rogers rocket belt. *Handy* was the word he'd use.

Across her face when she opened the door to find him on the doorstep (one thing hard to get in Henryville was telephone service; you'd have quit and moved back home before they got around to you) was that changeful flicker of hopeful, but maybe painful, feeling that he was getting used to. Such a small slight person, so full of emotions. Anyway all she said was Hello, and asked him in.

He'd asked her how had it gone the day before, at the train station. Well fine, except that that woman (she'd never ever say Francine's name out loud) had the crust to show up too, all dolled up and wearing a *veil* and carrying on like some mourner at Valentino's grave—as though she had a right! And Bunce himself, carrying the little bag Connie'd packed for him, had walked away with her down the platform, leaving his wife and son standing there. Just standing there! And after *she'd* gone away and Bunce had returned to Connie, well it was hard to wait for the train with him and say good-bye as she should, with all her heart, but she'd done it, she had. Was the wine for her? Oh that's so kind, she'd never had wine like this before.

He sat at her kitchen table while she gave her son a glass of milk, speaking softly to him and he to her. The boy's big brown eye fell on Prosper now and again, maybe as Connie's had on Francine—no, surely a little kid wouldn't know enough to be jealous of a man in his house. Connie ran a bath and dunked Adolph in it, talking on and on to him and to Prosper, who listened in a strange state of elevation, peaceful amid a family he could imagine might be like one he could have, while knowing it was Bunce's, who'd take it out on him if he ever learned of Prosper's sitting here at Bunce's table eating a piece of Bunce's own farewell cake and sipping pink wine from a tumbler.

Then after a quiet half hour spent alone with Adolph in the bedroom, while Prosper read a comic book he found there, Connie'd come out and shut the door softly behind her.

Prosper had intended to leave then, but of course he hadn't, and she hadn't wanted him to, that seemed evident, and they talked—she talked and he listened—and she tried the wine and said she liked it. The short night came down, and brought a lick of breeze—she called it a lick, tugging at the throat of her thin dress for it to enter there. Funny how, when the air cools, the sweat starts on your brow and lip, or maybe it was the wine. Could you put an ice cube in it? They decided you could if you wanted.

She made him tell her about himself, and he watched what he told her reflected in her features. He told funny stories and odd ones and she laughed and marveled, but through all these, in her eyes and in the parting of her lips and the tender double crease that came and went in the space between her pale brows, he saw an underlying something, a hurt for him, even when the stories were about what he was proudest of.

Then the wine was gone and they told secrets.

She asked him if she could ask him a question, and he said sure she could, and she asked if you were, well, with a man who you loved, in the bed, and if that person couldn't, you know, complete what you were doing or even get started because he couldn't—well did that mean he didn't love you, did it mean he hated you, or did it not mean that? What did it mean? And Prosper said he didn't know because it hadn't happened to him, and she said it hadn't happened to her either, she just wondered. And she wept a little. He came to touch her.

Still he could say that he hadn't meant to stay, hadn't meant to be still awake with her when the sky began to lighten again. Throughout she was as tentative, and yet as determined, as he was: they took turns. She never said, and he never said, *No we can't*. They just could and they did.

She was so slim and pale, breasts no bigger than apples, and yet between her legs golden fur thick as a beast's. Fascinating, but not to be remarked on, he knew that much. It crept up toward her navel and down her thighs, and seeing it and feeling it he noticed (as he hadn't before) the light down on her upper lip, the soft hair of her cheeks by her ears, and the drape of hairs over her forearms like a monkey's. They'd been there all along and still he'd expected a body smooth as a statue; now he knew better. What she'd expected of him she didn't say: he was always unexpected, he knew, and he made no remark on that, either, though she seemed surprised by the willingness of him and of his eager part, as though maybe she'd expected that to be attenuated or wasted too, like his legs. Wouldn't have been the first time for that either.

But he really hadn't expected all that or counted on it, and the proof was he'd not brought any of his Lucky brand condoms, still a couple left. When he said something to Connie that he hoped might make that clear—*we shouldn't, we should be careful because, you know*—she'd slipped out of the bed (near naked and aglow, as though she drew all the small light in the house into herself) and gone to the bathroom and then returned, a strange sweet odor about her, and just picked up where they'd left off.

What was it? he asked, afterward, and she whispered into his ear in the deep dark: Zonitor. What's that? You put it, you know, up there, and you don't get pregnant. She'd used it for a year with Bunce and never told him. Never told him.

A while after that they started again.

Then they'd come to the time at dawn where she'd wept about it, how she was cheating on Bunce with a cripple, and before she could answer his question to her (but he guessed the answer anyway because of the way she gasped in laughter at it, at his nerve), Adolph could be heard crying, then bawling: and in furious haste, as though the cops were at the door, she leapt up and struggled into her dress.

He got himself together and went home. That dawn walk back. He thought that, when and if it ever came time to assemble in memory all the most blessed moments in his past, then these dawns when a woman who had just allowed him into her life, maybe her heart, put him out because she had to return to her child, her work, her self, reluctantly from a warm bed or sometimes not so reluctantly—they would all be among the ones he would choose, though he couldn't say why.

9

Connie waited another day, exhausted and immobile, and then bathed and dressed and went to get a job at Van Damme.

First thing was to bring Adolph to the nursery and get him signed up and settled in. The nursery was in the same building as the huge cafeteria, occupying the whole sunny southern side, the curving spaces she'd seen in the magazine enclosing an inner space open to the sky, a playground with flowers and a little garden where the kids could grow their own vegetables (as she walked, Connie was reading from the little handout they'd given her). The principle the whole nursery and its kindergarten and classrooms went on was Learning by Doing. Prepare the child for successful adaptation to the school, the plant, the office, and the community. Good citizenship begins in cooperation, respect for others, and a sense of accomplishment.

It seemed a little more chaotic than that when she opened the glass doors and a wave of child and teacher voices hit her, a storm of babble, tears, cries of excitement. They gave you an hour or so on the clock to stay with your child so he wouldn't get a complex from being abandoned, but you didn't have to use it if you thought everything would go all right. Adolph clung to her as though to a rock-ribbed shore against the breakers.

"Well hello there, little fella," said the receptionist, bending over him, grandmotherly and gray; she reminded Connie of the woman at the United States Employment Office who had started her on this journey. "What's your name?"

Adolph made no answer, though he let go of Connie and smiled. Mrs. Freundlich somehow hadn't left him with a terror of strangers, thank goodness.

"His name's Adolph," Connie said.

The woman lifted her brows, regarding Connie over her Ben Franklin glasses.

"Well his name's Adolph really," Connie said. "But we always call him Andy."

"Andy," said the woman, whose own name was Blanche. It said so on her badge. She filled out some forms, asked if Connie would like to have the cost deducted from her pay when she got a position, and whether her son had any medical problems. No he didn't, he was fine.

"Well then, come on in, Andy, and we'll make you a card with your name, and get you all settled in." Blanche set off unafraid into the pandemonium beyond, sure-footed and broad-beamed, and Connie and Adolph went after her, his new name awaiting him, everything awaiting him, everything.

At Intake, they spurned Connie's little test paper with a smile, and nobody asked her for a birth certificate, though she'd brought it, which made her wonder why they ever had up north. It was as though the grimy and outworn Bull plant and its offices were located in some former age, as though she'd been transported into a grown-up world from a messy playroom. Next day she dropped Adolph, Andy, at the nursery and watched him totter off, as ready for this as she was. She started on the line, turning bolts with a driver, but as soon as she could she began looking at the training courses that you could take, get a better pay rate, do more interesting work. There were classes in Drafting, Engine Setup, Metal Lathe Operation, Blueprints, Calibrations. There were so many of them offered at so many different hours for different lengths of time that Rollo Stallworthy had made up his own computer to keep them straight, a piece of cardboard with wheels of cardboard pinned to it and little isinglass windows that lined up to show the date and the times and the rooms and who had signed up for which.

One of Henry Van Damme's ideas that his brother and his partners had rejected was a plan for training all new employees not just in one operation but successively in several—riveting, welding, engines, gunnery calibration, subassembly, anything—so that eventually in the course of a single shift a person could take a break from one job and do another for a couple of hours, and then another. It'd keep you alert, he argued, keep boredom from setting in (he feared boredom intensely himself), make for happier workers. Variety is the spice of life. The engineers and efficiency experts reacted with horror. The constant traffic of people from workstation to workstation would cost time, so would the training; most of the workers coming in were barely capable of learning one simple job, let alone five or six—this wasn't like down on the farm, where you milk cows in the morning and hoe corn in the afternoon. Very well, Van Damme at last said: but you'd better be ready for high turnover, and plenty of new trainees, and that's time and trouble too. If you haven't ever done it before, industrial labor is an awful shock, one or two simple motions performed every couple of minutes for forty-eight hours a week, plus overtime—plenty can't take it, and that didn't surprise Henry Van Damme any. Without bringing it up again he continued to brood on the matter and work up plans for how it could be done. The papers are in his archives today.

Connie signed up for Billing and Comptometry. When she was given a job, she was also sent to study Wiring Procedures. She'd be an inspector when she'd mastered those, a white band around her left arm with that word written on it, and the power—the *duty*—to make the workers whose work she inspected do it over if it wasn't done right. The first time she did that, and the woman whose work had failed inspection looked up wan and lost and hurt, Connie had smiled at her in a buck-up way and then gone off to the john and cried. Never again, though. Among the inspectors in her shop she was the most detested, particularly by the men: but she'd learned something about men, at the Bull plant and then here. Men—not all men but a lot, maybe most—didn't know everything that they acted as though they knew, and weren't as good at things as they let you think, tools and machinery and the tasks that those things were used for.

"They pat you on the head," Connie said to Prosper while Adolph got his supper, "or they look like they would if they could. Like you're a child. You ask them a question, they get all annoyed, as though sure, they've got it all under control. Then you look at what they did and it's not right. It's just not right."

Prosper—glad not to be one of the *they* she described, nobody could say he'd ever lorded it over man or mouse—shook his head in sympathy. He was all in favor of her, himself. He admired her for the hard skilled work she did, and the courses she studied for in her spare time, and the way in which, despite all that, she cared for her son with what seemed single-minded intensity. What he wondered was if she also undertook those many things so as to be too busy to have to decide to go to bed with him. He hadn't had a lot of welcome that way, quick as he was to pick up on any that he got. Sunday she'd take the church bus to St. Mary's in Ponca City, in her nicest dress and a hat; Sunday was his only day off, and hers. When Adolph's, no Andy's, supper was done she planned (she told him) to take a long bath and wash her hair and go to bed, and he understood her, the way she said it, very clearly. Not that she didn't want him there: she seemed to need him, greeted him with ardent hugs as soon as he'd got inside and away from neighbors' eyes. He'd stay till he wasn't wanted, then head home alone; come back another day, to knock on the subletter's door after night had fallen.

"I just can't help thinking all the time how jealous Bunce would be if he found out," she said to him when once he pressed her. "He'd go crazy. Thinking of that makes me feel, well, not so much like loving."

She sat at the kitchen table, where she was filling in a Suggestions form. Ever since she became an inspector she seemed to notice a lot of things that could be done better. Her Suggestions were growing longer. Sometimes they needed two pages.

"He is jealous," Prosper said thoughtfully. "I don't know how he can be so jealous when he . . . The things he's done. It's not exactly fair."

"All men are jealous," Connie said. "They just are."

"Well," Prosper said. "I'm not."

"No?" She looked up from the paper and twiddled her pencil. "Not jealous?"

"I'm not," he said. "But I can be envious."

"What's the difference?"

"Well," he said. The distinction was one he'd read about in an article called "Obstacles to Your Complete Happiness" in *The Sunny Side* long ago. "The jealous person wants what he has all to himself. The envious person wants what he wants, but he doesn't mind if other people have it too."

"So you can share," Connie said smiling. "Adolph's learning to share, in the nursery."

"Good."

"That doesn't sound like envy."

"It is if you don't get what you want that someone else has," Prosper said. "Or if another person gets more. It can drive you nuts."

Connie looked down at the form she'd been working on. "He is my husband," she said.

When she was done with her bath that night she let him just lie with her on the bed, the other bed from hers and Bunce's, maybe just too weary to resist him, and he embraced her from behind and reached around to touch her. He pushed down her damp pajamas, his hand searching in the fastness of her thick hair. She lay against him as still as a doll or a corpse (he'd never lain with either of those), but he did as Vi had taught him, wondering if maybe it only worked with Vi no matter what Vi said, but she seemed to melt against him, small adjustments of her into him, until he felt her breath quicken as though unwillingly, and hot with hope, as well as with the sound and feel of her, he'd kept on until she tensed suddenly with an animal's grrr, shook, and then softened; and slept. That was all. Every week a letter came for her from Bunce, somewhere in basic training: Prosper saw the envelopes. The number of glass Zonitor capsules in Connie's box, stoppered with white rubber, ceased going down.

Early in June the Allied armies landed in France. Even people who never cared to follow the battles, who didn't take out their atlases when the President suggested they should in order to understand his radio chats, now gathered at the radio and opened the papers, or listened to others who read from theirs aloud. Women with men in the services, sons and brothers and husbands; boys waiting for a call-up; older men remembering France in 1918. Connie in the hot night, hoarse from shouting all day over the plant noise, sat on the step of Pancho and Prosper's house and listened to Rollo read Ernie Pyle's column about what the beach in Normandy had looked like after those days, when the battle had gone on into the interior and it was silent there. Prosper lay asleep on his bed, and Adolph, who often as not was now Andy even to his mother, lay asleep next to him. Rollo read about the vast wastage Ernie Pyle had seen, the scores of trucks and tanks gone under the waters and lost, landing craft upended on the shore, the big derricks on tracks stuck in the sand or wounded and inoperable, the half-tracks hit by shells, spilling supplies and ammunition and *office equipment,* type-writers and telephones and filing cabinets all smashed and useless. Great spools of wire and rifles rusting and the corners of dozens of jeeps buried in the sand poking out. And Ernie said it didn't matter, that unlike the young men buried too in the sand or being collected for burial, that stuff didn't count, there was so much more where that came from, replacements a hundred and a thousand times over, you couldn't imagine how much more, a steady stream pouring ashore from that great flotilla of ships standing off to sea. Two young German pris-oners staring out at it all in dull amazement.

Even in this yard at the far edge of Henryville the sound of B-30 engines being tested, starting, winding down, starting.

Connie asked Rollo: "Why can't they do that without a war?"

Rollo looked up from the paper, shook it, out of habit, but didn't look back down at it; waited for Connie to explain what she meant.

"I mean why can't we just do this all the time, the way we're doing, that we've got so good at. Not to provide for war but just to provide for everyone. The way everyone's provided for here. Not just the pay, but everything."

"Well for one thing," Rollo said, "because the government had to borrow the money for all that. The country's going into debt making this vast amount of stuff that when the war is over no one will want anymore—guns and bombs and bullets and tanks. And they'll still have to pay back what they borrowed."

"But why can't we just turn around and order the same system, the one big system, to make things that people *do* want. Like those refrig-erators we all have here, or new cars, or better houses, or anything. Then people would be making a lot of money making the things and also be able to spend it, because the things they'd be making would be things people want."

292 / JOHN CROWLEY

"But who'd decide what people want?" Rollo had come to like Connie, and respect her too, and when his health wouldn't permit him to work, which wouldn't be long from now, he intended to put in her name to replace him as foreman, or forelady he guessed she'd be called. It wasn't unheard of. "Now it's the government and the army that decide, and sometimes they're wrong. What if they've built the B-30 for nothing, what if it's not the airplane that's needed? Well, who'd care, if the war got won? Waste wouldn't matter, like the paper here says. But after the war that wouldn't work—lots of things made that nobody wants to pay for, and the government not there to borrow money to buy it. It'd just go unsold. Businesses would go under. Jobs lost. Depression."

He put aside the paper and picked up his Roy Smeck model banjo. Connie didn't know how he could be so sure about this. Maybe there *was* a way to know. A science of knowing what people want. Their Passions, like old Mr. Notzing talked about. Not all people all the time, but enough. And not just the necessary things but silly things they'd want to buy that are fun and amusing for a while. Fashions. Sex appeal. But would there be any way to know enough about all people, each individual, so the system could work? You couldn't just order them all to go to Bethlehem to be taxed. They'd somehow have to do it themselves, associate themselves countrywide and maybe worldwide with their Passional Series of like-minded or like-feeling people, and be able to know hour by hour what all of them were doing and wanting and getting or not getting. Not even a worldwide telephone tree would be able to do that. Nothing could.

She looked at the radium dial of the new wristwatch on her wrist, which she'd bought out of her last paycheck, which had gone right into the Van Damme bank, she'd never seen it at all.

"Time to go," she said.

Connie's wristwatch and the big black-and-white clocks high up on the walls of the Assembly Building agreed that it was lunchtime, and bleating horns announced it for those deep in the guts of a *Pax* where they couldn't see. Connie'd been going over the wiring with a girl whose badge said her name was Diane, who watched Connie and listened to her in a kind of beautiful lazy way. She didn't fidget or get annoyed when Connie kept her there after the horn sounded, *let's just get this done*, though her dark eyes withdrew a little.

Just finishing up when she saw Prosper coming toward her, as he did now every day almost at this hour. Her friend Prosper.

"Okay," she said to Diane, the noise in this shop ceasing.

Then Diane saw the inspector's face alter, and something flew into it because of something that she saw. Diane turned to see what it was. The inspector was already climbing down from the platform, dangerously fast. At first Diane thought it was the crippled man coming this way with a smile on his face, but then that man looked behind him, as though he too understood Connie had seen something big. And Diane watched her rush past that fellow to a man in uniform now coming down the floor fast, snatching the cap from his dark curls and opening his arms to her.

"So. He's back, I guess."

The crippled man had come to Diane's station, and seemed to be hiding behind the scaffolding of the platform.

"Who's back?"

"That inspector's husband. I mean I guess he's her husband."

"Her name's Connie," Diane said, thinking the guy surely knew that. "Looks like she's not gonna come back and finish this." Connie and her serviceman were wrapped in each other, oblivious, drinking each other in. Workers went by them, some smiling. Diane climbed down.

"Were you," the man with the crutches asked her, "headed for lunch?"

"Well. Yes."

"Walk with me," he said, a little urgently.

He steered them not toward the cafeteria but toward a lunch wagon, one of many that served far parts of the plant, that was drawing up not far down the floor. It was a little trying, she found, walking with him; not only did she have to walk with an unnatural slowness to keep from getting ahead of him, but she also felt her body tense, as though she needed to lend him encouragement, the way you bend and make a face to force a pool ball to go right.

"So she was glad to see him, I guess," he said, looking straight ahead.

"Well heck yes. Sure. Who wouldn't be. You could just see it in her eyes."

He said nothing.

"That uniform too," Diane said, guiltily pleased to be able to tease him a little. "They come home in that uniform, it does something to a girl. I can tell you."

"Well." He seemed to pick up the pace a little, flinging his puppet's feet forward. "He was gone a while, I guess. I mean not long as these things go these days."

"No."

"I mean not actually gone at all, really, not yet. It's not like he's back from fighting the Nazis for years."

Diane laughed at that extravagance and at the grim face he'd pulled. "So actually you're a friend of hers."

"I'd say so."

"A special friend."

"Well she's got it tough," he said. "With a kid and all and her man gone."

"A kid? Jeez." Diane said nothing more for a time. "My guy's in the service," she said then. "My husband."

He looked her way, to read the face she'd said that with: it was a sentence you heard a lot, said in different ways, with different faces. "Army?"

"Navy. He's a fighter pilot." She was always shy to say it, as though it might sound like bragging; plenty of women didn't mind bragging, good reason or not, she'd heard them.

"So," he said. He'd stopped to rest, she could understand why. "My name's Prosper."

"Diane." She put out her hand, man-style, to shake.

They reached the lunch wagon, a Humphrey Pennyworth contraption with a motorbike front end and a driver in white with a billed cap like a milkman. They got in the line. The word up ahead was that It's-It bars—which Henry Van Damme had ordered to be shipped out every month from the Coast in refrigerated trucks—were now available, and the line got a little impacted with eagerness.

"It *is* hard," Prosper said, to her and not to her. "It is hard."

She'd rushed right past him unseeing, Connie had: seeing only the thing she aimed for. Bang into Bunce, as though he were her other half, found again at last. He had glanced back at them and he knew. For Bunce alone the lamps of her eyes were lit.

For that guy. For *him.*

Could it be that women really liked it that a man was jealous of them? Did they like jealous men better than those like himself who weren't? The furies that such men were capable of in *True Story,* the jealousy, it was always terrible and unwarranted and a man always had to surrender it before the woman would once again be his. But maybe that *wasn't* true of them, only they didn't like to admit it: maybe they could love a man who was mean to them and cheated on them, as long as he was deeply jealous, as long as he wanted them for himself alone.

He didn't know and didn't want to think so. But he felt pretty sure that for one reason or another no woman was ever going to look at him the way Connie had looked at Bunce as he approached, all her heart in her face; or take hold of him as she had Bunce, her man.

"They've got ham sandwiches and cheese sandwiches," Diane said, startling him.

"Ah. Um. One of each," he said, and she fetched them. "Thank you."

For some reason Diane kept running into this guy Prosper on the floor in the following days, or saw him passing by in the little *Aero* car with the reporter fellow, or in the cafeteria. Of course he was pretty visible, once you'd noticed him. They had a brief conversation now and then that never seemed quite to come to an end, one more thing to say that he didn't say.

Then she found a note in her little mail cubby at the dormitory. It was addressed just Diane, with a beautiful question mark after it of a kind she didn't think ordinary writers made. She unfolded it and it was all written in the same kind of beautiful script that only appeared in magazines.

Hello Diane, I got your name off your name tag the other day and I'm guessing this is you. It seemed to me if you don't mind my saying so that you were looking a little down lately, and I just wanted to remind you that over in the Bomb Bay tonight there's a real band playing, not just records, and I thought you might like to go listen, and dance—not that I'm claiming any ability to dance! Anyway I thought it might be fun, and it starts at 8 P.M. Your friend, Prosper Olander.

Sweet, she thought. She fanned herself with it; the day had already grown hot, too hot for the time of year. It was going to be awful in that plant.

Why shouldn't she go, anyway. What harm was there in it? She could maybe cheer him up too, a nice fellow, that funny crush he'd had on a married woman, married to a GI. She'd go: it wasn't like you were exactly stepping out with an actual fellow anyway.

A real band. She remembered the noise of the big band in the Lucky Duck, the mob on the dance floor, the sweet smell of the 7-and-7s on the table: it hadn't been much more than a year ago, but it seemed more than long ago, it was as though those weren't memories of her grown-up life but scenes from her childhood, or from the life of a kid sister she'd never had, a crazy kid sister she'd left back there and would never see again.

PART FOUR

1

Past midnight, and the Lucky Duck on Fourth Avenue was full to overflowing, as a continuous wash of people entering through two sets of double doors arose into the bars and restaurants and seemed to displace another bunch that spilled back out into the street and streamed away toward the lesser venues or toward the streetcars and the late shifts, the naval bases and the ships.

Harold Weintraub's Lucky Duck—that was the full name of the place, the name the maître d's spoke with unctuous exactness on answering the phones, the name printed on all the huge menus and the little drinks cards, that was written in neon and lightbulbs across the facade, the double name casting a backward glow and lighting the rooftop garden along with the Chinese lanterns and palm-shaped torchères—was stomping. It was the night that the band playing in the big second-floor ballroom changed, and the new band (their pictures inserted in the holders by the doors, the featured players tilting into the picture frame as though coming out to get you with their gleaming instruments and hair) was one everybody wanted to hear. The doormen were overcome by the people moving in on them, many of them men in uniform who of course got to go in, but what about the girls they claimed were sisters and cousins too, leaning on their arms, and the couples in evening clothes and opera capes who would certainly be buying a steak dinner and a bottle of champagne, and—the hell, why not everybody, even the unescorted dames you were supposed to be selective about.

Before the war the Lucky Duck had been a big and rather gloomy Chinese restaurant, and still now there were bead curtains in the doors to the cocktail bars and those big obscure plaques that were Chinese good-luck signs (someone always claimed to know this); there was still chow mein and chop suey and egg foo yung on the menus and little cruets of inky soya sauce on the tables. People ate a lot there, but the food wasn't the draw; when Harold Weintraub, whom nobody had ever heard of, decided to turn himself into Dave Chasen or Sherman Billingsley, he bought the huge place and added an upper storey and took over the five-and-dime next door too—nobody needed pots and pans and clothespins and washboards for now, not around here anyway, but they did need more room to have fun. "I want our uniformed servicemen to have a place where they can have fun," Harold (a strangely joyless and beaky fellow in drooping evening clothes) said to the papers on opening night 1942. The new lights spelling out his name were sadly unlit because of the blackout then in force. Harold was more successful than he could have imagined, probably, and as the population of the city almost doubled with war workers and servicemen the fun got so intense that he spent his own time just trying to keep a lid on the roiling pot so the authorities—the military police, city hall, the vice squads, and the DAR—didn't shut him down in favor of something more wholesome, and quieter.

That amazing rolling thunder a big band could make when it started a song with the thudding of the bass drum all alone, like a fast train suddenly coming around a bend and into your ear: a kind of awed moan would take over the crowd when they did that, and then all the growling brass would stand and come in, like the same train picking up speed and rushing closer, and the couples would pour onto the floor, the drumming of their feet audible in the more bon ton nightclub downstairs, where the crooner raised his eyes to the trembling chandelier in delight or dismay. Diane and the four girls she had quickly allied with at the door (easier to pour in past the hulking guy in epaulettes in a crowd) were swept out of their seats by a raiding party, three sailors, a Navy pilot with that nice tan blouse and tie they wore, and a sad sack soldier seeming no older than themselves. The girls couldn't turn them down, not with that surging rhythm sucking them all in, but they tried—it was part of the game to say No a couple of times, they all played it that way, even Diane knew that.

"Diane," she'd said to the other girls as they shook hands over the unbused table they'd claimed, giggling in glee about the dope at the door and their rush upstairs. She recognized a couple of them, she thought, probably from somewhere else on Fourth Avenue or Fifth where they all came together and floated, waiting to see where they could sneak in or who might come out and notice them. This was the first time she'd tried the Duck (that's what the other girls called it), and she was filled now with a kind of buzzing brimming triumph that she tried to hide under an above-it-all kind of smiling inattention.

Her Navy guy wasn't much of a dancer. He pushed her around in a halfhearted Lindy but mostly talked.

"You been here a lot?"

"Some."

"My first time. You know they can fit five thousand people in this place? What I hear."

"And they all want to use the washrooms at once," Diane said. It was a crack somebody else had made and she was proud she remembered it.

"What's your name?"

"Diane." She perceived he was talking in order to bend his cheek nearer hers, to make himself heard over the band.

"Danny," he said. "We both got a _D_ and an _N_."

"And an _A_," Diane said. Her name wasn't Diane, it was Geraldine, the most American name her parents could come up with. She'd been staring at it one day, written on a school paper, and suddenly saw the other name contained within it, the letters even in the right order, most of them. It seemed like a gift, even a sign. She knew how to be American better than they ever would. She told Danny that she'd graduated from high school the June before, but that wasn't so either. She had a year to go, and more than that if things went on the way they were going, but she didn't care, she just couldn't see it, why it was important now; she knew how much it meant to her parents, who told her all the time that she represented her people and her community and had a responsibility. Her brother'd got a beating when their father caught him trying to get out of the house in a pair of pegged pants and a broad fedora, watch chain swinging, the long collar points of his Hawaiian shirt spread over his jacket lapels—*pachuquismo,* their father yelled at him, *you got a knife somewhere you punk you,* but now he'd quit school and joined the Army and what was he doing, picking tomatoes on a government contract farm just like the *braceros,* so if that was representing the family, Diane didn't care: and the world was upside down now and crazy and people just didn't care and she was part of it. Because nobody cared, it was easy to get into the Fourth Avenue bars and get a Coke and then make it a Cuba libre, nobody cared, the bartenders and the soldiers and the older girls watched you and they were interested and you could see they liked it that you didn't care either, that you didn't give a hoot, you could see it in their warm eyes and smiles.

"You can meet some strange people in here," Danny said. "You can meet about anybody."

"I guess."

"I heard you could meet a morphodite in one bar. They come here."

"A what?"

"A morphodite. That's a woman that's half a man."

"You're kidding."

"I swear. You'd never know, to look at her. Him. It."

"I don't want to talk about it," Diane said.

He let her go at the song's end with a little mock bow, and she slipped from his attention to get back to the girls; though it seemed the wrong way to proceed, she knew it was the way it was done.

"He really likes me," one of them was saying. Her hair fell over her eye the way Veronica Lake's did, or anyway you were supposed to think that. "I know he does."

"Oh sure," another, a blonde, replied. "Khaki-wacky," she said to Diane, but for the other girl to hear.

"Don't you tell me," the other said. "You're no better. You're more khaki-wacky than I'll ever be."

"You clap your trap."

"Lucy Loose-pants."

The others were laughing and half rising from their seats to cover their friends and keep them from being heard. The khaki-wacky one looked over to where the sailors sat together and gave them a little brave wave, mostly for her friends' sake, just to show them that whatever she was, she was going to be it unashamed. Diane stayed in her seat. The girls were all about her age but seemed to her skilled huntresses, chasing uniforms with a single-minded intensity that seemed hot and cold at the same time.

"I'm getting a button tonight," the Veronica Lake one said as they pulled her back into her seat. "No bout adout it."

"Oooh, hotsy-totsy." The blonde blew and shook her hand, as though the matter were too hot to touch. The other looked away, cold-eyed, exploring the ice in her drink with the straw. Diane listened, a little afraid they might start questioning her. She knew they were after buttons, and had heard what getting one was supposed to mean, what you had to do. *I'll do it but you have to give me one thing.* She'd heard that the fiercest girls carried nail scissors in their bags just to get them with. The band started up again, a slow sweet number. Though she hadn't seen him come up behind her, she felt Danny the pilot lean close to her shoulder.

"Hey, sport model."

She turned to him a little coolly. It was rude to make reference to a person's height or weight or.

"I'm better at this kind of tune," he said. He really was cute. He offered her a hand.

"Ding-dong," she heard the blond girl say as they went away.

The Duck finally evacuated near dawn, and the crowds that were let out into the streets deliquesced, some walking away under their own power, the taxi fleet bearing away the incompetent and their supporters. Others remained to mill, unsatisfied even yet. Smash of a dropped bottle, girl-cries at a sudden thrown punch. One thing to do after such a night was to go out to the broad divided avenue that led to the park—Danny and Diane and the khaki-wacky girl, who'd snagged a soldier, did that—and wander down amid the flowers in the center plaza; overhead the royal palms lifted their shaggy heads on impossibly slim stalks, black against the dawn sky growing green.

"You know," Danny said to her, "down the other way, I mean back that way, there's some places where you can get a room. A nice room. They say. You don't have to stay all night."

"Go on," she said.

"True."

She kept walking, looking straight on, head held up.

"I mean," Danny said, by way of withdrawing what hadn't quite been a suggestion. They walked on, around them others, the last of the last, until they came to the big gates of the park, and inside everything was green and shadowed, and you could see (but you didn't look too closely) couples on the benches and on the grass, the tip of a cigarette maybe alight. Star-scattered on the grass. You went on till you got to the zoo, because the idea was—Diane acting as though she'd long known it, though this was the first time, the first time she'd been out all night with the others, and Danny not paying attention yet, not being from around here, not knowing—the idea was to come down at dawn after a night at the Lucky Duck or the Bomber or Bimbo's or places without famous names like those, to listen to the animals waking up.

Diane and Danny fell out of the line, like weary soldiers hors de combat and giving up; they found a stone bench. For a while they talked—neither of them was much of a drinker, though they tried to be, and tired as they were from the night and the dancing they weren't comatose like so many. He told her about where he had come from, far corner of the nation from hers. He was just out of flight training and would ship out for Pearl next week. Then who knows. Shouldn't even have said that much. Diane felt an instant of huge grief, and then warmth, then something like relief, then it didn't matter: there were so many gone and coming back and going out again, you wanted to care but you couldn't care. Then they kissed, blending each into the other in a way that surprised Diane, because she'd kissed some boys but she'd never had this before, when what you felt moved to do was just what somebody else wanted to do, you were sure of it, like you couldn't be wrong and didn't need to worry. She pushed his hands away, but when obediently he withdrew them, she pulled them toward her again. The lions, awakened, started to greet the Sun their father; startled birds arose from the trees around them. Danny looked up, as though the wild sound came from above.

"What the hay?" he said, but she drew him back. Other animals began to make noises, animals you didn't recognize and couldn't imagine, grunting and hollering; the big cats screamed, the baboons too but differently; the macaws and great crested exotics shrieked and hooted as day came on. Some of the humans joined in, in mockery or just catching the spirit. The Shore Patrol was coming through the park, fanning out, looking for their own.

They would get called *V*-**girls in the papers and the comic magazines, in** cartoons about willing girls with flipping skirts and lost undies amid wide-eyed delighted soldiers, and everybody could figure out that the V didn't just stand for *Victory*, though the jokes about *doing her part* and all that were constant, and the girls would sometimes even deploy them against one another—they could be cruel to their competition in ways that would have surprised the boys they competed for. But they weren't asking for money, or at any rate never considered those who did ask for money as belonging in the same sorority as themselves. Which made no difference to the civil and military authorities, since a girl could give a soldier a dose for free as easily as she could charge him for it (as the little booklets and the big posters filled with variants of the same cartoons kept telling him), and keeping the men off sick list and out of the infirmary was the big concern.

The Button Babes (as they called themselves to themselves) did get a lot of money spent on them, which wasn't the same thing. And anyway they were usually ready to spend it too if necessary, on their boys; except that you learned quickly that the offer didn't have the right effect most of the time, maybe only late at night when nothing mattered, when it was like shooting fish in a barrel and not much more fun (that's what Diane thought). No, the *shiff-shiff* of rubbed bills and clink of dollars and smaller coins had to go only one way, had to be shown and seen and then spent, the BBs didn't ask why, or why the transactions did what they did, raised the temperature, rolled the ball faster. Cigar lifted in his grinning teeth as he peeled bills happily from a roll. Presents could go both ways, though: Kewpie dolls and snapshots and locks of hair and things brought back from Hawaii or claimed to have been. Though that stuff wasn't what the BBs meant when they said *a present. It's okay,* you'd say when some other girl marveled at how far you'd gone, the chance you'd taken, true story or not—*It's okay, I bought him a you know, a present.* That foil-wrapped packet you could get for a quarter from the machine in the men's toilet while another BB kept watch for you (*get one for me too, well heck just in case*) or buy from a pharmacy unless the guy behind the counter was a fuddy-duddy and wouldn't sell them to a female, even one with a gold ring on. All the servicemen got issued their hygiene packets, but most didn't bring one along. So it was hard, but they were really scared of the clap, and even more scared of a good-bye baby, and the boys sometimes didn't remember or didn't care, and most of the girls didn't believe that the vinegar douche would work (or the one with Coke that the tougher girls claimed to use, all six ounces, warm, capped with a thumb while shaken, inserted), and anyway who was going to jump out of bed and into the john just at that moment, that precious moment, if you were even somewhere that had a john, or a bed.

All theoretical to Diane, whose greatest fear was negotiating her absences from the house on the Heights just to get to be on the BB periphery, where she remained for a long time: till she proved to have something not all of them had, not even the wised-up ones, the slick chicks; a thing that some learned to envy and some to despise in her— it took Diane a long time herself to know it. Come summer she convinced her family to let her go with other students from her school to work weekends at Van Damme Aero outside the city, maybe a night shift sometimes if it was really called for, and then during the week too when school was over. To do her part. Her mother weeping in some nameless mix of shame and pride to see her in her overalls and bandanna. If sometimes the hours she said she worked didn't match the money in her pay envelope, well they didn't need to count it, she was like a soldier now she said (clapping her lunch pail closed), and they had to trust her. Watchful as he was, her father always slept as deeply and lifelessly as his truck with the ignition off, the more soundly the later it grew (years afterward, alone in that house, he was going to die in a fire, awaking too late), and so he didn't know what time she came in. What her mother heard she didn't say.

Out with the BBs she wore the same sloppy socks and big sweaters they did, sweaters that slipped almost from your shoulder, so that you had to tug it back in place slowly now and then as if not thinking about it, as if wholly absorbed in the flyboy's face that you were holding with your eyes, except that his eyes didn't stay with your eyes, but stayed with you yes. It was flyboys that were the prized ones. They got just as crazy as the other boys, who were crazy enough; but they seemed to like girls who weren't silly and who didn't talk all the time, who could just let a moment like that (eyes, sweater, silence) come and stay. That was what Diane learned to do (by accident, sort of, at first just tongue-tied and keeping erect and still out of shy fear) and got good at: and when she did it and knew it worked she felt a dark sweet sensation that spread like a stain from its starting point, that point below, and spread all through her, and that he seemed to share. Just being seen and look-ing back, unblinking like women in the movies, like Rita Hayworth. The BBs wore thin silk scarves at their throats, and only they knew what the colors meant, what achievements or conquests—pink, white, blue, orange—but there was no color for causing *that:* it was unname-able, unclaimable, and the only one she counted. The BBs saw her do it without showing that they were watching her.

Fliers, because fliers could die. Of course any of them in uniform could die, except the clerks and the janitors and the orderlies, but the flyboys seemed closer to it, and more liable to die. As though surviving or fighting or marching or other things were the jobs of others, and dying, or taking that chance on dying, was theirs. It melted your heart: she'd always heard people say that, and now she knew that it was a real feeling you could have. But you heard of women, not V-girls and way on past girls who asked for money, who married fliers because of the government life insurance, $10,000 they said; and the flier was the one to go for, because you had the best chance of collecting quickly. Diane decided there was no truth to that.

Danny was a flyboy, but only in a way. He was back from his stint at Pearl now and training pilots at the Naval Air Station, going up with the student pilots in an old Bull fighter plane that he seemed to both cherish and hold in contempt, like a feckless older brother. So nobody was going to shoot Danny down, and he got a lot of leave, and pretty soon he was the only one Diane went with to the Duck and other places. He didn't realize she'd chosen him and forgone all others, and she didn't tell him; and because she thought the BBs might reveal it—

she knew which ones, and why they would, that cruelty that shot through their solidarity, it could catch you like a pin left in a satin dress—she started to draw him away from the places that that crowd went to and toward others. And maybe it was because they were alone together away from the BBs and the soldiers they followed, but their feelings, hers and Danny's, intensified in ways that surprised Diane, she hadn't expected it, becoming something not so much like a game anymore, and when he talked again about those rooms you could get she asked him whether he was pretending, just to tease her, or whether there really were such places and what they were like, nice or nasty. He told her, and he told the truth, and he never insisted; he pretended along with her that they were just considering a funny thing that existed in the world, places that others, people who weren't he and she, might use or go to. But once they were actually there in one of them (not nice, exactly, not nasty but bare and cheerless certainly, she made him leave the light off so as not to see, the only light falling on them then the red glow of the neon HOTEL sign that ran up the building's front), he refused the present she had brought, which one of the BBs had given her long before as a joke or a tease. I want to feel *you* baby not a sheep's gut. She felt his fluid absorbed not just into those parts but seeping, staining, proceeding—what was the word in chemistry for how it happened, it sounded like the thing it meant—into the whole of her, her heart and breast and throat. Rather than draining away like any other flooding would, the feeling went on increasing, and in not too long a time she knew why. She told him as they sat at dawn on their bench in the park. He held her a long time very gently and she said she felt a little icky-sicky now at morning. And without letting her go he told her that he was shipping out again in a week, to go fly real fighters, Hellcats, far away. He'd put in for the duty, wangled it, it's what he'd always wanted.

It didn't seem to be a disaster, none of it; it was lifted up with everything else that was being lifted up all around them, all around the world, as by a tornado, lifted and swung around to mean something it hadn't before. When they had been quiet a long time he lifted his head suddenly and clipped his hands together and shook them, in prayer or triumph, and she saw in the dimness the glow of his eyes looking into hers.

There was a lot to get straight between them, and it wasn't easy; faced with it she lost some of that lightness and carelessness she'd learned, she faltered and felt her eyes fill and then her heart grow small and cold. First she had to tell him she wasn't nineteen, had lied about her birthday, she had actually just turned eighteen, had been seventeen in fact when they. And he told her he'd guessed she wasn't as old as she said, he didn't know why he knew. She told him her real name too: wrote it on a paper and gave it to him, solemnly, and waited for his response.

"Geraldine," he said, and shrugged, having no preference and thinking it was funny she did. "Noo-nez? What kind of a name is that?"

Another reason she'd withdrawn from the BBs when she and Danny had got serious. They were always dropping hints about her when Danny was in earshot, telling her she ought to get up and dance to "South of the Border," passing her the chili sauce, things like that, though Danny had never picked up the hints.

"So it's okay for you to marry a regular white person? It's legal?"

"Yes it's legal. Silly."

"Hey, I don't know. There's laws in other states."

She didn't respond. He was studying her in a way that made her shrink, or swell—somehow both at once. She was glad there had been no Mexicans or anybody but palefaces where he'd come from—he said it that way himself. Nothing for him to think about except a funny name and some dumb songs. She told him her parents couldn't know, that if her brother knew he'd start trouble. She'd tell them after, when they were happy and everything had to be the way it was, and they'd be happy too.

He had nothing to tell her, was exactly what he seemed, all one piece from front to back. She loved him, the one single thing he was, and feared for him, and for herself; but she knew she could tell him she was afraid, and it wouldn't harm him or change him or pollute him. The tornado was carrying her on upward away from the city and her life and her family and all of it, shedding consequences, futureless, awake.

They had only a week till he was gone. There was another flier in his squad who was going to get married too, a fellow who had grown up just outside the city and had a car still parked in his parents' driveway. He was marrying his high school sweetheart, who was no older than Diane and whose parents would never allow it, so they were *eloping,* Danny said, as though the word itself were funny and sexy and good. The four of them could get out of the state and across the desert to where the wedding chapels were tying the knot for soldiers and sailors by the dozen, they all four knew about them, there weren't the laws in that state there were here, you could get the license and get married all in an afternoon. They could get back the next day.

They would leave early in the morning so they could get to the chapels in time to choose one. They had to have the Wassermann test, but the people at the chapel would do all the rest and by evening they could have the ceremony, which only took a minute, like the sudden weddings in old movies—Diane saw in her mind the comic judge or JP with wide whiskers, his fat wife playing the harmonium, the couple (as happy as any couple marrying anywhere) turning to each other in shy delight and expectation. *You may kiss the bride.*

Danny's friend picked them up before dawn downtown near the park, Diane wrapped in Danny's uniform blouse (she had started shivering violently in the chilly darkness). The friend was named Poindexter, but Danny told her to call him Bill, and his girl was Sylvia, big and blond and asleep beside Bill almost as soon as they started out. The car was ten years old, smelly and noisy, with a spare tire tied on the side that didn't look any worse than the four poor things on the car (that's what Danny said, laughing, unalarmed). In the trunk were tossed a dozen big bottles and a couple of empty jerry cans, which they'd fill with water somewhere as they came down into the desert, as much for the car to have as for themselves; and in there too was Sylvia's patent leather suitcase and now Diane's round hatbox and case.

Morning city, pale and unpopulated, they were all quiet putt-putting through the streets and out of the suburbs. At the edges of the wide farmlands, the low buildings where the picker families lived. Men and women and children, awake early, were climbing into the backs of trucks. Sylvia said it was an awful life but those people were grateful for the chance, they'd never had anything better. What Danny wondered was how they knew people would want that many artichokes: he'd never eaten one in his life.

They rose up gradually into pine mountains littered with sinister boulders as big as cottages, rose until they came to a place where a tower of crossed timbers was built topped by a lookout shack high up, you could climb up it if you wanted, but they had no time. From that last height they could see far into the brown lands they had to cross, and effortlessly the old car fell down over the folds of earth that turned at length into wind-combed dunes, as though any minute they would reach the sea. Bill and Danny joked about life in the service and told stories full of acronyms and abbreviations that the girls couldn't understand, but they laughed too. When the road stretched and straightened there was a big government sign warning travelers that the desert ahead was dangerous, that they shouldn't attempt it unprepared, that there would be little in the way of help for them: and on top of the sign a big black bird perched. "A vulture," Sylvia said in horror, but it wasn't really.

They stopped at a gas station building so low and flat it seemed to have been stepped on by God. It had a big warning sign too about the road ahead, handmade, with a skull and crossbones on it; the place claimed it was the last stop for water and gas until the city on the other side was reached. They filled the tank, and bought water.

"Gwaranteed alkali-free," said the dried old hank of a man working the pump.

"Alkali will kill you," said Bill.

Actually in a few miles there was another place that said it was really the last, and had rattlesnakes and lizards in cages to look at; and then another place farther on, the same. "The last *last* place'll be just when we get there," said Bill.

As the day reached noon Sylvia dropped her joking about vultures and mirages and Indians and who painted the Painted Desert; Bill drove the straight road with one finger on the wheel. Diane curled herself against Danny in the back, feeling suspended, shaken by the car but not in motion at all: becalmed, like a ship. She started awake (when had she fallen asleep? She didn't remember) and felt she was still in the same place. Danny's head against the seat back, eyes closed, mouth slightly open: he seemed not to breathe. For an instant she couldn't recognize him, a large stranger close to her.

Then there was a sudden band of green, as though drawn by a crayon, and a river to cross, they'd known it was to come but it seemed to slice across their journey with both a greeting and a warning. After that it was easy enough to see where they were supposed to go. Almost as soon as the iron bridge was crossed there were signs for competing places, billboards with pictures of linked rings, doves, hearts. It seemed not to matter which one you picked, but she and Sylvia rejected the first one that Bill tried to pull into, not feeling they had to give a reason, and the boys didn't argue. The next was worse, but the next, a white cottage under tall slim gray-leaved trees, a little pretend steeple on top and a picket fence, looked cheerful. It had a pretty rose-covered arcade to enter by and a discreet sign in front that was welcoming and mild and helpful and didn't say Cut-Rate like the others.

"Here," Diane said, and tugged Danny's sleeve.

Later on, a long time after, when maybe she told the story of those days to someone younger, Diane would try to think about having missed so much that was so important to so many people, things that she too had always thought, when she was a child, or a kid in school, would be important. Getting married, after a long courtship; a proposal, and a little plush box opened before her to show the ring and its promise inside, to put on her finger forever; and the church, with the smiling priest and the people and even the flowers seeming eager and impatient and glad for her in her hampering white dress coming slowly, slowly up to where he stood. Wedding night, and the gift of her innocence; honeymoon; house. How could she tell them that it never seemed to her to be a loss, or to be full of loss: not as it happened, and not as she looked back on it. Because what was important then, in that time, was not so much what you got as what you escaped. Escaping the worst was like joy. It *was* joy. It was freedom, it was freedom *from,* and just then that's what freedom meant. She thought she had been lucky. She knew she had been.

The two big hotels downtown were full and the others didn't look nice; at one a bellhop steered them to a place out of town that he said would do right by them, he'd call up on the phone, and Danny gave him four bits. They had some drinks and a steak dinner and it was deep dark when they reached the place, Desert Courts. The sign said MODERN COMFORT. TELEPHONE. FLUSH TOILETS.

"That's good to know," said Sylvia coldly. Then, laughing: "Hear about these Okies coming in from Arkansas or someplace, they've never seen a flush toilet but think it's mighty nice for washing your feet. Push down the little handle and you get clean water for *tother foot!*"

Yes, everyone had heard that, and because everyone had heard it Diane thought it probably had never happened. They turned in at the gate. The tourist cabins were low and heavy, made of adobe; a long trellis or breezeway sheltered their fronts and joined them like a happy family, and vines grew up from big red pots to clamber over them, and tall cacti too in bigger pots, fat and prickly. In the hot white moonlight it looked like the land Krazy Kat lived in. The motherly lady at the desk gave them keys and smiled on them all; Diane knew she was Mexican but didn't know if the others did: there was a cross on the wall behind her desk wrapped in last Easter's plaited palms. She and Danny parted from Bill and Sylvia in a sort of hilarity of embarrassment, a joke about getting some shut-eye, and then their door closed and she was alone with her husband.

He turned on the little fan at the window and watched its propeller whip the air. He was smiling as though at some secret thing.

"Danny."

"So you promised," he said, turning to her. "You'll go to tell your parents, as soon as we get back."

"Yes. I will."

She sat on the bed, on the broad red Indian blanket that covered it. He came and sat by her. "Show 'em that picture of me," he said. "The one I gave you. They'll like to see that."

"Yes."

"What were their names again?"

"Joe and Maria."

"Oh right. And your brother's . . ."

"Paul. He's in the Army."

"I'll be glad to meet 'em all. Uncles and cousins too."

She knew what she should say to that but she didn't say it. She lay back on the pillows and he turned to lie and nuzzle her, his arm across her. She took his wrist to stop him.

"Hey," he said. "What."

"I don't know, Danny, please. It might hurt the baby."

"What?"

"I mean if we."

"Why? Who says?"

"It's what I heard."

"Aw no," he said. "My kid's bound to be tough."

"Danny really."

He put his hands beneath her white skirt. "Maybe we can give him a little brother," he said smiling. "Come out as twins."

"Jeez, Danny. My God." The bed was as though afloat, about to lift and exit out the window into the desert night with them aboard; she lay still to keep it still, but his hands kept on, and everything within her flowed toward him.

"There's things we can do," he said. "Now that we're married."

"Oh Danny."

"Baby I love you."

"Just go gentle, Danny, you have to be very gentle."

"I'll sneak in. Just up beside him. Won't even wake him. I promise."

"How can you talk that way," she said, but he stopped her with a kiss, and stopped talking himself.

2

Somehow it was harder going back across the desert with the sun at their backs, not an adventure now but only drab miles to cover. It was cold till the sun rose high and Bill kept the windows rolled up and drove stolidly on, leaning over the steering wheel. Sylvia wasn't telling them what she knew about the world and people; once, pressed against Bill's arm, she wept, Diane thought: they'd soon be parted, and who knew what might happen then. Diane didn't weep: she felt herself to be living on a higher plane than Sylvia, where not weeping was required no matter what you felt, a duty to your man, your serviceman. Danny slept—she'd begun to think he could sleep anywhere, that he did it out of boredom, like a cat with nothing to mouse after.

For herself she was feeling sick, conscious of her insides in a way that was new, of a queasy fullness that was in her stomach and not in her stomach. She ignored it, or when she couldn't, she tried to stay calm and will it to pass by. But then, not rising or whelming but stabbing suddenly, she felt a new bad feeling, a real and distinct pain, not just in her middle but along a line she could trace from here to there. She shivered and made a sound, and Danny's eyes opened.

What if she'd been right, and they shouldn't have done what they did the night before? For a moment she was sure, just sure, they shouldn't have, and an awful premonition filled her from her bottom to her heart. Then when the pain passed it passed too. She said nothing. Danny slept again.

Back in the city the two flyboys had to make a run for the embarkation point, their car stuck in traffic, quick kisses and hugs and tugs away, Poindexter turning back just at the last minute to toss Sylvia the keys to the car before he and Danny were lost in the crowds. Sylvia got into the driver's seat, now overwhelmed with something that might have been grief but that had also begun to seem like it might be regret. Diane gave her a hug and lifted Sylvia's chin the way men tenderly lifted the chins of weeping girls in the movies, be brave, but Sylvia wasn't having it, so Diane wished her luck and all the happiness in the world, took her case and hatbox from the back and headed through the throng to the pier where the immense aircraft carrier was tied up. After a long time the crew and the fliers and everyone on board came crowding the rail, a vast distance above the people who waved and called, moms and dads and girlfriends and wives. A band played, its music coming and going with the breeze. She saw Danny, amazed that it was possible to identify him, it was as certain as anything, and she waved wildly and he waved back to her, and then there was nothing left to do but wait—even when it began to move, the carrier was going to take forever to be gone. When Danny had to leave the high deck from which he had looked down on her, not waving but smiling and holding her eyes—she could tell that he was looking right at her—Diane didn't turn away; she sat down on her case and watched the ship, which could now definitely be seen to be moving off, its tugs busy around it (Danny wanted her to call the ship *she* but Diane couldn't, it was silly). Its escort, too, oilers and other ships visible now standing out to sea, creeping out from other berths to be beside it.

The ship went on growing smaller very slowly. The crowd around her melted away. She remembered from school a teacher saying that you can tell the world is round because ships sailing away from shore sink over the curve of it and disappear, first their big bodies, then the funnels and the tiptops of their masts. Good-bye. Good-bye. She couldn't see that, though, because the haze out at sea erased the ship long before it could go beyond the horizon, drawing after it the other ships. Diane felt the thread of connection between her and Danny drawn out infinitely thin, until it broke with a hurt to her heart she'd known she'd have to feel, but worse than she thought it would be.

It was late in the afternoon now. She got up and took the suitcase and the other bag and started walking toward the streetcars; took the car to Union Station, where she checked her two bags, seeming as heavy as gold by now. Van Damme Aero ran their own bus service from the station around to the plant; she'd taken the bus often, bright yellow like a school bus, Van Damme's slim cartoon plane painted on its side, as though pushing the roly-poly bus along on its own curling speed line. Tomorrow first thing she'd go out there. In her handbag were her marriage license and birth certificate. She'd worked there before, on the Sword bomber, and she thought they'd give her a full-time job in a minute, the wife of an airman. For a time she'd leave out the part about being pregnant.

When her mother was eighteen and just enrolled in nursing school, first in her family to go that far, she'd found out she was pregnant, with Pablo as he would come to be, and she'd dropped out to marry and have her baby and take care of her man. And no matter that Pablito was everything to her, sun around which her planet turned, face always to him, she would still press her hand to her heart in grief and hurt when she thought of the degree she could have got, the white cap she'd have worn, the doctors' offices and hospitals she could have worked in. Diane in her senior year had won the scholarship to St. Anne's College for Women, the letter was there at home on the mantel next to the photo of Pablo in uniform. So Diane couldn't go home, tell them that all of that was for nothing, that she'd got a baby, been married by a JP, was going to be an Allotment Annie and sit on her *culo* just getting bigger and cashing her fifty dollars a month. When she had the job she'd get a room, somewhere. Her mother never came downtown, her friends wouldn't tell. It was as far as her thinking had reached.

She ate a hot dog at the station buffet, thinking she needed something, some nutrition, the baby too, but almost before she finished it she knew it had been a bad idea, and she spent some time in the ladies' lounge till it was all expelled. She wiped her lips with the stiff toilet paper and drank water from a paper cup. The attendant, small and dark as a troll, watched her with hostile eyes, proffering a towel, but that would mean a tip. She left the toilets and sat in a broad leather armchair in the lounge and for a while knew nothing.

When she woke she somehow knew, even in that place without windows, that darkness had come.

Where would she go now? Everyone knew that every place you might look for somewhere to stay was overwhelmed with applicants, that every shed and backhouse had a tenant in it, people were sleeping on the cement floors of garages and in the basements of unfinished houses roofed over with tar paper; hotels were impossible, even if Diane had dared to check into one all by herself; the YWCA was full every day. She could stay right here, in this chair that had seemed to become her friend, but she felt sure that the attendant would put her out before dawn. She got to her feet.

She could walk for a while. Something could turn up. She did walk, one second per step, wearing away an hour and another hour. Evening was soothing, the dark blue sky reminding her of childhood and trips downtown to the movies. Even as she thought this she saw ahead a movie theater, its great marquee projecting over the street, its tall sign rising with the name VISTA and the lines of lights chasing themselves around the edges. A lot of people milling around out front, a lot of them kids it looked like. Diane didn't notice the title of the show playing; she was only drawn to the booth where tickets were sold, as though to the gatekeeper of a realm of safety and refuge. Twenty cents. She passed inside. More children, coming out of the curtained entrance to the auditorium, going in again, sitting on the steps to the balcony looking weary or dejected, or running wildly. An usherette in pursuit like a comic cop. Diane went into the darkness and found a seat; the feature was just starting. It was called *No Room at the Inn*. Diane knew the names of the young people who would play the main parts but hadn't seen them in a picture before. The music covered her and filled her at once, like a kind of warm nourishing syrup, and she sank lower in her seat. Snow was falling in a dark city, people hurrying through the streets. The two young people had just arrived from somewhere else, they had an old car that was almost out of gas; she wore a white kerchief tied under her chin that seemed both humble and rich; he was unshaven and his pale eyes were worried. He had a job at a war plant and they were going to do all right but they couldn't find a place to live. The landladies and old men in carpet slippers who opened the door to them were mean and tight-lipped, or kindly but helpless. The girl was pregnant! They needed someplace safe and warm. The car busted an old tire and ran out of gas at the same time, which was funny and was supposed to be funny, you could tell, and it made you think everything would actually come out all right. They started walking in the snow and he was worried and gentle and she carried a little suitcase. They went to a sinister motel where a single light burned and you could hear laughter of the wrong kind, and a night clerk (Diane recognized the greasy-faced actor from a dozen pictures) got the wrong idea about the girl and the guy, and asked if they wanted to stay *the whole night,* and they were so nice they didn't even get what was going on or where they were, which was funny too for a minute and then horrid, you wanted them to get out of there. They went on through the snow and the hurrying crowds. Diane fell asleep. When she woke up, the man and his wife had somehow found a place to stay, only it was almost a barn, a shed with a donkey looking in the window, and it was funny again but sweetly serious too: something about the light or the music told you. The old man with a foreign accent who rented the space to them and helped them out talked to them about freedom and decency in a world gone wrong, his white hair like a halo. It was Christmas. Kids came caroling down the streets, singing about Peace on Earth, Good Will to Men. As though you were a visitor, some-one come to call or to investigate, you went into the yard and through the gate and up to the little shed, and there in a corner in a made-up bed of blankets is the young woman, and glowing in her arms, revealed to you as though you'd crept up to take a peek, the baby. Just before that— just as the carollers came in to see—Diane all of a sudden got the idea of the picture, no room at the inn, which she hadn't got all along because it had made her think only of herself and Danny and where she'd go and what she'd do. Her heart heaved and she started to sob, that awful won-derful sobbing that can happen in this darkness, where with all these people you were alone and spoken to.

The usherette of the Vista—the only one on duty late—was having a hell of a night. She'd come to believe that all the human beings in the city without a house of their own were sleeping in the movies. Or they just left their kids there to watch the show, and told them Mommy'd be back later when her shift was done, just stay there. Damn shame. Shame of the nation, she thought, these were war workers, doing what needed to be done, and no place for them or their families to go. Kids falling asleep in heaps on the stairs, picking butts out of the ashtrays to try out. When the owl show let out and the place finally turned its lights out at 2 A.M., the kids would still be there, and she'd have to put them out and line them up on the curb to wait. Then there were the older ones, "teenagers" they got called nowadays, in the back rows necking or worse, she'd seen some rather striking things and not been very descriptive about them when talking to the manager, who thought it was swell management to leave the whole thing to her for these last hours of the night. Every hour on the hour it was required of her to check each of the four thermostats in the theater, see that they all read right. One was up on the wall behind the last row of seats, and that's where she damn well went, flashlight aglow so they saw her coming, and still they said awful things to her. *Just doing my job,* said under her breath because after all the damn picture was playing, not that these types cared.

And where did they get the bottles they smuggled in, the smell of booze was distinct in the auditorium, floating here to there in the stale air like a wandering cloud. It wasn't her affair, except when the boys got into fights she had to stop or she had to hold some retching girl's head over the toilet, too young to drink, too young to be here, without anywhere else to go. If she kicked them out, what would become of them? Churches should stay open, maybe that'd help.

She'd already had it when in the littered and foul-smelling ladies' she heard some kind of moaning from a closed stall. What now? She knocked on the door with her flashlight, a harsh sound, and from inside came a startled cry. Then no more.

Something really wrong.

"All right in there?"

No answer, and she looked down at the tiles and could see what was certainly blood on the floor of the stall, which the someone inside had tried to wipe up and failed, oh Lord.

"What is it? Open the door. I can help." She could? Help by doing what, exactly, for who, a murdered girl, attacked, raped? The small sounds came again, but the door wasn't opened. She waited. There was some movement, and the latch was lifted but no more. The usherette pushed it open.

"Oh my Lord."

"I'm sorry."

Blood everywhere, all over her lap, her legs, the toilet, a pile of tissues reddened. The woman, child, girl, was gray, as though all that colored her had drained away.

"It came out, all this blood," she said.

"I got to call an ambulance," said the usherette. "You wait. Don't move." In the movies they always said that, for the first time she knew why.

"Don't," said Diane. "Please don't. It's over. I think it is."

"Dear, you could die. I know so. Don't move and I'll come back. The phone's right there."

Diane looked up at the usherette, whose great breasts strained the uniform she wore, little pillbox hat absurd on her wide wings of hair. Horror and pity in her face.

"I want to go home," she said. "Please."

3

The Bomb Bay was nothing but an extra building not far from the main assembly plant that had lost its use as more and more *Pax* components were being built in other plants in other places. It was square, low, and window-less, with a makeshift stage hung with bunting; it was decorated as though for a high school cotillion in crepe paper streamers and silver and gold moons sprinkled with shiny stuff (actually duralumin dust, produced when *Pax* parts were cut or drilled, but it glittered prettily in the light of a mirrored ball that turned overhead and reflected the lights). The main reason for the Bomb Bay's existence was that it was big enough to hold a crowd, bigger than any place in the city, and you could drink there. The Oklahoma dry laws came and went and came again in Ponca City, but the Bomb Bay had been established as a private club of which all the employees of Van Damme Aero were automatically members—just show your badge at the door, when there was somebody there to check—and the church ladies and dour legislators could go hang. The trucks rolled in from the Coast bringing the Lucky Lager, the unrationed tequila came from south of the border, and the rest of the array behind the long bar when and if. Waiters were in short supply; best get your drink from the bar and carry it to a paper-covered table.

"I'd like," Diane said—her cheeks flushed and eyes alight as though she'd already consumed it—"a Cuba libre, please."

"I'll have the same," Prosper said, not quite sure what it was. The volunteer barman filled two glasses with ice and snapped the tops from two bottles of Coca-Cola. He added a shot of clear rum to each glass, and then the Coke.

"Wha," said Prosper.

"Should have a lemon," the barman said, "but we're fresh out."

Diane picked up the glasses—both his and hers, without hesitation or inquiry, which endeared her to him immediately, and brought them to a table.

"Why Cuba libre?" he asked.

She lifted one shoulder fetchingly. She was a different person here than in the plant. "It means Free Cuba," she said. "Maybe from that war?"

"Remember the *Maine*," Prosper said and lifted his glass to her.

The band was just setting up on the stage, the drummer tapping and tightening his drumheads. There was a trio of lady singers, like the Andrews Sisters, going over sheet music.

Diane told him (he asked, he wanted to know) about Danny, her guy, flying a Hellcat in the Pacific. She got V-mail from him, not often: little funny notes about coconuts and palm trees and grass skirts, not what you really wanted to know, because of course he couldn't say. She lifted her dark drink from another war, and looked at nothing.

"So he," Prosper began, just a nudge, he had nothing to say; and though it didn't draw her eyes to him she told him more, remembering more. The Lucky Duck. The journey across the desert. At last the lost baby.

"Aw," he said. "Aw Diane."

She shrugged again, a different kind. "I really only knew him a couple of weeks. Not even a month, and I wasn't with him unless he could get a pass."

"Testing, testing," said the bandleader into the microphone.

"I can almost not remember what he looks like. Sometimes I dream of him, but it's never him. It's like different actors playing him."

"Hello hello," said the bandleader. "Hello and welcome."

Diane downed her drink as though Coke was all it was, and crunched an ice cube in her small white teeth. "We weren't even really married," she said. "Not by what the Catholic Church says."

324 / JOHN CROWLEY

"Oh?"

"That's what my mother thinks. Didn't count."

"Oh."

She smiled at him, her funny life. Around them men and women were taking the tables. Prosper lifted a hand to people he knew: pressmen from the office, engineers who'd appeared in the *Aero,* Shop 128 women. More women than men.

The bandleader, shoe-blacking hair and boutonniere, at last turned to his men and women—half the horns and clarinets were women—and with his little wand beat out the rhythm. All at once the place changed, filled with that clamor, always so much louder than it was on the radio.

"Like a school dance," Diane said. "The girls dance with the girls till the boys get brave." She'd begun to move in her seat as though dancing sitting down, and then without apology or hesitation she got up, twiddled a good-bye to Prosper, and went to the floor, where in a moment another woman was with her, jitterbugging tentatively. Prosper, new to all this except as it could be seen in the movies, felt that dancing itself must be a female endeavor or art, the men diminished and graceless where in other realms of life they were the sure ones. Not that guy in the flowered shirt, though, shined shoes twinkling. The three women singers, their identically coiffed heads together, sang in brassy harmony, reading from their sheet music, they hadn't yet got this one under their belts, about the Atchison, Topeka, and Santa Fe.

Big cheers for the local road, and the atmosphere intensified, but when the song was done Diane met Prosper over at the bar to which he'd repaired.

"Wowser," she said. "It seems so long."

"Since when?"

"Since I was dancing last." She touched his elbow. "Thanks."

So they had another Cuba libre, which seemed stronger than the first, and they sat again and drank. Whenever the right song was played Diane would pat his hand and flash him a smile and head for the floor, and Prosper could see that she moved differently from the others, at once forceful and supple, a snap to her waist and behind that no one else had; the men were taking her away from the women now and doing their best, but when the bandleader yelled "Ay-yi-yi!" and started a rhumba they fell away, all but the guy in the flowered shirt.

Whenever she came back to sit with Prosper, though, she'd take his hand under the table and hold it. Surprised at first, he thought he was supposed to figure out what she meant by this, if it was a secret signal, but soon decided it didn't mean anything, her face never turned to his to share any secret, she just did it: maybe it just meant that she'd dance with him if he could, or that she was dancing with him there as they sat. And it wasn't late when she yawned and said she'd had enough, really. He walked with her back across the still-warm tarmac, around the ever-burning main buildings, to the women's dorm.

"So have you seen your friend the inspector?" she asked as they walked.

"Oh. No. Not really. I mean she." Since Bunce had come and then gone again, Connie had seemed to lift herself above the plane where he and the rest of the world lived, her eyes somehow looking far off, toward where he'd gone, from where he'd return. "She's working over-time, I guess."

"Well." She turned to him at the door past which at this hour he could not go. "That was fun."

"I liked it. We'll do it again."

She aimed an imaginary pistol at him, one eye closed, and fired: you're on.

In her bed in her familiar room again she lay thinking, listening to her roommate's breathing in the other bed.

She thought what a nice fellow that was, how modest and funny and honest, seeming to be honest anyway, without any *designs* on her as the nuns used to say, easy enough to spot those.

She thought about Danny far away, trying to say a prayer for him, trying to remember in more than a dreamlike way his face, his laughter at his own jokes, his touch. She should write to him.

She thought about V-mail. About her mother fetching the little forms from the post office so that she could write one to Danny to tell him that she'd lost the baby. How many sheets she'd begun before she could say it plainly. His answer back, a month later, the dread with which she'd opened it, afraid of his grief, disappointment, anger even, though that was crazy to think, at her failure somehow. And his answer when it came not any of those things, just telling her it was okay, he'd come home and they'd make a dozen babies together, look ahead not back. She thought maybe you couldn't go to war, couldn't fly a flimsy little plane over an ocean, unless you could keep your head and your smile like that. The little shrunken gray V-mail letter, like a voice heard speaking at a distance.

She got up quietly from her bed and went to the window, having thought now too much. The sky seemed to have been heated to glowing by the plant and its lights. When she was well enough after the miscarriage to go to work again at Van Damme, they were offering jobs out here, and Diane signed on. She'd make more money and be far from that town, those places, from the movie-land hope that any day he'd come flying in again. Far from her mother's great sad reproachful pitying eyes, big enough to drown in. But now and then she wished, well she didn't know what she wished. *Ay mamí.* She put her hot cheek against the cool of the glass and waited for it all to pass.

Drawn through the nation, and passing somewhere near Ponca City, is that line below which everyone's glad to see furious summer depart and the cooler weather come. Autumn nights the height of felicity, sweet as June up north.

Pancho Notzing on such a night approached the Van Damme Aero Community Center, which formed the middle box of a big plain building; the box on the left was the men's dormitory, the one on the right the women's. Both used the Center, entering from their own wings: Pancho was reminded of the great meetinghouses of the Shakers, to which men and women came by different ways, to meet and dance and praise God in ecstasies.

He carried his jacket, neatly folded, over one arm. There were many on the path with him, coming from the houses of Henryville, from their suppers at the Dining Commons, from the far town, in groups and twos and threes, going in by the double doors, which gave out breaths of music when they opened and then closed again. Within, there were not all those satisfactions and challenges and innocent delights for the flesh and the spirit that would be offered, expected, assumed in the true Harmonious City: but there were more of them than Pancho had known in any human institution he had ever been part of. Pancho Notzing believed, though he dared not say it aloud until it began to come true—if it ever in his lifetime even began to come true—that enough human gratification could actually change the world, the weather, and the earth. Make the crops more abundant, fruits sweeter; the tundra bloom with grains. The days more provident. The nights and the air like this.

Well maybe it could begin. Maybe—Pancho's heart dilated at the thought—maybe it already had. Could it be that the heedless extravagances of war funding had combined with the genius of a single man, Henry Van Damme, to enact, to produce in concrete block and glass brick and Homasote and organization charts, what he, Pancho Notzing, had only been able to dream of and plan and think about? Pancho'd planned, down to the minutiae, for human happiness and its provision, because it was in the minutiae that Harmony existed or did not. Henry Van Damme had planned likewise, and planned well: Pancho simply could not deny it, however many faults he could find. For a moment, the first in his life, Pancho felt an impulse to hero worship. Henry Van Damme might be a Bestopian greater than himself.

But perhaps he was only induced to think so because of the present happiness he felt.

He came to the doors of the Community Center and entered in.

The walls of the wide entrance were covered with announcements printed and lettered, stenciled and handwritten. Tonight the *Pax* Players were doing scenes from Shakespeare; tickets were free, but the purchase of a War Savings Stamp was urged. The debate team was practicing tonight for its upcoming meet with Panhandle A&M, the thesis being "Farmers Should Not Be Draft Exempt." The course in Small Engine Repair was canceled for lack of interest. The Photography Club expedition to Osage Country was tomorrow. The movie tonight was *The Arizona Kid* with Roy Rogers.

While people turned off to this or that door or stair leading to various activities, Pancho kept on until he heard the echoey piano, already beginning. He came to the studio door and opened it. No it was no credit to Henry Van Damme that he had brought into this unlovely state so many people, mixed their multiple passions together in combinations too many to calculate. But here (he thought) they were, and what their freedom and Association could body forth was up to them. To *us*, he thought.

The piano had begun a waltz, but the instructor halted the piano player while she sorted her class into couples. She turned to Pancho, entering with solemn tread as into a church, and waved to him. He'd thought, when first he'd seen her here, that she was not someone who merely closely resembled the divine Clara Bow, It girl, freedom embodied, but the movie star herself: it was absurd, impossible, but heart lifting for a moment. And the real person who took his hand and welcomed him in had the advantage over Clara—Clara, his great secret impossible love, his Dulcinea—because she was after all a warm, living woman actually present to him.

"Hi there, Mr. Notzing," she said in Clara's own insinuating gay whine. "We're making up partners, but we've an odd number tonight, so I'll be yours, all right? We're going to start with a waltz, all right, and then we're going to try guess what?"

He smiled and went to her and didn't try to guess.

Over at the Bomb Bay meanwhile, Prosper and Diane were at their table, gossiping happily about the plant and people each of them knew, he certainly was a talker, he was like Danny in that respect though Danny was more dismissive of things that girls noticed. So it seemed. Danny'd listen but pretty quickly his eyes would go away. Why was she thinking about Danny anyway? She got up to get herself another Cuba libre, and one for Prosper too.

After a while the band finished what Diane thought was a pretty short set of numbers and claimed they'd be back. Cigarette smoke and the day's heat hung in the air. A smell of petroleum prevailed throughout.

"Know what would be great?" she said.

"What?"

"A drive. A night drive. Cool. Did you know there's a river just over there a ways?"

"I didn't."

"You don't explore. Did you know there's Indians very close by?"

"Yes I knew that."

"I'd like a drive," she said.

At that moment Prosper in amazement saw Pancho Notzing come

onto the floor, with a blond woman taller than himself on his arm, a woman dressed for dancing.

"I don't drive, myself," he said. He intended to make it sound like a choice.

"Well I do," she said. "Where I come from, everybody does." She regarded him with solemn certitude. "*Every*body."

Prosper made no answer to that but said, "Well if you want to take a walk, maybe we can get a car."

"Swell," she said. "One more drink."

"Really?"

"Oh Prosper," she said rising. "Don't be a better-notter."

The band was playing a waltz as Prosper and Diane went out, and the three women were singing mournfully about love and loss, and Pancho and his friend were turning each other with regal care.

The moon looked huge, the plant was far behind, the river—there was a river—was a trickle at the end of a dirt road, they'd almost slid off the bank and into it. Prosper's heart had turned cold when they'd discovered the key of Pancho's Zephyr actually already in the ignition; he'd supposed without much thought that they wouldn't be able to find it, and the plan could be given up. She'd driven just fine, though, mostly; she never could discern the switch for the headlights, but the night was almost bright as day.

It was cooler, truly: a little wind in the oaks, night birds and bugs he didn't know. From where they were the great illuminated refinery didn't look like an industrial installation close at hand but like a huge city far away. A flare of orange gas burned in the air, beneath the moon. Prosper and Diane sat close together, she leaning on him, he against the door.

"Well," she said. "Well well *well*."

He'd been telling her something about himself, the places he'd gone (not many) and the people he'd known. Also, because she wanted to know, about the women who had taken up with him, short time or longer. She listened with care.

"It almost sounds," she said, "like they picked you out."

He shrugged.

"I mean, *you*. I think you attract a special type."

"Like some women like soldiers. Or airmen."

That made her laugh, unashamed. He knew she wanted more, but he kept mum, suggesting it wouldn't be chivalrous: she could think there was nothing to tell if she wanted, or that there was.

Maybe to show she was ready to hear anything, she began to tell him about the Button Babes, and how they'd go after their prizes, the things they were willing to do to get them. She put her faintly bobbing head close to his to tell him: "You wouldn't *bleeve* what they did. Some of them."

"Well you tell me."

She considered this invitation. He was now her sole support; if he'd been able to slip out the door she would have slid down across the seat like a bag of meal. "Okay," she said. "Have you ever heard of people doing this?"

She whispered hotly in his ear, not quite intelligibly, her lashes flicking his brow, laughter distorting her words as much as drink and embarrassment.

"I've never heard of that," he said. He was lying, and that was wrong, and he knew it, but he did it anyway. "Never."

"Never? See?"

"What did they call that?"

"It doesn't have a name. It has a number." She drew it on his chest.

"How exactly would you do it?"

"Well see I don't know because I wasn't like that, but they said they did and they even said it was fun."

"They did."

She reared back a little, as though he was doubting her. "Wull yes."

"I mean I guess, but personally I'd have to see," he said, and she seemed just drunk enough not to guess where he was carrying this, or maybe he was all wet and she knew just where they were headed. His usual cunning was also a little blunted by those Cuba libres. He turned to put his arm across her lap.

"They did everything," she said thoughtfully. "But just to not get a baby."

"There's other ways not to get a baby."

"*I* know," she said, as though well of course she did. And for a moment she regarded him with goofy bliss, and for all he knew he did the same. He'd put before her a choice between the safe but unlikely and the regular but risky, and then taken away the risk of the regular, so it was not a choice but a banquet. Rather, he'd got her to put it before him: him, poor starveling who'd never partaken, as she was probably imagining. But he'd only think all that later. Now they kissed, her mouth tasting of the Coke and the rum and her own flavor. After a time she put her cheek against his with great tenderness and with one hand began unbuttoning his pants.

This was a first for him, as it happened, and she somehow seemed to know it; she was tender and tentative and didn't have the hang of it, no surprise, and he was tempted to help, but no, he just lay cheek to cheek with her as she did her best: she gasped or cried a small cry as she at length achieved it, maybe surprised. Confused then as to how to tidy up, the stuff had gone everywhere, like a comic movie where the more you wipe it the farther it spreads, never mind, they laughed and then she slept against him as he sat awake and watched clouds eat the moon and restore it again. She woke, deflated a little, not ashamed he hoped, and started the car—bad moment when it coughed and humped once and then failed, but she got it going as he looked on helplessly. At the dark house on Z Street she parked the car askew and said she was coming in to wash up, if that was all right.

What was marvelous to him then was that, when they were drawn to his bedroom by the force of some logic obvious to them both, she wanted to help him take off his pants and divest him of his braces, which she unbuckled slowly and unhandily as he sat on the bed. She raised her eyes to him now and then as she worked, with an angel-of-mercy smile from which he could not look away; he wondered if she thought that he needed her helping hand, as he had in the car by the river, and was willing to give it; this act seemed even more generous, unnecessary as it was. When that was done, though, he drew her to him with strong arms that perhaps she didn't expect, and divested her with quick skill, which also maybe she didn't expect.

When she awoke again he was deep asleep. She washed again and dressed. Now how had that happened, she'd like to know, but gave herself no answer. At least he'd known the use of *the present* as the BBs used to call it, oh so long ago that was, which was good because she'd never. She felt a strange trickle down her leg, reminding her of then, and she stopped, overcome with something like utter weariness. She guessed she'd drunk a lot. What must he think of her. She walked around the little dark house, so unlike a house, and found another bed. She'd have to think about this, and about Danny, and about everything: she'd have to think. She'd have to *remember*. Remember who he was; remember—she sort of laughed—who *she* was.

When Pancho came home after the Bomb Bay closed, he noticed that the Zephyr had somehow misaligned itself with the curb, odd, and when he went into his bedroom he found Diane in her blue dress asleep there like Goldilocks, one white-socked foot hanging off the bed, an unbuckled shoe falling from the foot, which just at that moment dropped off and woke her. She rose to see Pancho in the doorway. He stood aside as she walked past him with a nod and a smile, head lifted, and went out into the night.

4

This is the worst thing that's ever happened to me."

"I don't understand. I mean we did everything right." Dimly Prosper remembered Larry the shop steward, grinning at him in the pharmacy: *Lucky if they don't break*. "Are you sure?"

"They did that test with the rabbit."

"Oh."

"I guess I'm just real fruitful," Diane said, blowing her wet nose. "Oh Jesus what'll we do."

They sat perfectly still in the *Aero* office, talking to but facing away from each other, as though those passing by or working, who could look in, might discern what they talked about.

"Maybe it'll just go away, like the other one."

"I don't think you can count on that," Prosper said.

"I can't go home again. Not again. This time with a baby. Somebody else's."

Nothing more for a time but the periodic clang of work proceeding.

"You can stay here," Prosper said, drawing himself up. "Stay in the house with us, Pancho and me, and don't tell your husband. And then I can raise the. The child. Raise it myself. When the war's over and you go back, to, to."

He still hadn't looked her way while he made this huge statement,

actually unable to, but when he'd said it he turned, and she was looking at him as though he had spoken in some foreign tongue, or muttered madness. Then she put her chin in her hands and gazed into the
distance, just as if he'd said nothing at all. "This is the worst thing
that's ever happened to me," she said, once more. "The worst."

He thought of saying to her that after all it couldn't be the only time
in the war something like this had happened, it was sort of under-
standable, forgivable even, maybe, surely: but he hadn't said any of
that, luckily, before he had the further thought of not saying it. She
pulled from the pocket of her overalls a small sheet of paper, one of a
kind he'd seen before. "He's here," she said.

"Here?"

"Well I mean in this country, not way out there at sea. He was I
guess a hero out there somehow and he got hurt, he says not bad, and
he's been getting better in a hospital in San Francisco." She was reading the little shiny gray V-mail. "He's going back tomorrow, no the day
after. They gave him leave, a couple of days. He wishes I could be there
with him. That's what he says." She proffered the letter, but Prosper
didn't think he should take it.

"A couple of days?"

"I couldn't even if I could," she said, tears now again brightening
her eyes. "I mean can you imagine. What would I tell him? I couldn't
even say hello." She folded the little paper on its folds and put it away.
"So it's good I guess, that I can't get there."

She tried a smile then, for Prosper's sake he knew, but he couldn't
respond, and just then there came the beeping of an electric car, Horse
Offen's, just outside the office; Horse was standing up in the car waving
to him urgently.

"I gotta go," Prosper said.

"Me too," she said. She took the hankie from her sleeve and dabbed
her eyes, he got into his crutches and rose. Horse had his hat on, so
Prosper grabbed his.

"Diane. This'll be, this'll . . ."

"Don't," she said softly. "Just don't."

"This is going to be great," said Horse, turning the electric car out of
the shop and heading for the exit to the airfield. "I've never had a warn-

ing before, that they're coming, but this time I happened—I just *happened*—to be up in the control tower when they radio'd in. We'll get them arriving."

Prosper, gripping the rail of the car with one hand and his hat with the other, asked no questions.

"You do the camera," Horse said. He preferred to ask the questions himself on these occasions, Prosper used up too much attention himself and wasn't nosy enough. He had a good eye, though, Horse thought.

Prosper looked up, as Horse was now doing, his driving erratic. A plane was nearing, Prosper couldn't tell what kind, not large. "So who," he said.

"Crew coming in to ferry a *Pax* to the coast," Horse said. "A crew of wasps."

"Oh right." Not wasps but WASPs—Women Air Service Pilots. He'd admired them in the magazines—studying hard at their navigation, suited up for flying, relaxing in the sun, crowding the sinks at morning in their primitive barracks somewhere in a desert state. He began to feel anticipation too. Their planes had touched down here before, just long enough to let out crews, male crews, that would fly the finished B-30s to the coasts or farther, or the test pilots who'd bring them right back here. Prosper'd never seen a WASP in person. Now, Horse said, they were bringing in a crew all of women to train on the six-engine plane, after which they'd fly it themselves to wherever it was to go, at least within the States.

"There they come," Horse cried, seeing the plane bank and begin to descend toward the field. He gunned the little vehicle—it basically had one speed, and it wasn't fast—to where he had guessed the plane would touch down, then veering when it went where he hadn't. They were there, though, when it alighted, a single-engine biplane that seemed misbuilt somehow.

"Beech Staggerwing," Horse cried. "Fine little craft. Famous women won a famous air race in one, six-eight years ago, we'll look it up."

Prosper, doing his best to match Horse's urgency, climbed from the car and swing-gaited toward the plane as fast as he could, the Rolleiflex bouncing on his chest. The propeller ceased, kicked back once, and was still. Prosper had the plane in focus as the door opened and the pilot came out, then one two three other women, all smiles, waving to Horse and Prosper in what Prosper could only feel was an ironic sort of way, yes it's us again.

"Hi, hi!" Horse called out, waving grandly. He glanced back at Prosper to assure himself that shots were being taken and the film being rolled forward, and it was, Prosper watching and framing them, and they in the frame seeming to be some ancient painting in the *Cyclopedia,* stacked like strong goddesses on the step, the door, the ground, looking this way and that, all the same and all unique. They wore brown leather flying jackets and fatigues amazingly rumpled; each came out carrying her parachute and a kit. Warm boots in the unheated plane, cold aloft these days. How beautiful they were. How grateful he felt to be there then, and always would, there on that day of all days.

"How was the flight?" Horse asked, pad and pencil already out. "You ladies going to fly the *Pax,* is that right? Say, that's one monster plane, isn't it! Well you've flown, what, B-25s, B-17s, and yes what? B-29s? Well well well, Superfortress! Say, for my little paper here, can I just get some names? Martha, the pilot, okay Kathleen, Jo Ellen, Honora, that's *h-o-n-o-r-a?* Okeydokey!"

Prosper'd never seen Horse in such a lather, the four women just marching along, actually in step, answering what they were asked but very obviously on duty here, and tired. They each glanced at Prosper, their faces making no comment. He caught up with Martha, a dark-browed wide-mouthed woman who reminded him a little of Elaine. Seeing that he'd like to speak but was using all his breath to walk, she slowed down.

"Say," she said.

"Martha," Prosper asked, and she nodded confirmingly. "How long will you be here?"

"Just tonight. Fly out tomorrow for, lessee, San Francisco. 0500 hours."

"Where'll you stay?"

"They have this dorm here?"

"Yes."

"There."

"So you'll have the evening. I was just wondering . . ."

She looked again at him, as though he'd appeared from nowhere just at that moment, or had in that moment turned into something or someone he hadn't been before. He knew the look.

"All I want," she said, "is a drink and a steak. If I don't fall asleep first."

"Actually," he said, "that might be a tall order. The cafeteria's the only eats for a long way."

"Then that'll do," said Martha.

"For a drink," he said, "there's the Bomb Bay."

"The what?"

He explained, she thanked him, gave him a wave, and caught up with the other women. Meanwhile Horse had gone back for the car and now drew up beside him.

"What did you learn?" he asked.

Prosper didn't answer, and climbed into the car, thinking that some word, some name, had occurred in those minutes that meant a lot, but in a way he couldn't grasp, and he kept thinking about it as Horse, talking a mile a minute, drove him back and dropped him at the office.

"Get those films developed," he said, as he drove away.

"Yessir."

On Prosper's desk lay an envelope containing the new *Upp 'n' Adam* cartoons for him to letter. He sat down and slid them out, Bristol board eleven-by-fourteen inches, on which the artist had sketched his picture of the two fools—fat Upp blithely driving his forklift to disaster as Adam points at him and calls out to the viewer. The line that Prosper was to add was "Adam sez: If you *see* something, *SAY* something!!!" Prosper didn't think the picture was very expressive of what he took that phrase to mean, that the bosses wanted you to watch out for pilfering, waste, slacking, even sabotage: it was about getting workers to watch one another and report to management. Well it was hard to picture that using the two friends, with Adam turning Upp in. The blue lines of the initial sketch were overlaid in black ink, improving it here and there; those blue lines, the first thoughts, would magically disappear when the whole was photographed.

If you see something, say something.

Prosper remembered what it was that Martha the pilot had said that had tinkled a bell in his brain. San Francisco: she'd said San Francisco.

He got up, hoisting himself so fast he nearly tumbled over. If you see something say something. He made it out the door and down through the plant, people calling hellos after him, and toward the cafeteria. If she hadn't gone there, then the dorm, or the Bomb Bay. He was already speaking to her, making a case. Sure it's against the regulations but hell what isn't, listen her husband's an airman, *an airman,* a fighter pilot. And who'm I, I'm, well, I heard the story and gosh she seems like such a swell kid, so young, I'll tell you something, she was married *one day* and he was off to the Pacific, she hasn't seen him since. Her husband. Shot down in the Pacific, a hero. It's important, really. And Martha, you're the pilot, aren't you, and what you say goes in that plane, isn't that right?

The faster he spoke to Martha the faster he walked, hardly feeling the effort, the din of his blood in his ears. Probably, probably, it'd be harder to convince Diane of this than Martha, you could tell Martha was fearless and made up her own mind, but Diane? It'd work, it would, she'd just have to see, he'd *make* her do it. He invoked Mary Wilma, prayed to Mary Wilma for power, he'd *be* Mary Wilma and make Diane do his plan, by his will and by his certainty, he'd.

He stopped still, not only because his arms had at last got in touch with his brain and said No more, and his breath was gone: also because he had another thought. The thought was to not do this at all, no, to forget about it and not tell Diane and forget he ever thought of it. Because that might be better for him.

In the Bomb Bay she'd said to him *I don't even remember what he looks like.*

But *he* was here, Prosper, before her. She didn't need to try to remember him. Those good-bye marriages didn't need to last, everybody said they didn't last. She said this was the worst thing that'd ever happened to her, but what if it was for the best, what if she forgot Danny more and more until he was gone altogether, and he himself was still here, not going anywhere.

And alive. At the war's end he'd certainly be still alive.

At that shameful thought he started again toward the cafeteria. No. No. She was beautiful and she'd known how to be kind to him without diminishing him or treating him like an infant, she was just good at that and so he knew she was good inside, and inside her too was his own baby. But he had no right. Just *because* of that he had no right. No fair even making her the offer, posing a choice, it could only hurt her to hear it: the war was winding down and he'd soon be out of a job, maybe for life, and what kind of a prize did that make him? She couldn't say yes. He'd have to advise her not to. If he was her.

His heart hurt. Actually, even though the heart beat hard, it was the muscles of his chest that hurt, and the bronchia and throat through which the burning breath rushed; but he'd have said it was his heart. He reached the cafeteria, the vast spread of tables and people, not so crowded though at this hour, and after a minute they were easy to spot, the four of them at their table, it was as though the eyes of the other diners there, turning toward them, pointed them out to him.

Well so what, he thought. What he had, or would have, was a son, maybe a daughter, growing up somewhere, at one end of the nation or the other, and nobody'd know he was the father, nobody but Diane and he, and even she might talk herself into forgetting one day, though he hoped not, it wouldn't be fair.

Danny'd never know, but he knew. He knew what men don't know, what they don't get to know. They think they know but they don't know, because they aren't told, because they don't ask. But he knew, more than all of them, and better than that, he knew that he knew. And that was enough, would be enough, for now.

"Hi, Martha," he said, a little breathless. She'd watched him make his way across the floor with a kind of forbearance, not unkind, smiling even. She lifted her face in inquiry. "So. Can I ask you a question?"

She nodded and pointed to the chair opposite her, and he felt her eyes on him as he maneuvered to sit, unlock his braces, and turn to her, now an ordinary man. Then somehow his nerve went and he didn't know how to begin. "So," he said again. She pulled out a cork-tipped cigarette and he hastened to find his lighter and light it for her.

"So when'd you first fly?" he asked at last.

5

Summer 1936. Swimming was over for the afternoon and the girls were sitting on the dock or out on the slimy wooden float, looking down into the gray-green water or over toward the prickle of pines across the lake or at each other. Their wool suits of black, or navy edged with white, drying in the late sun: still damp tomorrow when the girls would have to squirm back into them for morning swim.

It came as a noise first, from where they couldn't tell because the bowl of the lake bounced sound from rim to rim unplaceably: new girls were known to wake up crying out in the night when the Delaware & Hudson night train passed miles away—it sounded like it was going to go right through the cabin.

Martha was the first to see it, turning and tilting as it rose over the pines in a way that seemed uncertain to her then but wouldn't later when she knew what the pilot was about. High up it caught the full sun, and white as it was it almost disappeared now and then against the sky, then came clear and solidified as it swooped down around the south end of the lake to approach the lake longwise.

"It's a seaplane," someone said, and now you could see that it was; instead of wheels it seemed to be shod in big soft slippers. Martha watched in awe as it came down fearlessly onto the lake's surface, seeming as light as a falling leaf and yet huge with power, the sound enormous now, the propeller nearly invisible in its speed. Then it struck the water—they gasped or cried out, but not Martha, as it seemed to bounce off and settle again, this time opening a long white rip in the gray fabric of the lake surface. Martha'd never seen anything so taking in all her life. She'd seen airplanes in the movies, where (like acrobats in the circus) they seemed merely impossible; even though you knew they were real they didn't seem it. But this one landing with negligent skill on the water—throttling its engine now and lifting softly in relaxation, turning toward the dock of the boys' camp on the other shore— it was real, what it had done was real and the pilot could have made a mistake and come to grief and hadn't; she could hear it, the power it expended, she could even smell it.

The girls stood and watched it even after it had tied up at the boys' dock and sat high and still and innocent there like any old skiff. Of course everything that occurred in or around the boys' camp was of interest. A long time afterward Martha would think how intense it had been, the two camps so near but with a great gulf fixed between, like life as it was lived then—the signals and displays from one side meant for the other side to see and decode, the thousand plans laid every summer but never acted on to cross the gap. It amazed her to look back and think how many camps there were in the great north woods like hers, boys divided from girls not far away. At Martha's camp the two had occupied spits or points that had seemed to strain toward each other, like Romeo and Juliet, like two bodies in movie seats; getting closer too over the years (so it seemed to Martha as she came back summer after summer and her legs grew longer). As though all of their cool nights and hot days and their talk and the summer's flickering endless contests about who had said a cruel thing behind whose back and who was snooty and who was whiny and who was definitely a part-time Liz were all caused, like a reflection, by what happened across the lake where the boys fought and played mumblety-peg and ganged up to humiliate the weak and snapped one another's bottoms with towels. Martha knew they did all these things because her older brother before his illness had gone to the same camp at the lake of the woods.

They could see the swarm of boys around the plane then. A tall counselor made his way amid them to where the pilot was just then

climbing out—he seemed to be wearing a Panama hat, of all things—
and the two of them met and shook hands, and the boys gathered
around the two and the girls could see nothing more. After a brief time
the pilot got up on the plane again, importuned obviously by the boys
asking questions and admiring the craft, and with a wave like Lind-
bergh, he shut himself in; then after a solemn silent moment the engine
started and the propeller kicked once, seemed to travel backward,
kicked again as the engine nacelle blew white smoke, then sped to a blur
in that way a propeller has, hysterical and self-satisfied at once.

What had happened—they learned at supper—was that a boy in the
camp, a first-year, had got bit by a copperhead, and they had no serum,
and so they'd radio'd out, and the plane had brought it in. Just like a
movie—snake, serum, radio, plane. It was thrilling but not as moving
to Martha as the plane itself, as it turned toward them—not toward
them, of course, toward the length of the lake, to take off again. But at
that, somehow all at once and without thought, the girls started waving
and calling and jumping up and down; and the plane seemed to pause
a moment, and then glided with an air of curious interest toward their
dock while the girls cheered in triumph.

It was a Stinson V-77 Gullwing, though that too she'd only learn
later, when she flew one. This summer afternoon she only stood trans-
fixed, but at the front of the pack, as Pete Bigelow (that would turn out
to be his name) stilled his engines to a mutter, and pushed his door
open, and asked if anybody wanted to go for a ride. None of the others
would—not in their bathing costumes, maybe not ever—but Martha
grabbed a robe and her espadrilles and presented herself before she
even knew she had.

"Two dollars," said Pete, tilting back the Panama. He was older
and uglier than she thought he'd be. Two dollars was a lot of money:
all that was in Martha's account at the camp store.

"Pay when we get back?" she said, and—seeing her there with no
money, no pockets to put it in—Pete Bigelow laughed, and reached out
a sun-red arm to pull her up and in, just as Martha glimpsed hurrying
toward the dock from wherever she'd been malingering with a cigarette
and a *Photoplay* the contemptible, the incompetent swimming instructor, her face a shocked mask of disbelief. Pete reached across her and
pulled shut the flimsy door. He kicked up the engine, a heart-seizing

noise, a noise that was not only loud but also large, as though it produced the whole scale of possible sounds from the lowest to the highest
and erased every other sound there could be. From then on it was the
strongest, most *easeful* sound Martha Goldensohn knew.

It wasn't until she was in college that she began taking flying lessons.
That would have been early 1941, and already the Air Corps was being
withdrawn from the routine jobs and organized into a fighting force,
and there was a need for fliers and planes who could take urgent messages or deliver those serums or search for lost hikers. She'd go down
in her little Austin runabout to the flying field whenever she could, and
pay for lessons at twelve dollars an hour, outrageous, nothing else at
school cost anything like that.

"Amelia Earhart, huh," the instructor, whose name was Doc of
course, remarked when she signed up.

"Ha ha," she said. "Anytime a woman says, I'd like to fly, you have
to say 'Amelia Earhart' right after, or you have bad luck all day—that
it?"

She did well, she had a gift, though she almost flunked out of college, which Daddy would not have been happy about, spending all her
time on the field or in the air. She managed mostly Cs that semester;
what mattered to her was that she got her pilot's license. She took a
little inheritance she got that year to go in with a couple of men around
the field on a six-year-old Cessna Airmaster that had been rebuilt after
a tipover on landing. She convinced her partners to sign up with her for
the brand-new Civil Air Patrol. Ten days later the Japanese bombed
Pearl Harbor.

Martha had felt since her first flight that if you'd once flown a plane
you'd never go to war, never want to, never see the point. Not only
because all those borders and their checkpoints and barricades would
be invisible or imaginary looked down on from above but also because
flight itself was better than fighting. She knew well enough that war
delighted men who could fly. She knew about the fleets of bombers over
London, so merciless; the Stukas that strafed the retreating British at
Dunkirk, the planes that shot up the lifeboats of sinking enemy ships:
you could think by 1942 that flying itself arose from an evil impulse

and ought to be banned. But she loved it, and her love, like any love, seemed to her innocent. She couldn't argue it and wasn't going to try.

The great thing about the CAP was that you got all the fuel you could use, though sometimes the supply itself was low. After all she and her fellow CAP pilots were helping to protect the nation. She never herself got to go out on coastal patrol and hunt for German subs (or sink one, as one heroic or lucky CAP pilot had done), but still she was showing what women could do in the war effort, and also, by the way, what Jewish people (as her mother always named them) could do, take that, Hitler, and all of them.

Silly, and she didn't need an excuse, but she took the ones she was offered. She flew packages and medical goods and government documents and ferried officials and searched for lost hikers all that summer, and then in the fall, she got a telegram: it was one sent to every qualified woman pilot that could be identified, and it invited her to become a pilot with the Women's Air Ferry Service.

Yes she'd go. She could go back and finish college when this was over. If she washed out, well, she'd go back to the CAP program, or go rivet things or weld things. She wasn't going to go read Shakespeare and Milton now, no, Daddy, not now. She convinced him and he convinced Mother, or Mother at least in the end didn't say no.

The week before she was to take the train south (she'd wanted to drive the Austin down but Daddy nixed that and got her a roomette) she stayed home every night and had dinner with her parents and her brother and her grandmother, helped her mother paste photographs in a family album and label the black pages with white ink, such beautiful handwriting she had, and she had lunch in the city with her father and drank a Manhattan and let him take her shopping to buy simple strong outfits they imagined would be suitable for her training (she'd send them home when eventually uniforms were issued them—she lived in those and her rumpled fatigues and a couple of skirts and blouses).

Her last evening before heading south she spent with her brother Norman, playing cribbage and joshing and drinking a cocktail Norman had invented that was so nasty you couldn't have more than one, it was more a joke than an intoxicant. Norman rolled up to the little bar in the library and pretended to know exactly what he was doing.

"Creme de menthe," he said, flourishing the Mae West–shaped bottle. "White of egg. Muddle the lemon with sugar."

"Oh stop, Norman."

"You'll love it."

He turned the chair to face her, with the huge murky drink in hand. "To you," he said. She took it from him and picked up his too; he needed both hands to move the chair through the room and down the little ramp that led to what Daddy called the card room. He locked the brake and with her help went from the wheelchair to an easy chair he liked, in which he usually spent much of his day.

"I like the mustache," she said. "It's so handsome."

Norman was an inordinately good-looking man, Martha thought, and everyone else did too, and a vestigial vanity about it had continued even after the polio, when (Norman said) good looks were about as much use to him as another ear. His thick black hair fell over his brow like Gable's, and the new mustache was like his too.

"You'll write," he said.

"Of course."

"Long letters. Every day."

"I might be a little busy."

She didn't mind the job of writing her life for Norman. Even when there wasn't much life. In fact it was easier when there wasn't much to say. Setting out on an adventure, in aid of the nation, to fly planes in the company of other women with nerve and skill: that was going to be harder, she could see that already, but she'd do it, she'd brag, she'd tell all, and not a touch of sorrow for him, not a touch of it. That was the agreement, never spoken. She could feel condemned down deep inside her that she could fly when he couldn't walk, she could feel that it was wrong in her to feel joy in any movement or possibility whatever when she sat with him here: but she knew also never, ever to show it.

"So any news?" she asked.

"No news, Martha." He smiled the smile that always came with that answer, and sipped his concoction. "Oh. This."

He put down his drink and made his way back into the wheelchair and across the rug to a table by the window flanked with shelves and drawers where his coin collection was housed. There were more albums in his rooms upstairs, but the trip upward in the clanking lift was one he took as infrequently as he could. He'd told Martha that making all that noise was as embarrassing as loudly passing wind in public.

"Here," he said. He took, from a stiff envelope addressed to him and sent from Mexico City, a small envelope of glassine. From that he removed and dropped into her hand a heavy coin of gray silver.

"Just arrived," Norman said. He often showed her his new acquisitions—reading history and novels and this collection were what he did—but this coin seemed to evoke not the usual enthusiasm but a kind of melancholy in him. He let her finger it for a moment and then took it back, to tell her (as he always did) its story.

"A Spanish milled dollar," he said, "1733, see? Reign of Philip the Fifth. That's the arms of Spain. This is a nice piece, and maybe was never circulated. Look on the obverse."

The other side of the coin said VTRAQUE VNUM and showed a pair of pillars with a scroll between them. Martha tried to remember her Latin. "And both one?"

Norman nodded, not bad. "Actually 'the one and the other.' Meaning the two worlds, East and West, Spain and the New World. But look closer at the pillars. Here." He picked up a Sherlock Holmes–style magnifying glass from the table and gave it to her. "Look at the little scroll. Can you read that?"

"No."

"It says *Plus ultra*," Norman said. He lifted his head, tossed back that falling lock of shining hair. "It means *Even farther.* Even farther, Sis." He put the cold coin back into her hand and closed her fingers over it. "Keep it with you," he said. "Go even farther. Just write."

She wrote: she didn't write that her first training base had no fire equip-ment, that they'd had no insurance, no hospital anywhere nearby, and they'd gone up in whatever planes were available and not always brought them down in one piece, partly because the mechanics disliked the idea of women flying their planes and pushed the checkout jobs onto the least senior men. She didn't say that, because he'd tell Mother and Mother didn't need to be more alarmed than she already was or more certain that Martha should come back home and go work with the USO. She wrote him funny stories and amazing stories and stories that were both, about being sent down to the Great Dismal Swamp, yes that's its name, to learn how to pull targets for antiaircraft gunners to train on, gunners who missed and hit the tow planes every now and then. She told him about the male pilot who was assigned to fly with a woman pilot and stormed in to his commander and said he was quitting if he had to fly with women, and tore off his wings and threw them down on the commander's desk; the commander said I'll tell you when you're quitting, pick up those wings and report for duty. So maybe that story wasn't true, anyway Martha didn't *know* it was true and the one or two male commanding officers she'd had anything to do with were as patronizing and horrid as any pilot, but it was the right story anyway. She told Norman how you used "Code X" on your orders to mean you couldn't fly because you had your monthlies, or "a limited physical disability" as they said. She quoted him the silly songs they sang: *The moral of this story, girls, as you can plainly see, Is never trust a pilot an inch above your knee*—but she didn't tell him when she lost her virginity.

She told him about flying: how at first she felt like she'd never learned to fly at all, the planes she was training in *landed* at nearly a hundred miles an hour, which was faster than any cruising speed she'd ever maintained. In a dive you could black out and blood would pour out of your nose. Her old Cessna had put out about 70 horsepower, and these things had *two* fierce engines that could get up to 1500 horse-power, there's the difference right there; they had retractable landing gear to remember to retract, constant-speed propellers, a hundred things to remember that she'd never encountered before.

She didn't tell him about the women she'd heard of who'd lost con-trol of a plane, or whose plane had failed them, who'd died in a crash.

Boredom and inaction were almost as large a part of it as danger, though: sitting around the duty room gossiping and "hangar flying" as they said, telling stories of this or that flight or near miss or cool bravery; riding the milk train or, worse, the bus back from ferrying a plane; doing paperwork; waiting; more waiting. Angling for the better jobs, for more flying, fewer ground lessons, watching other women get ahead. There was no way not to see that the WAFS, which became the WASP, was in some ways a lot like college, like sorority, like school, like, yes, camp. There was always a core group who never got in trouble for things that others had to pay for, whose records stayed spotless when others were washed out for minor infractions. They were the ones who shared a way of talking, a line of jokes, a kind of insouciance, the ones that male commanders thought of as their sort of woman. Many of them had got their licenses and their hours because they'd been able to fly their own planes, had families that could afford them, and been able to spend summers racing or barnstorming. She'd known such girls all her life, she was one of them herself at the same time as she could never be one of them, she didn't give a damn about that, but she didn't like getting sidelined or blackballed either, for the one reason no one would say: and fortunately, in this world and this time, what mattered most was how good you were, farm girl, working girl, college girl, Jewish girl. She was good. She loved the flying, loved learning she could fly huge bombers with as much ease and certainty as she'd flown her old Cessna. And she came to love her sisters. In spite of it all. Most of them.

"So now can I ask you a question?" Martha said to Prosper in the Dining Commons in Henryville. Her comrades had departed for bed or the Bomb Bay, and he'd told her his story and made his pitch, and she'd not said yes or no, though No was obviously the right answer.

"Sure," Prosper said. "Certainly."

"Is that polio you have?"

"No," Prosper said. "Something different."

"Oh." She looked around them, not as though she was about to tell a secret, and yet for a reason, he thought. "My older brother," she said, "has polio."

"Oh? Right now?"

"Well I mean he had it once. He's. Well he has a wheelchair."

"Oh."

"He's at home."

"Uh-huh."

He waited, ready to answer from his store of information and experience any question she might like to put to him; not many people needed it.

"So where'll you go when this is over?" Martha asked at length, seeming to change the subject. "Home?"

"Oh I don't know." He opened his arms. "Maybe see the world."

She took that for a joke, or at least a whimsy, and in fact he some-what drooped just after saying it. "You liked working here?" she said.

"It's been pretty wonderful. Actually."

"Because you got to do your part."

"Because there's no stairs."

Martha studied him in puzzlement for a moment, then laughed. "All right. I understand."

"Is your brother working?"

"Him? Oh no. No, he had planned to go to law school, but then."

Prosper nodded, nodded again, acknowledging. "Lots of stairs at law school," he said, "I'd imagine."

Martha laughed again, a better outcome than he'd hoped for.

"Maybe if there weren't," he said, "*I'd* go be a lawyer."

"Okay," she said. "All right."

He drew out his cigarettes, and shook one forth for her to take if she liked, but she waved it away. "So Martha," he said. "About this request. This, this appeal. What do you think?"

"Well why do you want to do this for her? I don't get it."

"She's. I mean she's just."

"I'm sorry," Martha said, "but I get the feeling there's something about this you aren't telling me."

"It's just important," Prosper said helplessly.

"You tell me why it is," Martha said. "Why it's important to *you,* and why you're here asking and she's not, and maybe I'll give you an answer."

He told her the story, Diane's, and told her his part in it too. It took a while. She listened. At the end she was leaning forward on her crossed arms, all ears.

"Well. Gee. I wouldn't have thought."

"Why? You mean a guy like me?"

She shrugged, smiling. "It's natural to think."

"Is it?"

"You're blushing," she said.

"Wouldn't you say, though," Prosper said, moving the ashtray around as though it were a fixed opinion he wanted to loosen, "that people are all the time thinking that only certain kinds of people can do certain kinds of things? And you can't change their opinion even if you know better? Even if, for you, doing that thing, that thing you do, doesn't seem so unlikely to you, if it seems to you the most natural thing in the world?"

She was blushing now herself.

"I just mean," he said. And he gestured to her. "You flying. The big bombers. Tell me the men all thought you could do it, oh no problem there. Tell me the other girls thought so. Tell me your *mom* thought so."

For a long time she looked at him, as though she was putting together from all over her life the parts of a thought she'd never thought before. Then she said: "Okay."

"Okay?"

"Okay I'll take her."

"Now you won't tell her I told you all that."

"No. Get her there at 0445 hours. That's quarter to five, A.M. No later or I'll leave without her. One little bag, no more. She should dress warm. Tell her if she pukes on me I'll push her out the door."

"I'll tell her that."

"Don't you dare."

They shook hands but then still sat for a while. Martha said she'd probably be back this way soon, with another crew. Maybe they could talk some more, she said, and Prosper Olander said oh sure, he'd definitely be here, he hoped they could meet, yes, he'd like that very much, to meet and talk: he would.

6

You remember my friend Poindexter," Danny said. "Bill."

"Of course I remember him. I'm not going to forget that."

They lay naked in the center of a bed big enough for three, faint light of a single lamp in a far corner, the room was as vast as a palace. Top o' the Mark. This was the room that Danny had been given, a suite actually, his buddies coming and going all day but all gone now, leaving it to Danny and Diane. She'd not told him how she'd got there, she'd put it a day back, a long train ride, not so bad though she said, not bad at all, because it brought her here to him. Actually she felt like she'd been carried here on a witch's broomstick, it was the most dreadful and terrifying thing she'd ever done, ever even imagined doing, which she actually couldn't have in advance. And that woman Martha just grinning at her and making small talk and pointing out the pretty lights below whenever Diane beside her could open her eyes.

"He got hurt pretty bad," Danny said. In this dimness his face was hollowed and skull-like, the sockets of his eyes deep and his cheeks sunken, as though he'd seen things that wouldn't pass from him, as though he went on seeing them always. "We had to land on the deck in the dark. We'd just made it back from hunting the Jap carrier and it was night. Lot of guys didn't get back. Almost out of gas, you had to set it down first try, couldn't go around again and again. They'd lit up the ship with every light they had, but it was still like landing on a nighttime parking lot in the middle of a city. That's when I got banged up. Danny almost made it, but his tailhook missed the cable and he went into the crash barrier and over the side. His plane broke up when it went into the water. They got him out, but he'd crushed his left side. He'll live, but he's lost an arm and a leg."

"Oh Danny." He'd said it all as though he were writing it in a letter, or reading it from one: as though it were far away from himself, something heard of or remembered from long ago.

"Yeah well. He's up and around, sort of. Sylvia's leaving him, though."

"No."

"Well." He moved his dark body in the silky sheets. He'd lost weight; his white north-land face was as dark as hers. "You can understand, I guess. I mean he was—well he's half a man. How was he gonna keep her."

"Oh Danny."

"I don't think I could do it," Danny said. "He was damn damn brave. Said he just wanted to live. I don't think I could do that, live with that."

"Oh Danny no." She covered her mouth, and her breasts.

"Don't think about it," Danny said and moved to hold her again. She'd been afraid up to the last minute that he might be so war weary or war torn or hurt that he wouldn't be able to or want to, and then where'd she be? But it was the reverse, he wouldn't stop, clung to her and pressed himself to her as though he could just disappear right inside her and forget everything. She'd asked Prosper—asked him once and then again, last thing before she'd climbed aboard that horrid plane—if there was a chance that the baby she carried could turn out, well, like him, Prosper. Whether the baby might have, you know, that. No no, Prosper'd told her, no, no chance, that was an operation he'd had that went wrong, not something in the blood you could inherit. The same answer twice. But just now she thought of what she hadn't asked: what had that operation been for? What was it supposed to fix, that it didn't fix?

"Oh Danny," she said, and said again, weeping even as she held him, all she could say to mean so many things she couldn't or didn't know how to say, the name of every grief endured or escaped, every misunderstood grace, every utter loss, every hope, every new fear, each one remembered as they embraced, felt as though for the first or the last time.

Prosper got a letter from her a week later. She told him she guessed the plan had worked. She'd decided to stay out there, she said, go home again to her parents, just rest and take it easy and eat good food and be careful for the baby until it was born. She'd write to her roommate, she said, and get her clothes and things sent home, there wasn't much really, the way they all lived out there; the dungarees and gloves and things could just be thrown out. She'd begun then to write something more and crossed it out so hard he couldn't even guess at the meaning, or why she'd crossed it out: something she thought would hurt him to read, or something she'd decided he shouldn't know; something she didn't want to promise, or offer; something.

In the Bomb Bay a new band was playing, an all-girl one this time, the Honeydrops. Their weary bus was outside, and their ruffled gowns looked weary too, but they themselves weren't, few as they were they beat up a big sound; their singer wailing high above the horns and clarinets, looking right at Prosper, as though the song she sang asked him and him alone a question: maybe the other men there felt the same but he was the only one who just sat and listened. Prosper was hearing one of the songs she sang for the first time. She sang it holding the microphone stand with tenderness and putting her lips almost to the bulbous mike itself to croon, he'd never seen that before. She'd kiss him once, she sang; she'd kiss him twice, and once again; it'd been a long, long time.

In the coming year, when Bing sang this song, and the boys were returning from Europe and then from the Pacific, it would be about how hard it had been for them over there, about coming home at last to wives and girlfriends. We'd hear it constantly; we can still hear it. But when Prosper heard it sung there in the Bomb Bay well before it was a hit, and with Diane's letter in his pocket, it seemed to be not about men but women. It seemed to be what those women, those hundreds of thousands left behind here, might say to someone they might meet, someone like himself: that they had waited a long long time, and were going to get a kiss and more than a kiss now where and when they could, until that man did come home, and everything would be different: but this was now and not then. Which in a way seemed to him dreadfully and wholly sad, even though he supposed he had been a beneficiary of that situation, and perhaps even had done some women some good that they wouldn't have got otherwise, which was somehow sad too. In fact he couldn't decide which was sadder, and tried not to ponder it too much. He guessed that there would be time for that soon enough.

He ordered a Cuba libre. Soon the band stopped playing and the singer softly and sincerely said good night.

Late December 1944 and there are fifty B-30s on the tarmac at Ponca

City, unable to be flown out until whatever's wrong with their engine cowlings or their oil tanks or ignition processes is discovered and fixed. We couldn't stop making them, for what would be done with us and all our skills and training, all our tools and procedures, then? So—a little more slowly, a little more thoroughly—we went on making them, the Teenie Weenies doing more standing around than before (as the Teenie Weenies in the comic pages are all doing most of the time while the active ones explore or labor). And then one more is drawn out the great doors to join the flock of others pointed toward the West and the enemy but going nowhere. When the doors open the icy fog rolls in and rises to the height of the ceiling above, to linger there like a lost black cloud.

How cold and dark that winter of '44–'45 was. In the North it was the bitterest in years; the lack of fuel oil was life threatening in some places, places far from Ponca City, we heard it on the radio, eyewitness. It seemed harder because for a while it looked like the war in Europe at least was almost over. War production was cut back and some items unseen since before the war began to return to the stores— irons, pots and pans, stoves, refrigerators. Then came the huge Ardennes counteroffensive and the Battle of the Bulge and the mad resistance in the Pacific at every atoll and beach, and the planners thought again. Some controls on metals and other things were reimposed; new ration books were issued, and not only that: all your unspent ration points from '44 were invalidated. Everybody started 1945 with a new damn book, same old rules to follow, now maybe forever: that winter suspicion that the sun's not ever going to return. Except now people didn't feel so ready to sacrifice, we were tired of all that, so tired, and so back came Mr. Black in a big way, the stuff you wanted was there if you could find it, gas traded for whatever you had, farm-butchered beef and pork removed from the system and sold out of meat lockers that you knew about if you knew.

Those who are going into the services now, boys out of high school, the rejects of the factories, the once but no longer deferred, know they will be the last: the boys mostly eager for the chance, desperate to grow old enough in time, others perhaps feeling differently. Now the lives of men killed and wounded far away seem to have been wasted, a loss insupportable, and more are dying now than in the frenzy of beginning—in the climb up useless Italy, in the frozen mud of the Ardennes, in the assaults on palm tree islands in nowhere, for nothing. It's beginning to be possible to think so, though you'd never say it. For the first time, photographs of the prostrate bodies of our men are shown to us, on beaches, in the snow: the dead in *Life*. Why now? Is it a warning, a judgment, a caution—you see this now but you will see far worse if you slacken? We don't know.

At Van Damme Aero Ponca City a woman walks down the long nave of the Assembly Building with a steady tread, eyes looking neither left nor right. It's Mona the mail girl, with a telegram. The edge of the yellow form can be seen in the front pouch of her bag. A mail girl's never seen on the floor if she's not bringing one, she never brings just mail, you get that at home or at the post office, they bring mail to the offices of the managers and bosses but not to Associates out on the floor. Of all the mail girls in their night blue uniforms it's Mona who is always chosen to deliver the telegram: tall and phlegmatic, vast black pelt of hair over her brow and shoulders, black brows knitted together in the middle over the prow of her nose—those who watch her pass know these details, there have been opportunities to study her. When she comes through the floor, her long slow steps, a zone of silence moves with her, leaving a stillness in its wake even if those behind take up their work again, spared this time; and the silence moves on ahead, and spreads around her when she stops.

"Mrs. Bunce Wrobleski?" Mona asks, drawing out the telegram. They know; they stop working but they don't—most don't, out of pity or to honor her privacy—look at Connie taking the flimsy form from Mona; Mona because she can do this task without weeping herself, can stand dark and silent there long enough for respect but not too long.

MRS BUNCE WROBLESKI
VAN DAMME AERO PONCA CITY OKLA=
THE SECRETARY OF WAR DESIRES ME TO EXPRESS HIS DEEP
REGRET THAT YOUR HUSBAND CPL BUNCE J WROBLESKI WAS
KILLED IN ACTION 05 JAN 1945 LETTER FOLLOWS=
JA WILLIAM THE ADJUTANT GENERAL

Once General Marshall wrote these letters in his own hand. Now there are too many, too many even to count yet. Nor can the silence of that moment last a long time. The women around Connie (the men won't come forward or can't or don't know how) shelter her, and help her to her feet from where she has sat helplessly down; and they hold her one by one and help her off the floor even when she says No, no, let me go, let me just go on, there's so much, so much to do.

After a time we do start up again, and the silence disperses.

7

Connie went back north with Andy to bring him to see his grand-parents, to leave him there for a while so they could have him with them; after a while she could come back, go on working. She'd got a letter telling her how to collect on Bunce's standard government insurance policy, he must have told her he had one but she didn't remember him doing so and she'd stared down at the letter and the huge amount of money feeling sick and horrified, as at some loathsome joke. She'd already been informed that Bunce wouldn't be brought home, not now, that there were just too many to bring home; he'd be buried with the thousands there in the land he'd died in, it hurt her heart to think of it, and to think what Buster and his mom must feel. She had to go back, for them. So she wrapped her son in the warm winter clothes he'd worn when they left the North, and they boarded the train, the same train.

"Good-bye, Prosper."

"Good-bye, Connie."

"I'll see you again soon."

"Sure. I'll be seeing you."

"Are you all right? What is it?"

"Yes sure. Just my back."

"Your back hurts?"

"My back hurts some all the time, Connie. Almost all the time."

"You never said."

"No reason to say. Get on board, Connie."

"God bless you, Prosper."

Going through the prairie and the river valleys Connie seemed to see all that she couldn't see when she had come the other way: the shabby towns and the weary old cars, the streets without people, unpainted storefronts, peeling billboards advertising things that no one could get or weren't for sale. All the hurt done to this country in the last ten years and more, the things not repaired or replaced, still left undone because the war came first. The light-less factories too, fences rusting, gates closed with chains. Rollo had told her that thousands of businesses had failed since the war buildup began, little shops and bigger places too that couldn't compete with the great names for the government contracts. Consolidation. More had failed than in the Depression.

Gold star in a window there.

Maybe she could see it all because of where she had been for months, that place all new and furiously busy. One of those that would come out rich.

Night and the train filling at small stations with soldiers, different somehow now from the crowds of them that had played cards and teased her on the way down. Different in her eyes. Outside, the land so dark, new regulations, all places of amusement had to close at midnight: no neon lights or floodlights to save power and fuel.

Dark, rich. She tried to remember what god it was in ancient times who ruled over the land below the earth, which was always dark but rich, because he was also the god of money, of gold dug in the dark earth. Pluto. *Plutocracy,* a vocabulary word. Did she travel home through Pluto's realm, money given and made, the great owners getting richer nightlong and every one else getting a little richer too, hoarding their money like misers and waiting? And the dead souls without rest among us, so many. Around her the standing men in their drab uniforms swayed with the train's motion like wheat, so quiet in the dark. Some of them, she hoped, some at least were going home.

That spring we watched in the newsreels the gleaming B-29 Superfor-tresses, long and slim and impossibly wide-winged like the *Pax* but coming smartly off the assembly lines of four different factories in working order and already winging over the Pacific. They could reach Tokyo now, as the B-30 was intended to do from bases in China; but those bases had never materialized, and the B-29s took off from the little islands of the Pacific, Saipan, Tinian. In March they were sent in a great fleet in the night to fly in low and drop not great blockbuster bombs but hundreds of thousands of little canisters of jellied gasoline. Tokyo they always said was a Paper City. Before the war, girls collected Japanese dolls with paper fans and paper umbrellas and paper chrysan-themums for their hair; the dolls were accompanied by little books about Japan and the paper houses and cities. In the newsreels we'd seen the jellied gasoline tested, an instant spread of white fire and black smoke, each canister making a disaster. The crowded city burned so hotly that the Superfortresses were tossed high up into the air above it by the rising heat, like ash above a bonfire. Later in the newsreels Tokyo was a gray checkerboard of streets, nothing more; no buildings, no people.

In April in Oklahoma, the lilacs purple and white bloomed along the little river where Prosper and Diane had watched the lights of the refinery in Pancho's Zephyr. In the middle of the first shift at the plant the loudspeaker announcer, whose inadequate and uncertain voice we'd all come to love and mock, came on unexpectedly.

"Attention attention. In a few moments the president of Van Damme Aero, Mr. Henry Van Damme, will be speaking to you, bringing you an important announcement. At this time please shut down machines and tools in Bulletin A5 sequence. Crane operators please secure lifted parts."

Silence, or at least quiet, passed over the buildings, the whine of machines going down, the ceaseless clangor ceasing.

"Mr. Van Damme will speak to you now."

There was a moment of silence, a slight rustle of papers, and Henry Van Damme began to speak, his voice oddly high and light, at least over this system. Most of us had never heard it before.

"Ladies and gentlemen, Van Damme Aero Associates. My office received a cable two hours ago announcing that President Franklin Roosevelt died suddenly last night."

Of course he couldn't hear us where he was, but he was wise enough to know he must pause then and wait. There was a noise of dropped tools, a woman's piercing cry, and a mist of expelled sound. There was weeping. A voice here and there raised in blessing or hopeless denial or distress.

"I knew Franklin Roosevelt," Henry said, and his light voice grew lighter. "I know that he would want us not to mourn but to look forward. The work is not done. And yet." Here came the sound of more papers shuffled, or perhaps a handkerchief used, and then Henry Van Damme began speaking again in a different voice, it was hard to say different in what way, but we lifted our heads.

"Oh captain my captain," he said. Then for a moment he didn't go on. "Oh captain my captain, our fearful trip is done. The ship has weathered every rack, the prize we sought is won."

Of course we knew the words, many of us, most of us. It was a verse we had by heart, one we'd spoken on Oration Day or standing at our desks while teachers tapped the rhythms. *Oh heart heart heart.* A few people spoke softly along with Henry Van Damme, as though it were a prayer.

"*The ship is anchored safe and sound, its voyage closed and done;*
From fearful trip the victor ship comes in with object won;
Exult O shores, and ring O bells!
But I, with mournful tread,
Walk the deck my Captain lies,
Fallen cold and dead."

The strange thing is that all through that April night there were rumors across the country of the deaths of other men, names we all knew, all of them found to be alive the next day. There was a CLOSED sign on Jack Dempsey's restaurant in New York City: surely Dempsey was dead. Jack Benny had died suddenly. Almost a thousand calls came into the *New York Times* asking about the stories. Babe Ruth was dead. Charlie Chaplin. Frank Sinatra. The rumors fled as fast as long-distance calls across the country. As though we thought our king and pharaoh, gone to the other side, needed a phalanx of great ones to conduct him on his way.

Henry Van Damme flew back that day to the Coast to talk with his brother and the relevant officers of Van Damme Aero about reducing costs on the *Pax* program as well as larger plans for the postwar world. As of that moment no industry fulfilling war contracts was permitted to begin conversion to peacetime production, since that would give an unfair advantage over others in similar case, but it had to be anticipated; they were all like yachts backing and tacking at the start line, eager to go. This miraculous over-the-rainbow collaboration between the military and industry was about to end—why would it continue?—and first across the line would be first into the new world. Competition though wasn't what it had been *prewar,* as we were already learning to say. It seemed more and more likely that Van Damme Aero itself would undergo dissolution into one of the even huger consolidated aircraft firms now in the process of forming like thunderheads out of rising plumes of heated air. Whether Henry and Julius would come out atop whatever entity would be born from that, or would remain somehow within the shell of the older company to fill out their days, was not at all clear. Henry Van Damme was so tired and sick at heart now that he began to believe he didn't care.

"It's necessary to begin now to reduce the workforce on the program, in fact throughout all the programs, including the A-21 and others that are still fulfilling orders, so that we don't release a tide of unemployed just as war work ends and peacetime retooling hasn't begun." That was the VP for labor, whose resemblance to the common figure of Death and Taxes with scythe and dark cowl had just become apparent to Henry. "The goal is to retain the skilled workforce. Unions are helping here; the Management-Labor Policy Committee we've had to set up has done a fine job of getting cooperation on all kinds of labor issues, the turnovers, the absenteeism, reconversion issues. So far. Unions will be willing to let go last-hired men, men with poor records, older men new to the union, and particularly women. Well they only ever admitted as many women as they had to anyway, and those few've got little seniority. Of course the women will largely want to quit as soon as peace comes, maybe before, not just because they'll be glad to get back to the home but because they'll see that their husbands and all the other young men being demobilized will need those jobs."

He turned a leaf of his report—that item dealt with—on to the next. "The handicaps will want to go home too, where they can be taken care of. They made a fine effort, many of them, but the limited tasks they were able to do can be redistributed now. It looks pretty certain that Social Security will soon be expanded to pay a lifetime disability payment to those people and they'll basically retire from the workforce. They'll not be our issue."

He began to describe other matters, colored and other marginal workers, recovering investments in housing provided at cost or on government loans; Henry Van Damme wasn't listening closely, though (as always) he'd find he remembered it all when he needed to know it.

"Henry," said Julius.

"Jet engines," said Henry. "One on each wing, underslung. It could give enough power to get the thing off the ground faster. Less strain on the other engines, less overheating. It's possible. Just a further modification."

Julius regarded his brother, the smart daring brother, the one who always made the wild right guess about what to do next. "The Army Air Force," he said, "is thinking of going with Boeing on that, Henry. Boeing's got a bomber in plan with about the specs of the *Pax* but with all jet engines. Our spies have just informed us. They've numbered it XB-52. The military's prepared to commit to it. I can give you the details."

"Well that's so wrong," Henry said, and pressed a hand to his heart. "That is just so wrong."

"It doesn't matter," Pancho said to Prosper.

Larry the shop steward had that day asked Pancho with a grin about Pancho's pink slip, knowing even before Pancho'd opened his pay envelope that he would find one, because (Larry didn't quite say it but everyone was free to assume) as shop steward and an associate member of the Labor-Management Policy Committee, he'd been personally responsible for its being put there. It was white, not pink, but it was what it was. Getting rid of the deadwood, Larry said to his circle of grinners and nodders. There's still a war to win here. Prosper had overheard.

"What's that mean?" Prosper now asked. "Doesn't matter?"

"I have, as the saying goes, other fish to fry," Pancho replied. He and Prosper walked the aisles of the Kroger in search of the makings of a dinner, which took a lot of time when shoppers were as judgmental as Pancho and as slow-moving as Prosper. "Understand, I came here chiefly for reasons other than permanent employment. I intended to refine some ideas I've had through observation of a new kind of practice." He lifted a potato from a bin and studied its face. "I've made scores of notes."

"Well I don't know where you'll get work now," Prosper said.

"I should tell you, dear friend, that I've long been in communication with many people around the nation. Around the world in fact. An inner core of associates as well. My ideas may seem to you to have come out of my own little coco, but in fact they have been tried and changed in argument and disputation. Anyway, these associates—I keep them abreast of my thinking, and they do their best to bring to fruition those plans I have long laid."

"Really." Prosper had seen him carrying his many envelopes to the branch post office in the plant, licking stamps, asking for special delivery on this or that. He'd thought it no business of his. He looked into the green porcelain meat case, checked his book of stamps.

"Now after many false starts it seems that matters are, coincidentally, coming to a head. I'm informed that a man of great wealth has expressed interest. Real interest. Wants to meet us, talk about these things." He leaned close to Prosper as though he might be overheard. "Oil money." He took up his search again amid the vegetables. "Of course not even the greatest magnate, the most repentant profiteer, could by himself pay for the establishing of even one Harmonious City. However much the world is in need of its example right now. No. But now perhaps a real start might be made."

"I thought this place, Van Damme Aero, was a kind of place you had in mind."

"An illusion," Pancho said with calm certitude. "I'm through with that."

"So you're going to meet this man? The oil man?"

Pancho said nothing, as though Prosper was to infer that it must be so.

Prosper had a hard time imagining these associates of Pancho's. He thought of the icehouse gang, of the Invisible Agent and his controllers. He thought that he, Prosper, was perhaps considered one of them in Pancho's mind.

They approached the counters, where a dull-faced woman awaited them at the imposing cash register to add up their purchases. Just there, crates of oranges stood, the first seen in a good while around here, things were getting better. While Pancho laid down their selections, Prosper studied the bright paper labels of the crates, which showed over and over a hacienda at sunset; primroses and cactus; a huge pot with zigzag stripe; and, holding in each hand a golden globe dropped from the rows of green trees beyond that led to purple mountains, a senorita just as golden. And he thought he'd heard about this place before. Hadn't Pancho spoken to him of it, as though from his own experience, that day they'd met beside the gas-less Zephyr? Yes just this place, where Prosper had thought to go and Pancho claimed to have gone, but maybe not. Well anyone could want to be there, now; surely anyone could believe, anyone who'd been long on the road and done poorly, that such a place existed, and could be reached.

"No matter," he heard Pancho say, to no one. "No matter."

April was over when Diane walked out of the house in the Heights for the first time since coming home from the hospital with Danny Jr. (her son's name till Danny agreed or insisted on something else, his letters had grown ever shorter and rarer as time went on). Danny Jr. had been born premature, small as a skinned rabbit and as red and withered-looking as one too, but the doctor said he was fine and he'd fatten up fine. And his back seemed straight so far: she couldn't bring herself to ask the doctor if he'd seen anything that was, well, and so she'd believe it was fine too, and stroked his tiny back and tried to guess. She'd insisted on the hospital, first in her family to be born in one, just because. It's healthful, *Mamí*, and I've got the money.

That day she'd told her mother she just needed to be in motion, and while the baby slept she'd just walk down toward the shore, make her legs work, walk without that ten-pound bag of rice she felt she'd been carrying forever. As she went gently downward past buildings and streets she'd known since childhood she began to see, there below her, people who were coming out of their houses; coming out, rushing out, and embracing others who were also rushing into the street. She kept on. More people were coming out now from the houses around her, excited, elated, frantic even. She heard bells rung, church bells. Sirens. More people in the street, hugging and cheering and lifting children in their arms, men kissing women. Girls rode on the shoulders of men, some in uniforms. In a moment she was surrounded, people taking her arms as they took others, the whole lot of them seeming about to fly up into the air in a group.

What was it? What was going on? She had to listen to them till she understood.

The war was over in Europe. It was on the radio. The Russians had taken Berlin, and the Germans had given up. They said Hitler was dead. It was over, over.

A fat man gave her a kiss on the cheek, a fat woman embraced her and she embraced the woman back, and they all went spinning and spiraling down the streets toward the ocean crying out that it was over. Some of them dropped out and went to sit and weep.

Over. It was so bright and sunny. Of course it wasn't over, not for Danny and not for her, but still it was over, and you could let your heart go for a moment to rise up among all the others, and you could link arms with strangers and laugh and smile.

8

Prosper Olander got his own white pink slip in an envelope stuffed
with bills and coins, a week's severance pay, which wasn't owed
to him under contract but given anyway. To him it would always
seem—well, symbolic, or appropriate, or suggestive of the shape
of time, or something—that his own employment should end on VE
Day, and later memorials and celebrations of that date would fill him
with a strange unease he couldn't quite explain to himself, as though
he should no longer exist. He thought at that time that Upp 'n' Adam
were going to be out of a job too, and so was Anna Bandanna, and
where they went he would now go, wherever that might be.

For a time he went nowhere, living in Pancho's house on Z Street
waiting for bills he couldn't pay to show up in his mailbox. Van Damme
Aero and the union had information about unemployment insurance,
which somehow Prosper feared to apply for; maybe it'd be discovered
he should never have been employed in the first place.

Mostly nothing arrived in that brass box at the Van Damme post
office, to which he had a tiny brass key. He had his monthly letter from
Bea, saying among other things that his uncles had got in trouble for
dealing in forged ration stamps, which didn't surprise Bea any. She
didn't think they'd go to jail, but it was dreadful that someone in your
own family, no matter how distant, could do such a thing.

(It was true: Bill and Eddy, attorneys, had a struggle getting the boys off lightly. Without Prosper their wares had grown cheaper and less professional, and they'd taken to pressing loose stamps on gas stations, who would then sell extra gas to special customers at a profit and turn in the fake stamps for it. Not every pump jockey thought this was a good idea, and the boys had started threatening some of them— their scheme was turning into a racket—until one plump little miss in billed cap and leather bow tie on the South Side of the city took the stamps with a smile and then turned them in to the authorities. Where'd she get the nerve? Mert and Fred also hadn't known that by now the paper used for the real government stamp books was specially treated, and if dipped in a chlorine solution would turn a pretty blue, and their paper didn't. George Bill put in evidence Mert's spotless record in the last war, and Fred pleaded he'd only got into the game to provide for his crippled nephew.)

The same mail that brought Bea's letter brought another envelope, the stationery of a hotel in a town in an adjacent state. Prosper thought he recognized the old-fashioned hand that had addressed it. Inside the envelope was a postal money order for four hundred dollars, and a letter.

Well, Prosper, I write to let you know what's become of me and of my plans, and also to ask of you a favor in memory of all the time we've spent together. Well it turns out that the group that I was to meet here and make some plans with weren't able, or weren't willing, to assemble. Not all or many of them anyway. And frankly the ones who did come were not the ones I would have relied on. I just can't work with that kind of material, Prosper, their good hearts and intentions (if any) aside. I have sent them all away.

Moreover, the big backer I was led to believe would be coming here to meet me and look over the plans for the Harmonious City, which I have had printed at some expense, he has declined to show up, having I suppose some more important or practical projects to interest himself in. To tell the truth he is not the first person to hold out before me a mirage of support with big promises that fade away like morning dew. I have never let disappointments like that touch me. I suspect that like the others he merely wanted to build a "Shangri-la" of his own atop my solid foundation, which would thus have failed even if he could have understood the thinking behind it. So there's an end to that.

I may appear to you embittered, and perhaps I am at least finally disillusioned, and being as old as I am and no longer employed or employable I find myself unable and more importantly unwilling to rise up off the floor once again. I have therefore determined on ending my life by my own hand rather than letting incompetence, ill-health, and poverty have their way with me. I have paid for a further week at this lodging, after which they will find I have no more to give them nor any use for their hospitality.

What I would ask of you, dear friend, is that in the next days you will come here to this town, where you would not want otherwise to journey I'm sure, and collect my remains, both my own poor person and more importantly the papers and plans to which with painful care I have devoted so many years, not to enrich or aggrandize myself, no, but for the increase of human happiness. What though I have failed? The plans, the philosophy of Attraction and Harmony, these remain, and if there is any hope and any justice in this wondrous world we inhabit, they will lie like seeds through winter upon winter, to be watered and nourished and grow in the end.

Well enough of all that, just get here if you can, I'll probably be on ice at the morgue on my way to the potter's field, but if you get here in time they won't throw me out. The enclosed for whatever expenses a simple burial might entail, the rest for your good self.

You know it's a funny thing how a plan of suicide simplifies your life. No reason any longer to pay the rent, answer your mail, wash, dress, even to eat. It's a strange relief to know that you've had to make a choice between ham and eggs and flapjacks for the last time in your life. But I maunder, my friend, and it is now time to bid you farewell in this life, and to ask

*your pardon for these obligations I have laid upon you. If you
don't fulfill them I will be none the wiser, of course, but here's
hoping.*

It was signed "Pancho," and on another sheet of the same stationery was a note headed *To Whom It May Concern,* that granted to
Prosper Olander the power to take possession of all his effects and
make such disposition of his remains as he deems appropriate, and this
note was signed Pelagius Johann Notzing, BA, Esq., and was dated
three days before.

"What the hell," he said aloud. "What the hell."

Sal Mass was there trying to open her box, standing on tiptoe with
her key to reach it, she'd tried to get a lower one but was told they had
to be assigned in alphabetical order. "What is it?" she asked.

Prosper held out the letter to her and watched as she read it. After
frowning over the first sentences she suddenly gasped, and clutched the
letter to her bosom as though to hush its voice, looking at Prosper in
horror. He gestured that she read on. When she was all done she looked
up again, a different face now.

"That god damn son of a bitch," she said.

Prosper knew who she meant: not Pancho.

Almost as though they'd instantly had the same idea, or communicated it to each other by Wings of Thought as the ads in *The Sunny
Side* said, Prosper and Sal together went out of the post office and
toward the Community Center where, unless the sun had stopped
going east to west, Larry would at this time of day be found in the
games room playing pool and jawing.

He was there. He saw Prosper and Sal approaching him and took
the damp unlit cigar from his mouth, grinning appreciatively. "Well if
it isn't," he said, but then Prosper had reached him and thrust Pancho's
letter on him.

"Read this," he said.

Larry looked it over. "It's not addressed to me."

"Just read it."

They watched him read, the game suspended, Sal with her fists on
her hips.

"Oh jeez," Larry said. "Oh for cripe's sake."

"You oughta," Sal said, "you oughta," but couldn't think what he oughta, and stopped.

"It wasn't my fault," Larry said. "I had no choice."

"Don't give me that," Prosper said. "We're quite aware."

"Get the hell out of here," Larry said. "That was business and I did what I had to do."

Later Prosper would try to think whether he'd actually had Larry's own advice in his mind as the next moments unfolded. A little crowd had gathered. "Somebody ought to punch your nose," Prosper said.

"Nobody's punching anybody," Larry said.

"We'll see," Prosper said, with all the implacable menace he could muster. "Come on." He whirled and started toward the door, Larry following him.

"Cut it out," he called to Prosper. "Don't be a dope."

"What are you, a coward? Scared of something?" Prosper said this in fury straight in front of him as he reached the door of the games room, grabbed the knob, and pushed it open. Larry was just exiting behind him when Prosper flung the door shut hard and hit Larry smack in the face. Then as Larry, dazed, pushed it open again to come after him, Prosper swung around on his heels and with one lifted crutch caught Larry a blow on the cheek that made the onlookers now crowding the exit gasp in horror or amazement.

That was all Prosper was holding in the way of an attack, and setting himself then as firmly as he could, he waited for Larry to fall upon him. His heart felt like it would tear him apart. Larry, red-faced and with teeth bared, seemed ready now to do terrible things, but after a pause he throttled down with awesome effort and backed away; threw his hand into the air, *Aw beat it,* and turned back into the Community Center, pushing through the crowd. Sal came squirming out almost under his arm, went to Prosper and stood beside him as though to shelter him with her own unassailability. "Bully!" she yelled back.

Ironic cheers for the two of them followed them out into the day.

"You're going to go?" Sal said. It was she who'd rescued Pancho's letter in the donnybrook.

"Of course I am." His heart still pounding.

"I'll go too," she said.

"No, Sal. You don't need to say that."

"Listen, mister. He was my friend too."

That was true: for all her mocking tone, Sal had sat as quietly as anyone could have been expected to as Pancho expatiated, and Prosper thought that was about what Pancho'd mean by a friend. "Well," he said. "What about your shift?"

"I'm quitting," Sal said, "if you want to know. I'm blowing."

"You are? What about Al?"

"Al and I," Sal said in that record-played-too-fast voice of hers, "are quits."

Prosper slowed down. Sal was about the only Associate around who had to skip to keep up with him. "What? That's hard to believe."

"I know," said Sal. "People look at the two of us and it's like the little man and woman on the wedding cake. How could they be apart? Well lemme tell you."

"I figured it was a love match. I admit."

"To tell you the truth," Sal said, "it was a kind of marriage of convenience. And it ain't convenient anymore."

"What's he done?"

"I don't want to talk about it. When do we leave?"

Sal and Prosper parted at the Assembly Building, Sal to go hand in her resignation (as she put it) and Prosper to go back to Z Street and prepare for a journey, a train journey with no aid but what Sal, who came up just past his waist, could provide. He was headed that way when he felt the presence of someone large coming up behind.

"Listen," Larry said, without other preface. "What are you going to do, are you going to do what he asked, go collect him and that?"

"Yes," Prosper said, looking ahead with dignity, and some fear.

"Alone?"

"Sal Mass just said she'd come too."

"Oh for Christ's sake. The two of you? That's ridiculous. You'll pull into town like some carny show. Nobody'll take you seriously. There's legal matters there to resolve."

Prosper kept on, following his nose.

"Look," Larry said. "I've got no responsibility for this. None. But I can help. I'll come along. You can't do it, you and her."

Prosper let that sink in for a few steps. "You can get the time off?"

Larry stopped suddenly, and Prosper did too. Larry fetched breath and looked to heaven. "Well," he said, "actually, I'm quitting."

The doors of the Assembly Building were rolling open, the little tractors arriving to do their duty. The nose of another completed *Pax* was revealed, then its wide wings.

"Well this is quite a day," Prosper said.

All that Prosper would ever learn about what had caused Larry to turn in his badge and resign his stewardship wasn't enough to make a story, and Prosper wasn't about to delve deeply. There was a woman, a woman at the plant, and an angry husband: Larry seemed visibly to break out in a sweat, like a comic strip worrier, when he let even that much slip. Prosper'd been tempted to say a lot then, maybe tell Larry Pancho's theories about war and the sex urge: but no.

"Well anyway," Prosper said. They were all three on the local train from Ponca to this city over the state line where Pancho lay dead. Sal in the opposite seat was asleep, her small feet not reaching the floor. "I'm sorry I whacked you with the stick there. I've been meaning to say."

Larry touched the side of his face. "Didn't hurt."

"Good. Anyway thanks for not punching my lights out."

"What?" Larry tugged at his collar. He was wearing a fawn-colored suit, a bit too tight, and his suitcase was in the overhead rack: he was headed farther, somewhere.

"Oh. You know." Prosper punched the air.

Larry was watching him with an odd look, a look Prosper had seen in the faces of women more than men: that look toward themselves as much as at you, waiting to hear their own permission to say something, maybe something they've never said before.

"Well," he said. "Look. There's a lot of stories about me. That aren't all what you'd call true."

"Oh?" The stories that Prosper had heard about Larry were all Larry's telling. Prosper removed all suggestion of an opinion from his face, but Larry seemed to strangle on the effort of saying whatever it was that might come next, and instead removed his hat and furiously wiped the sweatband with a large handkerchief.

Midday the train they'd taken toddled into the central station, which had no platforms, only a little wedding-cake building beside the tracks. Sal went out the door and down, leaping from the last step as the conductor looked on. Then Larry. Then Prosper, who stood at the door looking at the steep declivity. Easy enough maybe to go down the first two steps, handy rails to hold: but the last drop to the ground was going to take some thought. The conductor, ready to wave the engineer on, gazed up at him in a kind of disinterested impatience. Finally Larry, perceiving him stuck, stepped up.

"Come on!" he said. "I'll getcha!"

All the things that Larry standing there arms open was capable of doing or not doing passed as in a shiver over Prosper, but he didn't seem to have a choice. He dropped himself down the first step and then bent forward as far as he could so that Larry could take him under the armpits. Then he gave himself over to him. Strong as he was, Larry staggered for a second under the weight and Prosper knew they were going to go over, but Larry held and Prosper got his crutches set and propped himself, removing his weight from Larry. Larry blew in impatience or embarrassment, twisted his hat right on his head, and walked away; neither man ever mentioned the moment.

The hotel was across a wide bare street from the station, a wooden structure with a long front porch where a row of rockers sat. The words GRAND HOTEL painted across the facade were worn somewhat; they were supplemented by the same words in neon above the porch. Not the kind of place important oil millionaires would be found, in Prosper's view, not that he knew anything about it. Beyond this place and rising above, the newer buildings, like Ponca City's, plain or fancy. Even as they crossed the street to reach it, they could see what they should not have been able to see, and they could do and say nothing until they were entirely sure it was what it certainly seemed to be: Pancho Notzing, seated in a rocking chair, feeding bits of something to a little dog.

"*Now* what," Larry said, striding forward. "Now what in hell."

When all three of them stood before the porch Pancho said, "Hello, friends."

"You're supposed to be at the morgue," Sal said. "I came a long way to see that. If you just got out to come and greet us I suggest you beat it back there."

"What in hell," Larry said again.

"Hello, Pancho," Prosper said. "I'm glad to see you."

Pancho nodded solemnly but without seeming to feel that a quick explanation was in order. The little dog put a paw on his leg to remind him of what he'd been up to as the others arrived. For the first time it occurred to Prosper that Pancho, who spent his life and time and energy planning for the true deep happiness of men and women, every one of them different and precious, didn't really perceive the existence of actual other people. "Well as you see," he said at last, "I did not in the end take the step I wrote you about. I was on the point of sending you a telegram to say so, but approaching the dark door and then retreating took such an effort that I could do nothing further."

"It's all right," Prosper said.

"All those common questions and tasks that I said had flown away came right back again—in prospect anyway—and it was a bit appalling. Stops you cold."

"It's all right."

"Life," said Pancho. He took a bit of something from a plate in his lap and gave it to the dog, who snapped it up and looked for more.

"Who's the dog?" Sal asked, unable to frame a different question.

"A stray, belongs to no one," Pancho said. "As far as I can tell."

"So you mean to say," Larry said, "that we came all this way, ready for a funeral, wearing the suit and tie, and there was never a reason for it?"

"Larry," said Pancho. "I can't imagine why you've come, and I'm sorry to have disappointed you, but I am honored. I am deeply honored."

"Aw hell," said Larry, and he snatched the hat from his head, seeming to be on the point of throwing it to the dusty ground and stamping on it; instead he jammed it back on his head and turned away, looking down the empty street, hands in his pockets.

"Question is," said Sal, "if we can't bury you, what are we going to do with you?"

"And yourself?" Pancho asked.

"Well that too," Sal said. She'd taken a seat on the edge of the porch, her feet on the step below, looking more than usual like a child, and petted the little black dog, who seemed to take to her.

"We're all out of a job," Prosper said. "One way or another."

Pancho stared at Larry's back, and Larry's pose softened, though he didn't turn.

"Him too," said Prosper.

There seemed to be nothing for it except to go into the dining room of the hotel, where overhead fans spooned the air around and wicker chairs were set at the tables, and treat the dead man to a lunch; all his money was in the check he'd sent to Prosper. What should they do now? Some ideas more or less reasonable were put forward. For his part, Prosper knew he could go back to Bea and May's house, they'd take him in, and certainly there'd be something he could do somewhere in the art line, after all his experience. So long as he could get into the building and into a chair in front of a desk. It was the safest thing, and it was hard for somebody like him not to think Safety First. Safety was rare and welcome. He'd had some close calls; in fact it sometimes seemed that, for him, every call was close.

"I suppose you might not have heard," Larry said, tucking a napkin into his collar, "that while you were busy here, we won the war. Against Hitler anyway. He's done."

"I did hear that, Larry," Pancho said. "On that day I was reminded of a passage in a book I often carry with me. For consolation, though it hasn't worked so well that way lately."

He fished in his coat pockets, but found no book there, and then bowed his head, clasped his hands, and began to speak, as though he asked a blessing before their meal. " 'This is the day,' " he said, gravely and simply, " 'which down the void abysm, at the Earth-born's spell yawns for Heaven's despotism. And Conquest is dragged captive through the deep.' "

He lifted his eyes. "Shelley," he said. "Prometheus. The Earth-born. Friend to man. Unbound and triumphant."

The rest of them looked at one another, but got no help. Prosper wondered if this strange gentle certitude with which Pancho spoke had been acquired somehow in his trip toward the other side, as May always called it, and back again.

" 'And if with infirm hand,' " Pancho went on, and lifted his own,

" 'Eternity, Mother of many acts and hours, should free the serpent that would clasp her with his length' "—here Pancho seized the air dramatically—" 'these are the spells by which to reassume an empire o'er the disentangled doom.' "

He seemed to arise slightly from his chair, enumerating them, the spells, on his fingers: " 'To suffer woes which Hope thinks infinite. To forgive wrongs darker than death or night.' "

Sal and Prosper looked at Larry.

" 'To defy Power, which seems omnipotent. To love, and bear. To hope till Hope creates from its own wreck the thing it contemplates.' " Full hand open high above them: " 'Neither to change, nor falter, nor repent.' "

"Hey I have an idea," said Sal.

" 'This, like thy glory, Titan, is to be good, great and glorious, beautiful and free! This is alone Life! Joy! Empire! And Victory!' "

He was done, sank, put his hands on the table; lifted his head and smiled at them, as though awaking and glad to find them there.

" 'Scuse me, but you know what?" Sal got up and knelt on the chair seat to address them. "Right this minute, in San Francisco, California, the United Nations are meeting. You've read about it. All the ones on our side in the war, and all the others too, that's the idea. They're there talking about peace in the world and how to do it. How to make it last this time. About the rights everybody should have, all of us, how to keep them from being taken away."

"Four freedoms," said Prosper. "Yes."

"So, Mr. Notzing. Why don't you go there? Bring your plans and your proposals, your writings. That's the bunch that needs to hear them. Am I right?"

She looked around at the others, who had no idea if she was or wasn't.

"Oh," said Pancho. "Oh, well, I don't know, no, I."

She scrambled down from her chair and came to his side. "Oh come on!" she said.

"Mrs. Roosevelt will be there," Larry said, lifting his eyes as though he saw her, just overhead.

"We'll all go," Sal cried. "You've got a car, haven't you? We're all flush. Let's do it."

"Will you all?" Pancho asked with something like humility. Nobody said no. "Very well," he said.

"Yes," said Sal.

"We'll just take French leave. When we choose, we'll return for what we've left behind—if we think there's any reason to."

"It'll all be there when we get back."

"The things and the people."

"Yes."

"If you don't mind," Larry said, and picked up his fork and knife, "I'd like to have my lunch before we go. Maybe you people can live on air, but not me."

Outside on the porch as they all went out—Pancho with the two bags that he had intended to leave for Prosper, still neatly labeled as to their contents—the little black dog was still waiting, and happy to see them.

"We'll take him too," Sal said.

"Oh no," Larry said. "I hate dogs."

But she'd already picked up the mutt and was holding him tenderly and laughing as he licked at her face. Pancho led them to the side street where the car was parked.

"Best be on our way," Pancho said, climbing into the driver's seat. "Look at that sky."

A roiling darkness did seem to be building to the north, and little startled puffs of breeze reached them. Larry licked his forefinger and held it aloft. "Headed the other way," he averred. "Back toward where we came from."

"So we're off," said Pancho, and turned the key.

" 'Git for home, Bruno!' " Sal shouted from the back.

"There's no place like home," said Prosper; he said it though he didn't know and had never known just what that meant. It did occur to him that if seen from the right point of view, they in the Zephyr were like one of those movies where the picture, which has all along been moving with the people in it one after the other or in twos and threes wherever they go, takes a final stance, and the people move away from it. (Prosper, in the days when he'd come to pick up Elaine or wait while

378 / JOHN CROWLEY

she changed, had seen the beginnings and endings of many movies, the same movie many times.) Maybe there's one more kiss, or one more piece of comic business, and then the car with the lovers or the family or the ill-assorted comedians in it moves off, hopeful suitcase tied on, and it goes away from you down the road: and you understand that you're not going to see where they get to or what they're headed for, even as those two big words arrive on the screen to tell you so.

RECESSIONAL

I t was the fiercest tornado ever recorded in Oklahoma history, which made it remarkable in all the history of weather, because the tornadoes of Oklahoma are themselves top of the standings in almost any year. It didn't touch down long or go far, but what it touched it turned to flinders and waste, and left nothing standing.

Up north where it began Muriel Gunderson was on duty at the weather station at Little Tom Field, and took the astonishing readings sent in by the radiosonde equipment that she'd sent aloft attached to its balloon. Not that you couldn't already tell that something big was going to roll over the prairie within the next twelve hours or so: back on the farm the horses would be biting one another and the windmill vanes trembling in the dead air as though ready to start flailing as soon as they perceived the front.

The radiosonde was a blessing most ways. A little packet of radio instruments, no bigger than a shoe box, that could measure wind speed, air pressure, humidity, and temperature as a function of height, and send it all back to the radio receivers in the shack. No more following the ascent of the balloon with the theodolite—the instruments knew where they were, and kept transmitting no matter how far above the cloud cover they went. Women around the country were putting these little packages on balloons, sending them up, and then (the drawback) recovering them after they'd fallen to earth on their little para-chutes. There were instructions on the container for anyone who found it about how to mail it back, but in the daytime you just went out in the direction of the wind and looked for it.

Muriel was damp everywhere her clothes bunched. Tootie lay under the porch as still as though dead, except for his panting tongue. Muriel began taking down the readings that were coming in from the instruments. She'd had to have training in all of it, RAOB or radio observation, the Thermistor and the Hygristor, like twin giants in a fairy tale; it still made her nervous always that she hadn't got it right.

Well this number sure didn't seem right. It didn't seem that baro-metric pressure could get that low. Radiosonde equipment was mysterious: in the old method you knew you could get it wrong, and how you'd be likely to get it wrong, but now it was as though only the machine could know if it was wrong, and it wasn't telling.

Maybe she'd set the baroswitch incorrectly before she let it go.

Well who knows. Better to trust the reading than to guess, she guessed.

She went to the Teletype and began typing up the readings. The Teletype was new too, her words and numbers transmitted to other machines elsewhere that typed them at the same time she did. When Muriel got to the baro pressure number she put it in, and the time and height, and then put in a new line:

This is the number, folks, no joke.

Down under the porch, Tootie lifted her head, as though catching a smell, and ceased to pant.

The twister itself didn't touch down near that airfield, and Ponca City itself was largely spared too, a fact that would be remarked on in the churches the following day—the fine houses and old trees, the Poncan, the Civic Center, they all stood and still stand, the high school and the library. But out along Bodark Creek and to the west it churned the earth and the blackjack oaks and the works of man in its funnel like the fruits and berries tossed into a Waring blender. Those little houses,

A Street to Z Street, Pancho's, Sal's, Connie's, never firmly attached to the earth in the first place, were lifted up from their slabs and stirred unresisting into the air, block after block, with all their tar paper, bathtubs, bicycles, beds, tables, fretwork-framed proverbs (*Home Sweet Home*), Navajo blankets, Kit-Kat clocks with wagging tails, pictures of Jesus, potted cacti, knives, forks, and spoons, odds and ends.

It was bad, it was devastating, but it was one of those disasters that manage to inflict wondrous destruction without really harming anyone much. For in all of Henryville blown away that afternoon there was not a single—the word had by then changed from a colorless technical term to one that came into our mouths, some of our mouths, at the worst moments of our lives—not a single *casualty*. A beloved dog; a caged bird; some miraculous escapes beneath beds or sturdy tables. The reason was not Providence, though, really, or even wonderful luck; it was that there was almost no one in Henryville that day.

That day—it was the greatest in Horse Offen's career, the defining act of it anyway and certainly productive of an image that would remain before memory's eye—that day was the day the last rivets were banged into the five hundredth *Pax* bomber to be turned out at Van Damme Aero Ponca City, and Horse had persuaded Management (his memo passing upward right to the broad bare desk of Henry Van Damme) that every single person at the plant, from sweepers to lunchroom ladies to engineers to managers, ought to be brought onto the floor for one vast picture of the plane and themselves: a portrait of the greatest team and the greatest plane in the greatest war of all time. Everybody'd get a two-dollar bonus for showing up off-shift.

So we came and crowded in together, complaining—the heat, the closeness, the air like a fusty blanket, the spirit dejected, the mind dull. Under the shadow of those wings we sheltered, though of course not all of us were responsible for its coming into being, some of the smilers in the back having just been hired and many of those who had indeed riveted the dural and calibrated the instruments and hooked up the wiring already gone, dispersed, headed home. Anyway the picture—we nearly rebelled before the huge banquet camera could be focused and fired, Horse with bullhorn mother-henning us ceaselessly—the picture is that one you still see. Connie is in front, beside Rollo Stallworthy, and some of the other Teenie Weenies are scattered here and there; you can find their faces if you knew them.

Then as we stood there, about to break up, the twister came on, prefigured by the deep nameless dread induced in humans by a precipitous fall in barometric pressure, and then by weird airs whipping around in the great space and even rocking the ship we stood around, as though it shuddered. The windows darkened. Soon we could hear it, distant sound of a devouring maw, we didn't know that it had already eaten our houses and their carports, but the Oklahomans and others among us who knew the signs announced now what it was. As it bore down on us, the buildings all around were pressed on, the dormitories, the Community Center, and we heard them shattering and flinging their parts away to clang against the roofs and windows of ours, and there might have been a panic if it hadn't been clear to everyone that we were already in the one place we would have run to. We were warned to stay away from the windows, and we milled a little, but there wasn't much room, and we hardly even spoke or made a sound except for a universal moan when all at once the lights went out.

When it had clearly passed over, we went out. A little rain had fallen. The B-30s lay around the trash-speckled field like dead seagulls cast on a beach after a storm. One had been lifted up and laid over the back of another, as though "treading" it like a cock does a hen, to make more. One flipped halfway over on bent wing. They'd been made, after all, to be as light as possible. We walked among them afraid and grieving and delighted.

One death could be attributed to the big wind. A ship had been pushed forward, lifted, and fallen again so that its left landing gear had buckled and it slumped sideways. Connie and Rollo, assigned to the team checking the ships for damage, found Al Mass in the forward cabin, dead. He hadn't been hurt in the fall or in the crushing of the cabin, and the coroner determined or at least made a good guess that he'd died of a heart attack from the stress of the storm and maybe the sudden shock of the plane's inexplicable takeoff. Midgets aren't known for strong hearts, the coroner averred. Rollo and Connie gave evidence that supported the theory of a heart attack, but (without testifying to it, give the little guy a break) they both supposed that it might have come a little *before* the big wind, since Al was without his pants when they came upon him, and nearby was the abandoned brassiere of another interloper, who'd apparently left him there, alive or more likely dead: but who that was we'd never learn.

Al's buried in the Odd Fellows cemetery there in Ponca City; Van Damme Aero acquired a small area that's given over to Associates who died in the building of the *Pax* there from 1943 to 1945 and had no other place to lie. There are twelve, nine of them women. They fell from cranes, they stepped in front of train cars, they were hit by engines breaking loose from stationary test rigs, got blood poisoning from tool injuries, dropped dead from stroke. It was dangerous work, the way we did it then.

That ship they found Al in was actually the one that, years after, was hauled out to repose in the field across Hubbard Road from the Municipal Airport, wingless and tail-less. The story of Al and how he was found had been forgotten, or hadn't remained attached to this particular fuselage, and no ghosts walked. By then what was left of Henryville had been bulldozed away, unsalvageable and anyway unwanted, the land was more saleable without that brief illusion of a town, though the streets that the men and women had walked and biked to work along, and driven on in their prewar cars, and sat beside in the evenings to drink beer and listen to the radio, can still be traced, if you open your mind and heart to the possibility of their being there. There's a local club devoted to recovering the layout of it all, the dormitories, the clinics, the shops and railroad tracks, and marking the faint street crossings, A to Z. But that's all.

Afterword

To take on any aspect of the American military effort in World War II as a subject for fiction, especially any aspect of the air war, is to invite criticism from the very many experts who know more about it than you ever will—not only archivists and historians and buffs, but also those who remember firsthand the planes and the factories and the people that built them. In part to evade the heavy responsibility of accuracy, I chose in this story to invent a bomber that never existed, though it is modeled on a couple that did. Somewhat on a whim, I placed the factory that is making this imaginary bomber in Ponca City, Oklahoma, though there was no such factory there—the nearest was the Boeing plant in Wichita, Kansas. I have taken other smaller liberties with the historical record, some obvious, some perhaps not. Some things that might appear to be invented are true: the multiple suicides of Part One, Chapter Two are among these. The true story of the Women Airforce Service Pilots (as told by—among others—Adela Riek Scharr in *Sisters in the Sky*) is more extraordinary than any fictional account could suggest. I have drawn extensively on the personal accounts of the many women who went to work in the munitions plants, gas stations, weather stations, and offices, who drove trucks, flew planes, and succeeded in hundreds of jobs they had never expected to do. For most of them, and for the many African American

men and women, Hispanics, Native Americans, and people with dis-
abilities who also served, the end of the war meant returning to the
status quo ante: but things could never be restored just as they had
been, and the war years contained the seeds of change that would eventually grow again.

Among the hundred-odd books that a complete bibliography for
this novel would include, I am most indebted to *A Mouthful of Rivets:
Women at Work in World War II* by Nancy Baker Wise and Christy
Wise. The first-person accounts collected there are an enduring monu-
ment to the women of that period. Firsthand accounts like *Slacks and
Calluses: Our Summer in a Bomber Factory* by Constance Bowman,
and *Punch In, Susie! A Woman's War Factory Diary* by Nell Giles,
were helpful. *Don't You Know There's a War On? The American
Home Front, 1941–1945* by Richard R. Lingeman was important for
the background, as was *Alistair Cooke's America,* the recently repub-
lished account of Cooke's car trip across the country in 1941 to 1942.
*Freedom from Fear: The American People in Depression and War,
1929–1945* by David M. Kennedy was illuminating on the details of
policy, particularly the draft. Susan G. Sterrett's *Wittgenstein Flies a
Kite* was my source for most of the stories about early flight, including
the remarkable one previewed in its title.

Just as useful day to day were the Internet sites with information on
a thousand topics. From the official site of the B-36 bomber I learned—
after deciding that my bomber would be called the *Pax* and would be
struck by a tornado in Oklahoma—that the B-36 was called the Peacemaker, and a fleet of them was damaged by a tornado in Texas. I found
pictures of train car interiors on the Katy Railroad, studied salon hair-
styles of the 1930s, marveled at Teenie Weenies Sunday pages, learned
about the rise of sports betting in the war, read about poor posture and
nursing care for spinal fusion in 1940, and far far more.

I am grateful to Michael J. Lombardi of the Boeing Archives in
Seattle for spending a day finding references and answering my questions, and to Andrew Labovsky and all the crew of *Doc,* the B-29 being
lovingly restored at the Kansas Aviation Museum in Wichita, for allowing me up into the plane, as well as supplying me with facts from their
bottomless well. In Ponca City my very great thanks to Sandra Graves
and Loyd Bishop of the Ponca City Library for their great help on a

peculiar errand—casting their hometown for a part it never played. Bret A. Carter was generous with his collection of Ponca City and Kaw County photographs. I hope that they, and the reader as well, will understand that this book of mine is a Ponca City (and indeed a Home Front and a War) of the Mind, and that all digressions from the ascertainable facts, whether intentional or not, are entirely my own.

Many of the learned and curious correspondents, if that's the word, who read and comment on my online journal went in search of answers to questions I posed there, like the source of the phrase "Git for home, Bruno!" and the price of condoms in 1944 (about $1.50 for a tin of three; they found pictures, too). To LSB I owe the knowledge and understanding I have of what became of people with disabilities at that time, and before and after, which is at the heart of this fiction.